"Blast in t

A.J. found he was holding ~~his~~ ... *is doesn't work . . . we will have buried Helen and Joe so far under the ice that I don't think we'll ever reach them.* He closed his eyes and gave another silent prayer to whatever might be listening. *I don't care, too much, what happens to me . . .*

". . . six . . . five . . . four . . ."

. . . Just let us save her and my friend Joe.

". . . two . . . one . . . *Fire in the hole!*"

Compared to the quake that had caused all the trouble, the detonations weren't even a quiver. There was nothing to see or feel this far away, and the "technically an atmosphere" was a harder vacuum than almost anything produced on Earth; no sound would penetrate.

Europa's feeble gravity conspired to draw out the tension.

"We have separation, multiple areas," A.J. reported. He noticed some red dots. "Five charges still undetonated. Is that correct?"

"Confirmed," Brett and Madeline said simultaneously.

A collection of Faerie Dust near the doorway areas transmitted the scene; multiple showers of powdered ice falling ahead of the gigantic slabs now moving downward, destroying beauty a million years in the making for the sake of two lives that still might never be saved.

PORTAL

ERIC FLINT
RYK E. SPOOR

BAEN

PORTAL

A Baen Books Original

Baen Publishing Enterprises
P.O. Box 1403
Riverdale, NY 10471
www.baen.com

ISBN: 978-1-4767-3642-6

Cover art by Bob Eggleton
Interior Illustrations by Bob Eggleton

First Baen paperback printing, May 2014
Second Baen paperback printing, December 2015

Library of Congress Control Number: 2013001226

Distributed by Simon & Schuster
1230 Avenue of the Americas
New York, NY 10020

Pages by Joy Freeman (www.pagesbyjoy.com)
Printed in the United States of America

I dedicate this book (my work on it, anyway) to my beta-reading group (rykspoor_beta.livejournal.com); their constant encouragement, suggestions, assistance, and occasional direct pointing out of my failures has made all my work better, and without them *Portal* would have some gaping holes in it that I would never have filled on my own. Thank you all! —R.S.

ACKNOWLEDGEMENTS

Many people contributed vitally to the writing of this novel:

My wife Kathleen, who sacrificed many hours of time so I could write it.

Toni Weisskopf at Baen, who made sure it would be published.

Jim, Laura, Danielle, Joy, and all the other people at Baen who help make good books better.

And all of the readers who bought *Boundary* and *Threshold*, making it possible for Maddie, Joe, A.J, Helen, and the rest to finish this journey.

—R.S.

PORTAL

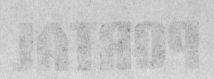

PART I

Recovery, n: 1) the act or process of returning to a normal condition, especially from sickness, a shock, or a setback; recuperation; 2) restoration to a former or better condition; 3) the regaining of something lost; 4) the extraction of something useful from materials or a situation which is otherwise useless or poor.

Chapter 1

I still have no answers.

That was the thing that kept him here now in an office lit mostly by the ruddy glow of Mars swinging regularly by. Nicholas Glendale was *used* to having answers, to knowing what he wanted to do and how to achieve it. By the time he'd been five, he'd known he wanted to be a paleontologist, and he'd succeeded—beyond his expectations, even.

Then when one of his best students, Helen Sutter, had discovered something impossible and the impossible had turned out to be true—a fossil of an alien creature whose species had built bases across the Solar System in the days of the dinosaurs—he had wanted to become a part of that, follow the dream into space. And he'd succeeded in that, too, and again beyond his wildest dreams.

But now that brilliant student, and her friends—*his* friends as well—now all of them were gone, and a hundred other people with them. The faces refused to leave, the crew of the half-alien vessel *Nebula Storm* kept coming and going like phantoms in his mind: Helen, with her blond hair tied back, looking at a dessicated *Bemmius Secordii* mummy sixty-five million years old; A.J. Baker, irreverent and irrepressible sensor expert whose blond hair, cocky smile, and not-too-well-hidden vulnerability had eventually led to his marriage to Helen; dark-haired, dark-skinned Jackie Secord, who'd found the first trace of Bemmie on her family's ranch and later become a rocket engineer for the first manned interplanetary vessel, *Nike*; Joe Buckley, brown hair above a face whose lines showed patience and acceptance of whatever the universe threw at him—good or bad. Madeline Fathom, golden-blonde, delicately built, the single most dangerous—and most reliable—person Nicholas had ever met, one-time agent for the least-known American intelligence agency, later Nicholas' own right hand and married to Joe; Larry Conley, tall and always somehow stooped over as though to apologize for his height, slow-talking but with encyclopedic knowledge of astrophysics.

But *Nebula Storm* was lost with its crew, as were over a hundred others on the ship she had been pursuing, the immense mass-beam drive vessel *Odin*, both vessels lost with all hands in what was in all likelihood an act of corporate greed gone utterly insane, or—possibly—a terrible accident triggered by misunderstanding.

And now he had to decide what to do. The others at Ares Corporation—Glenn Friedet, Reynolds Jones, and the rest of their board—were waiting on his decision as "Director Nicholas Glendale of the Interplanetary Research Institute of the United Nations."

He snorted at the pomposity of the title and stood angrily, the rotation of Phobos Station keeping him as firmly planted on the floor as if he'd been on Earth. Out of habit he began pacing again. *If I keep this up, I'll wear a hole in the exceedingly expensive imported carpet.*

It had all started so simply—as most disasters do. With the discovery of the first two alien bases, one on Mars and one on Mars' moon Phobos, it had become a virtual certainty that there must be other alien installations, possibly with incalculably valuable artifacts within, waiting for salvage elsewhere in the Solar System. The Buckley Accords gave the first discoverer to literally set foot on any other system body long-term rights to exploit resources on that body, within a certain range of that first footstep. That was the starter's gun on the greatest race in history—a race to discover these new locations and reach them first, claiming those resources for the country—or the corporation—that first placed a human being upon the planet, moon, or asteroid on which the alien base was located.

Larry Conley had made it three-for-three discoveries for the Ares Corporation; his coworker, A.J. Baker, had made the first earthshaking discovery within Phobos, and later found the pieces of the puzzle that led to a huge installation in Mars' Melas Chasma region, and now Larry had found unmistakable clues indicating that the minor planet or giant asteroid, Ceres, was the site of another alien base.

Keeping the discovery a secret, Ares and the Interplanetary Research Institute (usually just called the IRI) had prepared and finally launched an expedition to Ceres, locating and setting foot directly above the base—which turned out to be at least as extensive as the one on Mars.

And that, Nicholas thought sadly, *was probably the last straw.*

The European Union's flagship vessel, the *Odin*, had visited Ceres and remained there for some months. Cooperation had seemed to have been established, and many wonderful results had come of it—ranging from the commercialization of room-temperature superconductors found on Phobos to the discovery of structures which might hold the key, finally, to successful commercial fusion, and a completely intact alien vessel whose drive system and purpose was a mystery.

But the *Odin* had a secret agenda, and within the mass of scientific data one of their people—astronomer Anthony LaPointe—found indications of *another* alien installation on Enceladus, a moon of Saturn known to have many strange characteristics indeed. Keeping their discovery secret, the *Odin* prepared for departure, even as a meteor impacted the IRI-Ares base and took out her main reactor.

Except that it *hadn't* been a meteor, and A.J. Baker had been able to show that it was almost certainly a projectile from a coilgun, a magnetic acceleration cannon concealed—against all international and established space travel law—within the mass-driver elements of *Odin*. There was no *proof* of this, and neither the IRI nor Ares could afford to accuse the European Union of such things without ironclad evidence. The action showed that their worst fears had been true; the security officer of *Odin*, Richard Fitzgerald, was an old adversary of Madeline Fathom's and was just as willing to use extreme methods to assure the completion of his mission.

Ares and the IRI had, in the meantime, discovered the principle behind the alien vessel's drive system—something called a "dusty plasma" drive which acted like a solar sail combined with a magnetosail, requiring no physical "sail" to capture much of the Sun's incident energy to propel it—and using the most advanced nanotech sensor and effector motes had restructured the key elements to work again. For various reasons the Ares personnel decided to attempt to beat the *Odin* to the now-known base on Enceladus, and revived the sixty-five million year old vessel, launching it as the IRI vessel *Nebula Storm.*

The modified alien vessel had performed well and the *Nebula Storm* caught up with *Odin* near Jupiter, where both vessels were expected to perform an "Oberth Maneuver" to increase their speed and change their course to send them on a rendezvous with Saturn and Enceladus. The situation had been tense but Nicholas had felt that it was under control. Madeline's terse but informative final report had indicated that they had preliminary evidence that the *Odin* was indeed armed with up to four coilgun-based cannons concealed as part of the main mass-beam drive system, and thus was virtually certainly the cause of the apparent meteor strike that had temporarily disabled the Ceres base and almost killed Joe Buckley.

She had also stated that they were going to be able to obtain proof during the Oberth maneuver. From the specific way the former secret agent phrased her report, he suspected they were planning some actions which he, as director, would be better of not being aware of since he would be then required to advise against it, but he couldn't be sure. Still, he trusted...*had* trusted... Madeline Fathom (Buckley) to take no unnecessary risks four hundred million miles from home.

And in the normal course of things, he *still* would have at least known what *happened*. While professional astronomical instruments, both land and space-based, had more important things to do, WASTA would have been focused on the most exciting space travel event in history. The World Amateur Space Telescope Array (WASTA) had been a project started shortly after *Meru*, the Indian space elevator, had become fully operational, to deploy an inexpensive array of optical telescopes which would be able to be synchronized and controlled from the ground for amateur astronomers to use. It had been an ambitious and ultimately surprisingly successful project, with its multiplicity of smaller aperture space telescopes sometimes nearly matching the performance of some of the professional telescope arrays.

Unfortunately, only minutes before *Odin* and *Nebula Storm* had passed out of sight around Jupiter, WASTA's control system had crashed due to an adaptive virus infection which had taken a day and a half to eradicate, and another twelve hours had elapsed before the multiple elements of WASTA could be realigned properly; even a very small element of uncertainty in the positioning of the several dozen WASTA telescopes would eliminate their tremendous light-gathering capacity and resolution.

So instead of pictures of the ships down to less than a meter resolution—almost enough to read the Odin's *name on the hull—we lost them entirely for a few days.* Odin's *a shattered hulk, front half severed from the rear and most of two of its drive spines shattered, and* Nebula Storm . . . *is nowhere to be seen.*

Even radar had been misled, because whatever had happened, the two vessels had completely changed their courses. Instead of charging forward out of the Jovian system, both had for reasons unknown *decelerated* and emerged—or *not* emerged, he corrected himself, since *Nebula Storm* was nowhere to be seen—on utterly unexpected vectors. It had actually fallen to the Infra-Red Survey Telescope (IRST) to detect the wreckage of *Odin* and allow the others to home in on it and try to start making sense of the disaster.

As no trace of *Nebula Storm* had yet been found, the theory that made the most sense—a terrible sort of sense—was that she had for some reason slowed enough to drop orbit, scrape the atmosphere of Jupiter itself and be drawn ever closer until the friction melted even her alien hull and Jove pulled the remains down into the crushing blackness of its deadly atmosphere.

Nicholas shook his head and felt the ache not just in his head but in his joints, seeming buried in his bones. *I'm getting too old for this,* he thought.

It dawned on him with a faint chill that, in fact, he *was* getting old. *I'm past seventy now. It's been nearly fifteen years since Helen, Joe, and Jackie first dug up Bemmie. Ten years since I stood on Earth and watched* Nike *blaze its way out of orbit. Almost five years since we discovered a base on Ceres.*

These days seventy wasn't *that* old, true. When he was born—when personal computers were new and the web not yet worldwide—seventy was nearing the end of a man's life. People lived longer now and the last great medical advances had pushed active, healthy lifestyles even farther, so that he was physically a match for what his father had been at forty or forty-five.

But right now he felt more like twice that.

He sat back down and called up the almost blank

document which was supposed to be a press release—one he simply couldn't put off much longer. Oh, there'd been a quick one expressing everyone's shock and loss, with some hope that perhaps *Nebula Storm* would be located soon—but this was different. He would have to decide what direction he would take, both in public and behind closed doors, in placing—or not placing—blame for the disaster.

The European Union itself certainly wouldn't have resorted to such tactics . . . but the European Space Development Corporation might have; according to Walter Keldering, who was still the United States' representative here at Phobos Base, the ESDC's Chief of Operations Osterhoudt had some rather dark-gray, not to say black, operations history.

"Not *directly*, of course," Keldering had said, some weeks ago, "but he's connected. We're sure of it back at the Agency. And with the political pressure and having seen the benefits coming out of the discovered bases thus far . . . no, I wouldn't put it past him." He'd made a very expressive face. "And picking—rather forcefully—*FITZGERALD* for this? Sorry, Nick, but that pretty much screams 'dirty tricks.'"

He'd appreciated Keldering's honest input—the more so since he could *get* it now. The president who'd tried to screw Madeline over and, when Maddie foiled him by resigning and signing on with the IRI, sent out Keldering as a replacement was gone now, his final term marred by a completely home-grown scandal that put the opposition party in power. The new president was much more interested in cooperation, the more so since he could then rely on others to do a lot of the work while he focused on domestic issues. With those pressures gone, Agent Walter Keldering had become more an associate who simply had to be treated with respect and the same caution over proprietary information as any other, not a specifically-assigned spy.

He sighed again and started dictating. "The IRI apologizes for the delay in this announcement, but we have all been in a state of shock, and mourning, ever since we received the news that the *Nebula Storm* and the *Odin* had both been lost or suffered terrible damage, presumably resulting in the deaths of all aboard. We have lost friends and even family on those vessels, as have those in the European Union, and we extend our own sympathies to our brethren in the EU over this terrible accident..."

This was, naturally, the obvious and wisest course, to say nothing to anyone. Treat it as a terrible tragedy whose cause would likely never be known and perhaps arrange a true joint mission to Enceladus with the EU.

But he had to stop the dictation again, because the very idea made his gut rebel. *They killed my friends. How can I allow anyone to get away with that?*

He knew he couldn't really live with himself if he did. That was the reason Madeline, Helen, A.J., Joe, and even Jackie and Larry had gone out on that half-mad venture, chasing down the *Odin* in a vessel sixty-five million years old: because that kind of action, that sort of robber-baron treachery, could not be tolerated, *must* not be tolerated in the greater reaches of the solar system.

But at the same time he couldn't afford to lose the support of the European Union.

I really should have stayed a paleontologist. I had no trouble dealing with the petty politics there.

A light blinked on his desktop and he touched the icon. *A message from Ceres. Encrypted.*

Perhaps they'd found some evidence, at least. If he could *prove* what had happened on Ceres...

He was startled to find it was *heavily* encrypted. The standard decrypt key in the desktop wasn't sufficient; it was demanding a personal one-time key and biometric verification. *It must be something important.*

The screen lit up and his heart seemed to stop for a moment.

Then it gave a great leap and he felt a laugh of joy and relief rising as the golden-haired (if somewhat bedraggled) woman on the screen smiled at him.

"Hello, Nicholas," said Madeline Fathom. "I'm using the secure Ceres relay for this because I'm *sure* you'll want to decide what to do—and what you want *us* to do—very much in private.

"A warm hello from all of us here on sunny Europa."

Chapter 2

"Pull—*gently*, dammit, smoothly, don't jerk!" A.J. couldn't keep the tense exasperation from his voice as he barely reacted in time, commanding one of the three autonomous "Locust" drones, *Hopper*, to ease the tension on the all-too-vital cable.

"No need to *snap*," Dan Ritter said mildly. The dark-haired former environmental systems tech for *Odin* spoke English with only a trace of his native Germanic accent.

"Sorry. But *snap* is exactly what we'll get if we're not careful. We're crossing a hundred meters of ice frozen to minus one-seventy, and the cable's dropped a *lot* of flexibility."

A.J. felt his hair sticking to his forehead, barely kept himself from trying—futilely—to wipe sweat away. *That doesn't work when you're in a spacesuit.*

He stood between two spaceships—the *Nebula Storm*, half-embedded in a huge ridge of ice that had stopped her final slide after Madeline Fathom had, impossibly, managed to land her on Europa—and the *Munin*, one of *Odin*'s two explorer/lander vehicles, which had joined them after Richard Fitzgerald's

13

ill-fated mutiny led to *Nebula Storm*'s main reactor
being shut down and *Odin* being crippled and most
of her crew dead. *Six people on* Nebula Storm, *six
on* Munin; *the only survivors of this whole disaster.*

Of course, on *his* side that meant that *Nebula Storm*
hadn't lost anyone (yet), while the survivors of *Odin*
had lost a hundred of their friends and colleagues.

"Run the sheath heaters again?" Joe asked over
the radio.

So close now. Four meters, maybe five . . . but . . .
"Yeah, you'd better. If we break this we may be totally
screwed." A.J. heard his voice shake slightly and realized that he was far from recovered from the tensions
of the last few days. *Running on a few hours sleep
for days on end will do that to you, especially when
you're not twenty anymore.*

The cable he was helping string from *Munin* to
Nebula Storm was, quite literally, the lifeline for the
entire expedition. The superconducting coil batteries
on *Nebula Storm* had been heavily drained for the
landing—since her reactor was down—and the remaining energy was being quickly consumed by maintaining
the dusty-plasma "Nebula Drive" over the two crashed
vessels as a powerful radiation screen, diverting the
thousands of rems of lethal radiation that screamed
down onto Europa every day from Jupiter's hellish
magnetosphere.

Had *Munin* not been equipped originally as the
lander and exploration beachhead for the expedition to
Enceladus, they might have been out of luck already.
Fortunately, that *was* its intended function, with last-
ditch lifeboat a distant second, and that meant it had
Athena on board. The independent nuclear-powered

melt-probe was meant to penetrate the icy shell of icy worlds like Europa or Enceladus, and in the latter case to reach the presumed Bemmie base beneath—and for that it had a *lot* of superconducting cable.

So it wasn't, strictly speaking, the breaking of the cable that would be the problem; it was the fact that they didn't have time to do this over before the *Nebula Storm* and her barely-visible pearlescent shield shut down and let invisible, deadly hellfire in again. *If that happens, we'll have to splice cable and try to manipulate it almost all by remote, and I really don't know how well the Locusts will do in that kind of environment.*

"Activating sheath heaters," Mia Svendsen said cheerfully. *She's doing well,* A.J. thought. Possibly because she'd become so sure she was going to die at Fitzgerald's hands that she was still riding on relief. A.J. hoped she stayed that way, at any rate; they were going to need all the engineers they could get, and it was an incredible stroke of luck that they'd ended up with not one, not two, but three—four if you counted Eberhart, who was technically an engineer but focused more on computer software/hardware than the heavy gadget sort.

He set the cable down gingerly and waited; his suit's imagers showed the progressive glow of infrared marching down the length of the cable with its embedded heaters, and his other sensors reported the slow but steady rise of its temperature. He chuckled slightly.

"What's so funny, A.J.?" asked Helen.

"We're busy trying to *heat* a superconducting cable above the temperature that we used to have to cool them *down* to just a few years ago, so that we won't break the damn thing like a stick." The cable was considerably warmer already, but nowhere near room temperature yet. His smile faded as he looked to the side, at a counter projected in the upper left corner of the suit display; it showed the steady and inexorable drop in *Nebula Storm*'s power.

That'll have to do. "Mia, cut the power. Joe, Horst, I'm ready to pay it out again, you guys pull it through slow and steady on the count of three until you reach the interface. We don't have time to wait anymore, it's going to take you at least ten minutes to mate the adapter and get it linked in and then another ten to test before we can really throw the switch."

"Understood, A.J." Horst Eberhardt's voice was steady as a rock, betraying none of the tension A.J. knew he had to be feeling.

"On three. One . . . two . . . *three!*"

A.J. felt the pull begin and the cable began to move again. Behind A.J., inside *Munin*, Dan Ritter and Anthony LaPointe were feeding the cable through the ship. Outside it was just A.J. and his three Locusts— *Hopper*, *Kwai Chang*, and *Jiminy*. The sensor and exploration probes multiplied A.J., synchronized with his movements so that all four could feed the cable across the gap between the two ships with minimal chance of snags or miscoordination.

Now the cable rippled smoothly from *Munin*'s hatchway, through the manipulators of *Kwai Chang* and *Jiminy*, through A.J.'s hands, and thence from *Hopper* into *Nebula Storm*. One meter. Two meters. Three. Four.

"That's got it!" Joe's voice was triumphant. "We're starting to attach the adapter now. The rest of you lock down the cable and put the pads around it. Mia, I'll give you the go-ahead for the heaters as soon as soon as we get them connected and grounded—that's priority one in the adapter."

A.J. breathed a sigh of relief and told the Locusts to stay steady as he slowly released the cable. *One bullet dodged.*

But this far away from home, there's a lot more bullets on the way.

Chapter 3

"All right," Madeline Fathom said, her voice just slightly amplified by the walls of the common room of *Munin*. "Now that we're all reasonably safe for the next few days, we need to evaluate the entire situation and come up with a real schedule of action."

"Were you able to contact Dr. Glendale, Madeline?" Horst Eberhart asked.

"I was. He relayed a quick acknowledgement of our message through the secure channels, thanking us for bringing him up to date, and saying that he could delay a couple—but *only* a couple—of days to do a press release all of us can live with. So that's part of our agenda today, but I'd like to leave it for a bit later."

She looked around as the others nodded. The *Munin* was, relatively speaking, large, and had been built as a mobile command post and a vessel capable of entering and leaving atmosphere as well as airless environments. The common area was meant to hold crew for just such meetings, and the number of people there seemed to make it crowded, but a headcount would make it exactly one dozen, including herself.

Not very many to survive on a barren iceworld hundreds of millions of miles from home.

"First," she continued, "after this meeting we'll arrange a funeral."

"Not meaning to sound cold about it," A.J. said diffidently, "but is that a good idea? I mean, given everything else we have to do."

He winced and withered under a number of glares, which only subsided slowly.

"Yes, I think so," Maddie said, deliberately *not* sounding either hostile or exasperated—although exasperation was certainly a common emotion even with the new improved A.J. Baker. "*Nebula Storm* was incredibly lucky; we lost no one on board. But not only did *Munin* have two people die on the way here, but also *Odin* lost virtually all of its crew. We need to salute them, we need to say goodbye, we need to stay civilized and *human*."

"Sorry. I still think someone needed to ask. We'll be using power and resources for every thing we do here."

"I . . . suppose someone did." The Kentish accent belonged to Dr. Petra Masters, late the Chief Medical Officer of *Odin*. She was a moderately tall woman with the solid, heavy-boned build that was common in certain English families. "A question we will probably have to ask ourselves every day from now on." Her expression was controlled, but Madeline could still see traces of strain and sadness; she had fought hard to save both David Hansen and Titos Xylouris, but Hansen had been badly wounded in the devastating scattershot explosion that had crippled *Odin*, while Titos, outwardly appearing to be fine when he boarded *Munin*, had quickly succumbed to acute radiation sickness; he had, it turned out, been in a side section which had lost shielding—and the geometry had meant that the remaining shielding had actually caused *more* radiation to be channeled through that area. Even with modern medicine and some experimental anti-radiation drugs, there was nothing that she could do. Hansen had died hours after landing, and Titos followed him about half a day later.

Okay, let's get back on track. People need purpose. "Now that that's out of the way, let's focus on what we have to do. I don't think there's any argument that we are on our own in both surviving and getting home?"

Brett Tamahori shook his head. "No argument here. I've run some sims—being as that was my specialty—and worked with Joe, Jackie, and Mia on different assumptions, and the answer's always the same." The slightly dark skin tone was the only sign of Brett's partly Maori heritage, but the accent was, as Bruce Irwin would have put it, "pure Kiwi." He had been one of the few members of *Odin*'s crew not from one of the EU's member states, hired specifically for his modeling and simulation skills, which could be invaluable on a vessel that would have to evaluate situations constantly with limited information.

"There's just no reasonable way they can get us help in time," Brett continued. "The infrastructure was pushed to the breaking point to get us out here in the first place. If they start *right now*—within the next few days—to build a new *Odin*, or maybe a dusty-plasma sail rescue ship, *and* everyone gives it top priority, maybe. Maybe. But most likely we're looking at a couple of years before anyone else can make it."

"And even if we can survive a couple of years," Helen

said, "I suppose we'll still have to assume they're not coming at all, with that kind of timeframe."

"Exactly. So how long *can* we survive, Dan?"

"We're actually not in desperate straits there," answered Dan Ritter, calling up a display that *Munin* echoed to everyone present. "Thank the general for making sure *Munin* was prepped for just about every contingency. Even with scientific equipment on board, she was provisioned for eight people and an expedition length of one and a half to two years, and the general's decree of prepping her to be a lifeboat added to that. Your crew had planned on a round trip of three years and most of that's still to come. So provision-wise all of us together could make it at least two and a half to three years, especially if we're careful with rationing." He grinned and gestured toward the outside. "Water, of course, won't be a problem."

That was true enough; they were sitting atop a world-girdling ocean roofed over with water ice. "What about general environmentals?"

"We should be okay on that too. I'll have to keep up on maintenance on both ships, but with some good PHM programs and A.J. doubling our sensor coverage in those areas, I don't see any trouble. We've even got some backups if we have to scrounge—the large rover we brought has its own environmental plant. Insofar as power, *Munin*'s reactor can handle even a larger load than this for something like ten years."

Maddie could *feel* the tension drain from the room as the environmental technician made his cheerful, matter-of-fact statement of hope. "Thanks so much, Dan. Doctor, I think we need to hear about the rest of us."

While taking careful physicals of the desperate

combined crew hadn't been feasible, Dr. Masters had carefully gone over the medical records of the survivors and examined the telemetry of the extensive sensor suites in their suits. "Overall, that news is tolerable," Petra said promptly. "Naturally the majority of the crews of both vessels were chosen for physical health and capability as well as for their professional ability, and this is evident in my examinations. Some of us are getting older than the usual optimum, but that's actually not a terrible concern; everyone here has had a lot of preventative medicine applied and, speaking honestly, are likely in better shape even at fifty or sixty than they might have been at twenty-five or thirty in the early part of the century." She glanced over at A.J. Baker. "Mr. Baker's lungs are a matter of slight concern, but I'll keep a monitor on them."

Madeline saw A.J. wince reflexively, as he usually did when reminded of the horrific accident in which he had nearly died, and *had* lost his perfect health, inhaling enough superheated, toxic air to cause damage that even modern medicine could not completely undo. "Good. But I hear some reservations in your voice."

Dr. Masters nodded briskly. "Obviously I must be concerned with the gravity. Mars-normal gravity was shown by three IRI studies to be adequate to minimize many of the effects of microgravity, but indications are that anything below a third of a gee will be a serious problem. If we are here for a year, there could be long-lasting complications."

"I thought they'd figured out treatments for that," said her favorite voice in the world. Joe Buckley was seated over by the door, as though ready to exit in case of an emergency.

"Some," conceded Masters, "but the efficacy is still under research and there are clear side-effects. The intention at Enceladus was that we would regularly rotate the groundside scientists back to *Odin*, where they could reaccustom themselves to normal gravity in the habitat ring at periods which prevent bone loss or any of the other problems."

"This is a long-term problem," Maddie agreed, "but not an immediate one. I'd like you and the others, especially Brett, to work together to see if there are better solutions, but for now we need to concentrate on the mission-critical issues. Which really boil down to getting us off of here, which means fixing *Nebula Storm*."

"Exactly." Jackie Secord stood and floated up slightly before Europa brought her back down; she looked slightly embarrassed. "Ahem. That's going to be the biggest project." She called up simplified schematics of *Nebula Storm* to the room's projector. "Fitzgerald's bullet went through right about *here*. The problem is that *Nebula Storm* was a cobbled-together mess in some ways—no disparagement meant to you or A.J., Joe; she served us well and hopefully will get us back off this rock, but she was put together with not much time and some really crude compromises, which means that while I know it punched the core, I can't tell exactly *where* because I can't check the housing and angles as precisely as I'd like. I'm not sure we have all the tools I'd like to have, and it's going to be *touchy* work. We're talking about disassembling a nuclear reactor and fixing what's wrong—with tools never meant for that job. Which just emphasizes one of our biggest worries." Jackie glanced towards Dr. Masters.

"Oh, my, yes. Radiation. We have radiation meters already, of course—all of us going into the outer system knew this would be an issue. However, it is terribly more important now. Medical supplies are our most limited resource, and radiation illness . . . well, poor Titos gives us an immediate example. If you exceed your dosage, *you are dead*. You may feel fine, you may be walking, but you are dead and there is not one thing I will be able to do about it." She looked levelly around the room, making sure she caught everyone's eyes. "Remember that. *Nebula Storm*'s shield is protecting us from what would be a lethal dose every day, but nothing is perfect, and it is also always possible that something might go wrong and bring the shield down."

"They're all set to alarm automatically," A.J. pointed out. "And I can give us backups."

"That would be ideal, Mr. Baker. But anyone working on *Nebula Storm* will have to be doubly careful; radiation, please remember, is cumulative over quite a long period of time, and the more you absorb now, the less safety margin you have for later. I know this is repeating things said before, but it really *does* bear repeating, and I shall *continue* to repeat it at intervals until I am quite sure you have all got it. We will be here . . . a year? Perhaps longer. And during all that time we must be vigilant."

"We understand, Doctor," Joe said. "And repeat it all you want. Everyone should stay inside the ships when possible; they're built with shielding, especially the crazy stuff Bemmie used for *Nebula Storm*'s hull. But the big radiation shield from the *Storm*'s drive is our main interest, so we're going to be foolproofing that two ways. First we're going to armor the cable up so that you can drive over it without a problem, and second we'll be stringing a backup cable over another route. No power interruptions unless something can take out both."

The floor under their feet quivered and something rattled in another room. Madeline found everyone standing and looking at her.

"A . . . Europaquake," she said slowly. "Larry? Do we have something to worry about?"

The tall, slightly stooped astrophysicist glanced at his opposite number, Anthony LaPointe, and shrugged. "Hard to say. We might. The reason Europa has a liquid ocean is that Jupiter keeps squishing it around and generating heat. The following bulge moves back and forth every day . . ."

"And the one theory is that many of the cracks on the moon, if the ice is relatively thin, may be opening up every time this happens," Anthony finished. "We may have some very interesting times. Though the Conamara Chaos isn't *thought* to be a direct feature of that behavior; some people think it's the result of collapsing voids beneath the surface, I and some others think it's the remnants of a meteor strike, or maybe it's both. Still, significant quakes on a substrate that may be capable of splitting are not to be taken lightly."

"See what the two of you can come up with insofar as how bad the quakes are likely to be, how frequent, and what we can do to keep from getting killed or our ships and equipment damaged. The last part you'll probably have to work with Joe and Horst."

"Got you," Larry said equably. His even-tempered willingness to go along was one of his strongest points, especially in crowded spaceships. Anthony LaPointe also nodded his agreement.

"This," Maddie continued, making sure her tone lightened in a way to draw people's attention back to her, "brings me to the other major effort we'll be undertaking." The others looked at her in puzzlement, and she smiled.

"Let's be honest; we're going to be living here in very cramped conditions for probably over a year, with danger looking over everyone's shoulder almost every minute. I think we need to remember to give us something to do beyond just survival...especially if we can make it part of the whole effort."

Everyone's attention was fully upon her now. Jackie grinned, the sudden flash of white that always seemed to brighten the room she was in. "I see you've got something brilliant in mind as usual, Maddie."

"Just efficient. That's my job, after all. We're going to need a *lot* of reaction mass, what we sometimes sloppily call 'fuel,' for the main drive engines. We've used water in the past when we had to, but the ideal is hydrogen or at least some other lighter material. I know that our tanks are designed to handle multiple materials; what I want is a determination as to whether we can get away with just water for current purposes. It may not be as efficient but it is so much easier to work with that if we can, we probably should.

"In any case, whether we use water or hydrogen, we have only one real source: Europa's ice. Which we have to melt. Fortunately, we have a device *meant* to melt a *lot* of ice: *Munin*'s nuclear-powered thermoprobe, *Athena*. And it was thinking about that which brought the whole idea clear.

"We are all here on a journey of discovery," she continued, seeing some of the faces already brightening in understanding. "I see no reason we shouldn't continue to be scientists and discoverers even now.

"We can't protect Europa from our contamination really; we didn't plan on this landing, and we had no chance to sanitize our material in the manner required by international protocol. More, we can't afford the time and effort to maintain such strict controls, even if we had the resources.

"But we *can* continue our research. *Athena* was onboard *Munin* to probe Enceladus' interior, but she can tunnel into Europa's just as well—and provide us with all the water we will need. Unmanned probes have traveled through the system, but as we know from Phobos and Mars, all the automated probes in the universe still aren't nearly as good as human beings on-site, if you can get them there. Well, we *are* here, and we will not just survive. We will not just rescue ourselves. We will *learn*, just as we came all the way out here to do."

Helen suddenly laughed, and A.J. looked at her in confusion. "What's the joke?"

The blonde paleontologist shook her head bemusedly. "It's . . . so typically Madeline, three steps ahead of our own thoughts. If we were all thinking of this as survival and nothing else, we'd be doing our science all right . . . but feeling *guilty* about it, as though we were somehow wasting valuable thinking resources. She's already seen that and this makes it all *part* of our job—so we can just enjoy as much as we can."

Madeline felt a touch of pink on her cheeks, and—unlike in some instances—it wasn't entirely at her choice. "Anyone else taking a few minutes to think about it would see it. I just want us to remember to be human in *all* ways. Not just for remembering the dead . . . but for keeping us among the living." She looked up involuntarily, and—like the others—she wasn't really seeing the low ceiling of *Munin*, but the immense black sky with mighty Jupiter low in the west and Sun a tiny disc less than a fifth that seen from Earth. "Especially when we're the only living things within hundreds of millions of kilometers."

Chapter 4

I am the only living thing within hundreds of millions of kilometers, thought General Alberich Hohenheim.

The thought was not, he admitted to himself (there being no one else to admit it to) strictly true. There were undoubtedly a number of bacteria, possibly fungal spores and such, still living on the remains of the giant mass-drive vessel *Odin*, and there was the possibility that the water-oceans under the surfaces of Europa and Ganymede harbored some form of life.

But of course when we think such thoughts, we mean beings like ourselves—other people, or perhaps dogs or cats, something that feels as we do and would be able to alleviate our loneliness in isolation. And there is nothing like that *save for me until you reach—at least—the asteroid belt and Ceres.*

Seated—strapped in—at the engineering console of *Odin*, Hohenheim could see the exterior view displayed faithfully by the still-operating external cameras of *Odin*, or the half of *Odin* that remained at all. The forward portion, separated from the rest in Hohenheim's last-minute desperation maneuvers to prevent a meteoric crash into lethal Io, had impacted on the volcanic moon of Jupiter just scant minutes before Hohenheim's section had passed—just barely—by Io and continued onward.

In the following days he had gathered supplies from the wreck which seemed both far larger and more cramped than it had before. Sometimes he had to wriggle his way through crumpled metal that half-blocked a corridor, or find a way to force open a door whose frame no longer quite fit and which had no power to control it.

It was, he had to admit as he took a bite of the tight-wrapped liverwurst sandwich that was his lunch, something of a miracle that any of the systems were still functioning. Fitzgerald's shrapnel-filled shell had detonated at what might have been the worst possible angle and shredded the huge EU vessel like a bird hit by a shotgun blast at point-blank range. Angles of explosion and of other hardened components had protected engineering itself and some of the other core regions, but the damage was so pervasive, *so* heavy, that even systems which would normally have been able to recover some function were failing, and even with the references and augmented reality overlays that the central engineering systems and his own in-suit computers could provide, there was only so much he could do to fix any of them. Most of the status board showed red, with considerable splotches of yellow and virtually no green anywhere.

At least I can manage to spend a fair amount of time out of the suit. The suits had been designed well and a man could live in them for a long time...but everything chafes, everything becomes dirty, no matter how well designed, no matter what special functions or even self-cleansing materials and miniaturized systems exist.

The air of *Odin* was *almost* clean, but the sharp, urgent smell of burned electronics and heated metal still hung in the air, perhaps permanently a part of *Odin*'s surfaces by now. Still it was far better than being a prisoner to the suit, giving him time to take zero-g showers, clean out the suit, refill its vital reservoirs (and empty other, equally vital, reservoirs), and even to rest in a suspended hammock—with a helmet always nearby, naturally.

The lack of additional crew also meant that he did not have to ration out the better remaining supplies, such as the actual meat content of his sandwich; even though many storage areas had gone with the other half of *Odin*, the giant vessel had been provisioned for a hundred people for over three years. Even a very small fraction of that would sustain General Hohenheim for as long as he was likely to survive.

That might not be for too terribly long; the critical indicator of air supply was a brilliant amber and there were times he thought it was starting to shade to red. Overall, though, he was fairly certain of the integrity of the remaining hull of *Odin*, even if a large proportion of her main air supply had been lost. There were very small leaks somewhere, but whenever he could trace them he sealed them, and the cold, hard fact was that ninety-nine percent of his crew were gone; he didn't need all that much air. Oh, it would run out eventually with the slow leaks bleeding it away; a month, two months, three at the outside and he'd be reduced to staying in his suit, trading and refreshing air supplies until the rechargeable oxygen renewal systems finally gave out, but that didn't really matter. His real mission would be complete long, long before that. It was a simple mission, just one that had required a good deal of work, but was now almost complete.

Back to work. Hohenheim made sure he had no significant crumbs in the air and carefully placed the wrappings from his lunch in a disposal chute. He unstrapped, shoved himself with practiced ease over to his suit, and donned it, running through the full functionality checklist before sealing the suit and making his way over to his tool bundle. *One more set of connections to go.*

The theory was very simple, and the practice not much more complex. While *Odin*'s structure incorporated a lot of composites, it also included a great deal of metal, and some of that structure could be used as a gigantic antenna. Not, perhaps, the most *efficient* of antennas, but he could spare power to make up for that. Indeed he could, with virtually all other ship systems shut down, the mass-beam drive offline, and even environmentals only required for a fraction of the original vessel. The important thing was to make sure he could transmit with enough power—across a number of different bands—to make sure that he was heard.

Because what he was going to say...was going to be something many people did not *want* to hear, and he could not afford to be silenced. His honor—the only thing really left to him—demanded that much. The truth about Fitzgerald's actions, and those behind him, *had* to be known. That was the least that he could do for those on the *Nebula Storm*, as well as his own crew, who had been their victims.

It was in a way terribly unfair that he was the only survivor, but the *Odin*'s radar and remaining imaging systems—both infrared and visible—had found no trace of *Munin* or *Nebula Storm* since he had regained control of *Odin*. What had happened to them he could not guess; *Munin* had departed with the survivors many hours before *Odin*'s final rendezvous with Io, but perhaps it had been unable to escape that collision itself. *Nebula Storm*, crippled by Fitzgerald's brilliant if completely sociopathic attack, may itself have crashed somewhere, or merely lost power and dwindled into the distance, so far away that neither infrared nor radar could find her now. He had no idea of the full capabilities of these systems, nor was he an expert in their use.

Perversely, he still had an occasional flash of wishing that Fitzgerald were here; the security expert had hidden a tremendously able mind behind his deliberately-affected accent and had undoubtedly been nearly as omnicompetent as Madeline Fathom, his chief opposition. He would certainly have figured out a better way to accomplish this objective, and might even have been able to tell them what really happened to the others.

On the other hand, he'd simply have shot me for even trying to send the message I intend to send. He wanted Fitzgerald's competence, not his presence.

Hohenheim sailed with economical, efficient movements through the corridors and through rooms. Sometimes his passage disturbed the slow, drifting dance of ordinary objects—pens, paper, fragments of broken glass—in the air, leaving a rippling trail behind him that rang a distant bell in his memory, a fragment of one of the novels a younger Alberich Hohenheim had read while dreaming of space. *He was one hundred and seventy days dying and not yet dead...*

Indeed, though not that long has passed, or is likely to. Still, the memory was a sort of grim symmetry; like Gully Foyle, Hohenheim was trapped in the wreckage of his own ship, living only to strike back against those who had condemned him to this space-drifting tomb. The difference was that Hohenheim knew how to achieve his goal, and he needed no miraculous reawakening of the drive of his ship to do so.

The next door showed only vacuum on the other side. He sealed his helmet and opened the lock. The corridor looked superficially untouched, but a close look showed the neat hole, nearly large enough for Hohenheim to put his fist through, that had let the air out of this section. A distorted and frozen corpse—*Lieutenant DeVries*, Hohenheim thought sadly—drifted in the weightless emptiness. He tried not to touch the lieutenant's body as he went by—out of respect, not squeamishness. *I must devise some kind of ceremony after I'm done. There are at least ten bodies on board this part of* Odin *and if I cannot commit them to the deep properly I must at least pay the proper respects—perhaps make* Odin *itself a tomb worthy of their sacrifices.*

He opened a panel at the far end and checked. Power still flowed here. *Good.* He inserted the end of one cable into the power source and locked it to the repeater and transceiver box, then moved on. *Ten more meters...*

Naturally the door between there and here was stuck. He extracted the compact spreader-cutter rescue tool and inserted it into the gap. As he already had a power-connected cable, he removed it from the transceiver and plugged it into the spreader-cutter. The rescue tool hummed to work, the sound not audible through the vacuum but transmitted to Hohenheim through his suit as he held the tool in place. He could also feel and hear the groaning protest of the door as it gave grudgingly under the tons of force the tool could generate. A few minutes sufficed to force the door open wide enough for Hohenheim to wriggle through with the cable and transceiver.

He left the tool behind him for now; it was "compact" only in the sense that it could be carried around by one man, but it was still a massive and clumsy instrument, and he had no more barriers to pass, just a panel to remove. Behind the panel was one of the main structural members of *Odin*, metal and carbonan composite combined. He attached the antenna connections to the metal portion, reinserted the power line into the transceiver, and clamped all pieces down to make sure they stayed in place in the unlikely event that he made any maneuvers which put stress on them.

Almost impossible, actually, he thought. The neo-NERVA drive was no longer operable, its damaged nozzle having blown off in the final maneuvers, and the few functional reaction thrusters were very low on fuel—*or,* he corrected himself, *on reaction mass, to be precise.* With Jupiter's magnetic field available, *Odin*'s magnetorquers had been able to eliminate her unwanted rotation partially, with the field-parallel vector being dealt with by those few remaining reaction jets. Any maneuvers he *could* manage would be slow, ponderous, and unlikely to be felt by anything in the ship.

The main engineering console verified the connection and began running the program to characterize and balance the jury-rigged antenna system as best as could be managed. While that was ongoing, Hohenheim made his way back, picking up the rescue tool along the way.

The calibration run was nearly complete as he finished stripping off his suit and strapped back into the console seat. The computer had flagged a few anomalies for him to examine, and he sighed. *I am hardly a radio engineer, and if this requires more than a bit of look-up and basic calculation...*

Most of them, fortunately, were simply areas of signal loss that he'd expected. Most of the radio noise being received was what he expected as well; Jupiter's entire solar system was *filled* with it.

But...

He frowned at the last one. It was *narrow* in spectrum. And the cutoff bands were ...

"Gott im Himmel," he heard himself whisper. *It couldn't be...*

But there had been distinct peaks, peaks that corresponded to the movement of *Odin* in her drift through the Jovian sky, and that meant *direction*, a triangulation that would tell him if the impossible was true.

And when he had his answer, the amber warning of *Odin's* air supply was no longer irrelevant at all.

Chapter 5

Nicholas checked himself in the camera-eye view once more. Every stitch in place, every line correct. *And my hair going mostly white, I have to admit, has added an extra* soupçon *of dignity to my appearance.*

He also checked the VRD display, making sure the "augmented reality" display of his announcement would allow him to focus on the attendees while still able to see the announcement notes. *Good enough. Let's get to it, then, as Maddie would say.*

He stepped out onto the tiny stage that was in place in Phobos Station's conference room, and acknowledged the smattering of applause with a nod. "Please, all of you, sit down," he said with a brilliant flash of his trademark smile; he noted that for once there really were enough people present that addressing them as a group actually made sense. There were no fewer than ten other people present in the conference room—one representative from each of the five acknowledged space powers (the EU, the USA, China, India, and Japan), Glenn Friedet from Ares, and all four of the people who, in addition to regular jobs on Phobos Station or the IRI base below, acted as reporters for various news agencies.

"I know everyone's been waiting for a real announcement and some details, but I hope you understand it's been a very trying time for us all and we didn't want to make any announcements until we were absolutely positive of our findings."

That last bit was a deliberately ambiguous statement, and Nicholas thought he saw the slightest twitch of concern on the face of Giliam Maes, the EU representative from Belgium. *He probably doesn't know much, but there* has *to be some sense of worry pervading the EU space community right now. They've lost the most expensive ship ever built, at least by some measures, and it was at least to a great extent their own fault.*

But the idea of this conference wasn't to cause trouble, so he went on with a sudden broadening of his smile. "And the first thing I want to tell you . . . should be said by someone else."

On cue the display behind Nicholas lit up with Madeline Fathom's face; behind her could be seen a number of other people from both the Ares and the EU expedition. Madeline smiled and repeated the line she'd said first to him some days before. "A warm hello to all of you from all of us, here on sunny Europa."

It was amazing how a mere ten people then managed to sound like three times that many, and it took a few moments for him to get them to quiet down. "Please, everyone, I'll answer questions in a little bit, but let me get through my announcement; I'll undoubtedly be covering many of your questions as I do so.

"As you can see, by both tremendous luck and some absolutely heroic and inventive actions on the part of the crews of both *Nebula Storm* and *Odin*, there are some survivors of this double tragedy, and they are—at the moment—healthy and safe. They made a spectacular landing on the sixth moon of Jupiter, Europa; for those interested, the Institute will be releasing the footage of that landing as taken by the survivors themselves." *As if anyone in this group* wouldn't *be interested. I wouldn't be entirely surprised if that video clip becomes the most-viewed in the history of mankind.*

"Unfortunately, while—at the moment—all of the *Nebula Storm*'s six crew have survived, there are only six survivors of the *Odin*. In addition, these twelve people are currently marooned on a moon whose environment makes Mars look like an Earthly island paradise."

He paused for a moment, taking a sip of water from the glass on the lectern. The ten faces in front of him, five men and five women, waited tensely. "I know all of you want to know what happened—how we came to this point. The preliminary events are already known and I think we all want to put those behind us." He was referring, of course, to the fact that the EU had taken the information on Enceladus' possible Bemmie base and run with it, while concealing that information from the Ares-IRI consortium on Ceres. *No point rehashing it, either.* "I'm sorry to say that at this point we still only have partial information as to what happened in those crucial hours as both *Odin* and *Nebula Storm* prepared for their final maneuvers in preparation for heading to the Saturnian system, but I will tell you what we know at this point.

"As both vessels prepared for what is called an 'Oberth maneuver,' a method of using a combination of the interaction of the gravity well of a large planet with a ship's reaction drive to greatly change the speed and direction of your vessel, something went wrong with the automatic systems of *Odin*. Instead of firing her systems to accelerate out of the Jovian system, the ship swung effectively opposite the intended vector and fired to *slow down* the vessel. Subsequently there was a large explosion on *Odin*." *So far, I'm telling the truth—just leaving out a few details and confusing the timeline a bit. Now I have to add some bald-faced lies, however.* "Upon detecting this event, *Nebula Storm* changed her own maneuver to try to match up with *Odin*. This attempt was not entirely successful but did at least allow the two vessels to remain near each other."

He could see that Mr. Maes wasn't sure whether he should relax or not. *Don't worry. We've reached an agreement on how to handle this, and you'll be able to relax soon enough.* "We still have no evidence as to what caused this explosion." Strictly speaking one *might* be able to argue that this was true; he had some hearsay about what happened but no direct testimony by *Odin*'s personnel—yet—and he hadn't gotten copies of the sensor records from A.J. which would undoubtedly have demonstrated just what happened.

"What we do know is that it was violent enough to shatter at least one of *Odin*'s mass-driver spines and send shrapnel through most of the entire vessel. Most of the *Odin*'s crew, I am afraid, died within minutes of the explosion, as the shrapnel penetrated most of the living quarters in the 'hab ring' around the vessel. The damage also severely impacted the radiation shielding, which led to further casualties. Intraship communications were almost completely wiped out, and even in the areas of the vessel that remained liveable immediately afterwards, there was little to no way to communicate with other components, nor to reach them unless the people in question were fortunate enough to have their EVA suits with them. The vessel's magnetorquers apparently malfunctioned along with some of the other systems, and this caused a spin in the ship; this eventually revealed that serious structural damage must have been done, because in the end *Odin* broke up into two separate pieces."

"My God. How did *any* of them survive?" The involuntary question came from Diane Sodher, once a NASA information specialist on the *Nike* project, now main IT for Phobos Station and freelance 'stringer' for CNN.

The question fit into his narrative, so he went with it. "Fortunately, on the far side of *Odin* from the explosion was the bay with its remaining landing craft, *Munin*. Even more fortunately, General Alberich Hohenheim had directed that *Munin* be kept prepared for use at all times, even though arrival at Enceladus was not projected for many months to come. Because of this, the few survivors who were able to make it to *Munin* found themselves with an excellent and well-supplied 'lifeboat.'"

"Excuse me, Dr. Glendale," Giliam Maes said, "but . . . was the general one of the survivors?"

"I am afraid not," Glendale answered regretfully. "According to the survivors, he was still alive but remained onboard to make sure that, in fact, the *Munin* could launch successfully." *And that much is, in fact, true.*

The two successive questions had succeeded in

breaking the briefing into a question and answer session, but that didn't bother Nicholas; he'd gotten the main introduction out of the way and the rest could be presented in this format as well as any other. "Nick," Glenn said, "I'm confused by this. The *Nebula Storm*'s dusty-plasma drive isn't really limited by mass as such, and even if we assume that *Munin*, fully loaded, was maybe a thousand tons—I think it's considerably less—there's no reason for them to have *landed* anywhere. If the two ships could rendezvous at all they should have just made sure they were secured together and then headed home. It might have taken a little longer, but . . . ?"

"That would indeed have been the plan," Nicholas said, acknowledging Glenn's question with a nod, "but apparently fate was not quite through with our friends yet." Time for the next part of the big lie. "As they had slowed down to match with *Odin* and—later—with *Munin*, something struck *Nebula Storm* and penetrated the hull. It's possible that this was purely coincidence, or it may be that one of the fragments from *Odin* managed to take *Nebula Storm* with it. Be that as it may, whatever it was managed to damage the ship's reactor core."

"Christ Almighty," Glenn muttered, and similar sentiments rippled around the attending group.

"I see you understand. Without an operating reactor the *Nebula Storm* could not continue operation of the dusty-plasma drive, especially at full size and with full control."

"Dr. Glendale," Yoko Hyashibara, the Japanese representative, spoke up with an apologetic tone. "Forgive me for bringing this up . . . but as I understand it, the

Nebula Storm and the *Odin* were, in truth, the only vessels currently capable of outer-system travel—even if, for instance, the *Nike* or *Nobel* could be spared from their current support duties. Does this mean that we are only going to witness another tragedy as the survivors starve or freeze to death?"

"I believe not," he said with another smile. "We are already working on plans which—with, I hope, the assistance of the EU and others—will allow us to get a new outer system vessel constructed in the next year or so. But more importantly..." he activated the second clip from the interplanetary castaways.

"We're not just sitting on our asses here waiting to be rescued," Jackie Secord said from the display, smiling confidently at the assembly. She stood on the surface of Europa, the immense banded gibbous disc of Jupiter touching the horizon behind her, the black of space faintly pearlescent with some strange mist. "We have engineers. We have tools. We have food, air, and a whole *planet* of water, and we've got the Nebula Drive working some as a shield so that we can live and work right here on Europa.

"So you go right ahead and build a rescue ship—we need all the ships we can get anyway. But don't be surprised if we meet that ship halfway, because we're going to *fix* the *Nebula Storm*, and fly her and *Munin* all the way back home!"

Chapter 6

"I'm not seeing much of a lightshow," Joe observed as he watched A.J. hard at work. Of course the "hard at work" was more conceptual than actual; much of A.J.'s work looked more like a man reclining in one of *Munin's* pilot chairs, wearing a pair of reflective sunglasses and waving his gloved hands semi-aimlessly in the air in front of him.

"Give this iceball a decent atmosphere and you'd be seeing a pretty good one," A.J. retorted. "I've just finished retuning *Munin's* topside comm lasers and we'd already figured out the tweaks for those we put on *Nebula Storm*. They're all running now."

"Maddie mentioned you were working with the lasers, but she didn't say for what. So, for what?"

"We need all the resources we can get, right? Well, the most versatile single resource we have is, of course, Faerie Dust. I can't get any more of *mine* delivered here, but—"

Joe laughed. "You've still got it, I see. Of course, there's just *tons* of the *Odin's* drive-dust floating around out there. And the more of it we get, the better off we are."

"Right in one. Oh, it's practically chipped-flint level compared to my babies here," he patted the sealed bag he carried practically everywhere, "but even that stuff can do a *lot* for monitoring activities, basic PHM/CBM over every millimeter of both ships, be a sensor net over a wide area . . . and let us save the fancy stuff for when it's needed. Like if the Doc needs some very detailed imagery of someone."

"I thought you said your Faerie Dust wouldn't survive long in a human body. You know, when you went all Mad Science on Modofori." Joe was speaking of the not-so-distant time when some of Fitzgerald's agents (actually more unwitting pawns) had made the extremely bad mistake of kidnapping and threatening Helen.

"And that's true, but if one of us is hurt or sick, I'm not going to whine about sacrificing some of my toys to get our medical officer the best data she can use. At that point the very minor risk from the dust will hopefully be a lot less than whatever's threatening our crewmates." Another lazy set of gestures with a *glissando* ripple of the fingers. "Shouldn't *you* be working?"

"Break time. Those of us doing outdoor work—"

"—do pretty short shifts to prevent any chance of getting bored, overstraining the suits, and such. So do we need heaters?"

"Not so far. As you so aptly observed, Europa only has an atmosphere in the very technical sense that astronomers use—basically that it has a higher density of gas around it than the surrounding medium. So it's not conducting or convecting any heat from us, and only direct contact with the surface poses any kind of threat there. We're still trying to dump heat, not trying to keep it."

"That's good. I'm not sure how we'd retrofit some of these suits for heating."

A.J. suddenly sat bolt-upright, the motion bouncing him almost a meter into the air; whatever he was looking at in the VRD had captivated him so completely that he seemed utterly oblivious to the fact that he somersaulted halfway around and came down nearly on his face, breaking his fall with an instinctive and unconscious movement of one arm. "Holy flying *wrecks*, Batman!" he said.

"What?"

"The *Odin*! She's still flying!"

"No way. Show me! I thought we'd calculated that she was headed for a hard landing on Io."

The forward screen lit, to show a terribly mangled yet still somehow recognizable shape. "Damn. She looks even worse than the last time we saw her," Joe said slowly.

"A *lot* worse," A.J. muttered, his voice abstracted. "She's lost her entire forward half. More than half, if you're counting by mass—everything very far forward of the main engines and drive spines is *gone*."

"Could she have had a one-in-a-billion grazing collision?" Joe remembered an old video he'd seen of a huge meteoroid that had passed through Earth's atmosphere and then headed back out into space without actually hitting the ground.

"Umm..." More waving of the hands. "Not with the orbit we left her in. Something had to have shifted her orbit a bit. Not much, or maybe quite a bit, depending on *when...*" Some more motion indicated A.J. was trying to figure out how much change would be needed at what point in the orbit.

Joe stared at the mangled vessel on the screen, turning very slowly. "A.J.," he said finally, "What's that?"

"What's *what?* For an engineer, your dialogue is amazingly imprecise sometimes."

"That ... green flickering on the *Odin.*"

"What green ..." A.J. trailed off, then froze. "*MADELINE!* Get in here *RIGHT NOW!*"

The suit and ship control systems were not particularly smart by human standards, but they were very good at context-sensitive transmission. Not only did they immediately relay that order directly to Madeline Fathom (Buckley), they recognized the urgency and context and did *not* send it to anyone else. Joe, of course, stayed put. Anything that got A.J. that excited he wanted to know about right away.

The lock cycled and Madeline entered, retracting her helmet. "What's wrong, A.J.?"

The screen flickered, and suddenly, looking out of it, was a face. A face with a sharply-cut blond beard and a slightly-beyond-regulations haircut, looking at them with startlingly golden eyes. "*Nebula Storm* and *Munin*, please answer. This is General Alberich Hohenheim. *Nebula Storm* and *Munin*, please answer. This is ..."

Even Madeline seemed frozen in shock for long moments—though Joe realized later it could only have been for seconds. Then she snapped into action. "Can we reply?"

"Huh?" The question broke A.J. out of an incredulous stare. "Oh, yes. Certainly. He's using *Odin's* remaining dust-collecting lasers as a comm beam. Probably homed in on ours once we started them up." A.J. scratched his head, then tapped out invisible commands. "Didn't think the general was quite that tech-savvy, though. That was a fast response—I've only been working these things maybe twenty minutes." He nodded sharply. "Okay, that should do it. I've patched it through for you and you alone to speak, although anyone here—that's the three of us—can hear you."

"General, this is Madeline Fathom. We receive you. Over."

". . . and *Munin*, please answer. This is General Alberich Hoh—"

The repeating message abruptly cut off and the living General Hohenheim was on screen. The golden eyes showed hints of tears shed and unshed, but he was smiling broadly. "*Guten Tag*, Agent Fathom," he said. "A very good day indeed."

"A *marvelous* day, General! I won't ask you for the details at the moment, but . . . are you all right?"

The face paused for a few seconds before responding; A.J. said, *sotto voce*, "He's only about five hundred thousand kilometers away right now—figure about one point seven seconds each way."

The general then nodded. "I am, for now. I am afraid that there are no other survivors on board this vessel, however." His smile faded, as he asked carefully, "Might I ask . . . how many of my crew survive?"

"Only six, sir. I'm sorry."

The figure on the screen closed his eyes once enough time had elapsed to send the message back. "*Sechs* . . . Six." It was, indeed, a small enough number when his crew had numbered over a hundred in total. "Still, six is infinitely preferable to zero. Then you and *Munin* did indeed join forces. Still . . . why are you there, on Europa, instead of using your magnificent Nebula Drive to sail home?"

Madeline explained the situation. "So we expect to find a way to get home eventually, but we couldn't do it as things were."

Hohenheim nodded. "Yes, I see. Excellent thinking. *Munin* has more than enough power to bring both of you back into space, as she was designed to be able to reach Earth orbit on her own, and Europa has scarce an eighth of Earth's gravity."

"Pardon me for butting in," A.J. said, "but—no offense, sir—how is it you were able to lock your beams on ours so quickly? I'm not sure *I* could have pulled it off that fast."

"Unless," the general responded with a more natural smile, "you had that trick set up beforehand. Once we had recognized that you had captured some of our dust and were playing with the beam, it occurred to us that you might be planning to somehow interfere with our drive. I accordingly had instructed Mr. Eberhardt to create options within our control systems whereby our lasers—much stronger than your own—would automatically track yours and attempt to overwhelm any signals you sent. That particular application was not difficult to repurpose to using for a transmitter."

"Speaking of transmitters . . . General, you haven't communicated with anyone farther in-system, have you?" Madeline's voice was tense, and Joe suddenly realized why.

"No, not yet. I very nearly did, I admit, but just before I was prepared I detected radio activity and realized that it was coming from Europa." General Hohenheim looked grim. "I was going to transmit a detailed account of this entire affair—a completely honest account. But once I realized that your people might have survived, I decided to at least try to contact you and find out what your intentions were."

Maddie sighed with relief. "Thank you for that, General. As we proposed before Mr. Fitzgerald mutinied, we wish a cooperative venture—previously for the exploration of Enceladus, now in getting us off of Europa and home. Sending an unvarnished account would completely destroy that cooperation. Understand," she continued in a harder voice, "we have *every* intention of bringing this home to those who were behind Fitzgerald . . . but not in such a way as to make all of the EU our enemies by embarrassing them publicly."

After the pause, they saw Hohenheim nod slowly, his lips tightening for a moment. "As you wish. Mr. Fitzgerald himself is dead; while I cannot claim to have killed him—he was a terribly capable man, as I am sure you are aware—what little data I could wring from the computers indicates that in his attempt to reach the location on *Odin* where I had sent *Munin*, something happened which either killed him directly or, possibly, ejected him into space. Either way would be most certainly his end—and one far too good for him. But his backers . . . I assure you, we are of one mind on this."

Madeline was smiling narrowly, the kind of smile that sent a slight shiver down Joe's back; it always meant trouble. Trouble for the people Maddie didn't like. "And I think you, General Hohenheim, are going to be our secret weapon."

"I believe I have an idea of what you mean," the general said after a moment. "But you may only have me for a short time."

"What?" Maddie looked concerned. "Don't tell me the *Odin* is headed for a crash?"

"*Nein*, nothing so dramatic, I am afraid." General Hohenheim gestured to the ship around him. "The *Odin* is too damaged to work forever. In particular . . . she is leaking. In a few weeks—maybe a few months—there will be no air left on her that I can breathe."

Chapter 7

"We have to rescue the general." Horst Eberhart said the words emphatically, ending with a challenging glance at A.J.

"Damn right we rescue him," A.J. responded. At Horst's raised eyebrow, he continued, "Yeah, I raised the necessary question about the funeral, but that was about people we couldn't help anymore. If it weren't for the general, none of you people would've gotten off *Odin*—or if you did, Fitzgerald would've been on board. I can't see *any* way that could've worked out well." *And that's an understatement. That guy was someone who worried* Madeline Fathom, *and he damn near got everyone on* both *ships killed.* "So we all owe him big, since we'd never have landed alive without you people. We can't just let him drift out there and die if there's anything we can do about it."

"But . . . *is* there anything we can do about it?" Joe Buckley asked, reluctantly. "We're just starting to figure out how to save ourselves."

"I think there is," Larry Conley answered. He brought up a diagram of the inner Jovian system. "Here's big daddy Jupiter and his big kids Io, Europa,

Ganymede, and Callisto. *Odin* was originally scheduled for a grand finale hard landing on Io, but the general pulled off a genuine miracle and managed to shift his orbit to avoid that. The combination of his shift and the encounter with Io put him into *this* orbit."

A.J. watched as the dot representing *Odin* cycled through an obviously elongated orbit while the Galilean moons performed their effectively circular orbits around Jupiter. "He's orbiting between Io and Europa!"

"Exactly, and that's what gives us an excellent chance, if we can get everything working soon enough." Larry paused the animation. "Here, he's at maximum distance from Jupiter, and just a tiny bit outside Europa's own orbit. Here, he's at his closest, almost exactly on Io's orbit. Relative to us, he'll go through periods where he's really going quite slow, comparatively speaking. If we can rendezvous with *Odin* at those times, we can transfer people or equipment pretty easily without crowding *Munin*'s safety margin."

"Right," Dr. Masters said, "but I think the earlier bit there is the sticky one. *If* we can get everything working soon enough. Can we? The general said that he could be out of air in a few weeks."

A.J. opened his mouth but it was Mia Svendsen who spoke first. "General Hohenheim's managed some miracles so far, but he isn't an engineer. I would be very surprised if the engineers we have here can't give him some better guidance to stretch out his survival. Dr. Baker—"

"Call me A.J., please," he said reflexively. *I'm not quite as bothered by the title I haven't really earned as I used to be. But habit stays with you.*

"A.J., then. A.J., would any of your Faerie Dust still be operative on *Odin*?"

"Yes," he answered promptly. "I was going to say something about that just a minute ago. I'd concentrated a lot of the Dust into the control systems of the neo-NERVA drive and the drive spines—as you know. Some of it got lost in the disaster, but once we started talking to *Odin* I was able to focus some comm lasers on it and then use both *Munin* and *Nebula Storm*'s RF antennas to pick up some pings back from the Dust. Problem is that in all the hash of interference Jupiter likes to throw out, it's *really* hard to get anything decent out of the things at this kind of range."

"Would it help if you could have an onboard control node?"

"Well of *course* it would, but—" he broke off and then whacked himself on the head in reprimand. "Of course, there's got to be onboard comm and programming nodes for the drive dust. Maybe real simple—"

Mia shook her head and smiled. "Not very simple, no. We assumed that various types of nanodust might be used, including in the future some quite complex ones. All we need to use them as interfaces are your protocols and security codes."

A.J. hesitated, instinctively unwilling to hand control of his Faerie Dust over to anyone else—even if, as was true here, it was likely that all he was doing was just letting someone else *talk* to it so he could control it more efficiently. "Er . . . Yes, of course, you're right."

"What will we get out of that, Mia?" asked Anthony LaPointe.

"*Lots* more information, that's what," said Dan Ritter.

"We had a lot of built-in sensors throughout *Odin*, but the whole system was pretty much destroyed by the accident, and for all I know some of what Fitzgerald did might have wiped other parts by accident. We stopped getting any significant updates from the main PHM systems onboard once the main net went down. If we can get A.J.'s much smarter smart dust spread through the crucial areas, I'm *sure* I can figure out where the worst leaks are, help the general plug them, and maybe even find how to activate some of the backup air supplies that still have to be on his chunk of *Odin*."

"All right," Madeline said. "Let's assume we can help General Hohenheim seal *Odin* better and preserve enough air so that he has several months instead of weeks. We still have to get *Munin* filled with reaction mass, and we can't just detach *Munin* from *Nebula Storm* without losing our shielding."

"We're about ready to deploy *Athena*," Horst spoke up. "She was designed with piping to help dispose of water as it was melted, and Jackie and I have put together fittings that will take that water and put it directly into *Munin*'s tanks—and another set that will do the same for *Nebula Storm*'s tanks. Water is not the very best reaction mass, but it is the best compromise we have—abundant, stable, noncorrosive, easy to handle, no need for high compression or any of that trouble." As usual, only a slight hard edge on some of the consonants showed that German was Horst's mother tongue.

"*Athena* does a roughly one-meter bore," Larry said, "which means that you'll get a metric ton of water for every meter or so she goes down." He grinned.

"Which is what Maddie meant about doing science while we rescue ourselves; we'll be cutting a deep bore into Europa's crust, studying this cross-section of the moon, and getting our reaction mass at the same time."

"That's . . . a long bore." Hundreds of tons of water would be needed, A.J. knew—five hundred tons or maybe more for each ship.

"But actually pretty short compared to what we were looking at on Enceladus," Anthony pointed out. "Sure, where the vents are seen, there the crust must be very thin, but if we wanted a place thick enough to stay on without it cracking apart, we might have to find a place with kilometers of ice crust."

"Good enough," Madeline said, "but what about the *Nebula Storm* and the fact that we need to maintain a radiation shield? Those of us left behind *could* just retreat inside *Nebula Storm*'s main hull, I suppose, but . . ."

"Not necessary, Maddie," Joe answered. "Given the problems we've already had, Brett and I have been modeling various changes to the Nebula Drive interface, and there's ways of running a reasonable-sized shield version of the drive with a lot less power. If *Munin* fully charges our ring batteries before leaving, I think we can keep everything going a lot longer than we used to."

Maddie smiled. "Excellent. So we believe we can keep General Hohenheim alive long enough, we can get to him, and we can keep ourselves alive while we do it. That leaves just one more problem: why are we going out to *Odin*?"

Everyone, A.J. included, stared at her. "Er . . . what?"

Joe said after a pause. "We're going there to rescue the general, Maddie. Wasn't that what we were all just talking about?"

She shook her head. "Yes, and of course that's what we're doing. But what do we want *everyone back home* to think we're doing?"

Now A.J. got it. "Crap. Of course, we're trying to keep the general a secret. So we need a reason to go out there that makes sense but *doesn't* involve rescuing someone."

"Well, couldn't we be trying to salvage something from the wreck?" Helen asked.

"Maybe, yes," Horst said, frowning, "but it would have to be something *very* valuable—crucial for our survival. Look at how much we are risking. To help another survivor, it makes sense, yes, people will often do things that are very risky for that; but if we're not admitting that this is our reason, then we need a motive that's very, *very* strong."

"What about superconducting cable?" A.J. suggested. "We could say that a big chunk of *Athena*'s got heated too high during the landing." As with many other materials, heating the Bemmie-derived room-temperature superconductors too much could destroy critical parts of the metamaterial structure that made it work.

Maddie looked thoughtful, but Horst shook his head. "Never work; there's only one place on *Munin* that *Athena* would have been stored, and for it to get that hot, we'd have had a lot more problems. Ones probably ending with us all dead."

"Why not just say we're going to look for survivors?" Brett asked. "We didn't know there was a piece of

Odin intact before, now that we do we feel obligated to check."

It was Madeline's turn to shake her head. "That one unfortunately fails the strength-of-motive test. Oh, it could be assumed we had that discussion, but anyone would know that I would be against it—and, not to waste our time with false modesty, I'm fairly certain that I could make sure we didn't go down that road if I felt it was a bad idea."

No one seemed inclined to argue; the *Nebula Storm* crew had worked with Madeline Fathom for years and knew exactly how formidable she was, and of the former *Odin* crew, several knew that Madeline was the only person who had worried Security Chief Richard Fitzgerald.

There was a short silence as all twelve castaways tried to think of something that met the stringent requirements.

A rippling chuckle suddenly broke the quiet. Startled, all heads turned to the source. "What's so funny, Doctor?" Dan asked.

Petra Masters smiled. "Well, it's a tad trite, that's all. But why not medical supplies? I used up quite a bit of ours," her face was momentarily shadowed, "trying to save David and Titos. We're going to be working on a damaged nuclear reactor, on a moon—let's be honest, actually, a planet that just happens to be going 'round an even larger planet—that might be unstable enough to get us injured rather directly. And we still could get ill in other ways—that old hackneyed standby appendicitis could rear its head, to name one. *Munin* was supplied with the assumption that *Odin* would be orbiting overhead in case of any real emergency, at least in terms of medical supplies. Now we have twelve people and a *real* state of emergency."

A.J. found himself nodding along with Madeline; the delicate-looking blonde said, "I like it. Yes, I think that's excellent. Most of the experimental medications for low-gravity exposure are on *Odin* as well. That's really a very good idea, Dr. Masters."

"Well, we do tend to think of our own specialty first." The English doctor tried not to look overly pleased.

"All right then, people. Let's get to it. Keep the general breathing, get the tanks refilled, and prepare our stories to withstand any questions." Madeline said briskly.

"Concocting stories to mislead and confound the enemy?" Joe inquired as everyone stood up. "And I thought you gave that up for Lent."

"Oh, don't spoil her fun, Joe." Helen said, and gave a delighted chuckle herself as she saw a touch of pink on Madeline's cheeks.

"Wouldn't dream of it," Joe answered. "She's never quite happy if she doesn't have *someone* to confuse," he continued, with a fond look at Madeline, "and I'm just too easy a target to be worth it."

PART II

*Challenge, n: 1) a call to engage
in a contest, fight, or competition;
2) an act or statement of defiance; a call to
confrontation; 3) a demand for explanation
or justification; calling into question;
4) a test of one's abilities or resources in a
demanding but stimulating undertaking.*

Chapter 8

"So why *Athena?*" Madeline asked, watching the melt-probe's interface and prestart prep screen. *So far, all good.*

In one corner of the HUD, she saw Helen, who was helping position one of the anchor sections, grin. "My *goodness*, Maddie, I think this is the first time you've ever managed to surprise me by *not* knowing something."

She returned the smile at the gentle dig. "My publicity greatly exceeds my only very slightly super-human abilities. I know the *name* of course, Athena, the goddess of wisdom and warfare, sprung full-grown from her father Zeus' head. And I can, I suppose, see that a probe of any sort gathers information and so could be named *Athena*, but it seems quite a stretch."

"Very true," Mia Svendsen put in from her position directing the assembly of the anchoring structure for *Athena*'s deployment, "but as you very accurately stated, Athena was also a goddess of war, and it was she who, during the war with the Titans or Giants, plunged her spear directly into the Giant Enceladus."

"That *does* make it a much more appropriate name.

But you had the probe onboard long before we even discovered Enceladus would be the target."

Helen blinked. "Oh . . . yes, of course, they had to. They didn't have any opportunity to go back and get one built."

"That's right," Mia admitted, "And so the probe was originally just MP-N-1, Melt Probe, Nuclear, number one. We knew that there were several major bodies in the outer system which had icy surface layers which might require melt-probe operations, so such a system was included on *Odin*'s manifest as a matter of course. Once the destination was determined, a name became a priority and that one was an obvious choice." She raised her voice slightly. "Horst, Jackie, the support deployment is on schedule. How's the startup check going?"

"Everything looks good so far," Jackie answered. "Maddie hasn't seen any alerts, so *Athena* seems to have come through without any damage."

"How long before the support framework is ready?" Horst asked. "Prestart checkup on *Athena* will be done in a few more hours."

"Longer than that," Mia answered. "We are in very low gravity, which makes support less of an issue than it would be on Earth, but we cannot afford any level of preventable risk. Based on Anthony's analysis I've expanded the support radius considerably, with more anchor points. We'll be able to start *Athena* in two days or so, I would say."

Maddie nodded to herself. Anthony, with some input from Larry and modeling by Brett, had determined that there was a small, but significant danger from the quakes, and that they certainly should be bracing everything for potential shocks. A probe trying to tunnel into the depths of Europa was, obviously, one of the things most at risk, even though it *was* designed with that possibility in mind and could, in fact, tunnel backwards if it had to in order to get back up a partially-collapsed shaft. But it *did* need to retain a good connection to the surface to do that. "Good enough. Horst, I'll keep an eye on the interface, but I'm switching over to team two on the comm."

"Understood."

"Dan," she said, knowing the comm system would recognize and perform the switchover even as she spoke, "how are you coming with the *Odin*?"

"Slowly," Dan answered. He hastened to add, "There's progress, and I'm sure we'll get it all set soon enough, but right now things are going at a snail's pace."

"What's the hangup? A.J., is it the Faerie Dust?"

"Not as such, no. Or maybe yes, I guess. Between Mia and Horst—and me, of course—we were able to get their nodes to talk to my Dust well enough, and we're getting a lot of good data. But it takes *time* to get the stuff from one point to another, and that's one huge ship. I have to figure out how much to move, and where, and then it has to work its way, millimeter by millimeter, to the target. And the dust doesn't move all that fast on its own, even in zero-g."

"Aren't there key locations to focus on first, rather than trying to distribute it everywhere? And I thought you *had* distributed it through the systems before."

"Again, yes and no. When we first compromised *Odin*'s systems we entered through known points on the neo-NERVA drive, and after that I was able to pinpoint other entry locations. But even then, I was focused on one specific set of systems, the drive controls. I wasn't touching their environmentals, for a *lot* of reasons. So there's at least three places that I really could use a bunch of Faerie Dust in so it could disperse from there, but I never had anything all that close. So it has to go there, at about a hundred microns a second. And the routes aren't always very direct."

"Well, you concentrated most of it in Engineering," Maddie said after a moment. "Why not have it just go into a cup or a bag and let the general carry it to the main dispersal points?"

There was dead silence for a moment, and then the transmitted sound of a glove smacking the faceplate of a helmet. "*DUH! DUH!* Adric Jamie Baker... SOOOOOOOOper-Genius!"

Dan was laughing, but he said, "Don't beat yourself up *too* much there. None of the rest of us engineers thought of that, either."

"Sometimes you just need someone on the outside of the problem to show you the solution," Maddie said, trying not to let herself giggle; A.J. would get over it, of course, but there was no need to rub it in, as he was doing a more than adequate job of it himself. "Taking this into account—"

"—if I have the highly-trained commander of *Odin* act as pack mule for my ultra-advanced sensors, yes, we can speed things up a lot. Duh, again. Brett, can you model the dispersion if we have the general move some to the main areas in question?"

"Just a minute." In very little more than the named time, Brett Tamahori's voice came back on. "That cuts a *lot* of time out. We'll have most of the environmental and integrity monitoring network up within the next day and a half, especially if I assume the general isn't averse to actually dispersing what he carries in smaller packets to specific areas."

"I'm sure he won't be; after all, your initial tests *did* help already."

"True enough. We found two seals that had subtle leaks and one filter that had failed without tripping its built-in indicators. His air quality went up significantly after that."

"Brett, on another subject, how long will it take to fill *Munin*'s tanks?"

"That's an easy one. Assuming no breakdowns—and I think we pretty much *have* to assume no actual breakdowns, just occasional snags—*Athena* can manage about half a meter an hour at this temperature. As we go deeper the temperature may—has to, I guess—rise significantly, until you reach the water layer. It's got a melting cross-section a little bigger than I'd originally thought, just about exactly one and a half square meters, so you get about a ton and a half of water every meter. So...a month from the time we start melt, and she'll have gone about three hundred thirty meters, or a thousand feet for the Americans listening."

"Hey, I resemble that remark," A.J. said, "and I use metric all the time. I can't help it that my country insists that it's better to use arcane systems from the dawn of time."

"More to the point," Madeline said, ignoring A.J., "are you saying that we could launch to *Odin* in only one month or so?"

"That depends on how well we get everything established here. We can't afford to leave until the modifications to the Nebula Drive controls are tested and shown to work—both in reducing the volume and thus power demand, and in maintaining the same shielding effectiveness," Brett answered. "We sure don't want *Munin* taking off unless we are one hundred percent certain that we're not going to need *Munin* to keep us going."

"We are definitely agreed on that. One thing that we have to also do is check on the supply division; the last thing we need is to discover that while we have enough of everything, all of some vital material or component is on board *only* one of our ships, so that when *Munin* is gone one or the other of us is suddenly short."

"Food probably won't be a problem," A.J. said, "but the vital supply of Joe Dinners may be tight."

Maddie gave a small chuckle at that. "True, true," she said, "but if that's our biggest problem, I think we're in pretty good shape."

Chapter 9

"The EU, it did not advertise that its astrophysicists were expected to do heavy physical labor," Anthony LaPointe said with dry humor.

Helen laughed as she tried to position her piece of the huge gray-white mass of material. "I don't remember them specifying that for their xenopaleontologists, either," she said.

"Yeah," Larry said, "but at least paleontologists spend their time breaking rocks regularly. We astronomical types look at computer screens and expend our heavy effort lifting coffee cups." He pulled perhaps slightly too hard on his piece and it slid up and slightly over him so he had to back up, and tripped, falling in slow-motion. "*Bugger*, as some of our Down-Under friends would say."

Helen restrained another giggle. Larry's protest was of course mostly *pro forma* and exaggerated the stereotype; on Earth, the best observatories were generally in areas of the world which remained both remote and challenging, while any space-based operation required top-flight fitness; Larry had shown his physical capabilities while helping to build Ares' fledgling colony. "Is this thing built like our shelters on Mars?"

"Not really," A.J. said. He wasn't physically participating, but mainly because he was once more being the nerve center for coordinating several operations at once; it was something ideally suited to him, and Maddie had made sure to emphasize that, both to prevent anyone else from resenting the sensor expert's apparent indolence (not that many were likely to) and just as importantly to prevent *him* from feeling guilty that he was inside while most other people were doing "real work."

"On Mars," A.J. continued, while Helen and the others finished spreading out the largest of the shelter units *Munin* had been carrying, "we used mostly the old 'tuna can' hab units, like the ones we lived in on the way here to Jupiter system, plus the Cascade-SAIC designed subsurface inflatables. But there we could take advantage of the Martian soil, bury stuff underground and insulate with the native material.

"Here on Europa, we're dealing with ice frozen so solid that digging through it is like trying to take a shovel to steel. *Athena* can cut through it, yeah, but can you imagine how long it'd take to keep repositioning and running *Athena* in order to clear out anything of reasonable size? So we can't really go underground, at least not for quite a while."

"Actually, the original plan would put us underground anyway," Horst said, "but the excavation equipment was supposed to be brought down from *Odin* after the lander had verified the site, and the space for it was taken up by a lot of the additional supplies the general had us load up to make it a viable lifeboat."

"Yes," Anthony said. "We are lucky, I think, that these shelters stayed on board."

"All right, Maddie, you'll have to set the first hold-downs," Helen said, seeing that they had the fifteen-meter-long, ten-meter-wide structure spread out fairly well. "I think we can stretch it out a bit after you get a couple in place to keep it from sliding all over."

"On it," Madeline said. To set something down well into the steel-hard ice required something more complex and forceful than the standard tent stake, and that was why it was Maddie's job; the hold-down units were a combination of shaped-charge and spike, blowing a small hole into the ice and inserting a long spike which then extended anchor points.

"So to finish answering your question," A.J. continued, "These are more self-contained—though they need some power run to them from *Munin* or some other source—and designed for *much* more extreme environments. There's a big difference between operating in even a relatively thin atmosphere like Mars and going to hard vacuum, and sitting on ice that's cold enough to liquify air is another major difference. You've got a *lot* of specialized LTP aerogel insulation in the floor, carbonan-reinforced puncture-resistant layered synthetic walls—interior and exterior—plus a lot of built-in amenities. Well, 'amenities' by the Spartan standards of the Outer System; we don't have a Jacuzzi in any of these. But there's power, air filtration and renewal, temperature control, all the stuff to make it liveable . . . and give us a *lot* more space while we're here."

Helen cut in the private channel. "Which I am *so* looking forward to."

She saw A.J. grin and wink in her VRD. "I want to lay claim to our own hab unit again. And I know Maddie and Joe want theirs back . . ." he glanced sideways and she could guess where he was looking. "And it's hard for Horst and Jackie when there's like no privacy at all!"

Ain't that the truth, she thought. The two married couples in the group had established and assumed relationships, and the rest of the "castaways of Europa" had assumed and arranged—without, as far as Helen could call, even being *asked* directly—for occasional hours of privacy for those two pairs.

As Horst and Jackie had pretty much just *begun* the dance back...Good *Lord*, a year and a half ago...during *Odin*'s visit to Ceres, and had minimal chance for privacy since, no such automatic arrangements had materialized. It wasn't beyond the pale that another couple might materialize within their midst, either; Helen had no idea of the preferences or interests of the others from *Odin*, but—as Madeline had once mentioned to her—with two other women and (counting the general) seven other men in a highly emotionally-charged environment, she'd be surprised to see *nothing* else happening.

Besides, even without the romantic pairings, there was plenty of reason to want a few hours away from anyone else.

Maddie arrived next to her. "Stand *very* still." The smaller spacesuited figure bent down, did something with her hands; Helen felt a sharp shock or vibration through the soles of her boots, and a moment later Madeline straightened up. "Okay, let go."

The material tried to pull back but the spike held firm. "All right, then. Let's all get the rest of them stretched out and set at intervals. Watch for the indicator tags."

"You mean the square over the hold-downs?" Anthony asked. "It looks just gray and has not changed ever since we started working."

"That's because we haven't had any part of it anchored," Madeline answered. "The indicators sense tension and extension along the length in two dimensions. When they're pulled to the right distance and tension levels, that gray square will turn bright green. Pull too far and it'll go red. If you're too far off angle, determined by the way the spikes and other walls are set, it will start going either yellow for an angle that's too acute, or blue for one that's too obtuse. So you want to get each square as perfect bright green as you can before I lock it down."

"Understood."

The process took another hour and a half, by which time Helen was starting to feel awfully tired. Low gravity reduced the weight of the suits, but the mass remained, and it was actually in some ways a lot harder to move around in low-g with extra mass all over you—especially if you were trying to pull or drag things that didn't want to move to begin with.

But as soon as the last spike was in place, she heard Maddie signal A.J. "Okay, A.J., check status. If everything's green, pull the trigger."

"Checking now . . . nice job, everyone. That thing's within a *very* small percentage of being perfectly straight on all sides." A pause. "Maddie, the third spike near the center of the far wall—away from *Munin*—didn't set right. For some reason the anchor points didn't deploy."

"I can't move the hold-down, though. What do I do?"

"Pull the first spike, then take a new one and just

disarm the charge, then put it down the hole and I'll trigger it; hopefully it will deploy the anchor points. Normally I wouldn't really care about *one* being not perfectly set, but we're still not sure how heavy the quakes are going to get, and I don't want to take chances."

Neither do I, Helen agreed silently. A few minutes passed before A.J. confirmed the substitution had gone well. "A.J.," she began, "what if there's a *big* quake—one that really rearranges the landscape?"

A.J. shrugged. "Honestly? We may be totally screwed. Imagine one of these cracks opening up for a second. I think we have to assume we won't get something really big—like Richter eight. A five or six we can probably handle, though it's possible it would hurt *something.* But we need the space—for work, and for our sanity—and that shelter's built tough; I think it can take anything the rest of us can." He spoke more loudly and was broadcast to the whole group. "All right, I'm activating the shelter."

Helen stepped back; almost instantly she saw the almost shapeless mass, staked out in a rectangular pattern, begin to stir.

"Active composite elements responding. Constructing first level wall grid." The sides of the perimeter began to rise systematically, a low wall coming up almost as though being elevated from below. It reached a height of about one and a half meters before stopping. "First level wall grid complete. Interlocking supports connecting . . . connected . . . locked. Structure is solid! Looks like the design's working! Starting second level wall grid with reinforcement elements."

The shelter continued to raise itself under A.J.'s

direction; the main walls were three meters high, with the roof curving gently to a maximum height of four and a half meters. "That's deceptive, though," A.J. noted. "Insulation, structural flex capabilities, internal wiring and such, plus lots of cushioning and redundancy in the structure and leakproofing, make the walls about half a meter thick now that it's assembled."

Completed, Helen had to admit it looked pretty impressive up close; spaced-out transparent aerogel-filled windows would admit light and a view to the rooms that made up the interior (it could be divided up several ways). This was going to give them large, open, brand-new spaces where all of them could go around without suits. But *most* importantly . . . "A.J.? How long?"

"After you get the power line connected? I'd say . . . about an hour and a half.

"But for you, it's probably going to be at least another hour after that," he continued, and she could see him grinning. "Because I think our esteemed leader is willing to pull rank *and* her extreme badass nature in order to be the first one to get a real, if low-gravity, shower!"

Chapter 10

"Even with the reactor scrammed, the radiation in there's *gotta* fry the dust, A.J.," Brett said doubtfully, looking on as Jackie prepared to pour approximately three liters of Faerie Dust into an instrumented funnel-shape that was positioned above *Nebula Storm*'s main reactor, fitting precisely into the small but fatal hole in the casing.

"Oh, no doubt about that," A.J. agreed cheerfully, and Horst continued for him, "And if we had not access to the many tons of drive dust made for *Odin*, maybe we would not be risking our most versatile sensing method this way, at least not yet. But the drive dust was meant for long-term space exposure and was hardened by some complex metamaterial design to resist a great deal of radiation. Mostly beta radiation, admittedly, and I would caution against betting that it will survive long inside a nuclear reactor, but it should last long enough to give us the data we need."

The problem was, of course, that opening up a fueled nuclear reactor whose core had been punched was not something one did casually; in fact, with the tools available to the combined expedition it was something that only the insane or the desperate would attempt. Still, even something crazy was better attempted with the maximal amount of knowledge.

A.J. felt he'd redeemed himself slightly after his prior blindness to the simple solution of his Faerie Dust's mobility, by realizing that the tougher, simpler drive dust would provide a sacrificial method to obtain a clear idea of what the precise condition of the core was. A few devices back on Earth might have been able to look straight through the reactor casing, but—after all—the casing was specifically designed to *prevent* radiation of any kind from getting through it. While that was meant mostly to prevent radiation from leaking out, it was equally efficient at preventing any radiation from getting *in*.

He was actually pretty proud of how he'd solved the problem of knowing *what* they hit. Jackie and Brett had managed to put together a detailed model of the original reactor and core, and simulated what the drive dust motes would "see" as they encountered the various components. While there wasn't really enough data for the drive dust to identify, say, uranium versus steel in isolation—unlike his bleeding-edge Faerie Dust, it wasn't built with multimodal sensor components—but the way in which high-speed impacts would break the pieces apart would still yield a fairly good rule-of-thumb heuristic to recognize the different types of things expected inside the reactor.

So A.J. would run his custom sensor analysis software on the drive dust as it worked its way, probably quickly degrading, through the reactor casing, and then when he'd processed the data as best he could, he'd send to to Brett's model, where the interior would be mapped out and—with luck—the precise nature, position, and extent of the damage caused by Fitzgerald's last shot would finally be known, allowing them to proceed with precision; possibly they'd even be able to figure out a way to do the repair without actually having to *open* the casing, working through the already-extant hole as though doing a laparoscopy.

"Ready, A.J.?" Jackie asked.

A.J. checked all the displays in his VRD. "Telemetry's good for the whole mass. Since we're in vacuum we don't need to worry about any of the messy reactions that can happen in a reactor that's been breached. Yep, we're go."

"Brett?"

The New Zealander gave her a thumbs-up. "Model's ready to take input as fast as A.J. can feed it to me."

"All right. Starting the pour . . . now."

In Europa's roughly one-eighth gravity, the speed of the almost liquid mass of drive dust motes looked more like the lazy flow of stage fog off the edge of a stage, dreamlike, unreal. But there was nothing unreal about the torrent of data that abruptly filled the bandwidth A.J. had allocated. "Data stream coming in loud and clear." Another running tally started to rise. "Yeah, it's *lousy* with rads in there. Attrition rate is already noticeable. Progress isn't terribly fast, though. The motes are using gravity assist where they can, but that core's packed pretty tight. Lessee . . ." He made some basic assumptions, plotted things again. "Yeah, it's definitely going to be eating into the supply *fast*. Horst, I think we'll need twice that much to finish the scan, get it set up, would you?"

"Right away."

Jackie joined them in *Nebula Storm*'s control room, pushing back the helmet with a relieved sigh; A.J. knew that she was always—understandably!—tense when working near the damaged reactor. "When does Brett start getting anything?"

"Getting stuff now," Brett said. "Only starting the outline at the entry point, but enough to show it's working. Don't get too eager; it's going to be a couple hours, probably, before we get enough data to give you a look."

Jackie smiled. "It will take us *days* to take her apart, so a few hours to know whether we have to, or what *way* we have to? Priceless."

"A.J.," came Larry's voice, "You got a minute?"

"Now I do," he answered, leaning back a little in the seat. "What do you need?"

"We got another quake, about three-point-four on the adjusted Richter, and the dust we spread around the whole area did a lot of recording. Can you—"

"No problem. I actually have a suite of programs designed for deriving data out of that kind of return." He grinned suddenly. "Helen knows; you could almost say it was the earlier version of that suite that *got* us into this mess in the first place."

"You mean the analytical program you used that gave us a picture of the Bemmie fossil before we even dug it up?" He could hear the smile in her voice even if he hadn't seen it in the HUD imagery his VRD showed. "That's right, you set off little charges or something and mapped the acoustic, along with other signal returns."

"And the combination almost got me thrown off your expedition as a practical joker," A.J. finished, with a chuckle. It was one of his fondest memories; a revelation so dramatic that even the people who'd called him in very nearly didn't believe him—probably wouldn't have, if Joe hadn't known him so well. Plus, that was when he'd first met Helen. Not that he'd even imagined at the time...

A second firehose of data started dumping into his systems; this one, however, was for much more familiar analysis, and with even the relatively limited systems available on the *Nebula Storm* and *Munin* was much easier to interpret. In about fifteen minutes he was able to call Larry back. "Well, some interesting results for you to look at. Some of it I have no idea how to interpret, but I can tell you that it looks like there's a general discontinuity about a kilometer down; I'd say we've got evidence for the Thin Ice model."

"A *kilometer*?" Larry's voice was incredulous. "That's... almost ludicrous. Unless... lemme take a look." Several minutes passed, interspersed with Larry and Anthony debating some of what they saw in technical language. Finally Larry said, "Hey, listen up, everyone." The tone and his use of 'everyone' keyed the general broadcast. "Returns from that last quake gave us the data we needed. This whole area's part of something called the Connamara Chaos, and turns out it's an apt name below the surface as well as above. Everything's jumbled, no clear structure—and there's some really strange returns; I suspect that there's some subtle interaction of different phases of ice that's making it very hard to interpret some of what we're seeing.

"But I think we've got good evidence for an impact

several thousand years ago; that's what messed up this part of Europa, and it actually thinned the surface over an extended area; I think we can see the thickness trending up in all directions away from us. It's probably more like ten kilometers thick normally, but right around us the crust isn't much more than a kilometer thick."

"Does that mean that *Athena* may actually punch through?" Jackie asked.

"If we stay here long enough, and keep drilling in the one spot, I'd say certainly. So we've got a good chance of actually getting the first sample of a planetary internal ocean. Real science, guys!"

"That's about three, three and a half months of running *Athena*," Dan said after a moment. "But then she was meant to run for a long time. If everything else holds out, I don't see any reason we can't do that. And we're not going to be done with everything else before then."

"Does this have any implications for our safety?" Madeline asked. "I don't want to lessen the enjoyment of this discovery, but—"

"Completely understood, Maddie. We're still getting data on the . . . tectonic dynamics of this situation, so we can't really say for sure. On the other hand, there've been several unmanned probes of the Jovian system in the last thirty years which observed Europa pretty closely, not counting the Europa probe that glitched, and none of them have seen clear evidence of surface breaches even here, so I'd say we should be reasonably safe. Keep everything secured, is all I'd recommend."

That's a relief, A.J. thought to himself. If Maddie decided their current location was too dangerous, they'd have to figure out how to *move* the crashed *Nebula Storm* far enough to make it safe, and then land it safely again. *NOT something I want to even think about trying.*

He checked both sets of processes; the reactor analysis was still running, and the spread-sensor net was still running. *Hm. Another momentary spike of that lethal chemical dihydrogen monoxide.*

He'd seen several of these momentary, almost-in-the-noise readings of water vapor, but the net still couldn't localize them. Which meant he didn't have much to hand to the others.

It did occur to him that it might just be from the force of a quake, maybe momentary cracks vaporizing some of the ice somehow.

But the others were all busy talking about the ice thickness, so he decided not to bother. Yet. The scientists continued talking about the implications of this latest find while he leaned back and took a nap.

It was a curse that awakened him; the usually polite and cheerful tones of Jackie Secord saying "Oh, *shit.*"

That kind of thing immediately brought A.J. to full consciousness. "What's wrong?"

He could see by the expression on Jackie's face that it was even *worse* than he'd thought from the cursing. She pressed a control and the modified model of the interior of the reactor appeared.

It looks almost as jumbled as the damn ice! "What the hell . . . ?"

"Ricochets." The word itself was spat out like another obscenity. "That damned bullet penetrated the *Nebula Storm*'s hull, then the reactor vessel, then because the reactor was mounted directly on the lower hull it *bounced* off the hull the second time, and bounced a couple more times inside the reactor before it stopped."

"I guess that means it's going to take longer to fix." Larry said finally.

A.J. winced, and Jackie's face was grim as she answered. "No," she said, and took a deep breath.

"It means there's no way *to* fix it," she said slowly. "It's not a matter of one clean hole through; the whole *core* has been...almost scrambled, like an egg.

"Madeline . . . I'm sorry, but *Nebula Storm* will never fly again."

Chapter 11

"Got a minute, Nick?"

Nicholas Glendale looked up to see Walter Keldering standing in his doorway. "For you? Always. Please, come in, take a seat." He waved towards his coffeepot—the low-gravity device that Joe Buckley had designed for the station a few years before. "Coffee?"

"Don't mind if I do," Keldering said. "Always time for me? A change since the old days when Maddie would be finding the most *inventive* excuses to head me off." He inserted the coffeemaker's spout into the sealed hole in the coffee cup's top, and Nicholas could hear the faint hiss as the air displaced by coffee was vented through the other hole.

"And I find that just as much a relief as you do," Nicholas agreed with a smile. He noticed that while Keldering smiled, there was a faint tension to the way he moved while injecting a measure of creamer and sweetener into the cup, a wrinkle or two on the now slightly-balding forehead.

"Oh, I do. And between you and me, I never liked my prior boss much either. I'm glad neither of you decided to start playing ball with him." Keldering swung the chair around and seated himself, folding his hands around the cup as though to keep the heat in. He looked seriously at Nicholas. "Nick, I've got a lot of connections in a lot of places. You know that."

Glendale nodded and said nothing, waiting to see what was on Keldering's mind.

"Some of those people are in modeling and reconstruction for the government, of course; the kind of after-action analysts that do forensics on the big things, like weapons tests that go badly wrong, stuff like that," Keldering continued, watching Glendale's face narrowly.

Oh, my. I suspect I know where we're going.

After a pause, Walter Keldering shrugged and went on. "Well, I've had some of them going over the entire sequence of events with *Nebula Storm* and *Odin*, and things just don't quite match up."

"Match up?" Nicholas repeated carefully. "How do you mean that, Walter?"

Keldering gave him a look that said, as clearly as though he'd said it, *so we have to go through the whole dance? Fine.* "Well, you know, the whole bit with the *Nebula Storm* chasing the *Odin* never sat well with me anyway. Sure, *Odin*'s crew had pulled a fast one, but that whole emergency deployment of a ship you couldn't possibly even be sure would *work* didn't fit with the profiles we had of your people, at least not under those circumstances, especially given that Ceres base was still recovering from the accident and in the end actually had to give up its own reactor to get *Nebula Storm* underway.

"Leaving that aside, though, in all honesty the whole sequence of events starting with the pass by Jupiter just *stinks*, Nick. It's one of those barely-plausible sequences of events that no agent at my level can swallow as coincidence." He looked at Nick carefully. "But if it wasn't coincidence, then something *caused* it to happen...starting with that reversal of thrust on *Odin*'s final burn. And for that, I have a candidate named A.J. Baker, which would mean the whole thing was *caused* by Ares and the IRI!"

Sweet CHRIST. "Walter, you can't possibly believe that I, or Maddie, would try to kill a hundred people just because they stole a march on us? Or that we'd let A.J. do so, even if he was crazy enough to try, which he certainly isn't?"

"I would very much like to not believe it, Director," Keldering said, very formally, "but the fact is that there are multiple layers of redundancy built into the controls of *Odin*—and I would presume any spacegoing vessel—to prevent such mistakes, or to cancel or stop them if they were to begin. Such an inverted burn implies either a fundamental flaw in the embedded software—a flaw which never showed itself throughout all the prior uses of their drives—or, much more likely, a very carefully calculated subversion of the systems, so that even direct abort commands from the command deck and the core computers in the engineering section were ignored."

Glendale thought for a moment. "Before I make any comment on this, even unofficially, do you have anything else?"

"There's quite a bit more, Director."

He stood and paced to the window, then looked back at Keldering as Mars spun past. "I would think the whole destruction of *Odin* would be even more of an anomaly."

Keldering's narrow smile acknowledged the point. "It is. A most *interesting* anomaly in several ways."

"Let us suppose—purely unofficially and purely theoretically—that I were to say that it is possible your theory on the reversal of *Odin*'s drive is correct, but that if it were correct then there would have to have been considerable excuse, if not justification, for the actions."

"An excuse," Keldering said quietly, "such as an assault on Ceres Base by a coilgun cannon?"

Nick looked back at him sharply, but said nothing. *Where is he going?*

"Nicholas, the idea that coincidence destroyed both ships stretches to the level of the ridiculous. My people can't model any reasonable, or even reasonably unreasonable, scenario that would cause part of the *Odin* to explode with even a fraction of the necessary force, and the only sources of energy onboard which could have done that much damage were the neo-NERVA reactor and the *Odin*'s main power reactor—both of which are still perfectly functional, according to infrared signatures from the remains that are being tracked through the Jovian system. Even if we assume a high-velocity meteoroid impact that shattered a large portion of the *Odin*, it's very difficult to create a scenario that results in *any* fragments moving fast enough, on the right vector, to puncture *Nebula Storm*'s Bemmie-made hull." He stood and walked closer to Nicholas. "But it's not hard at all to model the possibility of a covert coilgun in the drive spines that could have had, to use a mundane sort of parallel, shotgun loads."

"The *Odin* was inspected by your own people,

Walter. Do you mean to tell me that the United States' own inspectors couldn't find a weapon—no, if you're right, *four* weapons—a thousand feet long, right in front of them?"

Keldering's face darkened momentarily, but he smiled wryly. "If this was the case, I assure you there will be several heads rolling. But of course we're talking a covert weapon, one that would be designed to *look* like a perfectly normal part of the vessel. The EU and its contractors are quite good, you know, and the fact is that there isn't that much *reason* to have major armaments in space."

Nicholas sighed, turned away from the window, and faced Keldering. "Walter, to be honest the point is moot. The *Odin*—and any covert weapon it may, or may not, have had on board—is a wreck, almost its entire crew is dead, and if your scenario is correct their arming the vessel cost them all their lives somehow. What matters isn't—"

"Nicholas." His name was spoken in a tone that cut him off instantly, something Glendale was not used to at all. "I think I know what you're doing, and I understand. There's no profit for the IRI in antagonizing the EU, and—if I'm right about what happened—right now you're potentially in a position of huge advantage with respect to them. But politically you're skating a lot of thin ice, and you're playing with the very, very big boys. If my scenario's correct, the EU—or, more likely, some private concern, the ESDC or one of their divisions or subcontractors—not only got that psycho Fitzgerald assigned as *Odin*'s security, they put a hypersonic cannon into his hands, in direct violation of the Mars Treaty and Accords. Maybe the EU itself was utterly blameless—I'd sure as hell like to *think* that even Bitteschell wouldn't be that stupid—but you *know* that we simply can't let this kind of thing slide."

Nick debated with himself for what seemed a long time, but was actually only a few seconds. *I have to trust him if we're going to make any of this work now.* "Walter, I agree with you completely," he said finally.

Keldering's look of relief was one of the rare uncontrolled expressions the agent had ever given. "You do? Then—"

"But this is not quite the time," Glendale continued smoothly. "You see—unofficially and completely off the record—I will tell you that you're entirely correct, and I'm very impressed by how you've put all the pieces together. But there are a few, very crucial, pieces that you're missing of this puzzle." As he explained, he found the sequence of expressions that crossed Keldering's face almost comical.

"The general is *alive?*"

"He is. And given everything else, I think you can see what we plan to do."

Keldering nodded, and then he began to look suspiciously at Glendale. "And you're going to need *me* to keep everyone else from jumping the gun."

"Please."

"Nicholas, do you have *any* idea what you're asking? If I have a reasonable bit of intel, I'm supposed to send it up the chain right away. Something like *this*—"

He nodded sympathetically, but then smiled. "I know, Walter. But on the other hand...you came here privately, unofficially, to ask me. You were already *trying* to keep it private. If you weren't ready to play ball, why did you come with your own bat and glove?"

Keldering couldn't restrain a snort of laughter. "Okay, you got me. I knew you guys couldn't possibly have deliberately killed people in cold blood, and I thought I knew the story...but you've added a few wrinkles. Damn. Nick, this isn't going to be easy. You want to keep the EU happy, stop anyone from blowing the lid off the truth, and get the rescue project well underway while your people try to pull off a by-their-bootstraps rescue on their own, before you go public."

"And we want to be able to get every one of the people responsible dead to rights," said Glendale, this time with a hard edge in his voice. "They nearly killed some of my best friends, and did kill a hundred people who had trusted their lives to those people's work."

"*That* is going to be the *really* tricky part," Keldering said slowly. "People like that—especially Osterhoudt, if he's involved—are insulated, protected, and very much prepared for any accusations. And he's not going to relax for quite a while." A sudden smile spread across his face. "But we still have a few cards we haven't played." Keldering stood up.

"Such as?"

Keldering stopped in the doorway and grinned. "You know, I can't attend his retirement party in six months, so why don't I give Director Hughes a call? He might like an update on what his favorite protégé is *really* up to on Europa."

The door slid shut, leaving Nicholas feeling better than he had in weeks. *We just might pull this off after all.*

Chapter 12

"So there's *no* chance of repairing the reactor?" Madeline asked, looking mostly at Jackie but keeping an eye on everyone else in the conference room of *Munin*. This was a crucial factor, and she had to make sure that no decisions were made without as much certainty as possible.

Like most engineers, Jackie instinctively shied away from absolute certainty. Centuries of experience had taught the profession that real life machines and structures would fail—or, sometimes, survive—in ways that you simply wouldn't have believed or anticipated. "Well…*no* chance? Um, if we were to…" She paused for a moment, clearly thinking, then shook her head. "What am I saying? No, Maddie, there isn't any way we're fixing it. Oh, I could come up with some ridiculous maybe-possible scheme with the combination of A.J.'s super-dust, all the engineers we have, and some luck, but in this setting? No, that reactor's shot, and it's not getting fixed."

Funny how we seem to go from triumphant confidence to crisis mode on a regular basis, Maddie thought. *Now to navigate* this *crisis.* "All right, the *Nebula Storm*'s reactor is shot. What's the next steps?"

91

"Well, first, we get the reactor and reactor-specific support components out," Joe said. "There's no purpose in keeping a damaged and potentially dangerous reactor onboard, and the thing—along with support components—weighs a *lot*. I know the "Keep our Solar System Clean" contingent will have kittens at the concept, but we've got to dump the weight when we can. No point in dragging our trash with us."

"Makes sense, and I wouldn't worry about the complaints; we'll deal with that if and when we get home for them to whine at. But what next? How do we get ourselves home?"

The silence was not encouraging. *But there has to be a solution. We have too many resources for it to not be possible.* "Horst, what about the *Munin*'s main reactor? Couldn't it run the Nebula Drive?"

Horst grimaced, wrinkling his usually handsome face so it looked like he was sucking on lemons spiced with habanero pepers. "*Ja*, yes, in theory. But ... Madeline, you remember we did connect our reactor to your systems for the travel and landing to Europa."

"Yes, which is one reason I asked."

"That worked for a short time, but that was because it *was* a short time," Horst said. "The connecting of the ships was done through an airlock for each of us and took up a great deal of space. We could afford that space for a few days, but it will be *months*—perhaps a year—for us to make it back to the Inner System and a location where we can be rescued or make a good orbit and landing for ourselves. As it is, we will have to be taking turns in the rotating sections to reaccustom ourselves to real gravity and minimize degeneration of our bodies from constant low-g exposure, yes?"

Maddie nodded reluctantly. "I think I see your point. The twelve of us—thirteen, after we rescue the general—are crowded enough as it is, even though with the equipment on board *Munin* we have been able to set up those self-contained living quarters—not to mention the absolutely wonderfully designed showers—in additional insulated structures intended for the exploration and study teams. We simply cannot afford to sacrifice room for such a connection." She looked over to Mia and A.J. Baker. "I don't suppose we could *not* use the airlocks? Put in a dedicated—and out-of-the-way—power conduit?"

Mia looked thoughtful, but A.J. didn't even hesitate. "No chance in hell, Maddie. Maybe for *Munin* we could figure it out, but to put a nice out-of-the-way power conduit into *Nebula Storm* we'd have to run it right through the *hull* of *Nebula Storm*."

She winced. No one knew better than she just how unyieldingly stubborn the composite alloy they simply called "Vault material" was. With what they had, she wasn't even sure they *could* put a hole in that hull at all, let alone do so with enough precision and control to prevent them from wrecking something else in the interior.

"There's another much bigger problem, too," Dan Ritter said after a moment.

"So what's *your* good news, Dan?" A.J. asked brightly.

"Well, it's related to that bit about gravity. In order for us to manage that at all, we have to spin the ship and use those habitation modules—"

Horst nodded glumly, and Joe smacked his forehead. "And *Munin* wasn't designed to spin, probably couldn't be balanced while attached to us, and making a harness that allowed you to be transferring the power from *Munin* that was stationary to a rotating *Nebula Storm...*" Joe trailed off, then finished, "It'd be twice as big, and a *huge* potential point of failure unless we did a lot of engineering work on it. Slip rings or similar tricks...they're just perfect invitations for wear."

Horst shook his head. "Worse than that, Joe. Remember that we need to take turns? Well, unless *Munin* is going to be just left empty and all of us crowd into *Nebula Storm*, how would we do that when the one available airlock between the two ships was filled with the power connection?"

They were silent for a moment, then Helen spoke. "Speaking of the hab modules," she said, looking at Joe, "Can we fix the one we sort of landed on?"

"Yes," Joe said with confidence. "It got bent and squashed, but all the pieces are still there and we've got everything needed to fix it. So we'll be able to spin up once we're back in space."

"That's good," Helen said.

Another silence. "How are we doing with *Munin* and preparations to visit the general?" Maddie asked finally. *Might as well touch on other subjects.*

"Going good there," Brett said. "We've got good models up on all the critical systems and we think we know how to fix them. It's going to take quite a while—our good friend Fitzgerald sure knew how to screw things up. But between the resources on *Odin* and our know-how...well, *Odin*'s never going to be pretty again, but she'll be a functioning space station, anyway."

The last line tugged at something. *Space station instead of spaceship.* But why? *Odin* couldn't move anymore, not in any significant way. She retained enough functionality to orient herself in different ways, but neither of her drives were...

"Joe," she said slowly. "And Jackie... When we threw *Nebula Storm* together, we used the reactor for the Ceres colony as our main power source, right?"

"Yeah," Joe said. "Plus a big bank of RTSC batteries to fake up the NERVA drive."

"And bolted the spare nozzle from *Nobel* onto *Nebula Storm*'s rear," confirmed Jackie. "Why?"

"Oh, oh, oh, I think I see where you're going, Maddie, and it might work, god*damn*, it just might work!" A.J. said, a grin spreading across his face.

The others glanced at him in puzzlement; he looked to Maddie; she just smiled and nodded. *He loves explanations, and I think he* does *get it.*

"Well," A.J. said, giving her a quick smile of thanks, "*Odin*'s pretty much kaput, but her *reactors*—both of them—are still intact, and the one is just a tweaked drive unit from the original *Nike*, just like the one on *Nobel*—"

Joe and Jackie started grinning too, and the smiles started to spread. Horst cut in: "—and the reason *Odin* can't use its NERVA isn't because the drive's completely shot, but because the *drive nozzle* was completely shredded! And—"

Suddenly it seemed as though everyone was talking at once:

"—well, that's not completely true, some of the secondary support systems were damaged," Mia Svensen said cautiously, but she, too, was smiling. "And we'll have to do some careful design models; I think *Nobel* had modified the nozzle design for its own applications—"

"—need to figure out how much water we'll need, might need several trips—"

"—and Larry, the orbital change needed, not much I think, yes?"

"—transfer valve to move the water from *Munin* to *Odin*, sort of a reverse, we never thought we'd have to do the opposite—"

"—cutting tools that might do the job—"

She raised her voice. "People. *EVERYONE, please!*"

The room went suddenly quiet. She smiled at them. "From the general look and sound, can I assume that we think this is a good solution?"

"It's a damn near *perfect* solution, Maddie," Joe said fondly. "With *Odin's* orbit going in to Io and out about to Europa, it's going to be tracing something like an old-fashioned Spirograph pattern around, which means over time it will get closer and then farther and farther around the circle, eventually catching up to us. But it does mean that it's going to be a pain to transfer back and forth, especially at different points of the cycle."

"And *Odin* has so many resources on board, even in its cut-down state, that we just don't have," Mia said. "If we can get it enough reaction mass and put on a nozzle that lets it shift orbit enough to turn to an orbit around *Europa . . . !*"

"... it becomes a satellite filled with resources we can access a lot more easily and reliably," finished Helen, who certainly understood the basics of the situation. "I guess we can't land it, though."

Horst snorted at the thought of landing the massive wreck. "I would think not."

"What about our other objections to the situation

with *Munin* and *Nebula Storm*?" she asked. "Do they still hold if we add *Odin* into the picture?"

"I don't think so," Mia said. "There are cutting tools and materials aboard *Odin* which I think could manage to put an access conduit through even the *Nebula Storm*'s hull; they would be too large and power intensive to be practical to transfer from *Odin* to us here on Europa, but if we assume that we will do all the design and preparation work ahead of time, we could bring *Nebula Storm* up when we're ready to leave, then shut her down and work on her in orbit; the *Odin* would provide more than sufficient living space, which is protected by *Odin*'s radiation shielding so that we wouldn't need *Nebula Storm* to maintain her drive at that time."

"So we would be able to put a connection for power that would still allow us to transfer back and forth," Joe said, "and with the tools and materials on all three ships we could probably make one that will survive the rotational demands for long enough."

Brett nodded, already starting on his simulations via remote. "It won't be easy at all, but I think it's all workable. The only question is whether *Nebula Storm* can actually tow *Odin*. I mean, whether it can tow it *effectively*. I know it's a matter of pretty much constant force so you could in theory tow *anything*, but is the Nebula Drive able to give us enough acceleration to get home in reasonable time?"

"Yes, it can," Jackie said positively. "First, *Odin* as she currently sits masses something like three thousand tons, maybe less, rather than ten thousand, especially if we dump most of the drive spines, which are pretty much useless now. Together, *Nebula Storm* and *Munin* are going to be about two-thirds that much, especially once we're topped off with reaction mass. So that's, say, one-fifth of our acceleration previously. But since it's *constant* acceleration, cutting it by five doesn't multiply our time by five—time's a squared term in there; so square root of five is the effect of decreasing the acceleration, it'll take us a little more than twice as long to get somewhere." She grinned again. "It took us about three months to get from Ceres to here. We've got food for more than a year, will have that much even after we finish all the work; in a year, I could get you across the whole damn *solar system*!

"Keep those smiles and make 'em bigger!" she said, and Madeline gave her own grin. "We're going home—and we'll be bringing *Odin* with us!"

Chapter 13

"Alone at last," Jackie said, deliberately using the old cliché.

"Yes," Horst agreed, looking surprisingly nervous. "We are."

One of the additional inflatable hab units had been transformed into Vacation Hotel Europa, as A.J. had dubbed it—a place where people could go for time separated from the group. The unit, originally meant as two separate living spaces, had been made into a single larger living space, with all the amenities that the castaways of Europa could manage crammed into it, including a shower, a large entertainment projector put together using smaller entertainment components, a larger bed than the standard near-bunk size, projective windows to allow the real view outside or replace it with other locations, a large proportion of the "Joe Dinners," and whatever other bells and whistles could be thought of.

Any of them—as individuals or groups—could schedule a "vacation" there when not immediately needed (which of course probably meant you worked twice as hard the day before). However, last week, right after it had been completed, Madeline had informed the two that Hotel Europa already had *two* full days reserved for them at the end of the following week, and that they were *not* to be working at all those days.

"You're looking awfully tense, Horst," she said, raising her eyebrow and putting a hand on his arm. "Something wrong?"

Horst gave an embarrassed grin. "Well... it's really very silly of me. But I somehow feel like... this is as though I brought a date home to my mother's house and we went to my room and locked the door."

Jackie laughed. "I guess that isn't so silly. Or maybe like coming home and finding your parents have Just Happened to step out for that night and have left a note saying they definitely will not be back until noon the next day."

"Ha! Yes, that is maybe much more like it." Horst took a deep breath and then exhaled, seeming to blow his tension out with it, and then turned and kissed her.

It wasn't their *first* kiss, of course, but it'd been a long time since they could just... take their time about it. Jackie took her time, and so did Horst.

By the time they broke slightly apart, her hair was slightly mussed and his would have been, if he didn't keep it military-regulation short. She smiled up at him and saw an answering sparkle in his eye. "That was pretty good."

"But it is important to practice your skills to make them better," Horst answered and suited action to words.

"Mmm," she said appreciatively after a while. "So, besides that, what do you want to do on our vacation?"

Horst glanced out the window, which was currently

set to an active view (based on recordings, of course) of Lanikai Beach in Hawai'i. "I would say a swim, but I am told it is actually colder outside than it looks."

"You goof. Yes, I think surfing and swimming is out. Though," she gave him a wink, "there is a double-size shower."

"Hmm. Something to consider carefully, yes," Horst agreed; his light Germanic complexion reddened noticeably. Jackie was pleased that her Native American heritage gave her dark enough skin that blushes weren't easily visible; it let her tease Horst, and sometimes other people, with impunity on her part.

"Well, I actually picked out some of the newest movies that Ceres was able to forward us. You like the *Kata Wandering* series, right?"

"Yes, yes! I did not know that the next one was already out. If that's okay with—"

"I wouldn't have brought it up if it wasn't," she pointed out. "Actually, there's lots of things to watch, if that's what we want to do. A.J. also set up a local Quest of the Seven Races server if you like that kind of stuff—I do sometimes—and there's some really good beach simulations if you wanted to at least *pretend* we're at the beach. Or there's old-fashioned chess or something like that."

"Or we could just talk, but I think we'd still end up 'talking shop' as you call it."

She shrugged, still smiling. *That's part of why I like being with him. Just any kind of talking with him makes me smile.* "Well, that's okay too—I mean, we talk shop because it *interests* us and we're still doing what we want to do, way out here in the solar system."

She signaled the window control and one window

shifted as she approached. "I haven't got tired of that view yet," she said softly.

Jupiter loomed over the horizon, about half above the edge of the jagged edges of the Connemara Chaos. Shadows from the sun were thrown in sharp relief of black against the bright surface, a black then tinged with the red-brown-cream light of the largest of the planets. Against one edge of Jupiter was a black spot, a spot with a yellow-orange crescent edge—Io, where they presumed the body of Richard Fitzgerald had finally ended its journey and where General Hohenheim had pulled off an impossible escape. The stars beyond dusted the black velvet setting of the sky.

"*Nein,* I have not either," Horst said, hugging her from behind and looking over her shoulder. "And the view will be changing for us again in a few days."

That was true enough; after their mini-vacation, she, Horst, Mia, Petra, Dan, and Anthony would be leaving to rendezvous with *Odin* and the general. As they were choosing close-to-minimum delta-v routes, it would take a few days to catch up with *Odin* on this trip, and depending on how long the work on board took, between a day and several days to get back afterward, but they'd also be able to transfer a considerable proportion of *Munin*'s reaction mass onto *Odin.* Several more trips would be needed to make sure there was sufficient water for the remains of the huge EU vessel to shift its orbit and have some reserves for later, but there seemed to be no barriers to accomplishing this.

"Sometimes I wonder where we'd be if you hadn't had Fitzgerald on board," she said after a pause.

She could see Horst frown slightly in thought.

"That . . . is an interesting question, you know. I suppose we would have still come to Ceres, but things would have been different almost from the beginning."

She glanced back and up. "Really?"

"*Ja*, no doubt. You were not on board *Odin*, so you perhaps do not realize he was main advisor to the general for most of the trip, at least in security and . . . hm, corporate espionage tactics." He looked somewhat embarrassed about the latter, which she didn't mind; the fact that it bothered him was one of the things that told her Horst was as decent as he appeared to be. "Oh, we would have been looking for things on our own, yes, but it may be that we would have simply made the proposal you did when you cornered us, except we would have done so when Andrew found the information on Enceladus."

She thought about that. *If it had happened that way . . . Horst would have left peacefully, we'd have had no reason to chase* Odin *down in* Nebula Storm— *hell, it wouldn't even be a named ship, just a museum piece—and I wouldn't have been going with them. Wouldn't have seen Horst for three years, probably.*

"I'd still be on Ceres, probably, unless I was shuttling back and forth on *Nobel*," she said after a pause. "That would be pretty exciting in its own way, I guess—you saw the announcements we downloaded?"

Horst snorted. "Your Nicholas, he knows how to work his P.R.; as soon as excitement from our survival dies down, he lets them release the news about the Bemmie fusion work."

She grinned. "Yes, he's good with that. And think about it; we *know* Bemmie had the technology working. We've seen the work they did carving out just *stupendous* caverns in Ceres and the digs on Mars, and we have those half-ruined pieces. Fusion isn't twenty years away; it's *five*."

"And that will change many things, maybe make us able to make a better *Odin* when we get back."

"Or maybe more; some of the stuff we've gotten passed on from Ceres through the secure channels..."

"You mean the plantimals?"

Horst was referring to some of the recent discoveries in Ceres, more advanced lab work with what appeared to be sessile forms of Bemmie-type life, or possibly animal-like plants from Bemmie's homeworld. "No, not those—though why they were apparently being developed as metal concentrators is still being argued about, and *Helen* is of course all over that stuff. No, I was talking about the hints from Rich and Jane."

"Eh? Maybe, yes," Horst said skeptically, "but I will believe they are close to cracking the Rosetta Disc when the translation is released. They thought they would crack it much sooner, remember."

She couldn't argue that. "I guess you're right. They thought they'd be giving lectures on its contents by now. I thought I'd be working on the design of a new and better ship for the IRI..."

"And I," Horst said, looking out across Europa again, "I had thought I would be here, in Jupiter system—but that was because we guessed there might be a Bemmie base here. Had not thought I would be shipwrecked on one of Jupiter's moons."

She grimaced and "And that *still* seems unreal sometimes. And frightening when I realize how close we came to dying...how close we still are, I guess."

"We are not so close now as we were, really," Horst

said. "Now we have backups for most systems and there is no Fitzgerald to damage them. And more engineers per square foot than some engineering firms!" He kissed her on the neck, making her giggle—she couldn't help it, she was ticklish there sometimes—and turning to the entertainment unit. "Now let's watch *Kata*, and we can have Joe Dinners, and then . . ."

"And then," she agreed with an impish grin.

Chapter 14

"Disconnecting in three, two, one—off." Horst, with Anthony's help, dragged *Munin*'s small section of the thick, insulated, double-wrapped cable back and stowed it securely near the reactor housing. "Everything stable?"

"No problems, Horst," answered A.J. "Batteries all full, we're running on them, drain shows what we expected. Get back here in a couple of weeks and we should be fine—though I'd a lot rather you get back sooner, if you can."

"Shouldn't be a problem, A.J.," Jackie said from her position in the copilot's seat. "But now comes the tricky part."

"Horst, are you sure you're comfortable with this?" Madeline's question, he could tell, was for his ears only. "If you'd rather, I'd still be glad to do the first part for you."

"Don't worry, Madeline," he answered, hiding the slight nervousness he was feeling. "Besides, that would mean you would have to set *Munin* back down and get off. The more ups and downs, the more chance for something to go wrong, I think."

"You're perfectly correct. Then good luck and take care."

"*Danke Schön*, Maddie. I will be very careful." He switched back to general broadcast. "Everyone, clear the area of *Munin* now, please. Is the power cable all stowed on your end?"

"Just got it in, Horst," Joe answered, sounding slightly winded, obviously still trying (with Helen and A.J. helping) to get the much larger and bulkier cable section into stowage.

"Everyone's clear, Horst," Madeline said. "I've just checked everyone's positions. A.J., will you verify?"

"Hold on, Joe," the sensor expert said. A pause. "According to readings on all sensors—mine and the primary suit and individual monitor chips—we have Horst, Andy, Mia, Jackie, Dr. Masters, and Dan on board *Munin*—"

"Might I ask," Petra Masters inquired mildly, "why I'm called by my last name and a title and everyone else is by their first?"

A.J. gave an embarrassed chuckle. "Always taught to be very, very respectful of *real* doctors, I guess. So, *Petra*, Horst, Andy, Mia, Jackie, Dan on *Munin*; Madeline's up front of *Nebula Storm* playing observer, me, Joe, and my lovely and talented Helen still wrestling this superconducting anaconda, and Brett and Larry watching over *Athena*. I check you, Maddie; all clear."

Horst finished locking himself into the pilot's seat, touched the controls, watched to see that Jackie was ready to back him up. "All right. *Munin* is preparing for liftoff. Cold maneuver jets first, to get separation."

The *Munin*'s maneuvering thrusters spurted in quick, controlled bursts, skidding the lander sideways.

Screeching, grating sounds echoed through *Munin* and a shower of pulverized ice rose and fell, a motion both too fast and too slow, alien and strange. Horst felt *Munin* wobbling on her skids, and—not for the first time—griped to himself inwardly about the winged design. Oh, he knew why *Munin* had been designed with wings—not merely for the possibility of skimming the atmosphere of one of the giant planets, which would be exciting but in his view far too dangerous, but much more importantly for the opportunity to land on Titan. *Not this trip, which means those wings are a complete waste.*

But they didn't cause him to tip, which was the important thing. "*Munin* now well clear. Engaging auto-launch sequence."

As with most vehicles, *Munin* could pilot herself most of the time, given the right circumstances and assuming nothing too terribly unusual; the last few flights had, of course, been rather decidedly unusual. A takeoff, however, even from a low-gravity moon with rough ice terrain, was something for which *Munin* had been designed. The onboard computer surveyed the area with LIDAR, millimeter-wave scanners, and optical imagery, and came to a decision. There was a staccato burst of activity from the forward nose jets, and *Munin* reared up on her tail—and then with a silent roar of flame blasted up into the black sky of Europa.

Horst grunted as almost two gravities of acceleration crushed down on him; it had been almost two months now since they had landed, and in that time he'd gotten far too used to Europa's puny grip.

The others felt worse. "*Jesus!*" came the strained voice of Jackie, and Anthony LaPointe croaked, "Horst...

is *Munin* running away? This acceleration, it is ... far more than you said!"

"I hate to tell you, Andy," he said, trying to force a relaxed tone into his voice, "but that is only one point eight gravities."

LaPointe said something obscene in French. "We are in worse shape than I thought."

"Which is precisely why we must cannibalize parts of the drive spine coils to make a controllable centrifuge," Petra said, her voice labored but clear. "Drugs may or may not work, but hours spent in heavy acceleration will definitely help. Brett and Joe should have the design perfected by the time we return."

Intellectually, Horst approved of this plan immensely. There was, however, a small part of him that was already complaining.

Real gravity was *tiring*.

"*Mon Dieu*." Anthony said softly.

Though he'd have phrased it in German, Horst would have said the same thing.

The wreck of *Odin* loomed large in *Munin's* forward port. They had of course seen the pictures A.J. had been able to capture ... but that was, somehow, completely different from seeing it in person.

The proud, sleek ship, the vessel that had stretched nearly one and a half kilometers from end to end, longest if not most massive vessel every constructed, was no more. Even the tattered, shrapnel-riddled wreck they had last seen when leaving to rendezvous with *Nebula Storm* was gone.

In its place, a truncated, sharp-edged hulk drifted through space, now silhouetted against a half-illuminated

Jupiter. Three long spines jutted from *Odin*, and for a moment she looked like an alien, long-taloned hand grasping at the largest planet to claw it from the sky. The fourth drive spine was of course gone, blown off at the base—almost in the position of a thumb, a ragged, torn thumb.

Odin looked dead, a tomb for those sacrificed to Fitzgerald's calm insanity. But there was a living voice coming from that metal mausoleum:

"*Munin*, this is *Odin*," the deep voice of General Hohenheim said, filling the cabin with its confident warmth, dispelling the momentary feeling of gloom. "I now have you by visual. Horst, the number three airlock is clear. I have activated its beacon and it should be visible to you."

He studied the screen. "I do not see—wait."

A small, steadily blinking green light was coming slowly into view as they approached. Zooming in, he could see that it was indeed the beacon light for Airlock Three. "Visual of target acquired, General. Proceeding to docking maneuvers." He activated the autopilot program, painted the target airlock with a target laser, verified target acquisition. "Transferring control to autopilot...now."

The little autopilot knew what it was doing. *Munin* slowed and approached the airlock with precise care, lining up, matching vectors, even rotating *Munin* to make sure that the airlock exit matched in orientation with the internal corridor layout as stored in *Munin*'s memory bank. There was a rustling *shifting* sound, followed by clear metallic vibrations transmitted through the hull. "Contact...locked. Telltales show airlock pressurizing."

He stood, his heart pounding surprisingly fast, and headed for the airlock; Anthony was right behind him, magnetic adhesive boots thudding clearly on the deck.

Munin's airlock door opened easily, pressure now equalized. He stepped in, closed the door, and reached out, spun the wheel to unlock *Odin*'s side.

There was hardly a whisper of air, showing that the equalization held for both vessels, and he heard— through his suit, in the air!—the door behind him open again. He removed his helmet; the smell was sharp, a lingering faint but clear burning odor that tried to send little spikes of worry through him. A waft of air from behind brought suddenly-clear other scents, and he wondered just how badly *they* stank from the point of view of another, presumably neutral, party.

Enough musing, he told himself, and pushed the *Odin*'s door open.

Standing on the other side, not three meters away, was General Alberich Hohenheim. He was drawn to his full height, in what looked like a carefully—if not perfectly—repaired dress uniform, rows of ribbons and medals showing bright colors in their lights, wide shoulders set straight, one hand up in a salute to just above the bright golden eyes. "Welcome back aboard, Mr. Eberhardt."

For a moment he was back in the *Munin*'s landing bay, watching the general stand proudly, alone, sending them off to live so that he could deal with the man who had killed his ship. He returned the salute, but heard his voice waver. "Thank you, General..."

Anthony LaPointe managed to stand next to him and return the salute as well. "We...did what you asked, sir."

The simple words broke the general's poise and he suddenly strode forward, caught Horst and Anthony in a double-armed bearhug. "I . . . thank you both, and it . . . it is *very* good to see you again," Hohenheim said. "To see you *all* again," he continued, looking past them into the airlock where Petra, Dan, and Mia were now waiting, and his smile was both bright and painful, the look of a man who had almost lost hope, only to find it standing before him. Horst realized that only now, with living, breathing survivors of his crew before him, could General Hohenheim truly believe that they were not all dead; only now was it *real*.

And as the general pulled away, straightening his uniform, Horst saw a sparkle in the air nearby.

In space, both tears *and* dreams could fly.

Chapter 15

"This," Helen said to apparently empty air, "is possibly the most boring thing I have ever done."

"Coming from someone who used to think spending weeks scraping away a centimeter of rock from some dead bone using dental tools was *fun*, that's a hell of a statement," A.J. said.

"It's nothing but the truth. At least with those rocks you got to *do* something. With this," she gestured to the images in front of her, "all I can do is stare at a lot of frozen nothing!"

The screen before her—several screens, actually—showed various angles of the same thing, specifically, the ice through which *Athena* was steadily, implacably, and very slowly moving. Half a meter an hour, a hair under twenty inches, or about an inch every three minutes.

"Sorry, Doc, but them's the breaks," her husband said in his usual not-very-sympathetic tones. "Everyone gets a turn at the boredom, and we're back to your turn."

"I'd *think* this would be something the machine could do *itself*."

"Yeah, you'd think that. And according to Horst and

113

Mia, it *would* have, probably, except that the prep and programming for specific circumstances was supposed to happen on-site. Turns out no one actually finished the smart-video suite that was tailored for this rig—or else someone *really* screwed up and failed to load it, but I don't really believe that."

"Can't *you* write it? You're the super-sensor expert, right?" Helen was aware that she was probably sounding a bit plaintive, but—despite the probably literally groundbreaking science that *Athena* was doing—she really would rather be doing just about anything else. Unfortunately, the emergency cutoff and other direct controls were integrated into *Athena*'s control station and no one had felt like trying to tamper with the design. Thus, someone had to sit right where she was during the entire time the melt-probe was active.

A.J.'s still-handsome, only slightly lined features popped up in a corner of her VRD. He grinned apologetically and shrugged. "*Could* I? Sure. Almost certainly, especially with Horst and Mia to back me. But that kind of work—which, for our current circumstances, would be absolutely mission-critical stuff, no failures of any kind allowed—takes a lot of time and patience. And a *lot* of checking. Even with our current software tools, that's weeks, at least. And there's so many more things to do here. So everyone gets shifts watching, because we're *already* good at picking out patterns." He glanced sideways, obviously looking at a feed of the same video. "And that wouldn't have been an easy analysis problem, let me tell you."

"No," she had to concede, "it wouldn't." Even naïve as she was with respect to the precise difficulties in smart image processing, she needed no explanation of this problem. The ice of Europa—at least, in this area—was filled with varying concentrations of cloudy colored materials ranging from cream to pale orange to dark brown, even black. A lot of those were from various organic molecules, which was certainly exciting and had Larry and Anthony in a constant running debate, trying to make sense of things; from Ceres and Ares Base on Mars, there were a large number of other scientists hanging on every transmission—especially, of course, the xenobiologists. Helen couldn't really restrain some smugness at being the only person even vaguely in that field who was actually on-site.

But all those impurities in the ice meant that it was often the case that even with bright lighting you couldn't see more than a few centimeters into the ice—and there had been at least three cases where the observing party had spotted something just before *Athena* melted through. The last time it had been a rock—probably an old meteorite fragment—which could have seriously clogged an intake pump if *Athena* had melted the ice away. They'd had to pull the probe up, lower someone—Joe, to be exact—down, and pull the stone manually. This wouldn't have been necessary if all of *Athena*'s components had worked perfectly, but the accessories that were intended to remove and eject such obstacles stubbornly refused to deploy.

Up until an hour or so ago, *Athena* had been passing through an area of relatively clear ice, visibility through it up to half a meter. But over the last hour or so, reddish-brown haze had come ever closer, and now almost entirely blocked *Athena*'s vision.

Which meant, naturally, that she didn't dare take her eyes away from the screen for more than a minute or so at a time. That meant that idle chatter would be her only real relief.

Fortunately, wireless connections meant never having to be silent. "I know you're refining the wide-area sensor network. What are Joe and Maddie up to?"

"Surveying the ice around us for the flattest, hardest stuff we can get for the centrifuge," Brett answered, interrupting A.J.'s attempt to reply. "I've pretty much got the design modeled and we're fairly confident we can drive it whenever *Munin's* down here to give the power. But we can't make it terribly huge—just don't have the resources—so it's going to have to spin pretty fast and hard, and the last thing we need is it to come loose and start walking like a badly-balanced washing machine."

"Well," Joe said, his own image popping up on the other side of her VRD, "we're going to try to counterbalance whenever someone's in for a run. Not hard to put opposing mass in the other chamber, at least I'd hope not." The blue-brown jagged mass of the nearby ridge showed in the background as he turned, holding some device pressed to the ice below him.

"No, not hard," Brett conceded, "but not hard to forget, either. A.J., we'll have to program in some failsafes."

"Already thinking about it, along with all the other 'leventy-dozen things on my plate. Not that you guys don't have all that same amount of stuff to worry about either," he added quickly. She couldn't repress a small grin. Her darling A.J. was still learning how not to casually insult people.

"And always one more than we thought," Maddie's voice said. "For example, we completely neglected to realize how important it was to figure out some substitute for gravity because we were so busy, and then it was two months gone by. Dr. Masters—Petra—reports that even the short burn to make Europa escape almost completely exhausted our crew. So now we work on the centrifuge and slow down other work."

"Well, it's not like we can really take the nozzle off right away," Joe said. "Until *Odin* is in a lot better shape, we won't even be able to *install* it. So that job has to wait. And . . . hold on . . ." he stopped, adjusted the device—a sort of geosounder, she thought—and put it down again. "And a lot of the work needs more people. Who're doing stuff on *Odin*."

"Is . . . is this going to affect our timetable?" Helen didn't want to sound *afraid*, and she wasn't, exactly . . . but there *were* some completely immovable limits, most especially food, on their survival, which meant that anything that significantly delayed them was eating—literally—into their time margin.

"Some," Madeline answered cheerily, "but not terribly much. Don't worry, Helen. We've got a lot of contingency plans. We'll get home one way or another, I promise you."

"Thanks, Maddie."

She glanced back at the screen. Now there was additional darkening in the center screen. *Wonderful. A thicker layer? Visibility is almost down to one centimeter.* "A.J., what do we do if I get to a patch that I can't even see a centimeter in? That's about one minute of decision time."

"Hm. Well, keep an eye on it is what I'd say. A minute is actually a long time, but much less than that and you might not have time to study what you're seeing and make a decision."

"All right."

The colors were not uniform either, but were often swirled through, like water with multicolored drops of dye added and then suddenly frozen. In the direct forward, or downward, view, the dark patch was becoming darker still.

Odd. The video processor is still claiming visibility slightly over a centimeter. No drop.

Most darker layers were a wispy swirl in basic shape—supporting the thought that they were frozen traces of various currents or specific processes. But this deep-brown phantom looked more defined, almost... almost oval...

And suddenly she was shouting *"STOP!"* and hammering the emergency cutoff, hitting it half a dozen times before it registered that *Athena* had already complied with her signal, had stopped instantly.

"What? What is it? Helen, *answer me!"* A.J.'s voice was concerned, worried.

She was speechless, staring at the screen in front of her; she was barely able to activate the feed for the others.

"What is... Holy *shit.*"

"Oh. My. God," Maddie said reverently, after a momentary pause.

For there, half a centimeter below the visible level surface of Europa's ice, was a small object.

An object that looked something like an oval shoehorn.

Just like the one Jackie brought me fifteen years ago...

PART III

Progression, n: 1) the act of progressing; forward or onward movement; 2) a passing successively from one member of a series to the next; succession; sequence; 3) MATHEMATICS : a succession of quantities in which there is a constant relation between each member and the one succeeding it. Compare arithmetic progression, geometric progression, harmonic progression.

Chapter 16

"You've *got* to be kidding me," Jackie said, glancing at the image of Helen in the upper-right corner of her HUD, then back at the crescent-shaped line cutter she was using to cleanly remove the cracked section of piping for part of the *Odin*'s neo-NERVA rocket nozzle assembly. "A Bemmie arm-plate? In the ice?"

At their current distance, the delays were only a couple of seconds, so she simply had to be patient. Helen answered in a moment. "I'm not saying it's a *Bemmie* arm-plate but it looks very like one and almost has to be from something like Bemmie, at two hundred twenty-seven meters under the surface."

"Is it a recent deposit?" asked Horst in an excited tone.

Helen chuckled. "Depends on what you mean by 'recent,' but, no, not really. Estimates on the ice we're going through run between twenty and eighty-five million years old."

"And my best guess is that the layer she's in there might be around sixty-five million years," Larry said.

"Oh," Jackie said, with a pang of disappointment. "So almost certainly something from when Bemmie was in-system, or not long after."

121

"That's my first guess," Helen said. "We knew they were working on water-based forms for use in enclosed areas, so the idea they were planning on colonizing Europa isn't crazy."

"But," came A.J.'s voice, without an accompanying video feed, "as we also know, they got into some kind of major spitting match in different factions, so all their work got cut off abruptly. So the likelihood they got past the basic testing phase...not very good."

"Still," said General Hohenheim, "it is a fine discovery and the first true xenopaleontological excavation ever performed, yes?"

Helen grinned. "Nice job not tripping on that word, General, I sometimes have trouble with it myself. Yes, that's entirely correct. Thank you."

"Where are you, A.J.?" asked Jackie.

"I'm busy trying to get the damn shoehorn out so Helen can take a better look at it."

"Wait a minute," Joe broke in, "Who's belaying you and watching topside? I just heard Brett mumbling about his model, and I'm over here with Maddie! Larry?"

"Whoa, slow down, sorry, didn't mean to confuse you. I'm not crazy, *I* am not actually down there picking at the ice, that's one of my Locusts. I'm just doing all the controlling by hand, so it's not a good idea for me to be looking at anyone else right now."

"*That's* a relief," Joe said.

"Look, Joe, I know I'm an irresponsible kind of guy but do you really think I'm dumb enough to lower myself down a seven-hundred-foot shaft with no backup?"

"Do I need to remind you of—"

"*That* was a long time ago, and I was younger and more stupid, and besides, people were in danger. Bemmie down there isn't likely to get any worse over the next few hours."

"No, probably not," agreed Jackie, unable to keep herself from grinning at her two old friends having the same good-natured arguments. "Well, Helen, keep us up to date and let us know if you find out anything else."

"Do you think you'll be able to *keep* me from telling you?" Helen said cheerily.

"Ha! Probably not. I'm going to cut out now, though, this is getting tricky."

"Talk to you later."

The others disappeared from her view, and she focused on the work at hand. The problem was that the transmitted shock and backpressure from the time when the *Odin*'s nozzle blew off had caused a lot of damage throughout the system, and some of it was quite subtle unless you were able to examine the piping and interconnects directly.

Examining the results of deploying A.J.'s Faerie Dust through the area, Mia had shaken her head dolefully, and Horst had winced. "There are at least thirty sections of pipe that need to be replaced," she'd said, pointing to a number of sections all around the base of the drive system. "We will need to route some of the power differently."

"Also have to cut away remains of welds and bolted fastenings that were broken off when *Odin* lost her nozzle, and devise new fastenings for the *Nebula Storm*'s nozzle," Horst had said.

General Hohenheim had nodded, looking over the

diagrams. "I will leave those repairs to Mia, Jackie, and yourself, Horst. Anthony, Dan, and myself will deal with the repairs to the life support and other related systems onboard."

Thinking of that, Jackie finished this cut and began prepping the replacement section for in-vacuum welding. "General, how is your work coming?"

"Slowly but well, Ms. Secord," the general answered promptly. "Anthony and I are only passable technicians, but Mr. Ritter is an excellent instructor. We are working on cutting off the direction of power or other resources to parts of *Odin* which we do not believe will require it again, and then will work on improving the function throughout the areas we shall be using now and on our journey home." His voice shifted to a heartfelt formality. "I also wish to express again my gratitude that you shall give me the chance to bring my ship, wounded as she is, home again."

"It's our pleasure—though, speaking honestly, it's purely practical as well."

"Perhaps. But it is still very gratifying."

"Let us not get ahead of ourselves," Horst said with a slight warning tone in his voice. "We have a plan and have begun our work on that plan, but there is so very much that is left to do. And much that could go wrong."

"Yes, your steadfast cheer is always something we could rely on, Horst," said Dan Ritter. "I'm looking on the bright side."

"I prefer to remain realistic about the situation," Horst answered, just the *hint* of humor hidden in his voice. "That way, if disaster comes—"

"—you get to say 'I told you so' in a very realistic way," Jackie interjected.

"Jackie!"

"Yeah, Jackie, don't interrupt our little snipefest."

"Even if we fail, it will not be total disaster," Hohenheim pointed out. "The EU and United States both passed the resolutions to work with the IRI to construct a new vessel that is expected to complete construction and be able to reach us here in reasonable time, and in the meantime Ares has apparently worked with the EU engineers to design a fast-time unmanned supply capsule which can use the drive dust here in Jupiter System to stop."

"I hadn't heard that last bit!" Jackie said, pausing momentarily in her work.

"Neither had I," the voice of Madeline Fathom broke in from distant Europa. "Where did you get *that* piece of intelligence, General?"

General Hohenheim's chuckle did have a small measure of pride in it. "You forget, Ms. Fathom; the *Odin* has been wired to act as a very large antenna indeed. The announcement was broadcast just now—or, I should say, a half hour or so ago, but reached Jupiter just now. Director Glendale would have to then take that news and convey it to you, so I would expect you to get a direct notification in a few minutes."

"Why the hell would they have kept the thing secret from us until now, though?" Jackie wondered.

"I would guess to avoid getting our hopes up and let us concentrate on what we were doing. Even now it might turn out something goes wrong with the design, so until we actually see it working we still have to keep working as though we're alone out here."

"I suppose," Jackie conceded. "Still, that's even better news."

"It is, indeed."

The network fell mostly silent for the better part of three hours, as both teams on *Odin* focused on their work. Jackie found herself remembering A.J.'s comment some time back about getting a method to wipe sweat out of his eyes while in his spacesuit. The suit worked hard to keep you comfortable but it was still hard to stay that way when you were cutting pipe, levering large sections of bulkhead out of the way in zero gravity, and other surprisingly strenuous activity.

Then Helen's voice came back on. "It's definitely *not* Bemmie itself."

For a moment Jackie was confused, then she remembered the subject area. "Really? How can you tell?"

"This one's noticeably shorter than the regular Bemmie plates. Judging from attachment angles for muscle groups, this was near the base of one of the tentacles, so if it were a Bemmie, this should actually be a *larger* shoehorn. I think the animal this came from was less than half Bemmie's length and an eighth his mass. Not small, but very small compared to Bemmie himself."

"Why," Brett asked idly, "couldn't it be a baby Bemmie? They were obviously here quite a while before their little civil war, they could've had children either with them or had new ones born while here."

"An excellent question," Helen said, her voice taking on the professorial tone of any academic warming to his or her specialty. "The main reason I doubt it is that while the muscle attachment groups are similar, I don't see any location for the primary precessional muscle groups—which serve for Bemmie's tentacles somewhat like our opposable thumb, allowing the tentacles to interact with each other in very complex ways. So either this animal lacked the precessional groups or had very, very underdeveloped precessional muscles, which makes him a different species.

"Additionally, our anatomical studies of the mummified bodies found on Ceres base indicate that their reproductive strategy involved relatively few children, rather than an R-strategy species. This means that they'd be extremely careful of their children, and with their technology it seems extremely hard to imagine one just wandering out to get lost on the surface. But I think the anatomical evidence of the muscle groups is fairly conclusive."

"Is it like any of the test creatures found on Ceres?"

"In some ways it seems very similar to some of them. Might have been part of a field test."

Joe asked the obvious question. "Well, if they were doing a field test . . . do you think any of them could be alive down there?"

Helen was quiet for a moment; the image of her that was visible was clearly considering things carefully. "*Could* they? I . . . suppose it is possible. But unless we assume they progressed a very long way along their research, or that they found an ecosystem already in place that was by some miracle compatible enough with their form of life that they could integrate their work with it . . . I would strongly doubt it. Sixty-five million years, after all, is evolutionary-scale time. Even if a significant population was developed and put in place, there are so many ways they could have gone extinct in the interim."

Jackie felt a sting of disappointment. "Well, I'll keep hoping."

"By all means," Helen said. "I'm not giving up hope that there's something amazing down there, I just try to temper that hope with realism. And even if there is nothing alive *now*, this fossil tells me it *was* livable a short time ago, at least for aquatic creatures, and—perhaps—we'll find *something* alive whenever we get there."

"Just as long as the finding something alive doesn't involve us breaking through the ice and then the screaming starting," A.J. said with a comically exaggerated cynicism. "You *know* that's how it always works. Besides, *I* still can't quite forget *Who Goes There*."

Jackie shuddered. A.J. had gotten her to read that story once, and even now, more than a century after it was written, it had the power to send chills colder than Europa down your spine.

"Don't worry," Helen said with a laugh. "I promise, if I see something that looks like freezing solid sixty million years ago just pissed it off, I'll let you and Maddie drop thermite on it before excavating."

"That's why I married you, always practical."

"*Almost* always," Joe corrected.

"Almost?" Helen asked.

"Well, like he said, you *did* marry him," said Joe.

Chapter 17

"Well, I've got good news and bad news," A.J. said to the others, studying the images in front of him.

"What is it? Can't you get *Athena* restarted?" Madeline, currently taking a break from outside work, was up beside him almost instantly—not surprising, he knew, since *Athena* was one of their most crucial pieces of equipment.

"Oh, I *can*, but I can't do it *here*. Now that I've got her down to her prior level, I find I'm going to have to haul *Athena* all the way back up the bore, move her over quite a distance—probably as far as we can practically manage it—and start her up again. Which means that until we get that done, we don't even have her supplemental power running some of the systems, so we're totally on batteries now."

"Hm. I'm presuming that's the *bad* news, A.J., so I'm also assuming there's good news somehow involved in this move?"

"Yes, though it's mostly for the beautiful and talented Helen Sutter-Baker."

"There's *more?*" He felt a grin spreading involuntarily across his face at hearing the excited joy in Helen's voice.

"*Lots* more, near as I can tell. I used the instruments on *Athena* to do some quick near-range sensing and there's a whole bunch of material scattered in a layer about, oh, a meter thick maybe, stretching out some distance from the bore. How far a distance I can't tell, and if we're still here when *Athena* reaches that level again we'll probably have to let her keep going rather than keep relocating her, even if there's even more stuff in her new position."

"My God. Let me see! Come *on*, A.J.!"

"Why," Madeline asked, as he transmitted the preliminary data to Helen to digest, "didn't you notice this *before* you sent *Athena* back down? Couldn't the Locusts have sensed it?"

He felt his cheeks go uncomfortably hot. "I . . . didn't think of it. She wanted me to retrieve it, so I sent the *Locust* down, had it get the fossil, then ran *Athena* back down as fast as I could so we got the water flowing again . . . and then of course this happens."

"Understandable," Madeline Fathom said, but her tone carried an unspoken "but I expected better from you" that made him wince. She continued, "A.J., can we afford that move? Sorry, Helen, but we *are* talking about survival-oriented equipment and limitations here, and we've already been without *Athena*'s water and significant auxiliary power generation for quite a bit already."

"But—" A.J. could hear Helen stop herself with an effort, take a breath. "I understand."

"Well . . . we've already set *Athena* up once successfully. We've seen the little snags that we need to watch out for and how to start her. There's enough power reserves so we've got plenty of time to do this. My only real concern is backing her up that far; we've already seen on this run backwards that the tunnel doesn't stay perfectly suited to her, so she's going to have to do backwards melt too. She's designed for it, of course, but then she was also designed to deal with rocks and stuff herself, and we know how well *those* gadgets are working. It went pretty smoothly *this* time, but every time I shift her gears I'm afraid something's going to go wrong. I'm *still* wondering if it's something in *Athena*, or one of our systems, that's causing those occasional readings of water vapor in miniscule amounts."

"Hmm." The deceptively delicate blonde rubbed her chin thoughtfully. "Taking the other tactic, can you and Helen—with your Locusts, naturally—actually make some significant additional scientific progress down there? Without *Athena* you'll have no way to get to the other specimens, would you?"

A.J. shook his head. "Not true. The Locusts can drill, bore, or even melt their way through obstacles. Just not hundreds of feet of obstacle, like *Athena*. Remember that when I designed them, the idea was that we might have to use them to explore and even extensively sift through remains of a base, as well as having them do heavier lifting type work or fast surface searches. They've got a lot of versatility, and since we patched together all our solar cells into a really large array, I've got independent power to keep them charged in rotation. So Helen will have her metallic grad students to do the gruntwork under her direction, and it shouldn't—I hope—cost us much except the time to reset. And of course we'd have to be willing to let Helen have the time to run it and study stuff."

"Hold on," Joe's voice came. "I don't want to rain on anyone's parade here, but I'd like to point out that I'm not sure the whole idea makes sense. If there's a whole layer out there, you're still going to have to drill through it the next time, and as you point out, every time we do something with *Athena* other than keep her running, we don't know whether one of those unknown glitches is going to get us in the nether regions."

A.J. could *just* hear a strangled sound, something like a cross between a whine and a grunt, which undoubtedly came from Helen desperately restraining her impulse to argue. He winced with sympathy for her; this was a technical and survival issue and she knew that would trump anything she had to present directly, but this was still *her* profession. As Madeline began to speak, he sent her a quick hug-and-heart icon. *I love you.*

"I can't argue the basic concern, Joe. I share it. On the other hand, it *was* my idea to emphasize that we do some science while we're here, and that was really the purpose of *Athena* as well. Helen, I know you want to say something; do you have anything that might have a bearing on the argument?"

He heard his wife take a deep breath. "Yes, I do, actually. First—as you say, it was your idea that we do science while we're here, and this is, in fact, the *only* science I'm really qualified for.

"Second, we have no idea what the extent of the layer is. It could be that it's just a very small preserved pocket, say the remains of a small ship, or a warm-ice bubble that sort of petered-out most of the way to the surface ages ago." A.J. could tell she'd been studying some of the ice-geology associated with models of Europa; he hadn't even *known* about the idea of warm ice somehow moving up through cold ice before they got here, and even now the idea seemed pretty strange. "Third, if we just keep going, without relocating, I don't get to study *any* of it because there isn't *room* for me to do so behind *Athena*. So if we're going to study any of this at all, why not pull up *Athena*, move her as far as we practically can, and then not only do I get something to work on, but we get another sample point giving us a starting idea of the size of this layer?"

"Well," Maddie said after a moment, "Those are reasonable points. A.J., how long *should* it take for you to get *Athena* back to the surface and ready for relocation?

A.J. thought for a moment. *Let's see . . . The probe's got a couple hundred meters to go. I could just try to winch it up as fast as possible, but I'm sure there's places the ice has deformed, especially with the pretty-much-constant quakes, so I should probably have it do the climb itself in active mode. It got jammed three times when I tried the fast winch last time, and that wasted hours. Climbing up in active mode's a lot faster than full-bore ice-melting but still not fast, about a meter a minute. Assume it doesn't run into anything that actually makes it stuck, which it shouldn't, that's a little less than four hours. Then I have to shut the reactor down, make sure it's cool, lock her into transport mode . . .* "Say, maybe six hours?"

"And if we move it as far as we can, set up, and begin drilling . . . that's going to be at least that long, I'd think," Maddie continued, thinking out loud. "So

we're talking basically two work days for you and one
work day for several of the rest of us doing the setup."

"That shouldn't be a big deal, should it?" Brett
asked sensibly from nearby. "We've made progress
reworking the pieces of *Nebula Storm* we could repair
as she lies, you've surveyed a good place for the centrifuge, and my modeling work's almost done. Until
Horst and the others get back with *Munin*, there's
not that terribly much for us to do other than basic
maintenance and such."

"Hm." Madeline stared into apparent space, consult-
ing some things on her own VRD, and then nodded.
"I agree. We have the resources currently, if an emergency presents we should still be able to survive until
Munin can make it, and—as I had said myself—we're
supposed to try to be doing science while we're here.
A.J., get it going."

"Yes, *ma'am!*"

Chapter 18

".. . and the rest will be up to Dr. Glendale. You all understand the timing and the necessities of the situation, Maddie." The well-loved face had a few more lines, but the iron was still in Director Hughes' voice—along with the underlying affection. "If you can maintain your timetable, while there will be questions about the official version of events in Jupiter system, the cooperation of Ares, the IRI, and the EU will be able to keep them to a murmur, I think. Maneuvering the right people into a position of potential vulnerability will take some delicacy, but I'm doing the best I can to make sure that the revelation of your *other* survivor, and the story he'll have to tell, will have the necessary effect."

Maddie nodded, knowing that the director wouldn't be able to see it but still feeling as though she was being briefed on an operation. She touched a button and paused the playback, smiling fondly. For just this short time, it was like being back in his office, back in her old job, and even though she had come to realize how very, very bad it would have been to stay in that line of work much longer, it was one of the most comforting feelings in the world to hear that voice, dryly outlining the latest developments and making sure she was prepared.

Keldering and Hughes, with their various contacts, had managed to verify what Madeline and Hohenheim had both suspected: the ultimate decisions which had led to *Odin* being armed and Fitzgerald being placed aboard lay with the ESDC and, specifically, Chief Operations Officer Goswin Osterhoudt. Multiple other people of course were involved, but only a few of them were the ones *responsible*, those who had made the decisions, arranged the double and triple blinds that hid everything, the amazingly deft and complex alterations of design that had—for the most part—hidden the entire installation of four capital-class coilgun cannon, loading mechanisms, and even ammunition and components from shipyard and inspection personnel alike.

At that thought, she shook her head again in chagrined disbelief mingled with unwilling respect. *Why can't people with such talent focus on something constructive?*

Of course, she knew—none better—the answers, the real answers, to that question, and those answers were the reasons she had worked for Hughes for most of her life. *To put a stop to them.*

She touched the button again and Hughes came back to life on her VRD. "I'll send a summary with the details as soon as you're prepared for departure." He leaned forward, in a posture that caused her, too, to lean forward tensely. "Be careful, Maddie. There is of course no way that Osterhoudt and his people believe the official story is believed by anyone close to you; they *know* you know the truth. They must for the moment assume that you are keeping quiet because working with the EU is so much more advantageous than getting into a fight with the ESDC and potentially embarrassing and alienating your current allies.

"Once you are back in the Inner System, they know that may change drastically; right now, you need everyone working together, but when you are safe? Perhaps not. You *may* of course continue in that vein, but you and I know very well how this sort of person thinks, how they work. They will assume the worst, and act, if they think acting will do them any good."

"I know, sir," she said, habit stronger than her knowledge this was a recording, "but by that point they may well realize that there's no way we kept everything secret from key people—such as yourself— and decide that their best chance is to push on the political angle to keep from being prosecuted."

As Hughes continued, she felt her face go from fond relaxation to the controlled coldness of HIA Agent Madeline Ariadne Fathom. *He's completely correct. People like Osterhoudt, despite being utterly brilliant, are at the same time terribly, terribly stupid in their arrogance.*

There was a short moment when fondness returned, at the very end: "... but I have faith you'll all come through this, and at the end you and the general will bring it to a satisfactory conclusion. I'll make sure everything's in place, Maddie, if I have to go back into the field one more time before I retire." He smiled. "A welcome-home present to my favorite ex-agent."

She deliberately held onto the smile for a few moments before activating private channels. "A.J., Horst, Mia, General, secure conference, as soon as possible."

"Secure...okay, hold on," said A.J.'s puzzled voice. Similar questioning tones came from the other two, but within five minutes all four confirmed they were on.

"Very well, Agent Fathom," the general said, with only a trace of humor at the use of her old title, "We are all in conference, if you can put up with a few seconds delay."

"I can. I'm calling this conference between us four because at this point I do not know if there is any particular reason to include any others." She summarized most of the update she had gotten from Director Hughes. "The director has delayed his retirement to make sure this gets done," she continued.

"Hold on, won't that draw attention to him, make people wonder what he's up to?" A.J. asked.

She smiled tightly. "Oh, undoubtedly. On the other hand, he's planned to retire at least four times, and backed out every time before, so this isn't really going to surprise anyone. More important, though, is that we're going to be in a lot of potential danger once we start back."

The general's image responded a moment later with a raised eyebrow. "Danger? Do you imagine they will, what, be preparing to fire a larger coilgun at us? That would be complete madness, would it not?"

"A coilgun, yes, that would be completely insane," Fathom agreed. "They aren't that stupid, unfortunately. Just as unfortunately, they *will* almost certainly be very arrogantly stupid in other ways. General, correct me if I'm wrong, but Mr. Fitzgerald had his own control protocols for the *Odin*, including the weapons but also other systems, yes?"

"*Scheiss,*" Horst said distinctly. "You are correct. I believe I understand what you are getting at, Maddie."

"Dammit," A.J. said. "They'll have backdoors into the *Odin*'s systems."

"That's one possibility, yes," Madeline confirmed.

Mia nodded and touched controls that were out of view. "During the . . . disaster, there were no fewer than four interfering protocols trying to direct the cannon operations. Mr. Fitzgerald had placed cutouts in other vital systems under his direct control. As he was not a master programmer himself, any more than you, Madeline, those were either present all along, or were at least making use of embedded hooks in the software that gave him priority access."

"The latter, I'd guess," Horst said after a pause. "The main control protocols were given to the general, once the need to reveal the existence of the weaponry was determined. Correct, sir?"

"Yes. He and I had access to other override protocols as well, but the ones he used were separate. I believe many of them must have been updates he received or created en route, once he began to suspect that I would not be . . . entirely cooperative."

"Then we must presume that these buried control systems are still at least partially operative. As we have not renewed full connectivity with the outside world for *Odin*, they have not had an opportunity to activate them, but as we get closer in-system and are using *Odin* as part of our rescue vessel, the chances that they will be able to make contact and in some way take control of shipboard systems increases."

"No, no, this is just stupid," A.J. burst out. "They couldn't possibly think we didn't send Nick the straight dope, can they? I mean, really, would they think *we* are that moronic?"

Madeline smiled sadly. "No, they will obviously assume that Nicholas has the information, and possibly Keldering. If they choose to act, it will be as a coordinated, multilayered operation that only something as large as the ESDC—and, speaking honestly, some of the other less-official organizations it is connected to—could manage. The goal will be to eradicate *all* first-hand data, including whatever authenticated data you have sent to Nick. As the old saw goes, 'three can keep a secret, if two of them are dead'; they also have the absolute certainty that Nicholas Glendale *cannot* have told more than a few people of the truth, because otherwise that truth would have leaked, not merely become suspected."

"They couldn't get away with—"

Maddie waved her hand abruptly, cutting A.J. off, then sighed, leaning back in the seat of the otherwise-empty cabin of *Munin*. "A.J., of course they *can't* get away with it, not in the long run. They'd have to have everything fall absolutely their way, all the way down the line, and miss nothing.

"But they will be *desperate* by the time we are getting in-system. Men like Osterhoudt *will not* go to jail. They will take *any* risk if they see the danger looming close. And they will convince themselves that if they can get rid of the two damning pieces of evidence—the survivors and the wrecks—then despite any circumstantial evidence, no one will try to bring it home to them, because the potential loss is greater than the gain."

The others were silent for several seconds. Then

the general nodded decisively. "You are completely correct, Agent Fathom. I know such people. Fitzgerald himself was such a man; there was no true way he could have gotten away with his deception in the end, yet he was still proceeding on the assumption that somehow he *could*. And he was, I am afraid, far brighter than those who hired him. Therefore..."

"Yes, General. We will all begin looking through the *Odin* for these trapdoors," Horst said.

"And taking them *out*," seconded Mia.

"But not *completely*," said A.J., with a devilish glance at Maddie.

As the others looked at him in puzzlement, Madeline could not restrain a grin. "You have gotten to know me too well, Mr. Baker."

"Evil knows evil, Ms. Fathom-Buckley," he said. "If they're going to be stupid, far be it from us to keep them from *proving* it."

"Ha!" Horst exclaimed, as both the general and Mia began smiling as well. "We will leave the access protocols and spoof the control reaction, yes? Make them *think* they can still control *Odin*—"

"—and record the whole attempt," Madeline confirmed. "In the true principles of your favorite aikido, A.J.; we will allow them to firmly and finally convict themselves."

Chapter 19

"You know," Jackie said, triggering a *Cancel and clear* on her workspace, "we've been wasting just a *ludicrous* amount of time on this hookup."

Horst scratched his head. "But we need to have the access to *Nebula Storm*, and it has to spin—"

"Yes," Jackie interrupted, "but we're going about it all *wrong*, probably because we were trying originally to figure out how to make it work with *Nebula Storm* and *Munin*, and then trying to make the connect to the regular airlock on *Nebula Storm*."

"So what's your solution?" Mia asked reasonably.

"Go back to what the *Odin* was originally designed for. If we stick the *Nebula Storm* in the center of the body along the main axis..." she paused.

She only had to wait a second before Horst struck his own forehead with a muttered German imprecation. "Of course. Rotate *all of Odin* at the same speed, and we don't need any special connectors; we just integrate the *Nebula Storm*'s forward end into the ship and we can enter and leave as though *Nebula Storm* were just one more section of *Odin*."

"And we can leave everything extended, as long as we can clear off any ragged pieces trailing around the area."

Mia was smiling now. "Oh, this will be *so* much easier, Jackie! I can't believe we didn't see this before. Yes, and there should be very little to clear away; remember that the forward portion of *Odin* was jettisoned on purpose, and the separation charges designed very carefully."

Horst checked the uplink. "Ah, signal is back to full; we have emerged from behind Jupiter. Brett, this is Horst, are you receiving me there?"

The round-trip delay now, at their maximum communication distance from Europa, was close to eight seconds, so Horst had to enforce patience while he waited; as they'd done this many times now, he was getting good at having conversations with significant time delay built in. It was only about fifteen seconds before he heard the reply. "Horst! Good to hear from you all. Yes, receiving you fine now."

"Glad to hear from you too. We trust that everyone is doing well there?"

"Good enough. *Athena*'s almost done filling *Nebula Storm*'s tanks, and I guess we'll have to start dumping the water until you guys get back for a refuel. Helen's been happily digging away in the ice by remote control, and we've laid out a centrifuge area and started putting together the components we can for that. How're you doing?"

"We've got *Munin* loaded with the pieces you guys specified for the centrifuge."

"What about power?" A.J. interjected. "Did you—"

"Solved," Jackie said. "There's a spare reactor for the low-g rover we have on board *Munin*, so we're sending that down to drive the centrifuge. That way you can keep the rover intact."

"Excellent," A.J. said.

"How about you, Petra?" asked Jackie.

"I," the British doctor answered, "have managed to get every duplicate piece of medical equipment into *Munin* as well." While the others had done the larger engineering work, Petra Masters had been carefully attending to the medical aspects of the trip. "Low-g compensation drugs have been loaded—I am currently working out the best schedule for testing each of us to verify whether any of us have unsupportable reactions to the medication, as we have no true emergency facilities."

"Take your time, Petra," Joe said. "No one's in any hurry to be a guinea pig if we don't have to be."

"I know," Petra said. "On the other hand, however, this is an ideal time to perform some preliminary field trials, and was after all the reason the drugs were sent along in the first place."

"Oh-oh." Joe's voice was so grimly dour that Jackie couldn't help but giggle. "Now she's going to experiment on us in the name of *Science!*"

"You need anything, Jackie?"

"Actually, yes, Brett—I realized we were all being so stupid with the linkup design. I want you to do a model and design trial assuming we're going to dock the *Nebula Storm* forward-points first along the axis of *Odin*."

The pause was somewhat longer than the expected eight seconds. "Along the . . . oh, *I* get it!"

"Yeah, I guess we *were* all being kinda dim," A.J. commented. "That'll work a lot better. I guess we figure on embedding up about halfway to the main lock, then run a corridor tube out to the lock."

"Something like that. And then we rotate everything at the proper speed. *Odin* was designed for that anyway."

"She *was*," agreed Hohenheim's deep voice cautiously, "but I remind you that my ship has been put through a very great deal in the last months, and we should be very careful about forcing her to rotate in that fashion again until we have surveyed the entirety of the critical support structure. We do not wish to have half of the *Odin* suddenly send itself hurtling into space."

"No fear on that," Brett answered quickly (or as quickly as time-delay would allow). "With A.J.'s sensors, my modeling, and *Odin*'s own PHM systems, we can make very sure."

"Any additional problems caused by this approach rather than the other?"

That was Madeline, Jackie thought, and then considered the question. "Umm...I don't *think* so. The only real problem I can think of offhand is one of the same ones we would have in the more complicated linkage designs—attaching stuff securely to that damn Vault material in the hull. It doesn't weld easy at all, and I don't think anyone's found a glue that sticks worth a damn, either."

"I'll model some alternatives," Brett said. "I'm thinking of just running clamps out to the bases of the four habitat extensions, and putting a ring behind them. It'd be a pain on EVA for whoever's doing it, but I think it'd work. We're not talking about terribly high accelerations in any direction, so structural integrity shouldn't be a big problem."

"Just make sure you model extreme cases," Jackie reminded him. "I know, that sounds like an obvious thing, but we won't get any do-overs on this. So modeling...oh, I dunno, say what happens if one of the habitat anchors gives way and suddenly we're rotating with only three of four connected? That's the kind of thing we have to be ready for."

"You're right. And believe me, I'll make sure all of you get to see the models I've done and let me know if I've forgotten anything."

"Good enough," Maddie said.

"Hey, Helen," Jackie said. "I had a thought while we were around the other side this time and wondered if you had an answer for it."

"Hold on, Jackie...All right, I've got the Locusts on hold. They're excavating something else for me now. Go ahead."

"Well, I know there's been all sorts of debate about aliens before we discovered Bemmie, and a lot of the arguments were about how and why they'd bother to come here," she said slowly." But it occurred to me that now we've got a better explanation.

"Maybe Bemmie *came* from Europa. That's why they were here. They didn't have to travel *to* the solar system because they're just as native to it as we are."

The airwaves were silent for several moments before several voices started to speak at once. "Hadn't thought of—" "Hell, that's an idea, I—" "No, I don't think—"

"Everyone," the amplified transmission of Hohenheim came, momentarily squelching the others, "let

us speak one at a time. Dr. Sutter, the question was addressed to you."

"It's certainly possible as far as I am concerned," Helen said after a short pause. "Since the ocean here is possibly very like Earth's, and both Earth and Europa must have formed at similar times, there were billions of years for Europan life to evolve. No reason that I can think of that Bemmie couldn't have gained sentience and sapience a few million years earlier than we did."

"And that would sure explain their presence," Dan said with some excitement. "They got to their surface, saw all the other planets, and Earth would have looked like a beacon to them, I think, close enough in that you didn't have to melt your way to the surface to see the stars."

"It has an appeal of simplicity about it in many ways," agreed Hohenheim. "But I believe I heard some dissent on your end, Maddie?"

"I think that was A.J., though I have some questions on the idea. A.J.?"

The sensor expert's voice held the slight edge of pride that it usually did when he was announcing an insight. "Sorry, Jackie, but no way. And there's a reason for that which any engineer would know—or any classical student, probably."

All right, what's he getting at?

"I'm not following you, A.J.," Joe said after a moment. "At least, I'm not seeing any objection to this that's anywhere near as bad as the ones for them traveling light-years."

Got it! She felt slightly better, having just figured it out instead of having to hear A.J. explain to her the vital hole in the theory. "No chance for Prometheus, is that your point?"

"Oh, excellent, you got both references." His rejoinder wasn't sarcastic—one thing about A.J., he liked people to figure things out.

"What do you mean?" Helen asked.

Maddie answered. "It's the first objection that came to me, too. The key to civilization as we know it really rests on two things, and one of them is the control of fire. How do you refine metal, manufacture a spaceship or tools or do any of a thousand other things when you can't build a fire, smelt ore, and so on because you're always underwater?"

"And I just thought of another," Helen said. "A more fatal one overall, actually, and I have to admit the 'no fire' objection is pretty close to fatal. Bemmie was an evolved *amphibious* form. But there isn't any land here."

"Oh, duh," A.J. said. "There I went coming up with the clever scientific objection and you figure out one that's so much more basic that I needen't have bothered. So that's that; they had to have evolved on a planet that, like ours, had an open water ocean and an oxygen-rich atmosphere, since all indications are they breathed air like ours, and they went from making fire to building starships, breaking the light-speed barrier to travel across the galaxy. Or at least the local stars."

"Eh?" Jackie said. "A.J., I seem to remember you accepting—way back on Mars, after we first finished looking over the Vault—that they'd come here using some kind of STL tech."

"I did, but I've rethunk it," he said. "These guys

could come all the way to another solar system with enough stuff to set up at least one and probably two major research facilities. They had enough time and resources involved that they could end up in a major war, and someone who won could do all that and then build the damn Vault as a message...and walk off." She could see his tiny image shake its head. "No, I reverse my old pronouncement; I'll bet everything I've got that they had something that was either FTL, or that violated some *other* rule of our known physics enough to make traveling to another solar system no harder than traveling to another planet in *this* system."

"So...why didn't they ever come back here, finish whatever work the side that won was doing?" Joe asked.

"No answer to that yet," A.J. admitted, "or, rather, there's about a thousand answers to that and I haven't really got anything that gives us a clue as to which answer we want."

"Doesn't really matter now," Helen said sensibly. "What's important is we're all alive to ask the questions. And that it looks like we're going to stay that way and keep asking them a while longer."

"As long as we keep working," Jackie said, reminding herself as much as everyone else. "Horst, I think we'd better go up and start looking at the areas we're going to need to prep for *Nebula Storm*'s lockdown."

"You and Mia had better do that," Horst said. "We need to get the first load back to Europa Base so they can build the centrifuge, and I can start bringing *Odin* back lots of loads of water for *Odin* to use. It's time to start launch prep."

She realized that he was right; if *Athena* was finished refilling *Nebula Storm*'s tanks, it was time to

start ferrying reaction mass from Europa to *Odin*.
"You're right. Okay, Mia, let's get moving!"

She swung out of her chair and propelled herself
quickly towards the far exit, where her spacesuit hung
on velcro, waiting. *We're really making progress!*

Chapter 20

"Argh!" A.J. said with articulate precision.

Joe looked over at his friend, who was currently settling back down to Europa's surface, still clinging to one of the wrenches designed for use in space-walk conditions. "Didn't lock yourself down again, eh?"

A.J. muttered something that didn't sound at all friendly. "I keep getting focused on getting the work done and forget where I am. Stop *grinning* at me!"

"I'm smiling at how well the centrifuge is shaping up," Joe countered, the broad smile still on his face. "Not mocking your inability to remember basic procedure. No, not at all."

"What about the time *you*—"

"—I know *exactly* what you're going to bring up, and that was about ten years ago, and I did it *once*. This is the third time I've seen you wrench yourself right up off the surface of Europa."

"Be kind to him," Helen said, but her image wasn't showing grave, serious concern either. "I'm using his only Locust right now, with the others having to do slow sequential recharge, so he can't sit in his master control center and have his robotic servants do his bidding."

"Focus on the tasks at hand, please," Madeline said calmly from her position on the other side of the centrifuge assembly. "We need to be sure everything is done properly. A.J., how's your IAA program tracking?"

The Integrated Automated Assembly application monitored the entire process of construction; similar programs had been in use throughout the assembly of all the current generation of spaceships—and, for that matter, planes and ships back on Earth. They made sure the right fasteners were tightened in the right order, grounding contacts properly made, and so on.

After a pause, A.J. answered. "Looks like . . . I have to give this one another tug or two, not surprising since I didn't really get a good grip last time." Joe managed to keep from interjecting anything else, not that this was an easy thing to do. "Maddie, one of the fasteners on module seven—I'm highlighting it in your view—is overtorqued. Back it off until the display shows green."

"Anchors?"

"No change since we started full assembly, despite that one big ground tremor. Looks like those got planted good, so it shouldn't walk on us."

"Is everyone clear for takeoff again?" Horst's voice interrupted.

Madeline did the official checkoff. "Yes, Horst, we're all over here with the centrifuge assembly, except for Helen, who's running her excavation in *Athena*, and Petra, who's relaxing in Hotel Europa. All clear."

So far, things are going smoothly, Joe thought to himself, then spent a few quiet seconds kicking himself for even *thinking* that. Still, the basic thought was correct. Having someone like Brett along to make sure the entire design was workable and help figure out the best way to assemble things sure helped. And Dan had pointed out—in another of the "we should have thought of that weeks ago" moments—that the best way to keep *Munin* shuttling back and forth would be to set things up so that the *Nebula Storm*'s tanks could be emptied directly into *Munin*'s; then *Munin* could take off, bring additional reaction mass to *Odin*, have the crew do some more work on the giant EU vessel, and then come back to tank up without having to wait for *Athena* to do the whole job. This way, when the time came, they wouldn't have to wait for more than the time it took to fill *Nebula Storm* back up.

So now *Munin* was taking off—there she went, impractical wings and all, straight into the black sky—only about four days after she'd brought the components back. And they were getting close to finishing the assembly of the magnetic-drive centrifuge.

"I know it's gonna be a pain," Joe said, "but I'm actually kind of looking forward to spending some time moving around in real gravity for a while."

"I think the novelty's going to wear off really fast," A.J. said, "but me too. I haven't been able to do decent exercises since we came here; the old 'dynamic tension' method doesn't cut it, and I've got at least an inch of padding I didn't have before."

"Not *quite* that much," Petra Masters said from her comfortable position in the artificially sun-drenched room of Hotel Europa, "but the little you have gained feels—and probably looks—like much more given the rather unforgiving designs of your suits."

"Thought you were on vacation, getting away from it all."

"I'm still interested in your progress. But think of it as a phone call from this marvelously sunny vacation flat. By the way, I compliment you, Dan—this really does feel like actual sunlight."

"Thanks, Petra," Dan Ritter said after a few seconds' pause, as Dan was still aboard *Odin*. "Visual triggers and biological ones for the light cycle are pretty important and widely studied; I just followed their advice."

"Well, wherever the basic idea came from, it is a capital one; I feel more ... myself, somehow, than I have in some time."

"You have trouble with SAD back home?"

"I do indeed. Seasonal Affective Disorder is common in my family."

Joe nodded to himself. "I guess that's more of a problem out here where the Sun doesn't seem itself at all."

"That's got it," Maddie said from the other side of the structure. "A.J., how about yours?"

"Done. Was that the last one?"

"I certainly hope so, or my beloved husband has been slacking terribly over the last few minutes. Instead of *asking* me—"

"—I should just check the screen ... okay, yes. We should be ready to connect up the power and test her out with a dummy load. Joe, would you go get in?"

"Is that supposed to be a demonstration of your brilliant wit? Helen, I think he's going senile." As he continued the usual banter, Joe went to retrieve the test load which, for his usually obscure reasons, A.J. insisted on naming "Buster."

"I've got the test dummy; putting it in place." He

picked up the stuffed spacesuit and entered the spin assembly, making his way to the acceleration chamber. The interior was adapted from one of the shelters in *Odin's* storage, meaning that it would have its own atmosphere and, within the very limited space, afford several options for exercise (pushups, tracked weights, chin-up bars, and about a ten-foot span for walking back and forth). He stripped off the suit, hung it on the rack set next to the airlock, and dumped the dummy in the middle of the floor.

A minute later he stepped down, having made sure the door was fully secured. "Okay, I'm out."

"Maddie, check the balancing readout. How much excess weight you reading in the acceleration chamber?"

"Just a moment, A.J." A pause, then, "I make it one hundred thirteen point four kilograms... and that's mass, not weight, A.J."

"Mass, okay, whatever," A.J. said. "Buster with his suit actually *masses*, according to my own numbers, one hundred thirteen point four two. Well within accepted margin of error and the balance limits that Dan and Brett gave us. All right, I'm loading that much *mass* into the opposite balance chamber."

A few minutes later A.J. said "All set. Everything shows green on my end. Anyone else see anything off?"

Joe checked his own systems. "No warning lights here. Power's set."

"Then we're ready for a spin test," Madeline said. "Everyone back to *Nebula Storm*. I'm sorry, Petra, that includes you—you'll get your additional hours back. But if anything goes wrong with something that large spinning fast enough to make a one-gravity equivalent field inside, it could send very heavy pieces scattering over the surface, and *Nebula Storm*'s the only absolutely safe location in that case. Helen, shut down the Locust and *Athena*, just in case."

It took about half an hour for everyone to wrap up and assemble in the now rather cramped confines of *Nebula Storm*'s control room.

"All right, Joe. Start her up."

"Engaging drive."

Joe fed power to the centrifuge. It was a simple enough design in concept, using modified magnetic acceleration components from *Odin*'s drive spines (and the hidden coilguns) to spin the modules around a track which was constructed at a precise angle. When the centrifuge reached the speed at which the side acceleration was approximately one gravity, the combined lateral acceleration and the slight contribution of Europa's downward gravity vector would make the floor of the acceleration chamber seem to be precisely down. "Centrifuge on."

Outside, the forty-meter-wide, spidery structure showed movement inside the wire-cage openwork which was the main accelerator. "Acceleration as predicted. Power draw is within one percent of theoretical. Increasing power."

The rotating component was a cross-shaped structure in the center, two carefully balanced weights at the end of each of two crossarms, the other crossarm having the acceleration chamber at one end and the counterweight chamber at the other. The display showed the spinning, like the spokes of a wheel— except in this case the wheel stayed stationary while the spokes moved faster and faster. "Up to two RPM now—nearing one-third gravity." The twenty-meter radius would require the assembly to spin at nearly seven RPM to reach the desired acceleration—non-optimal, because some of the crew might find that unpleasant, but there was no practical way to build the thing larger; Joe had been skeptical of their ability to construct something *this* large, and Dan and Brett had spent a lot of time figuring out a design which would be practical. Dr. Masters thought there were ways to minimize the vertigo or nausea, and that the benefits of acceleration outweighed the risks of discomfort for a few hours.

"Any wobble?"

"Very little. Anchors are holding. Okay, guys, I'm taking her up the rest of the way."

Faster and faster the rotating chamber passed by. Once every twenty-five seconds. Twenty seconds. Fifteen. "Almost there, rotational speed forty-two . . . forty-five . . ."

A green light blinked and a chime sounded in all their helmets. Joe heard a small cheer from the others. "One full gravity, spinning at fifty point four kilometers per hour. Congratulations, Dan, Brett—she works!"

"Then let's put her into service," A.J. said. "So all of us can . . . take our turns."

Joe resolved to wait until A.J. got out of his suit before he kicked him in the shin.

Chapter 21

"Welcome to Europa, General," Madeline said as he stepped out of *Munin*.

For a moment, he didn't answer. He had seen many spectacular and awesome views already on this journey, enough to make him fear at times that he would lose the capacity for wonder. But the sight of mighty Jove looming above the jagged-spiked horizon, looking down upon the small white-shining collection of shelters and the bronze-colored, alien shape of the *Nebula Storm* stopped him in his tracks, filled him once more with an achingly strong feeling of mingled triumph and awe that here his people and those of the IRI had survived, had *built*, had made this first foothold on a world in the Outer System, under the very eye of deadly, beautiful Jupiter, and he knew that there was much wonder left in the universe.

"I thank you, Madeline," he said. "I am very glad to be able to come here, to see this world and the base that you have all built together."

Left on *Odin* now were Jackie, Horst, Mia, and Anthony. Madeline had come out with the last crew to help fly the *Munin* back, as it had been universally agreed (before he was even asked) that he should have the opportunity to visit, and she was the only other even vaguely qualified pilot for *Munin*.

That of course is not quite *accurate,* the general mused to himself as Madeline and Joe followed him down the ladder. *I could fly* Munin *myself, if the occasion arose.* "Where should I expect to stay? Aboard *Munin*?" The fact that the two were carrying his personal belongings seemed to argue against that idea.

"No, sir, General. You get the vacation suite for the few days you're staying. We've cleared it out for you."

His initial instinct was to protest, but he certainly liked the idea of a shower, even under low gravity, a great deal, and of a place that seemed able to at least somewhat pretend to be on a safer and more comfortable world. "I am very grateful."

"Live it up, General!" A.J. Baker said. "The rest of us actually have had a few days there over the past few months. You should've had a turn a while back."

The general did note that the sensor expert's voice sounded oddly strained. "Are you all right, Mr. Baker?"

"Oh, about as all right as you can expect. Look directly across from you."

The large circular structure on the far side of the camp showed movement, and Hohenheim understood. "Ah, yes, you are in your gravity practice now."

"Yep. And still not used to it. You'll get your chance at that, too. Doc Petra insists."

"Yes, General. You really should have been brought down earlier," Petra continued. "There's no excuse for people not spending some time even in this . . . feeble gravity field, let alone avoiding the centrifuge now that we have it built."

"I look forward to it," he said with a smile. "I have had much time to exercise, of course, but actual weight on my feet is hard to come by."

He found himself slightly disoriented by that weight, in fact. After many months of weightlessness, the existence of a completely stable frame of reference was highly peculiar, and weight itself felt...*wrong*. It became clear just *how* unused he was to this experience when he suddenly tumbled across the ice.

"General! Are you all right?" Madeline Fathom drifted down near him as he began to carefully right himself. "What *happened?* That didn't look like an ordinary fall."

"I am physically unharmed," he answered, trying to keep the chagrin from his voice. "Somewhat embarrassed, that is all. I must pay more attention to my movements in future, until I reacquire the habit of gravity."

"Oh, man," Joe said. "Of course. You haven't had even *this* much ever since the fiasco."

"No, and I have developed excellent new reflexes for living in constant no-gravity. I stopped concentrating and in mid-stride my body tried to shift to prepare for deceleration against the habitat ahead."

"Yeah, I guess there's still a world of difference between zero gravity and one-seventh or eighth, like here," A.J. remarked. "And a few worlds' difference between that and *this*."

"Do not overdo it, Mr. Baker," Petra Masters' voice was stern. "I know you are proud of maintaining your physical condition and dislike the shifts you have seen, but you will make nothing better for yourself by pushing too far."

"Yes, Doc. I'll try to distract myself with that stuff Ares sent us on the monitor designs for the Mars colony."

Hohenheim raised his eyebrow; the motion did not go unnoticed by Madeline, who was apparently watching his imagery closely. "A.J. designed all the condition monitoring for the Mars Colony, and they've been having some problems expanding it. Now that we've managed to establish reasonably good contact through *Odin*, we're all able to get stuff from back home." She caught herself. "Well . . . almost all of us."

"Hm." He had actually been doing a great deal of thinking about that. It was hard not to, given that he was aware of the data traffic passing through his vessel and that much of it had initially consisted of heartfelt thanks and greetings from the relatives and friends of his surviving crew and those of *Nebula Storm*.

They passed through the airlock into Vacation Hotel Europa. He stumbled again in surprise. The interior did indeed seem to be lit by bright, real sunlight pouring through the windows. He caught himself this time, and took some time to slowly remove his helmet.

The air actually smelled . . . *fresh*. "How in the *world* . . . or perhaps I should say in the *worlds* . . . did you manage this?"

"Manage what?" Joe asked, perplexed, then, as he took his helmet off and saw the general sniffing the air, grinned. "Oh, *that*. Well, keeping the filtration systems up to top standard has of course been one of our top priorities, given that breathing is the first crucial survival necessity. Ours, of course, weren't as abused as poor *Odin*'s—we didn't really have fires, damaged insulation, all that kind of stuff forcing the recyclers and filters to take the insult of that level of aromatics. But it's really Dan who gets that credit."

"I just happened to be tracking a lot of the research being done on space environmentals. It's my job," Dan protested uncomfortably. "And while we couldn't get some of the unique filters and supplement cartridges shipped to us that the latest deployment on Phobos Station was using, I was able to get the specs and how they worked—exactly what chemical species had to be removed, and which ones had to be added, and the exact structure of the metamaterials involved in making it all work pretty much automatically. Still wouldn't have made any difference because I saw it as just theoretical. It was actually Reynolds Jones who pointed out that we were missing a bet."

"Jones? I'm unfamiliar with the name. Oh, wait a moment. Yes, he was one of the people from Ares who came out to assist you, as it turns out, with the vessel that came to be *Nebula Storm*?"

"Right. Ren's one of the best materials science experts around," Joe confirmed. "And so when we sent him the one report, I mentioned what a shame it was that we couldn't get one of those filters, and he replied—how'd he put it, A.J.?"

"Heh. He said, in typically polite Ren fashion, 'It's a shame that you can't adapt A.J.'s materials-repair dust to work on other materials.' That's about as close as Ren ever came to calling us stupid."

"And we *were* being stupid. Though I guess the fact we've been working on a thousand survival-type things since we crashed is sort of an excuse."

"We have all been guilty of various forms of stupidity, I suppose," the general agreed with a smile, finally stepping out of his suit into the startlingly warm air. "But what materials repair was he talking about?"

"Oh, yeah, you wouldn't know about that. Well, the *Nebula Storm* wasn't exactly in launchable condition when we found her, and the biggest single problem was the drive-control spines and related circuitry relied on a *lot* of the RTSC—room-temperature superconductor— stuff we discovered on Phobos," A.J. explained. "Since all the basic elements were there in *mostly* the right patterns, I had some Faerie Dust made that was tailored for fixing that kind of thing. Used it to process the stuff back into the proper metamaterial structure. So Ren was just pointing out to us that if I had something capable of doing *that*, there wasn't any good reason I couldn't—with Dan's help—make it generate the right structure on a filter, if we had all the materials available. It took a few weeks, but it worked. I'm not sure whether we'll be able to do that to all the key filters in the *Odin*," he continued, "but we might. But the one in Vacation Hotel Europa's special; we sent back to the Japanese, who'd come up with the process, and begged 'em to tell us what to do to give the interior of the place the smell of a seaside cabin. They turned that request around in less than forty-eight hours."

"Not too surprising," Madeline pointed out, hanging the general's bag inside one of the small closets. "As they have been focused on exploiting the entertainment and vacation aspects of space—and are doing well at it—I suspect they already *had* that figured out and were using it. The surprising part is that they didn't charge us something for it."

"I'll bet they have," Helen's voice said. "Welcome to Europa, General," she added. "They probably sent us the formula here, and billed Nicholas. And he probably paid the license fee for the patent without argument."

"You're probably right," A.J. said. "And it'd be just like him to not say anything to us about it, either. He's good people."

"He is," agreed the general, along with several of the others.

"Well, General," Madeline said, "I'll leave you to get comfortable and relax for a bit. You can have a tour a little later, if you want."

"I would like that. But if you would be so kind, Ms. Fathom, I would appreciate it if you would stay for a bit. I would like to talk to you privately. Nothing untoward, of course," he said, looking at Joe.

"General," Joe said cheerily, "you outweigh her by at least three to one, I think, and I'm sure you're a dangerous man, but I'm perfectly certain that if you *did* mean anything 'untoward,' Maddie would break you like a twig. I'll let you have a Commander's Conference in this lovely resort center while I go set up the water transfer connection to *Munin*."

"Thank you, Mr. Buckley."

Once Joe had left, Madeline looked at him curiously. "What can I do for you, General?"

Alberich Hohenheim let himself sit slowly in one of the chairs near the artificially-bright windows. "I have been thinking about the current situation—the fact of our likely conflict with the ESDC and any of their allies."

"I see," she said, taking a seat of her own. "And you're wondering if we need to keep your existence a secret any longer."

He blinked. "You are . . . a very perceptive woman, Ms. Fathom. Or do you prefer—"

"Fathom in this, which is my professional capacity. I'm only Fathom-Buckley when it's a social circumstance."

"Fair enough. Yes, that is indeed the question. I have some family at home, and a large number of friends. Not only are they mourning me, they are undoubtedly now processing my estate. This will be... complicated to unravel when I get back."

She nodded. "No doubt. And there's little point in my sending inquiries in that direction; just doing so could trigger suspicions in the wrong quarters."

"Unless we *do* drop the mask and let them know I am here," he said. "I am not married, so it is not as though I have a wife and children living through this—which would make this a vastly harder decision— but I do have a brother and sister, and several nieces and nephews who are very dear to me. I am unwilling to keep putting them through this pain unless it is necessary."

She studied him for a moment, with an analytical gaze that, he found, actually made him somewhat uncomfortable. *A dangerous woman in many ways. It may be that Mr. Buckley is a much more formidable man than he appears, to have won her apparently exclusive affections.* "So you want me to confirm that this is necessary, or to say we do not need to continue the charade?"

"I . . . suppose, in a sense. I don't expect you to make the decision by yourself."

"General, if you're waiting for me, I think that means that you already have thoughts on the matter, but were hoping *I* would make a decision and solve the problem for you." She shook her head. "You are a commanding officer, a military man who's made no few decisions in his life. You're not the sort to *not* have a clear opinion. And also, why just me?"

"But," he countered, "I am also human, and there are aspects of this that are very personal. I need to be sure that I am making the right decision, and not being either overly sentimental, or being deliberately hard-hearted in order to *avoid* sentimentality.

"As to your second question, your husband put it succinctly enough; this is a commanders' conference. You and I are equals in this mission, and this is a command decision."

She smiled. "A reasonable response. All right." She sat back in her chair and thought for a moment.

"General, as I see it, much of the damage of your silence is already *done*. It has been months. Once we reached the *Odin* and said nothing, it would be considered an absolute fact that you had perished on your vessel along with most of your crew. At that point, funerals would be held, wills would be probated, all the processes of a death would be set in motion, and most of them would have concluded by now, unless your will and estate were *most* complex to handle. I would expect that you would in fact have had a very straightforward will."

"Yes."

"On the other hand, the question is whether there is still any *benefit* to maintaining silence. We now have deduced good reason to believe that we are not entirely out of danger, and will not be until we have arrived safely at some destination in-system—most likely either Phobos Station or *Meru* at Earth; I think most projections of likely departure make Ceres an increasingly unlikely destination."

He waited as she paused, thinking.

Finally Madeline continued. "As the command-ing officer of *Odin*, you have certain unique traits. Perhaps the most important here is that you are a high-ranking military officer, rather than a civilian as are all of the other survivors of *Odin*. You were Fitzgerald's commanding officer, and you were *directly* aware of a number of his actions which led ultimately to this situation. You have the best grasp of the entire sequence of events as it happened aboard the *Odin*, and you were also the last one to confront the imme-diate culprit. Your testimony will be—if not absolutely critical—one of the most powerful arguments against our opponents. And while they can obviously antici-pate anything that your other surviving crew might say, or that we might say, it is very unlikely they will be assuming a dead man might come back to accuse them. It is also possible," she went on, "that they may try first to use overrides based on your personal com-mand codes; if so, you can counter those directly."

"So you are of the opinion that I should remain a dead man for now?" He felt some sense of relief.

"I think that if we were to do otherwise, we've then put your friends and family through *unnecessary* pain. These months of mourning and acceptance will have been a waste of time for no reason. Perhaps it will turn out that hiding your presence has no real effect on the outcome—but if it's even a small possible effect, I would say that it's worth it now to keep that ace in the hole."

He nodded decisively. "I thank you, Madeline. This was the tentative conclusion I had reached, but I was afraid I might have been selfishly justifying these actions."

"Selfishly?"

He smiled, feeling a touch of embarrassment again. "Yes. You see, I am a man who appreciates dramatics, and I cannot help but feel a great anticipation in revealing my presence in direct accusation when we arrive."

Madeline laughed, and shook her head. "You're not the only one that likes dramatics here, General, and I can't blame you. In fact, I'm sure we *all* would like to get a chance to see their faces when that happens." She stood.

He rose to help her with the suit. "I appreciate your willingness to help me see my way clear."

"My pleasure, General. I—"

Alarms screamed through Vacation Hotel Europa, as they must have been throughout Europa Base, and the artificial projected light vanished, replaced by the actual view outside the windows; Hohenheim watched in shock as the support framework for *Athena*, the absolutely vital melt-probe, suddenly crumpled under some invisible impact.

Chapter 22

"Holy *shit!*" A.J. did not apologize for the curse.

At nearly the same instant, Joe Buckley said, "God *damn* it!" followed by "Ow ow OW!"

"I see yellow and red on your telltales, Joe!" Petra said, having obviously switched in her medical monitors. "Talk to me!"

"Goddamn...stupid...universe..." they heard Joe mutter. "Got a hole punched through the suit."

"Through the *carbonan?*" A.J. said incredulously, jamming his way into his suit as fast as he could.

"Yeah, right through. My guess, something like one of the support fasteners on the rig snapped...god-*damn* that hurts...shot out like a bullet..."

"Joe!" Maddie's voice did not have its professional calm, and A.J. was struck again by the sheer intensity of her attachment to his old friend. *Not that Joe doesn't deserve her, or her him, but she's usually so* controlled. "How's the air?"

"Leaking like a sonofa...but it's through the leg, not chest. My *other* leg, so I guess I'll have matching scars." Joe was referring to the lovely scars he had from the one leg being severely fractured to the point

169

of bone poking through the skin after his crash on Mars. "Got a . . . temp patch in my pouch. Think I can get that on, and I'm heading into *Munin* right now."

"Dr. Masters?"

"Mr. Buckley's going into mild shock but still functional," the Kentish voice replied calmly, "and I'm seeing no indications yet that a major artery has been severed. I am on my way over, but I think that Mr. Buckley has once more, shall we say, dodged the bullet."

A.J. heard his sigh of relief echoed by the others as he bounced his way toward *Nebula Storm*.

Reaching the IRI spaceship, he dove through the airlock and was still stripping off his suit as he reached the control console, where Larry was staring at the panel, not even touching it for fear of making things worse. "What *happened?*"

"I don't know! Don't look at *me*, I didn't touch anything I haven't touched a billion times before."

"A.J., what's wrong? Is *Athena*—"

"Don't know yet, give me a few seconds." He brought up screens and telltales, connected his own displays and sensors. "Okay, everyone quiet down, and *nobody* go anywhere near the rig until we get a handle on what's happening."

"Understood," came Madeline's now-calm voice. "It's your call now, A.J.; we're on standby."

Normally, A.J. loved being the center of attention and having everyone hang on his words, but this was different. He might be telling them they were totally screwed, which was not at all the dramatic effect he wanted. A completely unfamiliar sickening tension knotted his gut as he tried to make sense of the sequence of events. *Support gantries crumpled under a* downward *force. Only thing that could have done that would be* Athena, *but how...*

Some of the connections in the control cable were misaligned, possible breaks in the fiber, or something else—he couldn't be sure. *Not getting full telemetry back...but the melt part's shut itself down, did that according to timestamp just seconds before impact. So not from damage or even a jolt, but from...*

"Well, *that* is interesting. I hope."

"A.J.—" There was a warning note in Helen's voice.

"Hold on, hold on, let me finish this." He keyed in overrides, activated the lights for a moment. A jumbled, confused image, lines and curves blurred at distance, appeared. And the cable monitors... "Whoa. Better check the gantry feed... Oh, damn, it's twisted half around. No way to get it loose right now. Argh!"

"What've we got, A.J.?" Joe asked finally.

"Not quite sure *yet*, but I think I know... Ha! Yes, I can check." He reviewed the telemetry from the scattered sensors around the bore from the time just before the event to some time after. "Okay, I've figured it out. It's not good, but it's not a complete disaster, at least not yet." A.J. opened up the communications links to full. "Let's go to full conference mode, people, and I'll fill you in."

It only took a few seconds for the images of his friends and colleagues to fill the display as though they were all sitting around a conference table; even Joe was there, helmet off, looking pale and somewhat sweaty but with Petra Masters next to him. "Okay, the short version is that *Athena* just broke through the crust, but instead of dropping—as we expected—into water, she fell into a void under the ice. A pretty big one, too—haven't been able to measure it, but it's at least ten meters high where *Athena* went through."

"How do you know that?" asked Larry.

"Simple; that's how much slack *Athena* took when she dropped. Which meant she fell for more than seven seconds and was doing about thirty or so kilometers an hour when the cable caught her. *That* was the stress that yoinked the whole support gantry down—like trying to stop a medium-sized car with one pull." He sighed. "One more thing that didn't quite go right—there were cable arrestor brakes that failed to kick in right away. I can think of a couple reasons but that doesn't matter right now."

"No, it doesn't, not really," agreed Madeline. "How do you know it didn't drop through the crust into the subsurface ocean we've been expecting?"

"Two ways. Indirectly, it's too soon, we're not quite four hundred meters down, and I *really* don't think there's water closer than a kilometer. More, though, the melter section shut down on its own because it was *overheating*. If it dropped into water it'd be cooled just fine by the water, though the boiling might cause other problems. But instead it was out radiating its heat in empty space instead of into ice. I confirmed that by checking the borehole sensors; a small but measurable wash of mostly water vapor came up the bore after she dropped through, from presumably really slow sublimation or maybe warmer ice farther down."

"Where the hell would such a void *come* from?" asked Dan.

"I am perhaps not entirely sure," Anthony said, "but I would be thinking it might be a result of the impact structure. If the crust came back together unevenly..."

"That's an idea," Larry said slowly. "It'd keep closing up, eventually erasing everything, but might take many thousands, even hundreds of thousands, of years to fill in all the empty spots. The pressure's not going to be anything like that on Earth—even a kilometer down is only equivalent to about, oh, a hundred thirty meters on Earth. You get plastic flow at about fifty meters in glaciers . . . but at these temperatures, ice is a *lot* harder. I wouldn't be surprised if the pressure a kilometer down is just barely into plastic flow at all on Europa."

"I guess that's an interesting theory, but it's not getting our problem solved, people. So now what?" Brett asked from the *Odin*.

"Now we've got some tricky work," Joe answered, having been examining A.J.'s data, obviously distracting himself from whatever Petra was doing to his leg. "The gantry sections got twisted and they've pinched the cable hard. We'll need to keep the cable anchored so she can't drop farther, then work *Athena* free, repair the gantry, and see if we can get the thing working enough to get her back topside and see what damage has been done. *Ow!* Watch it!"

"I've used anaesthetic, Mr. Buckley, it can't really be hurting, and would you rather I left whatever this is in there?"

"Well it still feels . . . wrong, even if *pain* isn't exactly the right word. But no, sorry, go on. Um, where was I? Oh, yeah. I'm betting that some of the dropout we're seeing on the data feed comes from the pinch, but some of it's almost certainly right near *Athena,* probably near where the cable attaches. Hopefully we can control her well enough

to melt any impediments along the way back up."
Joe cursed again.

*Oh, that's not good. Unless that's just another thing
Petra's poking at.* "What do you see, Joe?"

"Water feed tube snapped. At the top."

"Oh, son of a...it's going to be freezing solid all
the way down. Hundreds of frickin' meters of ice-
filled piping."

"Yep. We'll have to bring it *all* up and thaw it out,
patch it, and then send it back down when *Athena* is
repaired and ready to start up again." Joe shook his
head. "At least it *is* open at the one end, so hopefully
the ice will all push its way up and out rather than
busting the pipe longitudinally."

"How long?" Madeline asked calmly. It was, of
course, one of the crucial questions.

"Can't be sure yet," A.J. answered reluctantly; he
preferred to be certain, but there was no way to tell
yet. "Depends on how bad the damage is. I don't *think*
that *Athena* actually has any crucial damage anywhere,
and we've got enough feed to show that the I/O is
working. So *if* we can get her back upstairs I think
we'll be in good shape. Brett, can you—"

"Already on it, m'man." There was a pause. "Fixing
the gantry support structure won't take long with the
right tools. Which you now have, thanks to the runs
we've already managed from *Odin*. But until that's
fixed you won't have the gantry for support, and you
don't want to leave *Athena* hanging if you can avoid
it. I'd recommend doing a manual lift back to solid
tunnel, if you can do it."

"*And*," A.J. pointed out, "if we can get *Athena* running enough to start traveling up."

"There is that," Brett conceded.

"A.J., give me direct feed from *Athena,* as much as you have," said Mia.

"Sure thing...here you go."

Mia Svensen knew more about *Athena* than any of the others, A.J. knew. She was hopefully going to be able to do a better job diagnosing the melt-probe than he would.

A few minutes later, Mia's voice came back, noticeably more cheerful. "I do not think anything crucial is broken. It may take some minor trickery to get her to work under the current circumstances, but trickery is your business, yes?"

"I prefer the term *wizardry,* but close enough," A.J. said, feeling the knot in his gut slowly relaxing. It wasn't entirely gone—there were a lot more potential problems—but so far it didn't seem like doom. "Maddie, if you want a wild-assed guess, I'm thinking this will take about two weeks to straighten out. A month at the outside, assuming we don't find out that Mia's wrong and *Athena* herself is broken. That's the only thing we really can't fix—don't have the tools for most of what makes the key parts work."

"Even a month we can afford." They could all hear both relief and reassurance in her tones. "Once we get *Athena* and the gantry pieces clear, I would also like to send one of the Locusts down to see what's in that void. Would that be reasonable?"

"If Helen's willing to—"

"Of course I am," his favorite voice in the world cut in. "I've got a fair amount to work on by myself, so you're welcome to stop my digging to look at something new, at least for a while."

"Then in that case, since my talented and lovely wife has no objections, sure, I'd love to. Find out how big it is and how far it goes." He grinned. "Back to my original job, really, the same one that got us all here in the first place, so to speak."

"I suppose so," Maddie agreed with a quick smile. "All right, people, it looks like we've all got some real work to do. General, I'm sorry—"

"Do not apologize," the general said, having kept quite respectfully silent as the others handled the immediate disaster. "Let us instead consider this an opportunity; you now have another pair of hands available to assist."

"And one hell of a pair of hands it is, sir. We'll get started now," A.J. said, "but you don't have to come out yet, General. Really, enjoy yourself for a few hours." He looked at the damage report and the estimates of time and operations to be performed now coming in from Brett's simulations, and winced. "I can promise you," he continued wryly, "there'll be no shortage of work for you to do later!"

Chapter 23

Madeline checked the integrity of the support structure member again. *We don't want a repeat of the last time, that is for certain.*

The new gantry was being heavily reinforced. While they didn't expect to have this problem again, especially with a new set of modified automated brakes in place that Brett and Joe had designed and tested, no one saw any point in taking chances. *Athena*'s new supports would hold even if the probe fell a good thirty meters instead of ten.

"This one's good," she reported. "I'll finish checking the last two; if they pass, we're good for reassembly when everything else is. Joe, how are you doing?"

That was a double question; given how many times her husband had been the receiving end of near-lethal accidents, she couldn't help but worry, but he was also working on other aspects of getting *Athena* back up.

"Me personally, the leg aches like a bastard today, but Dr. Masters says there's every indication of fast healing working, and I don't need to baby it anymore, so that's good; hole like that could've taken a lot longer to get better than a week or two." His smile lit up a corner of her display and she felt immediately less tense. "I've just finished reattaching *Athena*'s main control cables, and everything checks out. Mia's working on part of the linkage for *Odin* but she's going to run *Athena* through a full workup in a couple hours. Unless she finds anything wonky, we should be good to start redeploy soon."

"What about the piping?"

"Making progress," Larry replied promptly. "We've cleared a hundred and forty-six meters of the stuff so far, clean-cut the one end in prep for splicing, and as we clear it we're stowing it neatly indoors to keep it as flexible as possible."

"Good work. At that rate we should have it clear by, what, this time tomorrow?"

"Think so."

"A.J., what have we got? I gave you the day you asked for after getting *Athena* out and doing the major repairs."

"It's . . . big. Really big." A.J.'s voice held both the irrational yet common pride of a discoverer in the thing that he's discovered, and unwilling awe. "It's a pretty smooth tunnel that's triangular in general cross-section. Near as I can tell, with some input from Larry, Anthony, and some of our brains way back home at the IRI, the impact theory has to be the explanation. Looks like what we have are three huge chunks of ice that clumped on top of each other, leaving this void—which was probably even bigger back then—and then they froze up in this position. Incline's only a few degrees, but the path got broken up, probably by crustal movements—some of those look like they're almost *circular*, dunno how *that* would work—"

"Heated ice and convection currents, maybe," Larry

put in. "Different states of ice might interact in funny ways."

"Maybe. Anyway, the path turns out to be sort of like a half-spiral made from long straight sticks laid together at angles, and it goes a long way down. I'm still getting trace water vapor coming up from the lower reaches, which makes me wonder if this thing actually gets down near the ocean itself.

"But you want the kicker?"

Ah, A.J., you and your sense of drama. But you wouldn't be you without it. "Of course we do. What's your big secret, A.J.?"

"The last part of the half-spiral almost reaches the surface only about a kilometer over *that* way," he caused an arrow to materialize on the display, overlaying a map of the crash site. "And it's got a crust so thin on it that you could break through with a few charges."

She blinked, realizing what he was saying. "A.J., do you mean to say that *we* can get into that tunnel?"

"Not just *us*. I said, this thing's *big*, easily large enough for that rover that *Munin* has on board."

"Mr. Baker," came the deep tones of General Hohenheim, "are you suggesting that some of us might actually *drive* into the interior of Europa?"

"And call yourself Arne Saknussemm! Why not, General? As Maddie said, we're here to do science as well, and exploring the interior of another world rather than just looking at whatever's exposed as we drill through it, that should be useful, I'd think." He grinned. "Besides, it'd be kinda neat to think that we'd actually get to *use* that rover for what it was meant for, rather than looking at it as a potential emergency refuge or extra reactor or source of spare parts."

"I thought you *had* cannibalized part of the rover," Dan said from the *Odin*.

"We almost did, yeah, but it turned out we didn't need to. LGT-1 is still fully operational, or should be once we prep her."

"I certainly won't say the idea's ridiculous," Madeline said cautiously. "We have the tools, the rover was meant for exploring low-gravity worlds, and while we have work to do there will also be significant downtime once *Athena* is back in business. A.J., you said the slope was reasonably gentle—that means quite a jaunt. If we assume that it goes to the subsurface ocean, and the minimum distance below us for that ocean is a kilometer, the total length of your path will be several tens of kilometers, am I right?"

"That's right. I think it's averaging about three degrees, which is pretty gentle for this kind of setting, and would mean that if it's a kilometer down you've got about thirty, thirty-five kilometers of tunnel to drive down."

"I wouldn't mind taking a look-see," Larry said slowly, "But what about the quakes?"

A.J.'s image shrugged. "Well, yeah, that's a danger, but look at it this way; near as we can tell this thing's stayed open for several thousand years, it *probably* isn't going to collapse on you guys in the next month."

"I still don't like the thought of the possibility," Madeline said firmly. "What if it *did* happen?"

"Well . . . we'd lose the rover, probably."

"Just the rover?"

"He's right," Joe said. "Unless the whole thing came down and just crushed them—and in this gravity I wouldn't bet against the rover being able to keep itself reasonably intact, at least for a while—the worst that's likely to happen is that the way back gets blocked off."

She raised an eyebrow at Joe's image. "That sounds rather grim to *me*, given that it would be an airless, frozen passage with no replacement air or food. Water I'll give you."

"Oh! Oh! I know the answer to this one!" Jackie's voice cut in. "*Athena*."

"My thoughts exactly," A.J. agreed. "As long as the rover's got reasonable supplies on board, all we need to do is reposition *Athena* over the tunnel near where the rover's stuck and melt down, then bring up everyone through the borehole. *Athena*'s borehole won't let the rover come up, but it's more than wide enough for a person. And we already have multiple tests and proof that she can cut fast and reliably through ice of whatever depth we've sent her to."

"What do you think, General?" Madeline said finally. "It *is* your equipment, after all."

He chuckled. "Agent Fathom, here we are a good socialist collective and we have contributed what we have to the common cause." He looked thoughtful. "Once *Athena* is clearly working again there will have to be several trips to *Odin* to supply reaction mass, and all of us appear to be approaching completion in the basic survival and preparation tasks. There will be much more, as you say, downtime. So perhaps it should be literal *down* time for some of us?"

She heard A.J. snort at the general's pun. "If you're comfortable with it, I have no problem," she said.

"Comfortable . . . perhaps not. There are many dangers. But we did not come these hundreds of millions of kilometers to be comfortable *or* safe, but to learn, and we have the equipment and the personnel to do the job."

"Thank you, General. Joe, you helped direct similar operations back on Mars when we got *Thoat* running, so I'll put you in charge of setting this operation up as well, once the other essential work's completed."

"Great! We'll figure out who to send when the time comes, I guess."

She nodded. "Some choices are obvious. I'm thinking no more than four people, though."

"Mmm-hm." Joe sounded slightly distracted, so she didn't say any more; he might be working on auxiliary components of *Athena*.

Midway through checking the next support, she heard a triumphant *Ha!* from Joe. "Something good? *Athena* running?"

"Hm? Oh, I wasn't working on her. Just trying to figure something out, and I got it perfect."

She smiled fondly. "And what was that?"

"Well, LGT-1 isn't much of a name, so if I'm going to be getting her ready to roll, she needed a name, and given what we're doing with her, it became obvious."

A terrible foreboding stole over her, but she couldn't stop the question from slipping out. "And the name is . . . ?"

"*Deep Thoat*, of course."

Divorce is always an option, she reminded herself as she heard A.J. dissolve into juvenile snickers. *Always an option.*

Chapter 24

"Careful!" Joe said reflexively as the huge assembly wobbled.

"Sorry," Horst said from the other side. "It is not easy, moving this thing while keeping it steady. Not exactly the best-balanced object we've moved."

He couldn't argue that. *Nebula Storm*'s rocket nozzle, once meant as a replacement for *Nobel*'s in case of damage, was a massive, bell-shaped assembly that looked deceptively simple from the outside. However, there were complex channels built into the bell to keep it cooled below critical temperatures, control and sensor runs, and other components embedded inside. The nozzle was essentially symmetrical radially, but much heavier towards the narrow end, and they didn't have any transport vehicle to move something nearly that big; it was nearly as far across as one of the smaller inflated hab units, and twice as tall.

So they were having to essentially drag it to the *Munin*'s bay with improvised rails and rollers. "I feel like an Egyptian pyramid slave," A.J. said, pushing with what feeble leverage Europa allowed.

"Actually," Maddie said from her vantage point

ahead, "the Egyptians didn't *use* slaves for the pyramids, at least for the most part. They were public works projects constructed by regular, paid workers, something like the large construction projects in the 1930s."

"Really?" A.J. sounded startled. "I didn't know that."

"I'd say I was surprised," said Madeline, "but alas, A.J., I've long since resigned myself to the fact that your education has . . . interesting gaps."

"Everyone has 'interesting gaps' from someone's point of view," A.J. retorted, but his defensive tone, Joe was pleased to note, was much less strident than it used to be.

"The only 'gap' I'm interested in is whether this thing's going to *fit* in the landing bay. I know the measurements say it should, but this nozzle seems bigger every time I look at it," Jackie muttered; the low-voiced comment was still picked up and transmitted by her helmet microphone.

"It will fit," Joe assured her confidently. "Now that we got *Deep Thoat* out of the bay. Wouldn't have before."

"Stop calling it that! It's the *Zarathustra*. You're *sure* the connectors will mate up?" Jackie continued. "On *Odin*, I mean. I know I've asked before, but . . ."

"Brett?"

A couple of seconds later, Brett Tamahori answered. "I'll guarantee it. I compared the as-built adapters with the designs, and then with the actual connectors on your nozzle, using A.J.'s high-res models made from the actual thing. It's all well within tolerances."

Brett rarely made such sweepingly confident pronouncements—anyone doing models knew how

the real world could trip you up—so just hearing
him state things so clearly with no "weaseling" made
Joe and, he guessed, the others feel a lot more
comfortable.

"All right, everyone," said Maddie, having moved
two of the rails slightly. "Another shot . . . one, two . . ."

On "three" Joe threw his strength into pushing,
as did the others around the rocket nozzle. This
time it slid smoothly forward several meters, and Joe
nearly lost his footing trying to keep up; his leg gave
a twinge, but that didn't really bother him; the fact
he *could* push was proof enough that he was pretty
much healed. "Whoa, slow down! Damn, this really-
low-gravity thing is a pain."

"Tell me about it," said A.J. dryly. Joe saw that
his friend was skidding slowly across the ice; as he
watched, A.J. hit one of the ripples in the surface and
was launched on a slow-motion arc into the nonexistent
air. The sensor expert took advantage of his position
to rotate his body and landed in a better position to
slow himself down. A few moments later he was slowly
bounding-walking his way back. The chuckles at his
predicament had mostly died down by then.

"How long will it take to get the nozzle fastened
on and working?" Helen asked.

"Well," Jackie answered after a speed-of-light pause,
"just putting it on will take a couple of days since
that's regular spacewalk work. Once it's on we're going
to do a *lot* of very carefully calculated tests to ramp
us up to full functionality . . . figure a couple of weeks.
No reason to rush and every reason to take it slow
when this is the *only* nozzle we've got left."

"How about the *Nebula Storm* coupling setup?"

"Still working on that, and it probably won't get finished until after we've verified the nozzle working."

"Once that is done," Hohenheim said, joining the conversation, "we will need one more load of water, if your prior calculations are correct, and then *Odin* will move to orbit around Europa. After that, we will finish filling *Odin's* tanks as much as possible before preparing for the final maneuver which will bring *Nebula Storm* back to space and bring *Munin* home at last." Joe could *hear* the smile in General Hohenheim's voice, and felt it on his face as well, as Hohenheim spoke so matter-of-factly about the final steps in their bootstrap-based rescue. "With *Athena* continuing to run well, we now have no reason to fear any other immediate disasters. Have you selected the crew for *Zarathustra's* exploration of the interior?"

"We have," Maddie answered, gesturing for another, more careful, push that moved the nozzle forward about one meter. "Either Larry or Anthony was an obvious first choice, and they elected to choose which by a random method, which Larry won.

"As we have also already found one layer with extremely interesting xenopaleontological significance, Dr. Helen Sutter was also an obvious choice. That covers the obvious scientific members of this expedition. With two other slots available, as we had agreed on four people, no more, I felt that I was one of the other obvious choices. Not to sound full of myself—"

"—but you'd have every reason to be," A.J. interrupted. "You're our best all-around everything, really, and if you run into anything you don't expect down there, well, you're the one who's going to deal with it better than anyone else."

Joe could hear that Maddie was pleased with the compliment. "Thank you, A.J., and that's my basic thinking."

"And your last crewmember?"

"That'd be me, General," Joe said. "There should be at least one engineer with them, I know *Deep* . . . er, *Zarathustra* better than anyone else except maybe Mia, and Mia's supervising all the work on *Odin*."

General Hohenheim gave a grunt of assent. "That all sounds quite sensible. Have you found the precise access location?"

"*Kwai Chang* located the thin crust area yesterday," A.J. said, while pushing. "At its thinnest it's no more than half a meter thick. Maddie's already calculated the charge points, and from the one side of the hole I think we'll have a drop of no more than two or three meters, which *Zarathustra* will handle just fine in this gravity. After that it should be all clear. If we run into an obstacle we can't clear, well, okay, that's that, but *Jiminy* didn't find anything when I sent him through before."

"Very good. Then once *Munin* has safely brought the drive nozzle here, I would expect you shall begin this exploration?"

"That is indeed the plan, General."

Joe had to admit, as he saw the nozzle slide a few meters nearer *Munin*—now only about thirty meters away—that he was excited by this prospect. Oh, sure, it was just an icy tunnel, really, but he'd be descending *into* a moon. And there might be more exciting finds; Helen had uncovered at least six pieces of something Bemmie-like, and other as-yet unidentified fragments of something that might be animal, plant, or something else. He remembered those long-ago times on Earth, driving or walking along weathering cliffs and arroyos, trying to spot something just a tiny bit different that might mean a fossil. *And we just might be doing the same thing here, six hundred million kilometers from Earth!*

Chapter 25

"My *God*, this is beautiful!"

It wasn't the first time she'd expressed those sentiments in the last hour, but Helen couldn't restrain herself, and the others didn't seem bothered.

The walls of the huge, generally triangular tunnel reflected the lights of *Zarathustra* in a blaze of color, as though coated with layers upon layers of diamonds. Stripes of color—brown, black, greenish, red-orange— ran through the walls at different angles, but the walls themselves shimmered in hues of transparent glass, glacier-blue, sea-green, with irregular surfaces that seemed faceted on every side. Some were like cubes, others hexagonal plates layered upon each other, and in other spots the wall shone pure white like new-fallen snow at high noon, or cast tiny sharp-edged shadows that revealed feathery, curling structures.

"Looks almost like something dissolved away parts of this wall," Maddie said quietly.

"Not dissolved," Larry answered with a grin, taking picture after picture from the data stream. "A process much more sublime than that."

Joe failed to restrain a snort, even as Helen winced,

189

knowing what Larry had set in motion. "Enough of your vaporing, Larry. What's your triple point?"

"Deposit yourself back in your chair and I'll explain. It'll be a gas."

"Enough." Maddie's voice held a tinge of amusement, but only a tinge, and there was more than enough authority with it. "I swear, every time I think you're getting older, Joe . . . and Larry, stop encouraging him. So you're saying that the . . . worn and eaten-away appearance here is from the ice subliming away in vacuum?"

"Partly, at least," Larry answered.

"But don't you usually end up with a dark, even blackish surface that way?" Joe asked, more seriously. "I seem to remember something about that with comets. And Ceres had a lot of blackish ice."

"Normally, yes. But . . . well, first, let's face it, we're still learning stuff about the solar system. Every time we've sent an unmanned probe somewhere, it's sent back information we didn't expect. Every place we've gone, something weird's shown up. Why should we expect Europa to be any different?

"Anyway, we're getting fairly deep inside Europa now. We've come, what, almost twenty kilometers, so we're down well below where *Athena* holed-through. Pressure on the ice is getting significant, and—much more importantly—up until *Athena* came through and we dropped *Zarathustra* in, this was sealed up."

"You think that makes a difference?" Helen asked.

"It might. You see, if this is a sealed chamber, or was, it's more like a crystal chamber on Earth, or a geode, than something exposed in a larger chamber with an outlet. Remember that A.J. detected a wash of water vapor come up when *Athena* broke through? I think there was *pressure* in here. Not much, you'd call it vacuum on Earth, but a lot more pressure than anywhere else on Europa. The ice sublimes slowly over millions of years, and redeposits elsewhere. As we get farther down, remember, the temperature goes up. It's already noticeably warmer where we are than on the surface—though humans like us wouldn't notice. So that might mean we've got more water vapor coming up from below, filling this space.

"And we've got more pressure on the ice itself, except at the very surface, which means that there's probably several phases of ice here. Hexagonal stuff is normal ice, Ice I_h, but some of those things there look more like octahedrons, which would be Ice I_c, and over there," he pointed to a set of squarish-looking crystals stacking up like a deck of cards given a half-turn, "those look rhombohedral, which would indicate Ice II. No one's really had much chance to study how a complex system with multiple ice phases like this could interact, and what we're seeing here could be a combination of crystals left after one phase sublimed, and crystals deposited later on."

"And, of course, there's whatever impurities we've got in the walls." He gazed at the rippled colors passing by. "I'm restraining myself from demanding we stop only because I want to see what's at the end of this ride as much as the rest of you." he added. "*After* that, we come back and do some ordered and systematic sampling."

"Of course, Dr. Conley. And whatever causes it, it's lovely," Madeline said. "A.J., I'm surprised you didn't draw our attention to this."

"Well," A.J. answered after a pause, his voice sounding slightly tinny through the multiple relays they'd left in the tunnel to assure transmission, "I'd *sort of* noticed that there were some neat formations, but I was really more interested in scoping out the extent and accessibility of the tunnel. And looking at the pictures my Locusts brought back...Well, they're okay, but they don't have the impact yours do. Remember, the Locusts were designed for close-up work mostly, and don't have the top-quality ranged imaging systems. The pics you're sending back are gorgeous."

"How are things topside?" Helen asked.

"Other than missing you?" he said, his sharp smile showing in the upper left corner of her VRD. "Pretty good. *Athena*'s performing perfectly, *Munin* docked successfully, and they're transferring the nozzle now. Everything's stable up here, no emergencies, not even a *hint* of emergencies, actually, so you don't need to worry. *I* just have to worry."

She shook her head, but smiled. "Everything's fine here too, A.J."

"Found any fossils?"

"Nothing obvious yet," Joe answered, turning the wheel of *Zarathustra* slightly to maneuver around a large chunk of ice sticking out into the passage. "We didn't see anything when we passed the rough level of the deposit that Helen was looking at from *Athena*'s old bore, so either it didn't extend that far out, or the layers were shifted."

"I'd guess the latter," put in Larry. "The patterns on the walls and floor that we can see through the—presumably—sublimed and redeposited material seem to at least tentatively confirm the theory that this passage is a void left by jumbled blocks of ice, which would mean that a lot of the surface might *seem* like a continuous thing, but it's a scrambled mess under the surface, like breaking up ice on a pond and then letting it refreeze. *Whoa!*"

Helen echoed him with an inarticulate cry as *Zarathustra* tipped forward and dropped into freefall for a heartstopping second, before bumping (surprisingly gently) back to a driving position.

"Don't panic," Joe said calmly, ignoring the consternation in A.J.'s sudden spate of inquiries. "Went over a shelf and dropped a few meters. I knew it was there and it's not like rough riding on Earth." Joe made sure *Zarathustra*'s two manipulator arms were still firmly locked in position, tucked under the forward part of the rover where they were least likely to get in the way or be damaged by anything projecting.

"So if it's a matter of subliming, temperature, and pressure," Madeline said, picking up the prior conversation, "we should expect more and larger formations as we get farther down?"

Larry looked suddenly cautious, with an expression Helen knew from her own mirror during the original *Bemmius* research: the look of a scientist trying to avoid making any direct statements on something that they haven't enough data about. "Well...*if* I'm right on that, and it's very wild speculation, and we haven't gathered nearly enough data...well, yes, I'd expect we'll see more as we go down. But like everything else in the solar system, I won't be surprised to be surprised on that."

Helen chuckled. "A perfectly scientific way of putting it, Dr. Conley," she said, and then checked her time and map indicators. "At this rate, we can falsify or verify your prediction in a few hours. We've got, what, about fifteen kilometers to go?"

"Fourteen point two," Joe said, "According to the sketchy map data A.J. put together. At that point the passageway appears to end. But it's going to get a little rougher and a little slower than you think."

"So tomorrow?"

"Yes," Madeline said firmly. "I'm not going to let us drive on for more than another two hours, and we will not reach the end before then. We'll stop and rest—and yes, go out and take a few samples, since we'll already be stopped," she said, seeming to be reading Helen's mind, and perhaps Larry's as well, given that the big astrophysicist's frame had leaned forward and just as suddenly leaned back.

"Time enough to see the end of the journey tomorrow."

Rationally, Helen agreed completely with Maddie; there was absolutely no reason to rush, and every reason to be cautious—and despite the startling drop and the casual byplay, Joe *was* being very cautious. And besides, pretty ice formations aside, the end of the tunnel was probably nothing more than that, the end of a tunnel in a lot of ice.

But I still really want *to see what lies at the end!*

Chapter 26

"Okay, everyone strapped in?"

Joe listened to the affirmations from the others, then put *Zarathustra* into gear. "Then we're on our last leg. Next stop, the center of the Earth. Well, way down inside Europa, anyway."

There was no grumble of a mighty engine, just smooth, silent acceleration as *Zarathustra* began turning its two-meter-wide wheels in slow, majestic synchrony; not only were they in vacuum, but the electric motors driven by the compact nuclear reactor only emitted varying levels of hum.

Joe had to admit to himself there was slightly less visceral entertainment in such a smoothly silent vehicle, but—as an engineer—he approved. Noise was wasted power, or worse, an indication that something was wrong. The last thing you wanted to hear, especially out in space where the parts suppliers were few and far between, was the increasing hum of a worn and failing bearing.

"Hey, A.J., were you able to send the pics and initial data back to Ceres or Phobos Station?" Larry asked.

"Yeah, and I got an acknowledgement that sounded

suspiciously filled with *squee* from the exogeologist types. I'd expect we'll hear something more substantiative from them in a couple days, at least about your theory, though even the initial responses included people excited about, and people utterly dismissing, the idea that you're seeing different phases of ice that I guess aren't supposed to exist at those pressures."

"I think we may be seeing something that *used* to be those different phases," Helen said.

"How so?" Larry asked.

"Well, let's say your other phases aren't supposed to exist when they reach the surface. If the conversion to the other phase isn't something instantaneous—and at these temperatures I'd think not too many things *are* instantaneous, and the other conditions are what you describe, I'm imagining you're looking at something more in my field." Joe could see her smile when he glanced in the rearview; he could also see Larry's momentarily perplexed expression.

"It's a mineral equivalent of a fossil, Larry. The shifting phase of ice lost molecules of ice as they shifted, but new molecules were deposited in the same location. Eventually, you end up with a structure of standard ice that's in the same shape as the old structure of a different phase of ice, just as a bone starts out made of, well, bone, and is converted over millions of years into a different mineral composition."

Joe maneuvered *Zarathustra* slowly around a slender column of feathery, green-brown tinted ice that looked something like a feathered vine as he heard Larry's grunt of understanding. "That...that might just work. It's sure a good alternative to multiple coexisting phases of ice that shouldn't be present. Bet we can get a few papers out of this, either way."

Maddie, seated in the copilot seat to his right, chuckled. "With everything we've seen on this journey, I wouldn't be surprised if you had enough to write papers until you both die of old age."

"What an exaggeration," Helen said. "I've only recovered a small handful of obvious fossils and a few other possibles. Why, I could hardly manage three dozen papers on that."

"Funny," A.J.'s voice said. "We still call them 'papers' though they're almost never on paper anymore."

"Language changes, but phrases stick around for a long time," Joe said, slowing as he approached a tilted area of the tunnel. "I still hear people say they're 'running out of steam,' when I'm not sure any of them have ever *seen* a steam-powered vehicle. In fact, I'm not sure *I* have except in old videos."

"I like your theory, Helen," Larry said, continuing the main thread of conversation, "and we also don't know what effect the various minerals in solution might have for replacement or crystal formation. If some of them crystallize first, they become nucleation sites for other crystals, including water."

"But," Anthony LaPointe's voice broke in, "additional dissolved minerals should lower the freezing point. Would that not affect the formation of other phases of ice?"

"It might. But it's not really the temperature, but the pressure. Even at the bottom of Europa's ocean, if it's a hundred kilometers deep, the pressure won't be even as high as it is at the bottom of Earth's ocean trenches. Now, I seem to remember that under some conditions you can recover several other ice phases at standard pressure, but..."

Joe tuned out the more technical discussion as the icy road ahead got rougher. *Zarathustra*'s tires were a unique polymer blend, nanotextured as well as formed with carefully-designed tread patterns to maximize grip on icy surfaces, but even that sometimes wasn't enough to prevent skids and slips on ice in an environment with an eighth of a gravity and at temperatures that made the ice more a solid rock than ordinary frozen water.

Zarathustra skidded slowly as he braked into a turn to avoid another column; the huge rover barely brushed the column, which held firm—and then seemed to explode in a shower of shrapnel as he edged *Zarathustra* by. "Holy *crap!*"

Other shouts of consternation echoed in the rover's cabin as he brought *Zarathustra* to a halt. *What could possibly have caused that?* "That column just *blew up*, Larry, A.J., everyone." He scanned the telltales and checked the feeds coming from the onboard sensors, slowly relaxed as he saw no sign of damage. "What the hell caused *that*? Are some of these formations so unstable they're *explosive*?"

Larry scratched his head. "That...doesn't seem likely. Even if there's a reasonable concentration of oxygen in the water below, like some theories claim, it's not going to be available for an explosion *here*. And at these temperatures..."

He trailed off suddenly, then gave a deep chuckle. "When, exactly, did the column blow up?"

"I was almost past it, though we were just about brushing on the right-hand side."

"Which means it was exactly next to the main radiators."

Joe slapped his forehead, feeling more than a little like an idiot. "Temperature differential?"

"Temperature differential. What with our environmental requirements and the reactor itself, we're radiating a lot of heat into this environment. And at *that* range, you've got maybe three, four hundred degrees of differential between the one side of the ice and the other. Wouldn't have too much effect on larger chunks, probably just take chips off them, but on something that long and thin..."

"Yes, that *would* do it," Madeline said, nodding. "I've seen really cold ice-cubes shatter pretty energetically when you drop them in water that's just warm."

"It's not *quite* that bad," Joe said, checking the readings. "At this depth, we're reading a balmy minus one hundred ten. Still more than enough." He started *Zarathustra* moving again.

"If we're radiating that much heat," Helen said after a few moments, "are we endangering what we're seeing?"

Larry frowned. "Probably, at least to some extent. These regions have never encountered the temperatures we bring with us. Hold on." A pause, during which Joe got them over a ridge. "Yeah, it's affecting the area. We parked in a fairly wide area of the tunnel, and examining the formation pictures before and after I can see they changed or eroded overnight. Not *terribly* much, but if we stayed there for a few weeks there'd be quite a bit changed. On the plus side, we *are* dealing with water ice, which has a high heat capacity compared to a lot of things, so it's not like dealing with spires of solidified nitrogen or something."

"Then we cannot stay down here long," Madeline said reluctantly. "Since we are nearing our goal, I see no point in not reaching the end before returning; we will be emitting essentially the same amount of heat as we pass the same areas whether we do so now or a day or so hence. But we can't spend more time down here than a day or so, or we risk causing significant damage to structures which may be unique."

"I wouldn't be surprised if there are at least one or two similar regions," Larry said. "I *suppose* we could have just happened to land near the one and only example, but I would bet heavily against it. Still, you're right. If there's anything worth seeing at the end, and it's big enough, we could stay there a few hours, but we should make tracks back as soon as we're done."

The thought did put a slight damper on Joe's enthusiasm—he'd hoped they'd have time for some actual research—but he couldn't argue the point. All those beautiful formations they'd seen couldn't survive their presence for long; staying nearby would be like observing sugar sculptures while misting them with water. "Well, we're almost there. I can also try to drive us out a little faster than we came in."

"Dunno if that would help much," A.J. said. "Move faster, you're cranking the generators more, which means more waste heat per minute. Maybe it would, though. But even though you've been down the path once, driving faster in the other direction might be the key to a disaster. I think we'd all agree that while we want to preserve all the scientific data we can, we don't want to do it at the expense of any of you."

"Exactly," Madeline said. "No, Joe, take the same caution going out that we did coming in."

"Okay. Just felt I should offer."

A few minutes later, *Zarathustra* rolled smoothly into a moderate-sized cavern. To the left and right were a profusion of icy formations—hexagonal branching plates, feathery columns and spines, interpenetrating cubes. The far wall was mostly bare, however, a smooth sheet of white frost with slight tinges of other colors.

"End of the line," Joe said. "We've come as far as A.J.'s map says we can go. There's a lot of formations here that we could do some quick sampling and examination of."

"Where will you park?" Maddie asked.

"Not near either of *those* walls," Joe said. "The far wall's got pretty much no formations on it, except up on the higher edges and some on the far sides, so if I park there we should be endangering as little as possible."

He suited action to words, trundling *Zarathustra* over the now fairly smooth floor towards the far wall; as there was enough room, he turned around and backed towards the wall, so that *Zarathustra* would be already facing the exit when they left.

As he backed towards the wall, the high-intensity rear lights shone directly on it, and with a few meters to go, Joe suddenly caught sight of *another* set of glints, glints and shadows *within* the wall he was approaching.

He slammed on the brakes reflexively, and that would have been more than enough; he'd intended to stop a meter or so short of the wall anyway. But *just* as he did so, a small tremor jolted the ground, three of *Zarathustra*'s six tires lost contact with the

ice, and the rover slewed sideways slightly, bringing
the left-hand radiator into direct contact with the
white-crystal ice.

With a silent detonation the entire wall shattered
like crystal struck with a sledghammer, fragments
ranging from the size of daggers to boulders raining
down. Within *Zarathustra* the slow-motion cascade
of shattered ice sounded at first like a quiet tapping
hiss, then more insistent rapping as though a dozen
elves were knocking on the hull, building to a rattling
cacophony that nearly deafened all within. Subsidiary
blasts of pulverized ice showed as larger chunks hit
the radiators.

"I think you've disturbed the environment," Larry
said dryly, as the last of the chunks banged off the hull.
"I hope..." He trailed off, as Joe slowly unstrapped
from his chair, eyes fixed incredulously on the rear
window which a moment before had shown shadowed
white blankness.

Beyond the wall was an immense space, so huge
that the brilliant lights of *Zarathustra* could not even
begin to illuminate the entirety of the cavern. The floor
descended in regular, rippling terraces to a smooth,
ballroom-flat area that extended beyond the lights' range.
In every other direction—walls, ceiling, even parts of
the floor set away from the descending terraces—were
icy growths of impossible delicacy and size: feathery
draperies of arching beauty that would have shattered
of their own weight on *Mars*, let alone Earth, stratified
columns that seemed to have telescoped from floor to
distant roof, scatterings of hexagonal plates embedded in
clear ice like the honeycomb of some inconceivably huge
bees, fairytale spires rising from the floor and dusted

with incredibly thin and diamond-sparkling needles of ice that reflected the light like a shining halo, a thousand wonders of translucent and diamond-clear and ripple-tinted crystal that held the entire crew of *Zarathustra* in complete and utter thrall for long moments.

Finally, Joe shook himself and resumed his seat. "I think," he said, "that we've found a place I can park."

Chapter 27

Hohenheim shook his head in pleased amazement, looking at the fantastic images transmitted only seconds before from Europa. "I believe I speak for us all on *Odin*, Ms. Fathom, Dr. Sutter, Mr. Buckley, and Mr. Conley, that we truly do wish we were there." There was a murmur of assent from the others, and an added "Us up here on the surface, too!" from A.J.

"Larry," Anthony LaPointe said, with an unmistakable note of envy in his voice, "I am doing calculations with Brett now, modeling that interior with the help of A.J., who has produced a general model from the stereo images you have sent. With your permission, General, I will increase priority to get the results as quickly as possible, so that we can advise as to how long you can spend in that region."

"I'd sure appreciate it," Joe put in. "None of us want to leave before we have to, but none of us want to do significant damage. Well, aside from blowing up the odd wall or two."

Hohenheim considered briefly. The main number-crunching for other tasks aside from those related to the nozzle and the eventual unification of the three vessels was over, and none of the remaining tasks were time-critical. "As you wish, Dr. LaPointe. I agree with all here; we want as much initial data as possible, with as little damage as possible."

Other than some continued exclamations of "Wow!", "My God..." and "How gorgeous...", there was silence for a time. Finally Brett spoke up. "Okay, mates, here you go. The size of that room gives you a reasonable cushion, and the fact that the average temperature there seems to be something like a mere minus ninety, warmer down at the bottom, means the temperature differential isn't quite as bad. So you can spend about twelve hours there before you really should be getting out."

"Make it eight," Hohenheim said, adding, "If you concur, Ms. Fathom?"

Madeline's answer came after the current second and a half pause. "I do, General. I trust Brett, Anthony, and A.J., but there's no point in taking chances we don't have to. A full workday, and then we start back. Joe, it'll be hard on you, though. As we've already done some damage, I'd prefer we return to the last cavern we stopped in before resting for the night, which means you'll be up a lot longer—"

"No, I won't," Joe said. General Hohenheim could hear both fondness and reluctant decision in those words. "I'm going to take a nap for about four to six hours right now, so I'm fresh for the drive back. I'll still be able to help out for a couple hours at the end and I won't be driving tired."

The small image of Madeline wore a relieved smile; Hohenheim shared the emotion. Telling any of that small group that they'd have to give up any of the few hours they had to view and explore the alien wonders would be hard; by choosing to volunteer, Joe had made things easier.

Which seems to be his general personality; he makes things easier for those around him. I begin to truly understand why, of all the people she knew, Madeline Fathom married Joe Buckley. Perhaps she is just as fortunate as most of us have assumed Joe is. "An excellent decision, Dr. Buckley. Now, while we are already talking, allow us to bring you up to date. Jackie?"

"*Nebula Storm*'s nozzle mated perfectly with *Odin*'s connectors on the third try—it wasn't easy to align everything at first. Good work, Brett, A.J., Joe. Horst and Mia finished the control integration and calibration this morning," Jackie said cheerfully, "and we're working on checking out all of our repairs to *Odin*'s reaction mass systems now."

"So you're going to be able to do a test burn today?" A.J. asked.

Jackie shook her head, something easy for Hohenheim to see as she was floating near one of the engineering panels only ten feet away. "Don't jump the gun, A.J.; there's a *lot* of *Odin*'s systems to check and double-check first. Remember, she had a lot of subsystems for the drive and auxiliary jets, and a lot of that got shredded when Fitzgerald's frag round went blooey in the coilgun. We can't afford to find out there's a weak point in the system when we test the new nozzle—no second chances this time."

"No, you're right. Sorry, I just want to see you guys up in orbit around here, and not just to cut down that really *annoying* delay, either."

"We are *all* looking forward to losing that delay, and to being in close and constant contact, Mr. Baker," Hohenheim agreed. "In the meantime, Horst and Anthony have also completed another project which we were not sure would succeed, but has."

Horst grinned from the general's other side, and hit a transmit switch. The images showed the interior of a large room on *Odin*, with huge doors slowly opening. "The *Munin*'s landing bay was jettisoned with most of *Odin* when the general performed his successful maneuver to save himself and *Odin* from Io, you all know. But we do not want to lose *Munin*, yet putting *Munin* outside the *Odin* and locking her down will be difficult.

"The general pointed out that there was at least one major loading bay in this section of *Odin*, and calculations showed that we could probably fit *Munin* inside if we moved everything else out, and if we could fix the doors.

"So the doors are fixed, you see, and the bay is empty. We have had Brett model also the exact maneuvers and it is in fact practical to bring *Munin* home."

A small spatter of applause—strongest from the other crewmembers of *Odin*—filled the little conference of airwaves. Hohenheim found that he was also grinning broadly. The *Munin* had saved all their lives in one way or another, and it would have been a great tragedy to leave the landing vessel behind. Now, he wouldn't have to make that decision.

"I commend both of you for your work. It seems, Ms. Fathom, that we are approaching the time for departure."

"Only a month or two, yes, General. I did receive

a communication from Dr. Glendale earlier today, updating us on progress there."

Hohenheim leaned forward reflexively. "Indeed? How goes the construction of *Bifrost*?"

"The joint rescue and exploration vessel is well underway, but launch won't be possible for at least another six months. The name is actually still under debate," she added, "but you're correct that *Bifrost* is the front runner in the names so far. It's symbolic of the bridging of the gap between the UN, Ares, and the EU, and the extraction of the name's the same as that of *Odin*, so the EU seems to generally approve."

The general shrugged. "I will welcome her by any name, but I believe *Bifrost* will be the one chosen. Six months?" he repeated. "In that case, I believe we shall be bringing ourselves home before the rescue itself can launch!"

Madeline smiled and nodded. "I certainly hope so. After what we've accomplished here, I think all of us would like nothing better than to pull into Mars or Earth orbit on our own—with a unified ship built from the pieces we were left."

There was a loud murmur of assent, including a "Damn straight!" from A.J. and similar sentiments from Horst and Joe.

"Then let us impede you no longer," the general said. "Finish your exploration of the interior, and by the time you return, *Odin* will be a living ship again—and we can begin the final preparations." He looked out the *Odin*'s screens to mighty Jupiter. "In two months or less, we set sail."

Chapter 28

Helen squinted uselessly at the darker area underneath a profusion of impossibly delicate icy growths. "I swear there's *something* there. A.J.?"

"Sorry, sweetheart, I can't get any more out of your onboard cameras. Borrow the one Larry's got for a minute and I can at least tell you if you're seeing things or not."

"Larry?"

The astrophysicist sighed. "I was *going* to have it do a full panoramic imagery scan of the cavern from the edge of the first step...but okay, just for a minute."

The camera Larry let her take was a high-resolution scanning camera that used multispectral lasers at low power to provide highly detailed, full-color images of the targets while also deriving full three-dimensional spatial data from the laser signals, so that the pictures could be rendered accurately into full immersive environments for study. In addition to the obvious advantages, this meant that—properly arranged for the scan—they projected high-intensity light into even the darkest regions and thus got excellent detail from areas the viewer couldn't see even with a powerful standard light (which projected diffused white light rather than pinpoint laser scans).

Helen aligned the camera carefully so that the laser scanner had a clear line of sight to the dark region at the base, and set it running. "Okay, A.J., data coming your way." The radio relays were still doing their business well, although with so many hops to get through and overhead involved in maintaining the link reliably this far down the line, there had been a slight degradation in bandwidth.

"I'm on it." A few seconds went by as the camera finished the scan. "Okay, got the raw data. Hold on."

She spent the time looking around. Larry was waiting for his camera back, while Maddie was up on the wall, to the left of Helen, suspended by belaying lines as close as she dared get to a feathery-looking crystal outcropping whose miniature feather-like branches appeared to end in tiny flat hexagons. Joe, presumably still sleeping, had parked the _Zarathustra_ as far out of the way as possible, near the center of the cavern.

But not _too_ near, as the true center of the cavern was that series of concentric, descending terraces that ended in the flat area which, Larry guessed, might be a shell only a few dozen meters thick above the Europan ocean. "We'll go down and check it a little later, but the key point is the temperature differential. Up here it's almost a hundred below zero, but down there the ice reads as about forty below—no colder than a really cold day in North Dakota. My guess is that means that we can't be far at all from the actual ocean. If we had an atmosphere in here, it'd probably even stay breathable since the CO_2 wouldn't be freezing out."

"Well, will you look at that." A.J. transmitted the image to her.

Revealed in the scanning image, embedded perhaps a few inches beneath the ice at the base of the profusion of ice growths, was a squat, three-lobed shape of unmistakably organic design, looking to Helen's startled first gaze like one of the plant samples preserved back in the Vault on Mars. "Oh my God. I've *got* to get better images, better data on that!"

"You can't go bulling in there and breaking things up," A.J. reminded her.

"I *know!*" She restrained herself from saying anything else. In most paleontological digs, it was the *fossil* that was delicate. No one was usually worried about the *rock*. "What about...um...the remote probes? We have acoustic, a couple of laser probes, and you had a magnetic one?"

"There's several, yeah. Let me check the specs..." she saw his usual rippling gestures, heard the half-vocalized commands. "Um. Okay, you can use the acoustic, the near-field sensor probe, and the ultraviolet imaging probe. They're long enough to extend to the base and the specs show they *should* continue functioning cooled down to ambient there. But make *sure* you cool them to ambient first, which means take them out of *Zarathustra*, extend them, and put them on the floor for about ten minutes before you go try using them near that area, okay?"

"Got it." Helen moved carefully around the perimeter of the room; the combination of ice beneath her feet, the very light gravity of Europa, and the fear of damaging any of the multiplicity of unique formations around the room meant it took her half an hour to work her way back to the big rover. *Almost five hours now. We'll have to leave in three.*

She entered through the main lock and glanced over, saw Joe looking up sleepily. "Hi, Joe. It's—"

"I see, five hours almost on the dot. Guess I'll get up, get ready to help out for a couple. You didn't just come here to wake me up, though?"

"No," she said, heading for the storage bins. "I need the—"

Without warning the whole rover shuddered and bounced. "Another quake—" Joe said.

Helen expected the movement to subside, but this time it didn't. A second, stronger shock hit, bouncing *Zarathustra* entirely into the air, the rover coming down slightly tilted as the ground continued to shake; the shaking motion shoved the still-imbalanced rover sideways, and Helen shot a terrified glance towards the forward window.

It all happened in an almost comedic slow motion. Sliding with ponderous grace, *Zarathustra* began to rotate as first one wheel, then two, then all three on one side went over the edge of the first terrace. Though Joe was lunging for the controls, trying to get the wheels to grip and it was moving slowly, no force they had could stop it now, a multiton mass already in motion, tilting, pitching farther down, rotating now so she was looking down, right at the bottom of the cavern.

That was why she saw the *crack* as it opened, gaping wide, wider, steam *exploding* into the air as water at thirty-two degrees Fahrenheit, zero centigrade, met near-vacuum at an ambient temperature considerably lower, columns of water *screaming* upward, boiling and shattering ice in all directions, and she realized they were plunging directly for that black, erupting chasm, and that if they entered that raging storm of water and ice they would be hammered to pieces. She remembered A.J. telling her, "...so a kilometer down, the pressure's about like a hundred thirty-five meters down on Earth—say thirteen atmospheres."

You can survive a dive to that pressure... she thought with growing fear, *but being equalized in pressure all around is completely different from being hit* with it!

But now they were sliding faster, another *bump* as they hit the second ledge, and now *Zarathustra* was really tumbling, bouncing outward, all the way across the gap as it fell. To her surprise and confusion, the thundering jets of water seemed to be faltering, but it still sounded like a battery of sledgehammers as *Zarathustra* passed through one of the bubbling, foaming geysers. They rebounded from the wall, spinning, passing the third terrace at a velocity that was no longer laughable, *smash* against the wall below the fourth terrace, bouncing again as Helen herself was hammered into the wall near *Zarathustra*'s front port.

The others were shouting something, she couldn't make sense out of any of it because it was all jumbled together and the big rover was still spinning. *Larry was wrong*, she thought in an almost detached, clinical fashion. *The floor was less than two meters thick, we were walking on the top of the ocean itself.*

The pressurized fountains of water, the rising waters that should have filled the vast cavern in moments, were faltering, the pressure dropping even as ice seemed to be appearing everywhere in midair. The

water was not going to smash the capsule to pieces...
but that was not an unalloyed good, because they
were now plummeting straight into the crack that
now yawned twice as wide, bubbling and spewing icy
mist. A smaller object might have been deflected, a
falling person buoyed up or even hurled back by the
vaporizing water, but *Zarathustra* was ten metric tons
of unstoppable juggernaut moving now at nearly thirty
miles an hour, as fast as *Athena* had in her near-fatal
plunge and ten times more massive. There was no
time for screaming, just the sound from inside the
rover of Joe cursing the universe, and then an impact
that stunned her.

And then the slow settling sensation galvanized her
to action. "Joe!" she shouted. "We're *sinking!*"

"Helen! *HELEN!*" A.J.'s voice was near to panic,
and she shut it out, because she knew that to panic
now could get her killed.

Joe tried to scramble up from where he'd fallen,
but succeeded in throwing himself against the wall
when *Zarathustra* shifted. *The quake's still going!* she
realized with horror.

Lazily, yet inescapably, *Zarathustra* rolled over,
dropping into the water another half-meter, and plunging the entire cabin area into the ocean of Europa.

PART IV

Transformation, n: 1) a change in form, appearance, nature, or character; 2) LOGIC *: also called transform; one of a set of algebraic formulas used to express the relations between elements, sets, etc., that form parts of a given system; 3)* THEATER *: a seemingly miraculous change in the appearance of scenery or actors in view of the audience.*

Chapter 29

No.

That was the only word in Madeline Fathom's mind as she saw the rover with Helen and her husband in it beginning to sink into the endless Europan depths, even as the fairyland formations around her whipped slowly around and then disintegrated in a shower of shining fragments.

The whole thing had seemed a dream; the monster quake beginning, the shock felt through her feet of something collapsing—and not far away—then the deadly surge of water that she was sure would envelop them all in seconds. At this pressure, the water should blast from the ocean of Europa and drag everything with it in a surge of unstoppable fury, a freezing tsunami that would solidify in a few more seconds, trapping all of them forever like flies in amber.

But for some reason that *didn't* happen, the iron-straight columns wavering, foaming furiously like monstrous fountains of soda, and she neither watched *Zarathustra* battered to scrap nor watched black, freezing water engulf her.

Just watched as the rover plunged into the jagged, boiling, gnashing chasm.

No.

She looked sideways, up, down, judging angles, distances, gravity, while a crack lazily traced its way along the side of the massive cavern and, in the very dim distance, she saw slow, ponderous movement of a fall on a scale she didn't want to contemplate. At the same time the water boiled *up* again, buoying the sinking rover momentarily, rising higher, and incredulously she realized she was *hearing* hisses. *The vapor's filling the cavern faster than it's leaving. For a few minutes, we have a water atmosphere in here!* But even through the steam, the shimmering icy dust that was condensing everywhere, she had to keep looking...

There.

Madeline Fathom-Buckley launched herself from the blue-white shining wall, ignoring the now-incomprehensible babel of questions, shouts, screams, from those nearby and those far away. *I have one chance.*

Even as she leapt, *Zarathustra* sank lower, unmistakably, inexorably. Designed with mass to maintain stability, the tires made of solid if deformable material, the overall density of the rover was considerably greater than that of the water she was now in, and though the water was rising she was sinking, and there was nothing now to stop her.

Nothing except me. Larry was too far away, and frozen with shock. *But he has to move* now! "Larry! *Catch my line!*" she shouted; out of the corner of her eye she saw Larry shake himself and move towards the wall she'd just left. The line anchors released their grip on her line at her signal, and she was in midair now, a human arrow, her own focus narrowing to a single target, the hold-down eyelet under *Zarathustra's* prow, exposed now that the rover had temporarily completely inverted.

Exposed but not stable. Even as she passed through a shimmering mist of shattered ice-dust and entered the roiling fog of erupting molten water not ten meters from *Zarathustra*, the rover started to roll again, the ice gaping wider and allowing center of gravity to take over.

But the roll wasn't fast, not with Europa's puny gravity the only driver, and she was close now, line in hand, a meter of it held out in front of her, one of the explosive hold-down spikes she had on hand as pitons in her other hand. *Don't let me miss this one, please.* It was a silent prayer to whatever might be listening, that her training and practice would let her pull off the impossible just one more time.

The stiff line bumped the edge of the eyelet, which was now coated with ice, narrowing its diameter, and for an instant her heart stopped. But it bent, twisted, and went through, almost half a meter through, three quarters, let go, *grab* again on the other side.

She twisted her body around, faint crunching-crinkling sensations echoing through the suit as a thin coating of ice she'd gained in her passage through the mist shattered. She reached out, hooking the hold-down onto the line, and then feeling her boots touching down, her body almost parallel with the ice-cave's floor, slowing, slowing, tension starting on the line, *now!*

She triggered the hold-down spike, and its focused-energetic charge hammered a long sharp anchor into the rock-hard ice. *Please hold, please hold . . .* She skidded, hit the opposite wall, rebounded across the cavern in a great leap even as Larry grabbed the rope and pulled desperately, fighting with all the pathetic friction he could achieve to keep the rope from loosening, from letting *Zarathustra* sink farther.

But she *was* sinking farther and they had to stop it, had to, the rover was settling, less than one-quarter of it still above water. The water was subsiding now, layers of new ice added to each terrace as it descended, dropping, *Zarathustra* pulling more and more line down with it, down, down to the original level, settling. *Why is it settling? It shouldn't be dropping . . .* Traceries of ice began to form around the open crack, then shatter as the shudders of movement continued, as *Zarathustra* continued to descend, and her radio suddenly went deathly quiet, as thought not merely Helen and Joe, but all the rest of the Europan survivors had sunk into the black depths.

She couldn't think of that now, couldn't even contemplate it. There was an unbroken ice column there, not too far, "Hold *on*, Larry!" she shouted, and as she reached him she grabbed, swung around, *kicked* off the ground sideways, and the two of them moved laterally and inward in a low, curving arc as the sinking rover pulled the rope down.

But they were swinging now around the icy column, all the way around, crossing *just* over the rope on the other side, and she grabbed the length of rope behind Larry, who grunted in understanding as she kicked off from his suit.

The rope's tension slowed Larry, began to draw him back in a deadly whipping motion, but in that instant Maddie passed just *under* the part of the rope they'd just gone *over*, and with bare inches to spare bounced upward, pulling the line through.

Larry Conley released his part of the rope and joined her, pulling, drawing in the slack on the improvised knot, backs to the *Zarathustra* as they braced and pulled harder.

The line went rigid, and through the line she felt a vibration. Maddie shot a terrified glance back, and the *Zarathustra* was almost gone now, only a fraction visible, but the little hold-down spike held, showed no sign of movement.

She braced her feet against the column along with Larry, pulling harder. The movement of the rope slowed . . . ceased . . . and the knot pulled in on itself, tightening. The cavern's shaking was subsiding, and the knot was tense . . . and holding.

It was holding.

But when she turned around, all she could see was the rope disappearing sharply into the water from both sides—water that was changing now, shimmering with white and diamond sparkles as crystalline ice formed and raced out from every side, a frosting windowpane in demonic fast-forward, solidifying, hardening, even as she shouted *"Joe!"*

"Hold on, hold on," Larry said, grabbing her arm. "The line's not moving, it's got them. You did it, you crazy woman, you actually pulled that off!"

She took a deep, shaky breath and allowed herself to lean against Larry for just a second. "I *had* to, so I did."

"You sure did." He shook his head and frowned. "Things sure ain't good, but *man* they could've been a lot worse." He looked around apprehensively. "This whole cavern could've come down on us. Still might if we get another shock like *that.*"

"That was the worst we've had, by a *long* shot, though. Look at how many of those formations came down. They'd never have grown out that far if quakes even close to that level were common. Am I right, A.J.?"

Silence.

She looked at Larry, who looked back and shrugged. "I dunno," the astrophysicist said. "The comms went out while all that was going on."

Madeline thought a moment, then managed a smile. "Ah. Of course. We were relaying through *Zarathustra*'s transmitter for power and range—and to save our own radios' power. We did drop relays every so often along the way, though. Let's see..."

After a moment she managed to figure out how to get her radio to stop looking for *Zarathustra*'s network signal and scan for one of the relays. Nothing.

"I think," Larry said slowly, "there's a default power saver limit on these things?" He said it as a question.

Yes, there is, she thought. A.J. and Horst had mentioned something like that. A quick search through the control menu and she found it, turned it off, scanned the airwaves again. *Got one!*

"*Nebula Storm*, this is Madeline Fathom, do you read?"

"Maddie!" Unsurprisingly it was A.J. who answered first. "Thank *God*, when the connection went dead I thought..." His voice wasn't entirely steady.

Other voices started, and then Hohenheim's overrode

everyone. "Let us quiet down and get a report. Agent Fathom, are your people all right?"

"I . . . believe so, General."

"You *believe* so?"

She *had* to believe so. "I presume everyone above felt that quake."

"Worst we've ever had," A.J. confirmed.

"We received the readings, yes," Hohenheim said dryly, "but that is not an answer to the question, I believe."

"General, when the quake hit, it . . ." She took a breath. "No point in all the details, but *Zarathustra* went through a crack in the ice which went straight to the Europan ocean. We have managed to catch the rover with a belaying line, and *Zarathustra* appears to be stable at this time."

There was a moment of silence. "Was anyone . . . in the rover?" A.J. said slowly.

"I'm afraid Helen and Joe were both inside when she went under."

"God*damn*." She knew he must be already half-standing, trying to *do* something, then realizing he couldn't actually do anything now.

"Which brings me to the most urgent question, General, everyone: is *Zarathustra* watertight to a depth of . . ." she eyeballed the line, calculated the angles she saw, ". . . of between five and ten feet in the Europan ocean?"

"Brett?" A.J. said tensely. "You've got the full models."

"Hold on a minute."

The minutes seemed to pass like hours. Maddie found herself shifting in her suit, and the crinkling noises—along with a rapidly-obscuring view—warned her that she'd better keep doing that. "Larry, turn up your heaters and move around. The water vapor's condensing back out and solidifying on everything— including us."

"Yow!" Larry actually found it momentarily difficult to move; some of the ice had started to affect the suit joint areas. "Never a dull moment here. Hey, am I nuts or have I been *hearing* stuff from outside?"

She checked her suit readouts and history. "No, you aren't. We just went through a *huge* pressure cycle. Pressure in here peaked at..." she blinked. "That *can't* be right."

"About one point three megapascals?" Larry asked.

"Yes. How did you know?"

"When that hole opened up, the water vaporized while it welled up and pressurized the area until the pressure was enough to keep the water from coming through, or at least let stuff start freezing and slowing the flow." Larry grimaced. "That *also* means that we're sealed off, because the pressure wouldn't have built rapidly enough to save us from being *all* embedded in ice otherwise. Must've caved in not far up and then the water vapor condensed, sealing any leaks. One in a billion chance, let me tell you. I'm surprised those radio relays are working at all right now, but I'm not looking a gift communicator in the mouth or whatever."

"That will make this whole operation...interesting," Maddie said slowly. "If I understand you right, that means that if we *do* break through to get *Zarathustra* out, the water's going to do the same thing again."

"Yeah," agreed Larry, "And that'll be a bitch and a half. Well, we *could* just drill a hole and let the water vaporize to fill it, but I wouldn't want to chance whatever it was sealing us again."

"Okay, everyone," Brett's voice said. "The answer is yes, *Zarathustra* can hold the pressure at that depth, at least for a while. It was designed with both positive *and* negative pressure seals for use in a wide variety of environments, ranging from Europa to Titan or pretty much anything else the designers could reasonably foresee, and with very hefty safety margins. It's *pushing* the limits heavy, and if she got damaged on the way down . . . but let's assume not. The environmental systems are going to be strained—temperature issues when you're surrounded by water instead of vaccum mean it's going to stay very chilly inside, but their suits can take up some of the slack."

Maddie felt a huge knot in her stomach relax. *We're not out of the woods yet . . . but there's still a chance. There's still a chance to save them both.*

Chapter 30

Helen wasn't ashamed of having screamed as *Zarathustra* took a final sinking dive into the depths. If any occasion called for a scream, finding that you were about to plunge into a lightless, freezing ocean a hundred kilometers deep, drifting ever deeper until the rover you were in collapsed like an empty beer can in a sailor's fist, was exactly that occasion.

But she suddenly realized that they were slowing, coming to a halt. *But there's nothing under us!* she thought. The lights were still working, and the water was empty below them.

Joe chuckled, then broke out laughing. "I *thought* I saw someone go past as we went down. Maddie, you *genius!*"

"What did she do?"

In answer, Joe climbed up the seats in the now nearly vertical *Zarathustra*—in fact, angled slightly more than vertical, tipping backwards a few degrees—and pointed up, to a point just below the front window.

Helen had to move upwards herself to get a look, but finally she spotted it: a sharp V shape, two white lines pointing directly at *Zarathustra* and then vanishing up into the bright ice above. "She got a *line* on us in *that?*" she said incredulously. "Maybe she *is* Supergirl."

"If she was, she'd have lifted us out of the ice rather than leave us hanging," said Joe, sounding like his usual cheerful self. The tone lifted Helen's spirits just by its comforting familiarity, even as she winced at the inevitable pun. "Still, I can't complain, since we're still alive."

Helen noticed that her face was feeling chilly. "Oh-oh. Joe, I remember we had a discussion a while back about how vacuum wasn't cold, so keeping warm wasn't a problem. But—"

"But *this* isn't vacuum, yeah. This could be a problem." Joe was instantly serious, and lowered himself down to sit on the now-upright back of the driver's seat, examining the controls. "Water, just about the worst-case, except maybe liquid helium or something. Still, I seem to remember..."

He fiddled with a few more controls. "Ah-*ha*! That's it, the environmental offsets. Lessee...Well, they don't go up *quite* that high, but she *was* meant to operate in places with atmosphere as well as vacuum, so I can crank our heat up some." After a moment, "There, that's got it. I think she'll stabilize somewhere around ten degrees C—that's around fifty Fahrenheit."

"Is that all?" Helen felt a bit relieved. "We've camped in much worse, and these suits can handle the rest easily."

There was a faint creaking noise as an unseen, lazy current swung *Zarathustra* around. The two froze, staring out in silence. "Can *Zarathustra* handle this, though?"

Joe shrugged. "I'm sure she wasn't *designed* for an

underwater plunge, unlike the probe capsule on *Athena*. But the fact I'm not seeing water down there at the bottom is a good sign. She's holding the pressure—and it's a fair amount of pressure. If we live through this, I'll want to give her designers a big ol' hug. She could spring a leak any minute, but we just have to hope that doesn't happen."

The elimination of immediate panic gave her a moment to realize something else was wrong. "Maddie? Larry? Anyone? Are you there?"

"Don't bother," Joe said. "Radio waves won't penetrate water, at least not at the high frequencies we usually use."

"Can we change the frequency?"

Joe thought a moment. "You know, we probably can. Most radios these days are actually just given a factory setting that locks the wavelength. They're not like the radios from forty years ago that were built to handle only a very narrow band. And I'll bet somewhere in the settings of *these* things there's some flexibility. Maybe not enough, though. Getting through..." he glanced again at the rope, measuring, "...um, two, three meters of water and another half to one meter of ice with *stuff* dissolved in it, that's going to be a challenge. In *theory* the software-defined radios are capable of almost any frequency, but in practice I dunno if I can get us down from the gigahertz range we generally play in—higher for some applications—and into the low megahertz I'll need to penetrate the water."

"Worth trying. We need to get some kind of contact going." She glanced up again. *So close*. "Will they even be able to *receive* a signal like that, though?"

"If I don't miss my guess, A.J. will be scanning every wavelength known to man until he gets you back. Don't worry, if I start transmitting and it gets through, he'll hear us."

She sat on the back of one of the other chairs for a few moments, thinking. "What *happened* up there? I mean, I understand we had a quake, but I thought the water would keep on going up."

"So'd I. I'm not sure, but I'd guess the cavern got sealed off, the evaporating water filled it with gas, and the floor was rising in the quake, squeezing the pressure higher." He shrugged. "The fact is we've done a lot of lab playing with these things, but as anyone who's worked with models can tell you, sometimes you get very strange shifts in behavior when you get enough bigger or smaller. We've never actually spent time on a planet at cryogenic temperatures and played around with massive amounts of water and supercooled ice. The physics doesn't change, but the interactions of all the elements can surprise you sometimes. Probably some factor, or factors, that we just don't know right now."

He looked up from the panels he had been checking. "Well, it doesn't matter what happened, it happened, and we didn't get crushed, or worse, caught in a short-lived tidal bore that froze with us inside it. And we're not going to freeze to death; temperature's leveled out at twelve degrees C—almost fifty-four Fahrenheit."

After a pause, she glanced down. "You know, the water's actually not all that clear. I mean, it's *clear*, so to speak, probably clearer than any water I've seen in an ocean back home ... but there's stuff drifting in it." She let herself drop slowly to the rover's rear window, stopping herself just short. "I can stand on this, can't I?"

"Probably, but it's taking a lot of pressure from the outside. Be on the safe side and don't."

She got her face closer to the curved reinforced diamond laminate window. "Definitely little particles. And the way the light shades—you can see that the water has very slow currents in it with different distributions of dissolved material, probably why you get that wavy striping in the ice."

"So it's circulating? Interesting. Why would that be happening? There's no open ocean, no winds, no interaction with an atmosphere."

"Well, you've got the squishing motion of Jupiter, first of all. If it's dissipating enough energy to keep a hundred kilometers of ocean liquid, it's moving it quite a bit." She found the view somewhat vertiginous; there were no steady reference points, and as they were in fact over an effectively infinite abyss... "Larry and Anthony were torn over whether there'd be enough energy to give Europa an active rocky center, but if it is, then you'd have rock movement affecting things too. And—"

She froze for a moment, long enough for Joe to turn and say, "And?"

"Joe," she said, very carefully, moving nothing but her lips, "get me camera three, the one we left in here. Make sure it's set for minimum distance."

"What's up?" Joe asked.

She stared at the window, or rather, at what lay just a few inches beyond it.

Something almost transparent, a shimmer like a tiny sliver of ice.

But ice did not move against the drifting current with the blurred beating of tiny legs.

Joe arrived with the camera, followed her gaze, and stared. "No way."

"It's *alive*, Joe. Moving, eating, breathing *extraterrestrial life!*"

She started the camera running, glanced up at Joe, whose grin was slowly widening to match her own. She turned back, making sure the camera followed the little creature precisely. She couldn't make out exactly what it looked like, but enhancement of the imagery would help there. The important thing was just to make sure this moment was recorded. *Even if we don't live to be rescued, someone may recover* Zarathustra *eventually. And this will be there, waiting.* "Joe, since we *are* in this ocean, can you give me a reading on the oxygen concentration?"

"Do I look like A.J.?" Joe said, but without rancor. He clambered back up. "The external sensing suite wasn't made with this in mind, but lemme try."

A second creature joined the first, and the two moved around each other in a slow spiralling dance that she captured in the memory of the camera.

"Quite a bit," Joe reported. "I can't be sure, but I think it's about ten to fifteen milligrams per liter. There's a bunch of other stuff dissolved in it too."

"My God. That's...that's more than enough to support just about anything from Earth. Anything water-breathing, anyway. And the temperature's not much below normal freezing." She shook her head, amazed. "And that colored stuff...has to be nutrients. Don't know the source, but there's an *ecosystem* here, Joe!"

The smile suddenly faded from his face.

"What's wrong, Joe?"

"I just realized, we were looking at the whole situation wrong."

Helen tried to figure out what he was saying, gave up. "What situation? What do you—"

"*Our* situation, here, Helen." He looked up. "It's not *comfortable* in here, but we can survive—as long as *Zarathustra* doesn't suddenly decide to give up the ghost—for a long time. But Larry and Maddie—"

Oh, God damn it. Joe didn't have to spell it out. "They've got no real shelters, only whatever food their suits have in the units, and however much breathing their current charge can give them."

He nodded. "Now, that's not terribly limited—we all charged up prior to this cycle, and if Maddie doesn't overdo things, they might have a week or even two of air. But by that point the waste recycler will be full. Long and the short of it is that *they're* the ones in trouble."

"But *Athena* . . ." she trailed off.

"Yeah, *Athena*. That option was predicated on the—entirely reasonable—assumption that we'd all retreat inside *Zarathustra* and live in cramped but not impossible style for a few weeks while *Athena* bored down to our level."

"Can't they speed her up?" Helen realized just what horror they were contemplating. If the tunnel had collapsed, there was no way out.

"Some," Joe admitted, "but I'm not sure that *Athena* could make a kilometer in that time even if they redline her and ignore all safety interlocks and protocols.

"No, the fact is, Maddie's not going to be able to rescue us. *We* have to rescue *her*."

Chapter 31

"We're not getting out of this alive, are we?" Larry said slowly.

"I'm not giving up yet, Larry," Madeline said, staring down at the pathetically small collection of equipment, "But I admit I'm not immediately seeing an answer to this problem."

Besides the tremendously strong carbonan-reinforced rope, of which they had another hundred meters not committed to the vital task of keeping *Zarathustra* in place, they had about a dozen of the explosive-driven spikes or pitons, three cameras of three different types, small sample collection devices, two space-qualified rock hammers of an alloy that remained tough even in extreme low temperatures, two suit multitools, a couple of scientific instruments, and one recharging pack.

"Well, the recharge pack can recharge our suits, right?" Larry asked.

"It's a universal connector, so yes." She checked the charge. "And just about enough for one recharge for one of us, or half a charge for both. If we do a lot of exertion, which I have to assume we will, that leaves about a week of life support, maybe a week and a half, for both of us. The concentrates in the suits will last a few days, so starving won't be the problem."

"We *might* be able to get to you in that time," A.J. said. "The quake and collapse actually gave us a route down to the tunnel region that goes at least halfway down to where you are. No telling how long the crack will stay open, but we're bringing *Athena* up fast and we'll drag her over and get down—"

"Absolutely *not*." Madeline said. "I don't want *more* of us getting potentially trapped down here!"

"Agent Fathom," Hohenheim's voice said, "as a commanding officer I appreciate your sentiments, but I believe that there is not one of us who will accept them, any more than you would accept such orders in our circumstances. If you and the others still have even the slightest chance of being rescued, you must realize that we must, and will, do all in our power to do so."

She smiled wryly. "You're . . . correct, General. I would not accept anyone telling me not to effect a rescue, I shouldn't expect anyone else to pay attention to me in that area. But—*realistically*, A.J.—what chances do you think we have?"

"To rescue you . . . fair. If that gap doesn't close up on us, which it sure could. Depends on where the blockage is. Without another rover, we'll have to drag *Athena* there and lower her with hand devices. None of us are decent hands with explosives, and anyway, even if we were, and had enough, no telling what would happen if we tried to blow our way through whatever obstacles there are, so melting's our only option."

Something about "melting" nagged at Madeline, but rather than try to force the thought out, she just noted it carefully for later contemplation. "You'll have to run her laterally. Can she *handle* that?"

"Er...not my department. Mia, you have anything?"

"Let me think." A few moments went by. "If we can fabricate something like some simple rails for it to rest on...Brett?"

"If you'll help me with the design, we should. The heavy workshop equipment from *Odin* made the rails for the centrifuge, the same basic operations should give you what you need. It just has to be portable enough to go down with *Athena*, and we have to figure out a connector that allows the probe to keep the rails sliding forward with her."

"That still leaves Helen and poor Joe," Jackie said quietly. "How can we get *them* back?"

"Assuming they're still alive," Horst said bluntly. "There is no telling if there was damage to *Zarathustra*. You have heard nothing from them yet, yes?"

"No," Maddie said, trying to ignore the chill that had nothing to do with her surroundings. "But based on the angles and how much line was used, they're hanging suspended in water slightly more than two meters down. Their radios simply can't reach us through that."

"Can they adjust the wavelength to get through?"

"I...don't think so," A.J. said glumly. "Water's a bitch to transmit through at reasonable frequencies, and from what the sensors picked up during that... event, there's a fair amount of salts dissolved in that water. At the power levels they can transmit, they'd have to drop the transmitter wavelength to about forty to fifty kilohertz, and it's not designed to vary *that* much."

There was a pause, a dead space of air that caused the waiting gloom to try to close its cold, aching hand around her heart. Then General Hohenheim spoke.

"Well, we have limited time. Jackie, right now Mr. Baker is the only man topside on Europa, and he cannot move all the components by himself. We must immediately go to help. Is it possible to perform orbital transfer with the reaction mass we have?"

"General, you're saying you want to move *Odin* now?"

"If it is possible, yes. There is urgency now that there was not before, and if we can place *Odin* in orbit about Europa, the entire operation will be made easier. Can it be done?"

"Well . . . Yes. We wanted another load from *Munin* so we had more margin, but there's enough to make the transfer of orbit now. I would feel a *lot* more comfortable if we could take some more time to check the auxiliary systems, but in theory we could start right now. Well, whenever we hit the right point in orbit for transfer."

"And when will that next transfer window arrive?"

Andrew LaPointe answered immediately. "Twenty-seven hours, seven minutes, General."

"Then you have a full day, Dr. Secord. I would recommend we take full advantage of that time to ready anything else we believe will be useful."

"Thank you, General," Madeline said. "The major remaining problem I must still discuss, however. Assuming that we can be reached, the problem is still reaching our friends under the ice."

"I do not wish to sound pessimistic," Dr. Masters said, "but are we sure it is 'under' and not 'within' the ice?"

Maddie winced. "I... hadn't really thought of that, but conditions here simply aren't the ones I was trained for. Andy?"

"Brett, allow me the use of your models, yes?" A few moments passed. "I believe yes, they are under, suspended in liquid water. Your records showed how thin was the layer beneath, and more importantly we should remember that *Zarathustra* is herself generating much heat. The water surrounding her, that will be a degree or more warmer than the normal. Yes, they will be in liquid water."

"Still doesn't help much," A.J. said. "The real problem is that if we *do* manage to break through to them, we'll just have a repeat of that explosive pressure release—and no guarantee you'll get lucky a second time. Do we even *know* why you all didn't get inundated?"

"I think—" "Yes, maybe—" said both Anthony and Brett simultaneously. Brett chuckled, as did Anthony. "Go ahead, Anthony, it's really your field; I just ran the models."

"Well, we have taken A.J.'s sensors' data, and combined it with what we have learned so far, and models of various material behaviors," Anthony said. "What happened is that the crack Madeline saw, and into which our friends have fallen, was not the only opening. From the pressure waves there were at least five simultaneous openings which were releasing into the tunnels a huge amount of vapor.

"That vapor, most importantly, was *not* just water. You recall, I think, the appearance of the water? It was foaming a great deal, yes?"

Madeline nodded, remembering the white-brown

surge of destruction. "Yes, a lot—like a shaken soda bottle."

"That, it is a very good example. It is precisely correct. From the readings, at least the top portion of the Europan ocean is saturated with both carbon dioxide and ammonia. When the pressure was relieved, all of these, plus water, vaporized into the surroundings. The volume released, it was *immense*—and because of expansion, it was also *dropping* temperatures drastically.

"At the same time, movement of the surroundings uplifted most of the cavern system, crushing much of it, compressing the atmosphere within."

His image smiled. "This was most fortunate for all, as the compression, it heated the mixed vapor, kept most of it from condensing out immediately, maintained and even increased the pressure for those few critical moments. But more was boiling out and cooling at the same time, so the end result was that the water subsided and solidified swiftly, partially by self-cooling, rather than continuing to expand."

"One in a billion, like I said," Larry commented. "Good work, Anthony."

The thought she had set aside was starting to grow. "So if I understand correctly, normally once the pressure reached some—much lower—level the water wouldn't have continued boiling off, so without the external compression it would not naturally reach a high enough value to keep things stable?"

"Unfortunately, yeah," A.J. said. "I think a few kilopascals would be enough to stop the boil if it was pure water; it's a lot higher with the other gases, but still, you need over a megapascal to keep the pressure equalized. If you were thinking of punching controlled holes to give you a constant equalized atmosphere, it won't work."

"But," she said, slowly, "when *Athena* is drilling, she's giving us liquid water, not steam, right?"

"That's because *Athena* is sealing the area and draining it as she goes," Mia said. "No chance for the water to depressurize and boil off."

"But what if there *was*?" Madeline asked.

The airwaves went silent for a few moments. Then Mia said, "That... might just work."

"You'd have to keep her moving constantly, feeding in more ice—"

"Seal the entrance, too, and really solid—"

"—get the control and power cables stacked up in there—"

Madeline laughed. "Slow down, slow down. Do you really think it could work?"

"It's not entirely impossible, anyway," Jackie said, her voice as well as her transmitted face echoing her relieved smile. "If you can keep vaporizing water into the cave—water with its extra cargo of carbon dioxide and ammonia, too—and it stays sealed, you'll be creating a pressurized atmosphere. Do it long enough, you'll also make it significantly warmer in there, which will keep the stuff from immediately trying to solidify out. *Athena* puts out a hellish amount of heat, so you might actually be able to keep that area pressurized long enough. Then you could try to break through to *Zarathustra*."

"Which," A.J. said, grinning, "would be dead-easy with *Athena*."

"No, no, bad idea," Mia interjected, making A.J.'s face fall. "*Athena* is not a precision instrument, and down there you'll be trying to control her by hand, in extremely non-optimal conditions. If *Athena* were to drop onto *Zarathustra* for even a moment, the rover would be severely damaged. This leaves aside the even greater danger of the heat affecting the cable that is currently holding *Zarathustra* in place." Mia shook her head. "No, we will have to try to break through with the tools we can bring down with us."

"Still," Maddie said, "that's a much better situation than we were seeing a short time ago. We need to work out some way to communicate, to find out if," her voice hesitated the merest moment, "find out if Joe and Helen are still all right, but the rest . . . at least we have a course of action. Since most of it will have to be on your end to begin with, Larry and I had better rest and conserve our energy—literally."

The others agreed. "Then we shall begin, Agent Fathom, and in a day or so we should be on our way to Europa. Good luck."

"Thank you, General."

Madeline made herself sit down against one of the icy columns and relax. That was, at least, possible now.

We're not dead yet. And we're not giving up.

Ever.

Chapter 32

Joe sighed loudly, then glanced with concern in Helen's direction. Fortunately, she showed no sign of waking up. *She needs her rest, and I damn well better not deprive her of any.* Joe had insisted she rest once she'd filled an entire archive chip with ultra-high-detail images of the tiny creatures which had danced—were still dancing—in front of the windows of *Zarathustra*. She'd dropped off to sleep almost instantly, showing that the panic and stress of the day had definitely taken a toll on her.

"They're not good for *me* either," he muttered. But he had to admit that one advantage of apparently being God's chew-toy was that you got used to perilous situations. He didn't feel utterly strung out yet. Of course, he'd also had that nap in preparation for driving them back.

But that doesn't solve any of the immediate problems. He grimaced and finally dismissed the suit radio's option menu. After he'd recalled some of the design and instruction work, he'd managed to figure out how to call up the customization functions, but the lowest he could reasonably configure the radio for was about

150 MHz, which at the power he could generate—even with the power he could relay through *Zarathustra*, if her antennas were still intact—would never penetrate the four meters of ice and water that he estimated lay between them and the surface.

Assuming that there *was* a surface above. He winced and tried to shove the thought away, but he remembered the last glimpse he'd had of the cavern, tons of ice formations crumbling and dropping in slow-motion catastrophe. There wasn't any guarantee that the entire cavern hadn't collapsed afterwards; they might be suspended here because the mass of all Europa was holding those ropes in place.

He shook his head. If that was true, they were dead right here; even if *Athena* could be pointed directly at them, it might take longer than their supplies would hold out to get that far down, and even if it did, what then? If she punched through, *Athena* would most likely end up getting shot up her own bore like a bullet from a cannon, or would have to *stay* there as a plug. Which would make a rescue... rather difficult.

Communication's the key. He had to find a way to talk to the surface. If Maddie was alive (the *if* hurt more than he really wanted to think about), or if A.J.'s sensors were active above, any reasonable signal would get through. They'd figure out a way to understand him, however he did it.

"Okay, Joe, think," he mumbled to himself. "Radio's out. I'm sitting in salt water, no transmission I can make will get six inches in this crap. Never deployed the umbilical, so we've got no direct connection to..."

And he trailed off, gaze resting on the perfect "V"

of carbonan-reinforced line holding them suspended in the ocean. *There's a connection, all right. But can I use it?*

He considered using it as a transmission line somehow. *Electrical won't work. There's a carbon core, but soaked in water I'd never get a signal through. Besides, I'd have to run a line to it.* That would require him to go outside. *Zarathustra* did have an airlock, but he seriously doubted that the pumps could handle water, or the extreme pressure needed. It was something of a miracle that the seals were holding as well as they were.

But it still was a connection, and a tight one. He connected his suit to the controls and slaved the forward manipulators to his arms. Now when he reached out, the manipulators moved with him. He could also switch his helmet view to *Zarathustra's* external cameras.

He reached out and plucked at the cable. *Zarathustra* weighed in at about ten metric tons, but it wasn't *that* much more dense than water given the large volume of air inside, maybe one point fifteen or so. That meant that buoyancy supported eight point seven tons of her mass, leaving one point three tons to exert a downward force; in Europa's gravity, that meant roughly seventeen hundred newtons, or a little over three hundred eighty pounds. That made the slender line pretty taut; a faint, deep thumping twang thrummed through the ship. He tried plucking and striking the line in different ways. He was pretty sure that this sound would carry a long, long way in the water, but the problem was, as he thought about it, that the two meters of ice it was sealed in would probably damp out the vibrations. *Maybe* A.J. could pick it up, but probably not.

Still, that wasn't the only way. The line would be very poor at transmitting energy from one side to another. But it could have another use.

The manipulator arms were rated at a pull-and-lift capacity of well over a ton, Earthside; that meant that a hundred seventy kilos was easy. Joe reached out and grabbed the line and pulled gently.

Zarathustra rose slowly in the water, closer to the icy surface. Holding with one manipulator, Joe pulled the other back and then punched forward.

Tactile feedback gave him the feel of punching through water, but there was a significant jolt from the impact with the icy surface. He struck several more times, then turned on the external microphones.

The result startled him. Instead of the effectively dead silence, there was a sensation of *sound* everywhere, a background level that was like standing in a forest with breezes going through the leaves. Faint sounds that grumbled or moaned or squeaked, with a rumbling tone behind it. The sounds were almost familiar.

After a moment, Joe recognized it. The sounds were similar to recordings he'd heard from near the "black smoker" vents on Earth, places where the magma below the crust came in contact with seawater and vaporized it, sending boiling water at hundreds of degrees, filled with dissolved minerals, spewing back into the chilled ocean above. *That explains a life cycle here where no sunlight will ever penetrate. But it still doesn't—*

He froze, then smacked his forehead. *That's it!*

Once more he levered *Zarathustra* up, up until the nose was almost touching the ice above . . . and then he triggered the headlights, on, off, on, in the old pattern that even the most casual fan of adventure novels had to know: three short bursts, three long bursts, three short.

S. O. S.

He repeated it three times, waited. Then did it again. *Even two meters of cloudy ice can't stop those lights completely, not when everything above's going to be blacker than Hades.* Wait. Still everything above was dark as pitch.

A third time he triggered the cycle, but in spite of himself he was feeling his gut tighten. *Anyone up there would see it, see it pretty easy. They'd have to.*

If there's anyone there.

The third repetition ended and he stared up into velvet darkness.

And then the darkness flickered. Flickered again, and again, in a rhythm too fast to easily follow. But he had the signal processing on board to do vastly harder problems, and old Morse Code was in *Zarathustra*'s onboard library. Decoded, the flashes read:

Thank God. Are both of you all right? End.

He barely restrained a whoop of triumph combined with relief. He realized also that Maddie—it almost *had* to be Maddie, he doubted Larry knew Morse code—was using "end" somewhat the way old telegrams used "stop," except here it also signaled the other person that they could send—since if the two of them were to try to signal at once, the reflection of their own light from the surface would drown out the fainter signal from the other.

Both fine. Line holding us. No leaks yet. How are you? End.

Larry and I both fine. Cave-in trapped us. Plan to get us out. Maybe you. Take time. End.

Get A.J. to rig comm scan and code, he sent back. *Use different light wavelengths, modulate signals, can talk after that. End.*

He can't program Zarathustra. *End.*

Tell him simple encoding, send me parameters. Can tweak Zarathustra's *systems myself. End.*

Understood. Wait. A few minutes went by. *A.J. says will have answer in ten minutes. End.*

Got you. End.

The next ten minutes dragged by like an eternity, but he wasn't going to interrupt them. Sure enough, after about eleven minutes, the flashing started, but this time accompanied by a much brighter and more defined spot that sparkled. *Using multispectral scanning probe,* Maddie sent. *Set for distinctly different area of spectrum than* Zarathustra *headlights.*

Several more messages were sent, detailing the characteristics of the simple amplitude modulation scheme A.J. had devised, with Mia's help. Joe had to do a bit of hacking on the code for the rover's headlights in order to allow high-speed amplitude variation, but the sealed solid-state emitters were more than capable of it. He then keyed the modulation to go to the radio receiving portion of his suit, transmitting a copy to Helen's update buffer for whenever she woke up. *Here goes...* "Maddie?"

"Joe!" Her voice was distorted, muffled, but it was Madeline's voice. "Neither of you are hurt?"

"No. That slow-motion crash is pretty deceptive—I

got my leg wedged between two seats and it could've broken bad—but the suits are designed to keep that from happening. Helen's sleeping now, but she's fine."

"Glad to hear that," A.J.'s voice came blurrily on. "Good thinking on this approach, Joe. Light penetrates just fine at this range."

"Hey, I haven't been working with you all this time without learning to think about sensor stuff," he said quietly. Helen was still sleeping, stretched out across the backs of two chairs. "What's the bandwidth on this?"

"A little less than three kilohertz," A.J. answered.

"Ick. No data transfer worth talking about," Joe said, disappointed. "It'd take me, what, five minutes to send a megabyte down that pipe."

"We're lucky to get that with this MacGyvered rig. Besides, what data do you need to send?"

"How about photos of extraterrestrial lifeforms?"

The light-radio was silent for a moment, and then so many voices tried to talk at once that it was nothing but a hash of noise. Finally it quieted down and Maddie was speaking: ". . . enough, enough! Joe, are you *serious*?"

"Dead serious. Helen made the discovery and we've spent about half the time we've been down here filming them." He summarized the analysis of the water and what they'd seen thus far. "Sometimes I see faint glints that might even be from something bigger farther down, but we weren't built for sonar or anything."

"*Unglaublich*," Hohenheim said. "Unbelievable that you would happen to encounter life so soon. What sort of odds are those?"

"Not as bad as you might think, General," Helen's voice said, making him glance down in startlement. The xenopaleontologist grinned back. "The oxygen concentration is much higher than in the deep oceans of Earth, and something's circulating it. If there's some sort of nutrient and energy source like our black smokers—"

"I think there is. I heard something that sounded like that," Joe interjected.

"Well, then, there's nutrients, oxygen, energy, and the squeezing motion from Jupiter is circulating it all. This ocean's probably *full* of life. The top part of the ocean may be their equivalent of the bottom, the desert area—and everything might be attracted by *Zarathustra*'s presence. Heat, vibration, maybe even light, all these things mean *change*, and change can mean nutrients."

"Do you think this is actually *native* Europan life, or is this . . . seeded, I guess you'd say?" Madeline asked.

"That's a good question, Maddie," Helen said. "A lot of what I've seen—past the microscopic scale—*could* be something descended from Bemmie's biosphere, I see a lot of trilateral symmetry so far. But there's nothing saying that kind of design couldn't develop naturally on Europa, either. We'll have to get samples and do extensive testing. Somehow."

"If the Bemmies did this kind of thing regularly," A.J. said, "I'd bet you'll find a mix. If they're bio-forming colonizers, they'd want to be compatible with whatever was there to begin with, so that the stuff already present served a useful purpose for your colonizing species."

"Assuming there *was* anything here before they arrived," Maddie said.

"A much smaller assumption now that we know for a fact that at least two separate solar systems evolved life; this means that life isn't the terribly unique phenomenon some people thought it might be," Helen said. "We already had good reason to think life evolved separately at least two or three times on Earth alone, so it would seem likely to me that Europa had life on it to begin with. But samples will tell the story for sure."

"And we won't get any of those until we can get out of here," Joe pointed out. "Have you guys got an answer for that?"

"A jury-rigged one, yes, but it might work," Maddie said, and described their current plan. "*Odin* will be on its way to Europa orbit—actually, one of the Europa Lagrange points, a bit more than a hundred thousand kilometers away from *Odin* at the moment—in about, what, General, nineteen hours?"

"About that, yes. Once on-station most of us will be free to assist."

"Sounds like you guys have everything under control," Joe said, grinning. "I guess all Helen and I have to do is hang around."

Chapter 33

General Hohenheim dropped lightly from *Munin*'s hatch. "Good morning, Mr. Baker. You are no longer alone."

A.J.'s grip was a little tighter than it had been the first time they shook hands, and the eyes showed immense relief. "And I can't tell you how happy that makes me. So *Odin* is in orbit around Europa now?"

"Technically," Jackie said, coming up and giving her old friend a hug—Hohenheim suspected A.J. needed one, given the circumstances—"*Odin* is in orbit around Jupiter, at the L1 Lagrangian point. Which puts it very close to Europa, as Europa's mass is very tiny compared to Jupiter's."

"Oh. Well, whatever, as long as it's a better setup than we had."

Dan's voice cut in. "How's this? No transmission delay to speak of."

"That's sure a lot better," A.J. agreed. "Is it just Dan up there?" he asked, seeing Horst coming down.

"Not quite," Anthony said. "I am here with Dan, and so also is Brett. We can continue the work, make sure *Odin* stays on station—because, you realize, the

L1 point is not a stable place—and assist with comput-
ing solutions if needed. Brett felt he was more useful
here with the most powerful of the computers."

"He's probably right," came Madeline's voice. "Welcome back, all of you."

"Shall we get to work?" Hohenheim asked. "You
have made many plans, I think, Mr. Baker—"

"A.J., please."

"A.J., of course."

The sharp nod was easily visible. "Been setting up
the machines to fabricate the rails for *Athena*, just
like Brett designed. Mia, I didn't want to try anything
like putting a cradle on *Athena* without you here."

The Norwegian engineer nodded with a smile. "I'm
sure you would have done fine, A.J., but it's best that
we take no chances."

"Sure as hell I'm not taking any as long as she's down
there," A.J. said. It was spoken so quietly Hohenheim
suspected that it had been intended to be private;
the general decided he would take it that way, and
none of the others commented. More loudly, A.J. said,
"I agree. Now, the hard part's going to be getting
Athena down the rabbit hole. If you'll look here," their
helmet displays suddenly showed a 3-D map of the
region, "you'll see that the quake caused the ice to
split and then collapse over there, about a kilometer.
I've mapped the area and it gets us down pretty darn
close to the level we want—but it's not really stable.
Right now, it's closing at about three centimeters a
day, which isn't too bad, but there's no telling what'll
happen if we get another strong jolt."

"All the more reason to move quickly," Hohenheim
said. "Mia, can we move *Athena* into *Munin* and fly

her to the target location faster than we could drag *Athena* by hand?"

"I'd say almost certainly, General. That's rough terrain, even in this light gravity, and our experience with the *Nebula Storm*'s rocket nozzle showed that the light gravity is almost completely counterbalanced by the difficulty in exerting significant force by hand."

"*Athena*'s almost all the way up," Horst said, obviously studying the telltales on the local systems. "As soon as she is clear of the ice, we will shut her down and detach her from the supports. The rest of you can disassemble the support framework and we will all move to *Munin*. Yes?"

"Works for me," A.J. said. "Glad to see you here too, Doc," he said to Petra Masters.

"I hope my professional skills won't be needed, but it seemed much more likely that they'd be needed here than up there."

"So how long until you have *Athena* set up to descend and start cutting through to our location?" Madeline asked.

A.J. looked at Mia, who shrugged. "I do not know that we can make a terribly good guess at that, at least at this time. If all goes well, it may be a matter of a day. If not, it could be several days."

"Not to pressure you, but Larry and I are on a very limited timeline."

"We understand that most keenly, Agent Fathom," Hohenheim said. "And we shall make *every* effort to get to you soon. But at the same time, I believe you would not argue that we must proceed with utmost caution. We shall get only one chance to succeed at this, I think. Especially since reaching you will be only the first step."

"No argument there, General," Larry said emphatically. "Don't forget to assemble anything that's remotely likely to help seal leaks *and* break through ice."

A somewhat distorted voice—clearly that of Joe Buckley—joined in. "And when you say proceed with caution, remember to think of backup plans. Like, say, if that pit A.J. found collapses on you."

"Here is hoping that won't happen," Horst said. "Because, honestly? I cannot see there is a backup plan if it does."

Hohenheim didn't think there was one, either. Half a kilometer and more down, they had nothing to stop that huge hole from closing—probably there was nothing on Earth short of carefully designed mine bracing that could—and while *Athena* might be moved laterally, there was no practical way he could imagine to bore *upward* with her. "So we must assume it will not happen. If it does, however, let there be no regrets or recriminations, yes?"

"General," Helen said reluctantly, "I really don't want you to take the chance. The rest of you can still get *home*. We've done so much work to make that possible. Maybe I'm the only one—"

"You certainly aren't," Madeline said emphatically, and Hohenheim felt a twinge of...what? Pride, perhaps, although that seemed utterly nonsensical. These people weren't his crew, he had no hand in selecting or training them.

"You most certainly are not," Madeline Fathom repeated. "General, all four of us don't want to die, but even less would we want to think we got everyone else killed. I know we began this conversation before, but I don't want to cut it off this time."

"She's right," Joe said calmly. "Believe me, this isn't a pleasant death we're looking at, and I'd rather not be looking at it at all. But we *all* survived what we shouldn't have, some of us more than once." The gallows humor hurt Hohenheim more than it amused, and judging from the stiff pose of Mr. Baker, hurt him much more. "We've done goddamn amazing things here, all to get us home, and I think we'd be *proud*," his voice wavered just a tiny bit, "to die knowing all that work wasn't in vain, and you guys got to go home."

"Yeah," Larry said, echoing the sentiment. "And hell, where better for an astrophysicist to end up entombed than here?"

For a long moment, no one said anything.

"Yeah. That makes...sense." A.J. said slowly, quietly. He straightened slowly. "But *I* don't want it to be a waste, either."

Hohenheim nodded. "Indeed, Mr. Baker. Agent Fathom...Dr. Conley, Dr. Buckley, Dr. Sutter...I am—I think we *all* are—touched by your sincerity, and your courage. If you were my people, I would be able to tell you that I was proud to have you as members of *Odin*'s crew. But instead I can only say this: that you may think of regretting the waste if we do not go, but—even upon careful reflection—we would find it an *utter* waste to leave without having done *everything* that we could, even if it risked all of our lives—to rescue our friends. We are not leaving...unless *all* of us are leaving."

"So we will stay and try—even if it may get the rest of us killed." He looked around at the others. "Are we all in agreement?"

"Undoubtedly, General," Horst Eberhardt said firmly.

"I will not leave my friend Larry under the surface of our Europa," Andrew said simply.

"A fossil I dug up got Helen—all of us—into this," Jackie said, with a spark of humor. "I'll just have to dig up a couple more fossils now."

"Oh, that's cruel," Helen said with a chuckle.

The others agreed with the sentiments—and with Jackie's cruelty.

A.J. slowly straightened and nodded. "I'd stay and try if the rest of you left," he said quietly. Hohenheim realized he meant it quite literally. *And perhaps that intensity is what brought him together with the paleontologist willing to risk her career for a discovery.* "But I'm *damn* glad I don't have to!" he said, with a cheery brightness that did not quite mask his near-tears to anyone listening. "Damn glad."

Chapter 34

"*Move,* you stinking piece of—" A.J. expressed his feelings with a kick to *Athena's* side.

"It's frozen to the rails again," Jackie said with a sigh.

"There's *got* to be a leak somewhere," Mia Svendsen said tiredly, trying to push hair back from a forehead that was sealed away inside her suit. She muttered something in Norwegian that didn't sound at all polite. "But all the systems claim they're working."

"Dammit—" A.J. restrained himself with great difficulty.

The hardest part is knowing that we don't have that far to go. That we could have been there by now if Athena *didn't decide that it had to do a stop and go every few meters!*

There was little communication from Maddie and Larry now. They were conserving their energy and food as much as possible, and it was running low.

Two and a half days getting Athena *set up. Two more days getting us down here, setting up a motorized winch that allows us to do shifts downstairs and then go back up. Now four and a half days drilling through this crap a meter at a time!*

It didn't help that they had to make *Athena* do what amounted to a wiggle up and down constantly, in order to allow enough space for them to follow, slide through the rails, and so on.

"I do not understand," Horst's voice came up above in *Munin*, where he was resting. "The hydrophobic coating should exclude the ice. Why is it not working?"

"That stuff was studied at milspec tolerances, not cryogenic," A.J. answered absently, staring with both fury and longing at *Athena*, willing the massive melt-probe to start moving again. "Lots of stuff that works at a mere minus forty goes screwy at minus one hundred fifty. Plus it wears off with that much mass on it."

"A.J.," Mia said, "can you check the integrity of all seals again?"

"Okay," he said, "but I doubt I'll find anything."

The Faerie Dust worked passably here . . . most of the time. If he didn't demand too much of it, or could channel a lot of power to it with a transmitter. He'd brought down a portable transmitter and tuned it to one of the frequencies they could receive acceptably, so the dust on *Athena* should be working reasonably well.

Based on the signals, the Dust was doing its job. But the data coming back insisted that there was nothing at all wrong with *Athena*—other than that she was stuck and having to wait until enough heat could be built up to melt the ice. Then they'd have to deploy *Athena*'s lower side anchors as jacks, slide out the rails, dry them, coat them again, and slide them back.

We don't have time *for this.* "Nothing, Mia. Everything's intact, not even a pinhole in any of the connectors, the pipes, the flexible hose, even the forward nose seal. All intact."

He was about to shut off that view when some anomalous data came in. *What the . . .*

There was Faerie Dust on the rail. Dust he had not put there, as there wasn't any particular reason to instrument the metal. As the Faerie Dust was capable of its own (slow) movement, it tended to stay where it was put even in the face of significant vibration. *So where the hell . . .*

A.J. connected to his main control and data collection system back on *Nebula Storm*, through *Munin's* link, and had the individual dustmotes send back their UID—Unique IDentifier—codes. *Now, track their history. Where'd I put those motes originally? Is there any commonality?*

Slowly, an image built up in his VRD—the tiny dots, a fogbank of lightmotes, crawling backwards in time . . .

To all converge on the upper edge of the forward nose seal.

He stared for a moment, then felt a tiny thread of understanding starting to work its way through. *Data history for that period . . .*

Sure enough, they had all showed a quick spike of humidity and pressure when they were suddenly thrown from their position to end up on the rail. Checking, he found quite a few more motes scattered all over the place, trying rather unsuccessfully to make their way back to their assigned locations in the mobile network.

"Mia . . . I take it back. There's a tiny, tiny, intermittent leak in the upper portion of the nose seal."

"I thought you said it was intact."

I did. And it still is. "Yeah; and it *is* intact. So I don't quite know what's happening to—"

"Gravity," Brett said suddenly.

Mia froze. "*Uff-da*," she said with exhausted realization. "*Athena* is meant to be working vertically. The pressure evenly distributed—"

Now it made sense. "—but we've put her kinda on her side, so the pressure's less at the top. And so every little bit, when it goes over something that's not quite perfectly smooth, a tiny bit of water vaporizes past it."

"Yes." Mia frowned. "That leak is very small compared to the amount of water, yes?"

"Tiny. So small that we weren't noticing the loss in what was going upstairs." Refilling *Munin* was proceeding along with this operation; they weren't about to waste the water right now. "Hell, its small enough that we weren't noticing the mist. Playing back the video and enhancing, I can *just* make it out in a couple frames, but you have to be staring at it just the right way."

Mia stared at the nose of *Athena* for a moment, then went through a series of gestures and muttered commands that reminded A.J. of himself. "The nose seal material is a smart seal—it can be adjusted. But it has no fine control and direction." She looked up suddenly. "A.J., do you think—"

He felt a broad smile starting, as an immense weight seemed to lift from him. "Oh, I very *much* think, yes! I can embed enough Faerie Dust in there to tell you exactly what to do. Hell, if you need it I can have enough of it embed itself into the material so that it will act as a *conductor* for the signals."

"That might work. Brett, we need a model right now, tell us, optimum distribution to assure sufficient control of the seal, prevent more leakage?"

"Have it for you in ten minutes," Brett said promptly.

"Without the leak," A.J. said, "Mia, it won't freeze anymore, right?"

"I would be very surprised if it did," she said. "If we can keep any significant amount of ice from being available to adhere to the rails, we should be able to progress much more quickly."

"I sure hope so."

He wasn't religious—never had been. But knowing that Helen was so near, yet so utterly out of reach, in so much danger . . . he was tempted to pray, but he had no idea what *to. Just . . . let us save her, somehow.*

"Here's your model," Brett said suddenly, and he realized he'd been standing there for some minutes, doing nothing.

"Got it!" he answered. *Okay . . . whoo, that's going to take a fair amount of the Dust I have left. But who cares, if it works?*

"All right, Mia—try it!"

Athena lunged forward, eating its way through ice as fast as they could drive her.

And this time, it didn't stop.

Chapter 35

Not with a bang.

"But not with a whimper, either," Madeline Fathom-Buckley whispered to herself. She'd cut out the microphone and transmitter for now; there was no need of it and even the relatively small power drain could add up over hours.

Not in that *bad shape.* The last time she'd checked, *Athena* was chugging its way through the ice, with an ETA not long from now. If they didn't encounter any more problems. *Which I have to assume they won't, if I want to live to see Joe rescued. And I do.*

So if they didn't encounter any more problems, and she stayed still, kept the power usage minimal, she figured she'd have at least an hour, maybe two, left. Plenty of time.

As she thought that, she felt Larry's hand squeeze her suit. At the lowest power level—range only a couple meters—she activated the radio. "What is it?"

"Having...trouble...breathing." Larry spoke slowly, but she could hear the incipient panic. *And I can't blame him. Suffocating in a human-shaped coffin is a damned terrifying way to go.*

But why? We had the same charge at the same time, so—

Madeline would have kicked herself if it would have done any good. *Larry's twice my mass. Efficient or not, the suit's using more power to keep him going than mine does, and he's probably on his last reserves.*

"Control, Larry. I'll see what I can do, just hold on!" She grabbed the recharge pack. *It shows empty, but maybe there's a tiny bit left, enough to give him a few more minutes while I think.* She linked it to the coupler on Larry's suit. "Anything?"

"A...little." The big astrophysicist's voice was tense, but he tried to relax, visibly sagging back down. "The charge needle twitched. But I guess that might have gained me, oh, four minutes before it goes back down."

Not nearly enough. Need more time, lots more time for him.

The charge packs on the cameras were integral, and there was no way to connect them to either of their suits. She stared at the pitiful collection of useless objects: cameras with unusable powerpacks, explosive spikes only good for last-ditch suicide, multitools that couldn't conjure air or power from nowhere, and a completely compatible and compact recharge pack that was now utterly empty. *Any more empty and it'd suck the power* out *rather than put it . . .*

And the answer was there. If it was possible.

She almost made the mistake of activating the radio to ask A.J. or Joe the question, but realized in time what a stupid error that would be. *We'd spend all the time Larry has left arguing before they'd answer. I need to spend that time* finding *the answer.*

The key was the suits' configurability. The circuitry

had been made adaptable for numerous tasks, and she thought she recalled that the gloves specifically were used to induce low-level electrical flow in things like the multitool. She called up the suit's technical references. *I wish I dared ask A.J. but I know I can't. And I'm no slouch at this.*

Larry sat quietly while she worked. She guessed that he realized that if there was nothing she could do, she'd have said something. *He's been with us since the first days of the project; he knows me pretty well by now. He's not going to jog my elbow if he can help it.*

Voltage regulators . . . charging circuit . . . microcontroller, code. *Warning! Do not tamper with these settings!* She cancelled the warning with one of her override codes, grateful that she'd made sure there *were* override codes for just about everything, with A.J. supporting her in the argument. "There may be a reason to do just about anything, and if someone's willing to ignore the warnings and override, I'll assume they *have* exactly that kind of reason. The override will be logged, of course, so we know what was done and by whom . . ."

Well, let it be logged that I overrode the warnings and deliberately messed with the microcode running the entire power system of my own suit.

Time was running out, but now she was into the editor, looking for the flags she needed to set. *One chance at this.*

For a moment she was back on Earth, staring at a maze of wires and circuits, blinking ominously in rhythmic red and blue, knowing that she had only moments to deactivate the bomb; it had a timing circuit which would certainly go any second, and a movement sensor so she could not move it from where it lay. *Lucky it doesn't have a motion sensor, or I'd be dead already. But I have to choose right the first time* . . . "Sir . . ."

"Don't you think it, Madeline," her boss's voice came, calm and certain. "You'll be working for me for a good long time. Just take a breath, and do what you think is the right thing, and it'll work."

Do what you think is the right thing.

All right, sir. Let's do it. She didn't feel at all embarrassed for holding her breath as she set the revised code running.

Her suit's lights flickered for just an instant, then steadied. *Please, please—*

Madeline grabbed up the recharge pack, plugged it in.

"What . . . are you doing?" Larry asked faintly. "Nothing left in that . . ."

"There *will* be."

And she saw the indicator light on the pack glow green. *Charging.*

Of course, along with that, she saw the indicator of her own charge dropping swiftly. *He's still going to burn through this faster than I will. No good data on that—but I'll give him two-thirds of what I've got. At least the transfers are efficient, we won't lose more than five percent in the trade.*

"Wait a minute, Maddie—"

"Do not even *think* of arguing. There's a reason I didn't try asking the others how to do this." *That's it, as much as I dare transfer.* "Stay still."

Unlike someone like A.J., Larry apparently knew when not to argue. Silently he let her recharge his suit. "Did you leave yourself any?"

"I'm not trying to commit suicide, Larry. Now, we have to lie down and be as calm and quiet as we can. One way or another it won't be much longer."

Larry nodded, and they both cut their radios.

Madeline lay there, staring into inky blackness. *Had to dim indicators and telltales to minimum, no suit lights. I'll bet Larry's thinking he's been panicky, but he's doing better than he knows; plenty of people would be unable to even* try *to relax in this situation.*

Of course, she had to admit that this group of people was probably unique. Larry, herself, A.J. and Joe and Helen, Horst and Andy and Hohenheim, all of them were used to conditions in space, living in small spaces, working in tiny suits for hours. *If anything could have prepared us for this . . . well, it's the lives we've led.*

Time had little meaning in darkness where nothing moved. Occasionally she did see a glow, a flash from the center of the room, where Joe was signaling his presence. But he must realize now that they had no energy to spare to communicate with him. *Poor Joe. He must be frantic. And there's nothing I can do to help him feel better. Just . . . hope.*

A faint chime sounded, and her heart sank. *Into my reserves now. And if Larry isn't yet . . . he will be in a few minutes.*

Slowly the air became heavier, sharper. *Joe went through this back on Ceres. And he never panicked, never even let us know how terribly close he was to dying.*

I'll do my best to match you, love.

She felt Larry's grip again, but this time she knew it was simply saying "Thanks. This is it. Goodbye," and she returned the grip for a moment.

My vision's already going. Even with nothing to see I'm starting to see red . . .

She could see the rim of her helmet, edged in dull crimson.

A shot of adrenalin went through her, and she turned her head, half-sat up.

A point on the far wall was glowing, red to white, now blazing. *Athena!*

But could they get through in time?

She forced herself to lay back, prayed that Larry would do the same—if he still was conscious. Every breath was worse than the last, and her thoughts were starting to lose coherence. *No . . . not giving up . . .* She was trapped in a closet . . . *he's waiting out there . . . No, he can't be . . . Not LaFayette, no, he's dead . . .* But her disjointed thoughts conjured images from a childhood she'd erased, trapped, parents enthralled by a madman. They were calling her name now . . . *Oh, Madeline, you're growing up so well . . . the Senator will be so pleased . . .*

"No!"

She sat up, fighting off the hands, drawing great gasps of air into her lungs.

Air?

Her vision was clearing, and two figures were tumbling across the floor of the cavern; she herself was skidding to a stop against one of the columns. She keyed the suit to full activity.

"—totally freaking out! Get away from her until she comes out of it!" A.J.'s voice was a combination of exasperation and concern; he nearly went over the edge into the depression where *Zarathustra* had fallen before he got a grip on the ice.

"Oh, God, I'm sorry, A.J.," she said, sinking back in relief. "Some welcome that was to my rescuers."

"S'alright, I oughtta have expected something like that when you were half-conscious. You didn't go through twenty years of cloak-and-dagger without being ready for the worst all the time, I'd bet."

"How's Larry?"

"We are trying to wake him now," Hohenheim answered.

She looked over, seeing Petra Masters bent over the prone form of Larry Conley. A chill went through her and she accessed Larry's suit readouts.

No breathing. No heartbeat.

Wait . . . "He's in fibrillation!"

"Exactly. *Mr. Baker!*" snapped Dr. Masters. "*If* you please, how do I connect with your suits' controls to trigger a defibrillation pulse?"

"Jesus! Hold on, I haven't had to do that—"

"We have little *time*, I do not know how long he's been in this state! His suit's recorders were not working!"

Madeline found she was already skidding to a halt near the two. *No way to perform standard CPR, but maybe, just maybe . . .*

The suit was now charged, a recharge pack still hooked to the inlet. *And I know how to control the suit rigidity, so . . .*

She lifted Larry and gripped him from behind. Squeeze, *relax the suit in just the right places . . . release . . .* Squeeze . . . *God, this is* hard, *usually you use gravity, your whole weight,* Squeeze . . . *this is like doing chin-ups, lifting myself by arms alone . . .*

"Defibrillating," Dr. Masters said tensely. Maddie felt the body twitch.

And suddenly the jerky, rhythmless pulse shifted, spiked, spiked again, and the heart's beat was started. Larry gave a huge gasp, and his oxygen levels started to rise.

"Thank God..." she murmured, realizing that she was suddenly so exhausted she didn't have the energy to move out from under the astrophysicist's suit.

"Get these two up to *Munin* immediately," Petra said. "They've been without food for days and nearly died before we reached them. They need to recover."

"On it," A.J. said, and with Horst's help lifted Larry up. Hohenheim bent and picked Madeline off the floor with great care.

"Really, I can still walk," she protested.

"Maybe...you can," Larry's voice came, faintly, "but...not me." His tone shifted. "Maddie...thanks."

"Just doing my job," she said, lightly. "But ...you're welcome." She looked at Hohenheim. "We can't waste much time on us."

"I am aware of that, Agent Fathom. But we also will not risk your lives any further. You will rest until you are fully recovered." He smiled behind the faceplate, and she realized she *was* even weaker than she had thought. "And as you are now medically incapacitated, the others have agreed that I am in command—so that, Agent Fathom, is an order."

"Yes, General." She sighed, then laughed.

"What's funny?" asked A.J.

"Being ordered to take it easy, A.J.," she said. "This is undoubtedly the hardest order I will ever have to obey."

Chapter 36

Joe sat up suddenly. "I think I see something."

Helen squinted up. There *did* seem to have been a couple of very, very dim flickers. "I think so too."

"Please," she heard him murmur, so quiet she suspected he didn't intend it to be heard. "Don't care about me, but...please have gotten there in time."

Helen refrained from pointing out that this also implied he didn't care what happened to *her*; instead, she patted the shoulder of his suit. It was bad enough for her, sitting in the cold darkness of *Zarathustra* with no word from above (since neither Maddie nor Larry could afford the energy for the lights). She couldn't easily imagine what it must be like for Joe. He'd kept sending pulses periodically up, maybe just to say "I'm here" to Maddie and Larry, keep them from being in utter blackness all the time. But as days wore on he'd checked the time more frequently, redone calculations, and she knew he had realized that the suits had to be running low, perhaps had already run out, of power.

Even if the others had gotten *Athena* working

perfectly, even if no more disasters had struck, the others still might simply be too late.

And then words came in a blaze of almost-painful light like the dawn of the first day. "Helen, Joe, you guys both still with us?"

"*A.J.!*" Both of them said the same thing simultaneously, and she felt a tremendous wash of relief at the sound of that much-loved voice. Though she'd never tell him—A.J.'s ego didn't need any more inflation—just hearing him made her sure that things were going to be all right.

But Joe was talking. "Maddie! *Maddie!* Is she—"

The familiar warm soprano answered immediately. "I'm here, Joe. Larry's passed back out, but we're both going to be all right." Madeline Fathom's voice was exhausted, a little shaky... but alive.

Helen saw Joe sag back onto the vertical seats, tears of relief running down his face. "Thank God, thank *God* she's all right."

"And Larry," Helen added, but she knew that even Dr. Conley wouldn't be particularly surprised that Joe wasn't thinking about him at that point.

"*And* Larry," he agreed, voice a bit thick from the quiet tears. "A.J., cutting it a little fine, aren't we?"

"That's in my contract. Thrilling last-minute rescues, desperate improvisations, heroic wisecracks a specialty." Despite his usual lighthearted tone, Helen could hear the unsteadiness of tension and relief in her husband's voice as well. "Give credit, or blame, to *Athena*, who spent a lot of time balking us before finally giving up her secrets so we could make her move forward at double-time. And a *lot* of credit to everyone else, especially Mia. She managed to coax another twenty percent speed out of *Athena* in the last stretch, getting us here something like a half hour faster—which made all the difference."

"Then thank you, Mia." Helen had never heard those words invested with such intensity before.

"You're welcome, Joe," Mia answered simply.

For a few minutes Joe seemed content to just relax, letting the tension of the last few days drain out of him. The others weren't quiet, though, so Helen had to respond.

"Is everything all right with you two?"

"So far, yes," she said. "Temperature in the cabin's been holding fairly steady. No leaks yet, thank every god out there." She glanced down. "Native life activity has come and gone; a couple of times both Joe and I thought we saw something else, something much larger, but if so it never came very close, and to be honest right now I really *don't* want to see anything bigger. As a biologist it would be amazing, but..."

"No need to explain, Dr. Sutter," the general said. "I do not think any of us want any unexpected visitors of any size right now, regardless of the wonder they might inspire. Now, you understand it will take time to effect your rescue, yes?"

"Yes," she answered. "It's not comfortable in here, I'll admit, and Joe says he has no guarantee the seals somewhere won't fail in the next twenty minutes, but as far as we can tell we should be fine for at least a few weeks."

"It may take almost that long," Jackie said. "You understand the basic procedure we have to set up?"

"I think so. The idea is that you can't crack the ice over us without bringing the area up to pressure at, or extremely close to, that which the ocean's at at this depth. So you need to make an atmosphere in there with *Athena*."

"Right, but it's a lot harder than that. First we have to seal off as much of this room as possible, since we want to minimize the size of the pressurized area—easier to hold pressure that way. Then we need to create some kind of airlock, because we can't just blow the seal to leave; that might trigger a rupture and all of us get caught in the uprush. Then finally we have to make the atmosphere and pressurize it to a pretty impressive level, which probably means that this place has to be warmed up to something vaguely Earthlike in temperature before the ice stops precipitating out automatically."

"Can we *do* that?"

"Brett helped model the design; we've unshipped and modified two of *Odin's* internal pressure-breach doors from areas we aren't planning on using. We'll embed them in ice a short distance apart, and some simple piping embedded around them that can be used to flood or depressurize the chamber. That gives us our airlock. Sealing the rest of the cave . . . if we can get the volume down to something reasonable. Parts of it are close to collapse already. The real tricky part is letting that collapse happen without taking the whole cave with it. Sealing can be accomplished with enough ice—probably just boiling water near it will accumulate quite a seal as it vents and precipitates, but we'll try more direct means."

"Whoa, whoa, whoa," Joe entered the conversation. "Did I hear that right? You're going to try to collapse *more* of the cavern?"

"The areas that are unstable already, yes. We need to minimize the volume. If I dared I'd want to just cap off this center depressed area, but I don't think we can manage that," Jackie said. "It's too small for me to feel comfortable operating *Athena* in it without being sure of missing you guys. But I'm going to have A.J. use the rest of his Dust to give us a perfect-as-possible picture of the exact structure in those areas; if it's actually more stable than we think we'll have to live with the volume."

"The rest?" Helen blinked. "Have we used it all?"

"Damn near. Oh, I recover some whenever I can, but the fact is we're often using it for things that either destroy it, or that turn out to need it to be *left* there, like *Athena*. Until we're done using *Athena* down here she'll have to keep a lot of Faerie Dust instrumenting her. Every little bit piles up, and this maneuver will need a *lot*. And more than likely I'll *never* get most of that back. So yes. We'll have plenty of the El Cheapo knockoff version that was being used for drive dust, and I can make that do a lot of interesting tricks, though. But I'm going to lose at least a couple of wizard levels for a while after this."

"Hey, A.J.," Joe said, "your transmission's showing a five percent decrease. Are you using lower-powered lights or something?"

There was a pause. "No . . . and you're showing the same dropoff."

Joe's eyes narrowed, and suddenly he stood up, reaching the back of the control chair and lifting himself into it. He reached out, controlling the manipulators. A moment later he spoke. "Okay, guys, you'd better get cracking. I can see the problem, and it's not pretty.

"The ice is getting thicker."

Chapter 37

"Okay," A.J. said, hearing his own exhaustion in his voice. *Short shifts for, what, three days? Four?* "Dust reports complete seal and solid ice around both doors. *Finally.*"

"*Na endlich!*" Horst agreed emphatically. "I would call for drinks all around, but we have no drinks to speak of. I suppose a sip of water and a few minutes break instead?"

"A few minutes, yes." Jackie sagged back against Horst, who gave her a quick hug. From experience A.J. knew this was mostly a symbolic gesture, even thin as the suits were overall. "But we've got to keep working."

"I can't *believe* it took this long to set the damn things in ice. It seemed so simple on paper. Heat 'em up and melt 'em in." A.J. shook his head. "This stupid moon is such a crazy combination of hospitable and utterly hostile. Even *ice* doesn't act the way you expect."

"I *did* warn you it probably wouldn't work," Brett's voice said, with only a *touch* of smugness; after all, he would much rather have been wrong, and A.J. knew it. "Temperature differential and vacuum."

"Well, I know it *now*. I suppose it's not so bad, it gave us small-scale practice on the cavern."

In the end the only way to make it work had been to seal off the area temporarily with ice and pressurize the volume to a high enough pressure that the water no longer boiled off when liquified. This allowed it to flow long enough to enter all the cracks, cover the whole doorframe and lock it solidly into the very structure of Europa.

"And we won't know for *sure* that it's going to work until we get the pressure up in the main cavern. When can we start *that*?"

"I will be setting the demolition charges to bring the cavern down in a specific manner in three hours," Madeline said. Two days had been enough for her to recover and get back into the game; Larry would be resting still for another couple. His brush with death had been *very* close and Petra was not going to take chances. *And none of us want her to, except Larry. We've been damned lucky so far, and we're not even close to out of the woods yet. We can't afford any chances above and beyond the ones we've already determined we'll take.*

"Why three hours?" Horst asked.

"Because I'm going to take a couple hours nap and get a bite to eat, because any time you work with explosives you want to be very, very sharp."

"Indeed, Agent Fathom," Hohenheim said. "And as all of you will then be working in an area just recently blasted, and this is of course itself quite dangerous, I insist that all of the rest of us take the same opportunity to rest."

He's almost always using our titles and last names.

Which ought to feel cold, mused A.J., even as he heard himself say "No argument here, General." *But it doesn't.* In point of fact, A.J. realized, he found General Hohenheim's constant formality to be somehow comforting. He thought about *why* that might be as he put down an insulating pad and leaned back to rest. *I think it's because it's so* civilized. *You get in a lifeboat situation and things get informal, which is sort of nice, but also it can remind you that you're a long way from the real home, the real* control, *that you're used to.*

A.J. had long since learned to take rest when the opportunity presented itself; he took a nap.

Sometime later, his suit buzzed. "What?"

"You actually slept four hours," Madeline's voice informed him cheerfully. "Which is good, because I'm almost done setting all the charges and I want your dust to verify that it's in exactly the right places."

"I'll be ready momentarily. Lemme grab a bite." He bounced his way to the pressurized shelter they'd put in one of the caves outside the pressure doors, dropped his helmet after entering, and grabbed a sandwich wrap. Once his initial hunger was satisfied, he brought up the displays. "Okay, I used drive dust for this, after Horst pointed out that I ought to be able to get that level of operation out of it. But that means it'll take a little longer to build up a picture."

It did *lag*, A.J. had to admit. It reminded him of the old days—what, almost twelve years ago?—when he'd had to wait, and wait, and wait for *Ariel* to send back the pictures from Phobos and then respond to his commands. Slowly, sketchily, a shadowy outline began to build up in the 3-D Virtual Retinal Display image. "Okay, starting to get something...*Damn*, this thing's complex. Horst, it's a good thing we *are* using the drive dust on this. Mapping out everywhere it's cracked, all the angles, the sheer *volume* we're having to cover.... It's ugly. Okay, Brett, you've got Maddie's placement and the characteristics of the charges, I'm sending you the full-scale map. Near as I can tell, she's in the places she wanted to be, but I haven't *any* idea if that's the right place to do the job she wants."

"Received you fine," Brett's slightly New Zealand accent answered. "The model will take a few seconds to run, it's incorporating everything we've learned so far plus the regular models."

Mentally A.J. crossed his fingers. They had to depend on Maddie's demolition skills, and the models Brett could give them. They could get *some* advice from back home, but in the end it came down to what they could do *here*.

I love my automation, USVs, all of them—no one loves 'em more than I do. But there isn't yet an automated system built that could do half the stuff we've had to do on Europa, it's still all really clever artificial stupidity. Of course, on the other hand, if human beings weren't here, we just wouldn't be bothering to do all this crazy stuff—the ships would be left to stay where they crashed, the probe would be stuck under the ice and whoever built it would have to suck it up and take whatever data they'd already gotten.

"All right, Maddie. As best I can tell, you're in the best position to do the job. No idea if it will really work, though."

Madeline gave a tired laugh. "*No* idea? Aren't your simulations giving you *some* idea?"

"Yeah, but I'd rather not look at that."

Her voice was as serious as A.J. suddenly felt. "Odds aren't good?"

"They're great. Given the situation. Which is unprecedented."

"Never tell me the odds," A.J. muttered.

"On reflection, I agree with A.J.," Maddie said, and he saw her flash a grin at him in the display. "Tell me *after* we succeed how bad my chances were."

"As you wish," Brett answered. His smile was only slightly forced.

"All right, everyone. I'm coming out." A.J. watched her make one last check of the position and securing of each of the charges, then come through the two airlock doors. "This is it. Everyone confirm your positions, please."

"Me and Helen, still under the night-black sea of Europa," Joe answered dryly.

"Thank you, Joe," Maddie said with a wry smile; A.J. gave his friend a thumbs-up. "I mean, of course, those on Europa who are in any position to *not* be affected by this maneuver."

"I'm in the base tent," A.J. said.

"Same here," Jackie said.

All the others on Europa echoed this, except for Petra Masters and Larry Conley, both of whom were onboard *Munin*, and Hohenheim, who simply said, "Beside you, Agent Fathom," since he, also, was standing just the other side of the exterior of the two makeshift airlock doors.

"Then . . . blast in ten seconds. Nine . . ."

A.J. found he was holding his breath. *If this doesn't work . . . we will have buried Helen and Joe so far*

under the ice that I don't think we'll ever *reach them.*
He closed his eyes and gave another silent prayer to
whatever might be listening. *I don't care, too much,
what happens to me . . .*

" . . . six . . . five . . . four . . ."

. . . Just let us save her and my friend Joe.

" . . . two . . . one . . . *Fire in the hole!*"

Compared to the quake that had caused all the
trouble, the detonations weren't even a quiver. There
was nothing to see or feel this far away, and the
"technically an atmosphere" was a harder vacuum
than almost anything produced on Earth; no sound
would penetrate.

And Europa's feeble gravity conspired to draw out
the tension. For a moment, it appeared that all the
preparation, all the worry, had been for nothing; A.J.
couldn't see a single sign of movement anywhere.
"Um . . . Maddie . . ."

"Wait," she said calmly.

There. The telemetry showed movement now, one set
of Faerie Dust staying where it had been, the other
sets moving away from their prior comrades. "We
have separation, multiple areas." He noticed some red
dots. "Five charges still undetonated. Is that correct?"

"Confirmed," Brett and Madeline said simultaneously. "Five charges remain to be detonated."

A collection of Faerie Dust near the doorway areas
transmitted the scene; multiple showers of powdered
ice from detonation points, the powder falling ahead
of the gigantic slabs now moving downward, shattering the remaining ethereal decorations to powder,
destroying beauty a million years in the making for
the sake of two lives that still might never be saved.

And I'd sacrifice this and every museum on Earth for Helen, he admitted to himself, even as he winced in sympathetic horror with the breaking of each unique, irreplaceable formation.

Three huge slabs were in motion now, their bases striking the cavern's floor almost simultaneously, then tilting ponderously, majestically, terrifying in its vastness, white and deep blue and gray and black moving through the air like the descent of a Jotun's axe, and suddenly they were shadows, dim suggestions of movement as two of the lights remaining were crushed.

But now the unstoppable collapse was visible in an eldritch outline of innumerable tiny flickers and flashes as the ice collided, cracked, split. "What the hell is *that?*" murmured Horst.

"Triboluminescence, or more precisely, fractoluminescence," Larry said, awe in his voice as he answered. "Light's generated by the breaking of the ice itself. I've seen it in miniature... but this ain't miniature."

Two blazes of actinic light momentarily illuminated the entire cavern, a strobe-light picture of cataclysm in progress; colliding slabs of ice the size of skyscrapers filled the space with flying icy powder. "Oh my God..." A.J. heard himself say. *There's no way this can work, no way, we've* killed *them!*

"Second-stage detonations complete," Brett's voice said calmly. "Alpha slab now cut at the sixty-percent mark. Rotation beginning."

Watch, dammit. If it works, if it doesn't, you damn well better watch!

The simulations hadn't given the impression of size, the chaos of collision, and he still could barely make out what Brett was talking about, how the largest slab's top had just been cut by two charges so it was folding over and sliding slightly backwards. *God, this is* insane. *Yet . . . it's the only chance we've got.*

"Contact on all primaries," Brett said. "Box forming. Top coming down."

A three-sided box. It was such a simple idea, yet so impossibly hard to imagine even Maddie could pull this off. *And Brett's tied into the data feeds now, he can see more than* I *can right now.* "Brett, are the sides intact? Are they *holding?*"

"No sign of cracks in the primaries yet," Brett said. "Top closure impact in four, three, two, one . . ."

The slab slammed down atop the other three—still settling into uneasy equilibrium—in a spray of atomized ice and a blaze of fractoluminescence. *Stay intact,* please . . .

"Third-stage detonations on schedule."

Now the final charges went off, and *this* was the most insane part of the entire crazy idea. The area had to be sealed off and held down, held down so securely that over a megapascal of pressure, a hundred fifty pounds per square inch, could be held back over such a volume that the total pressure would be millions of tons. Not all the mass ever lifted into space by the entire human species could hope to resist such absolute power.

But the power of an entire moon just might.

Slowly, inexorably, the top of the cavern crumbled, began to come down. First a shower, barely a trickle, a few thousand tons of granite-hard ice sifting down about and over the ice-box, which now looked utterly vulnerable, tiny compared to the slow-motion juggernaut of destruction that was bearing down upon it. As more and more of the cavern collapsed, larger chunks rained down, greater fall meaning greater impact... but the box had been designed to reinforce itself, take pressure, and once the first shower started building up around it, that would brace it some, but... *but the model only said it* could *work, not that it* would.

And now there was nothing to see, the aggregation of Faerie Dust that had served as a camera hammered and scattered, some even crushed, by the impact of the ice all around it. Only scattered sensor readings now, things moving too fast, too *huge*, to be apprehended in their entirety by scattered little sensor motes.

The chaotic vibrations reached a crescendo... and began to diminish. "Topside sensors show a settling in corresponding area. Fractures propagated all the way to surface, settling now."

"A.J.," Madeline said quietly. "Your turn."

For a moment he couldn't make himself do it. *What if we failed?*

But he'd never know one way or another if he didn't try. "On it. Trying to reestablish network connectivity."

The problem was of course that he had to force a signal through the ice, and then get it relayed. The motes could vary their transmission frequency quite widely, but the power at their disposal remained exceedingly low even at full charge. The motes were also going to be very low on power at this point; unlike places on Earth or even Mars, there simply wasn't any energy around to scavenge. What they had left was whatever they hadn't used yet. He'd charged them fully before this stunt, but still...

Getting something. "Okay. Preliminary results show I'm down about seventy-three percent in connectivity.

Packet relay's going to be a bitch, especially through ice rather than free space. Network rebuild proceeding from inner lock." He set the network up to update the free-space transmission range in the direction of *Zarathustra*.

Well, there's the first good news. Free space transmission distance: 2.4130 meters. "Integrity of inner lock and surrounding ice appears to be complete. No sign of additional cracking. We've lost about half of the entry hallway to the door, but it's still got two, two and a half meters of clear space on the other side. Rest is filled with ice.

Now the hard part. God my gut hurts, I'm so tense. "As we expected, all connection with *Zarathustra* was lost; no relay circuits survived and if any internal relays near the floor of the cavern still exist they can't transmit through this much ice anyway. Network rebuild continuing."

He tried to keep the tension and fear from his voice as he went on. "Network now extends ten meters out from original entryway." *Free space transmission distance: 0.0005 meters.* "Ice is still compacting, some sign of slow pressure-driven flow."

"That's good," Jackie said, her tone not fooling A.J. any more than his was probably fooling them. "That'll do a lot of the sealing for us, before we start venting water vapor."

"Twenty meters, still all ice." He swallowed. *Zarathustra's one hundred twenty meters out and about thirty down. And we need at least twenty meters of clear space around them to operate Athena in.*

Free space transmission distance, 0.0060 meters. "Forty meters, ice mostly larger chunks here, but still cracking under pressure. Picking up some fractoluminescence. Ice sand is sifting down, probably will end up binding to the larger chunks."

Free space transmission distance: 0.0000 meters. Damn. "I think I've hit the edge of one of the slabs. *Huge* solid block, beyond the limits of the current network to resolve. Sparse nodes at this point, having to build network around edges to find route farther in. *If there is a route farther in.* He felt nausea, now, and swallowed. *There* has *to be a way in.*

Transmission distance: 0.0023 meters. "Found corner, definitely intersection of Alpha and Beta slabs." He brought his rush of relief up short with two inarguable facts. "Power for network dropping rapidly. Even duty-cycling among all candidate nodes won't let me keep this going much longer. And we've still got a ways to go."

Have to set up a cycling wave, move out, come back with summary data, minimum calculations, do the calculations at the base station here. Won't have much left even then, given the volume of data's going to be pretty big with the incoming relay. Free space transmission distance: 0.0002 meters. "Solid ice at seventy meters. Seventy-five. Eighty..."

Almost out of power. He heard Jackie whispering something under her breath. It might have been a prayer, or maybe just hope.

"Still ice at ninety meters. Network response very sluggish. Ninety-five meters, *still* ice, dammit, I—"

Free space transmission distance: 52.6010 meters.

For a moment he couldn't quite read the numbers; they were suddenly all blurry. But he didn't have to read them after seeing them once. "There's an empty void fifty-two meters wide at the ninety-six-and-a-half-meter mark. *And there!* A flash on the emission band of *Zarathustra*'s headlights!"

He stopped talking. He couldn't talk for a few minutes, just sat there, feeling tears streaming down his face in relief, and he didn't give a damn that everyone in the base tent could see it, was probably staring at him. "You did it, Maddie. God*damn*, you *did it!*"

It sounded like ten times as many people were cheering as were actually available in the Europa system. When it finally died down, he heard Maddie's voice—*was it just a tiny bit unsteady? I guess she's got every right to be worried too*—say, "We *all* did it, A.J. Almost everyone had something to say about this—and I admit it freely—crazy idea. And we were lucky."

"Seven times lucky," Brett said. "Best guess was you had one in seven of pulling this off, after all the numbers were in."

There was a moment of quiet. "Then thank *you*, Brett, for not telling me earlier," Maddie said finally. "A.J., can we get a message to Joe and Helen?"

Damn again. "Not now. The last power of my nearby relays is kaput. We've got to get into the cavern before we'll be able to do anything more."

"Then we should begin doing that immediately," Hohenheim said. "All those near end-of-shift, please go rest. The remainder, join me and Mia. It is once more *Athena*'s turn." His smile was bright. "And this time she has only ninety-six meters to go."

Chapter 38

"I *hate* this silence," Helen said. The too-cool interior of *Zarathustra*, its vertical and thus alien orientation, and especially the *not-knowing* were beginning to wear on her, even through the fascination of where she was and what she was learning.

"We're still alive to hear the sound of silence," Joe pointed out. "That's a good thing. And I can give you some more good news."

"What's that?"

Joe pointed up. "Well, we knew they detonated the charges—we saw some of that on the relay before it went dead. And I just did some test flashes, and according to the calculations it's still going into empty air—or rather, vacuum—at about the same level as before. Which means they didn't completely bury us."

"That *does* sound like good news," she admitted, but she couldn't ignore the nagging nervousness. "They *could* have buried us enough to make the whole rescue impossible, though, couldn't they?"

"Maybe," Joe conceded reluctantly. "Though as long as they can reach us at all there's still a chance. I admit they really *do* need space to work *Athena*, and

if *Athena* hits *Zarathustra*—even a glancing blow—
we're probably done. And the vibrations of impact
were pretty big, so they *did* bring down one hell of
a lot of the ceiling."

That sparked a thought. "I wonder..." She grabbed
up the camera and carefully made her way down to
the bottom. "Dim the lights a bit, would you?"

Joe complied. "What's up?"

"Well, it's effectively always black down here, so any
living creatures would either have to make their own
light, or they'd have to sense things by other means, just
as deep-sea creatures on Earth do," Helen answered,
trying to let her eyes adapt to the blackness below.
"One of the most common senses would be acoustic
or vibration sensing. And any kind of unusual vibration
would probably be worth investigating—it might be a
new food source, unless the type of vibration seemed
dangerous. So all the activity up there, culminating in
the huge vibrations involved in collapsing the cavern—"

"—might draw something to investigate. Yeah, I see."
Joe glanced up. "But the quakes have got to make a
lot of vibrations too, so why would our—comparatively
tiny—activity be different?"

"Patterns, Joe," she said. *Was that...something?* It
was very hard to tell, sometimes, if you were seeing
anything. Everything from the other tiny creatures
moving across the glass to the annoying "floaters"
inside her own eye could seem for a moment like
distant, phantom objects barely visible against the
velvet darkness. "The exact pattern of the sounds
will be like a fingerprint." She smiled. "Remember,
I'm married to Mister Sensor himself, he's given me
lots of lectures on the subject of detecting particular

signals. Animals are very, *very* good at discriminating
between various signals, and I'm sure that the acoustic or vibration signature of a deliberately detonated
and collapsed cavern is a lot different from that of a
general earthquake."

Something is *moving.* She triggered the camera. "I
think we have company coming, Joe."

Joe Buckley did not have an enthusiastic expression
at the thought of something unknown being on its way
to visit, and—to tell the truth—she wasn't entirely
happy about it. But on the other hand, there wasn't
much either of them could do about it, so she might
as well at least record it. "What, exactly, is coming?"

"I haven't any real idea, Joe. I just know it's a lot
larger than anything we've seen before." The undefin-
able shape disappeared into the unrelieved gloom.
Then it reappeared again, from its original direction,
but this time she thought it was just a tiny bit closer. *I
don't know if I like that.* It reminded her of something,
and as she watched it vanish again and slowly reappear
from another direction, this time definitely closer, a
faint luminescence outlining what seemed to be a long
winged cylinder, she realized that its motions were very
much like those of a deep-ocean shark, slowly examining
some unknown object in its patrol area.

"*How much* larger?"

"I'm not sure, it's hard to tell without any sense
of scale." She thought for a moment. "You know, I'll
bet we *could* get a sense of scale if your computers
are up for some instant triangulation."

Joe raised an eyebrow. She glanced back down,
saw the unknown creature disappearing again. "If
you flash both side rear lights at max power, and

take an image from both rear cameras, you'd get two shadow-cones going off from it which would give you a really good..."

"...stereo match, yes I would. You'll become one of us engineers yet, Helen. That kind of image comparison's built right into *Zarathustra*'s autonomic nav circuits. Let me just tweak the parameters a bit... Okay. Next time it shows up, tell me when and I'll hit the lights for a split second; close your eyes so it doesn't blind you, you want to still be dark adapted afterwards."

"Got you." She watched closely, waiting.

Once more the unknown swam lazily into view, the vague luminous outline hinting at undulation and texture. "Hit it, Joe!"

She closed her eyes; even so, the blaze of light was momentarily dazzling. She blinked her eyes clear. "Joe, did you get it?" There was no sign of the phantom creature visible now.

"Got it. Range was...a hundred meters away. The visible part of the thing covered eight degrees, which means it was about fourteen meters long."

"Jesus. That's almost as long as a T-Rex."

"And ugly, too," Joe said. "Take a look at—oh, *SHIT!*"

Helen looked back down and leapt backward reflexively, smacking herself into the forward port.

Flashing in multiple colors, in patterns sharp and clashing, the creature was rushing up from the depths. *The flash...it must have seemed like a challenge or a threat.* The winged-torpedo shape, something like the body of a squid but tripartite—a familiar body plan indeed, the same body plan that had got her *into* this mess—the thing was several times longer than *Bemmius Secordii* had ever been. Backward-pointing spines covered its exterior surface, which in the lowered glow of the rear lights seemed nobbled, gray-green and tough like rhino hide. It broke off the charge only ten meters from *Zarathustra*, and the wash of its passage made the whole ten-ton rover wobble. In that moment it had snapped at the water, a threat-gesture that exposed a three-sided mouth with black cutting planes and shredding points farther in. Short, thick grasping tentacles writhed at each corner of the mouth, and at the base of each tentacle glittered a small, but unmistakable yellow-green eye.

"Dammit, that's pissed it off. What do we do now?"

Helen had no idea. On the one hand, lighting it up had triggered the problem; on the other, if they didn't do it again that might be taken as a sign of weakness. *Compound the error or be too cautious?* Still...the thing had other senses. "Wait and hope, Joe. We're *not* living, and this thing might be able to tell that in a few minutes."

"Maybe, I guess." She saw him strapping into the seat. "You'd better get braced, though."

She had already had the same thought; even so, she had barely grabbed one side of the seat straps when the thing tore through the water at them again, this time missing *Zarathustra* by less than five meters, the short tentacles lashing out at closest approach and nearly brushing the rover's side. "What the hell can we do?"

Joe's face was grim, reflected in the curved forward port. "Improvise."

As the thing appeared again, Joe engaged the drive, spun the wheels quickly; the force against the water bounced *Zarathustra* upward and sideways, and at the unexpected movement the monster balked, sheered off at the last minute. She shuddered as she heared a rumbling shriek and realized the exterior microphones had just transmitted the thing's vocalization of anger.

This time it arrowed in from the side, coming in to grasp the entire rover, tentacles whipping out, curling around the rear end of *Zarathustra*.

The jolt nearly gave her whiplash as the creature let go, *thrust* the rover away and ran with a screech of obvious pain. "Ow...What happened?"

Despite the gravity of the situation, Joe chuckled. "Grabbed the radiators, that's what happened. Bet he's sucking his burned little tentacles and wondering what *that* was."

Helen wondered if it was over, now. But she remembered studying about apex predators. It depended on what *type* you were dealing with, and exactly what instinctual triggers you set off. She was suddenly very afraid she knew what was coming next.

And there it was, looming up, cruising at speed along the very top of the ice. *We're a rival, something challenging it in its section of this huge ocean, and once a duel like this happens it won't back down unless we beat it in some way it understands.*

The thing curved around, circled once, then shrieked another challenge and lunged.

But at that same time she saw Joe make a convulsive movement in the control chair.

Both manipulator arms, rated at a ton and a quarter lift capacity, lashed outward. One of the reinforced carbonan arms tore straight through one of the Europan monster's grasping tentacles; the other smashed directly to the side of the open mouth, shattering two of the cutting plates—and plunging into the yellow-green eye.

It wasn't so much a sound as a red-hot dagger slammed through both her eardrums, and *Zarathustra* rang like a bell with a final smashing impact. But the thing was fleeing, trailing phosphorescent blood, yielding the field to this immobile yet painfully dangerous foe.

"Good work, Joe."

He grunted. "I hope so. As long as he doesn't have any friends." He indicated a light on the control panel. "And as long as *our* friends don't take too long."

She could see the slow amber blink, and a sinking lead weight seemed to form in her gut. "What is it?"

"Outer lock seal," he said. "I'm not showing any water in the lock *yet* . . ." he continued, "but it's damaged somehow. In some ways, we'd better *hope* it's going to start leaking soon."

She stared at Joe, puzzled. "Um . . . why?"

"Because one of the *other* ways it could have been damaged is to have the door warped enough that it *won't open.*"

Chapter 39

A dull *thuddoom!* echoed through Madeline's suit and vibrated in her boots as all the compressed water vapor in the tunnel abruptly vented, the momentary hurricane tearing at her and the others before turning back to essential, silent vacuum.

"We're *through!*" Jackie shouted, and Maddie joined in the cheer. "Maddie, A.J.'s sacked out. Do you think—"

"No problem. Just get *Athena* far enough out of this tunnel so the rest of us can get out too. Then I'll want to check the whole area's integrity before we start faking up the atmosphere."

"You've got it. Mia?"

The Norwegian engineer nodded, and she and Jackie quickly got *Athena* to move forward now that there was no impediment between her and open space.

Maddie bounced over to the jury-rigged lightbar which served as the communication interface and hooked in fresh power packs. "Joe?"

"Maddie!"

The instant response made her feel suddenly ten years younger. "You're both all right?"

"For now."

Tension returned. Joe wouldn't say that if . . . "What's the bad news?"

"Well, the *good* news is that we've got some spectacular footage and evidence of a really advanced ecosystem here on Europa," Joe said in his usual overly-casual description of disaster. "The *bad* news is that the local wildlife got very frisky with *Zarathustra* and the lock's gone to amber alert."

Oh dear God. "Are you leaking?"

"Not yet, but sensors show an increase in humidity in the seal area. It's *going* to leak, and it's not going to take all that long. Now, I don't know if the *inner* door will have any problems or not, but it wasn't designed to hold *water,* just varying types of atmosphere, or lack thereof. I'm pretty damn sure the pumps won't handle it. Now, the *other* good news is that I don't think it's jammed shut—I can't *test* it, but all the indicators are that it should be able to open."

She took a breath and made herself relax before she spoke again, and gave silent thanks that almost everyone else was currently resting. "Do you have a guess as to when the real leak will start?"

She heard him sigh. "Not really, Maddie. But when it starts, it will get progressively worse, faster and faster; ten atmospheres is no joke, and the seals weren't made for it."

"Well, it hasn't started yet, and we're here, so we'll be getting you out of there as soon as we can." She stood. "I've got work to do, so I'm cutting out for now. I love you."

"Love you too, Maddie."

She made sure the connection was off, then took

the RF transmitter off her back and started it running. Slowly, the display in her VRD began to sparkle with the awakening of the Faerie Dust, which was now scavenging power from the powerful transmission. "Okay, we're in business. I'm checking the walls. Now, Jackie, you said that leaks will tend to be self-sealing?"

"With a vengeance, yes. Water vapor going out will condense and freeze almost instantly. That's both an advantage and part of our problem."

"I had a feeling you didn't sound as confident lately as we did a while ago."

"Oh, the plan sounds great on paper, but there's a big practical problem. Brett's models say we still *might* pull it off, but..."

Maddie knew that dancing around a problem was a way of trying to cushion the blow, and she appreciated the consideration... but sometimes it was like pulling teeth! "Mia, do you know what Jackie's talking about, or will I have to drag it out of her?"

"Do you understand how a steam turbine works?"

She raised an eyebrow, thinking. *Obviously this has something to do with the problem.* "High-pressure steam pushes a set of blades around, condenses, gets reheated until it boils, and around it goes again, heating to pressure, cooling, boiling... Oh, damnation."

"Yes, I didn't think I would need to do the full explanation. At somewhat over a megapascal, the boiling point of water is about one hundred eighty C."

She closed her eyes. *What's the point, then?* But she remembered what Jackie had said. "So the water will be condensing out as fast as we make it into steam?"

"That's the key," Jackie said, in a tone that sounded like she was working on convincing herself. "Brett and

I don't think so. *Athena* is a nuclear reactor *made* to melt ice, and melt it *fast*, and that means it can make one hell of a lot of steam. As more of the steam condenses, it will both be sealing the chamber *and* making it *smaller*, because it will mostly freeze on the inside. That will make the chamber very strong, and have lower volume, so we're now sure it can hold the pressure. And we *think* that *Athena* will be able to vaporize water fast enough to outpace the freezing, especially since freezing releases heat—heat of crystallization—and the temperature will rise significantly, and of course because we'll have the carbon dioxide and ammonia coming with the water.

"You can't melt this mass of ice easily, or very fast, just from air temperature alone, so pretty soon we'll hit an equilibrium volume and pressure will go up; water will still condense, but *Athena* will be throwing steam and gas up faster than it can condense out. We think."

Madeline *desperately* wanted to believe this would work. "But *Athena* was only going through a half meter or so per minute."

Jackie managed a grin, and in her nervousness seemed to be trying to emulate A.J. "Ahh, yes, but that was ice at almost minus two hundred, and we had to be careful because of the things we might hit on the way down. I'm not having to deal with *either* of those here. The ice here is almost at melting point already and we're going to drive her around boring holes as fast as she possibly can go, pulling her up when she gets near the surface—until we get close to the right pressure, and *then* we'll let her go down and vaporize the water as it tries to get past her.

I figure if we brace her really well in a bore she could hold something close to four atmospheres back by herself, so if we can get up to point six or point seven megapascals we can use the ocean itself to push things the rest of the way."

Madeline was already working the scenario over in her head—she wasn't an engineer as such, but rule-of-thumb estimation and jury-rigging was something of a must-have skill in her old profession. *Jackie's trying not to emphasize just how hard this is going to be. I can't blame her, really. We need to get the story straight for everyone else, because we can't have doubts slowing us up.*

"A small chance is better than *no* chance, Jackie," she said finally. "I'm not going to describe the problem to Joe and Helen. Joe might—probably already has—guess at the challenges we'll be facing, but I'll let him decide if he wants to drop it on Helen; I won't tell them myself."

Jackie nodded, then glanced at her. "You didn't sound all that relaxed *before* we gave you the bad news," she said. "What'd Joe tell you."

Maddie summarized the situation. "So we have even more reason to hurry."

"Then it's time to sound the starting bell," Mia said. "*General*! We are ready to begin! It is the last stretch of this race, and we need everyone on the track!"

Madeline looked down, where her husband and friend lay suspended in pitch-black water. *Somehow, this has to work. Somehow we will* make *it* work.

Chapter 40

"They should have started trying to break us out by *now*," Helen said. She knew it sounded like she was whining, but it had been more than two weeks since they had been stuck under Europa's steel-hard ice. Quick sponge baths, especially ones taken in ten-degree-C air, did not make up for lack of even the Spartan cleaning regimen available in *Nebula Storm*, let alone the comparative luxury of the hot showers in Europa Base.

And *Zarathustra* was starting to *stink* as well. The air was okay to breathe, but she suspected that being suspended vertically was impairing the plumbing. *If there'd been more of us, I bet the tank would be overfull by now...and we'd have a pool of something unmentionable on the bottom.*

"It's not all that easy, you know," Joe said. "There's a lot of space to fill."

"I'm not entirely innumerate," she snapped, then closed her eyes. "Sorry, Joe. I shouldn't take it out on you. But I could look up a few things, and make a few guesses, and things don't make sense. When you turn ice to steam you get about sixteen hundred times as much gas as you had water, a little less with ice because it expands a few percent. But even if the area they had above was a box sixty meters on a side and twenty high—and I know it's not, it's more a cut-off triangular pyramid, which has less volume—that's only about forty-five cubic meters of water they have to vaporize to fill it. Even at its old speed *Athena* should have gone through that in an hour and a half."

Joe grinned, but there was a sad edge to the grin. "That's not bad back-of-the-envelope guessing there. Actually, if all your principles held, they only needed about fifteen cubic meters. But . . . they don't hold. First, a lot of it's freezing out as they go, so they have to replace it. Second, that volume's at standard temperature and pressure. We have to build the pressure from *nothing*, and then keep going. Remember, ten times the pressure, which means we need a *lot* of melted ice."

A low humming rumble transmitted itself through the air as she absorbed that. *Athena*'s violent conversion of ice and water to steam caused vibrations throughout the ice that echoed into the ocean. The noise grew louder as the nuclear melt-probe drove downward, then stopped for a short time as the probe was pulled back up and repositioned, to start faintly again and grow louder. So far she hadn't seen any new visitors, but the longer that utterly-unknown noise went on . . . "You've known this for a long time."

"Figured most of it out as soon as I realized what the situation was, yeah. And I didn't tell you because there wasn't much point." Joe shrugged. "Now that you've asked—the lowdown is that I'm giving us a one-in-five they can pull it off."

She nodded. "Better odds than I guessed." She looked at the control panel. "Have we got a leak yet?"

Joe studied readouts on the panel and in his VRD. "Not yet, but...I'm guessing soon. No liquid water, but the humidity keeps going up in the seal area."

"How soon is soon?"

He shrugged. "If I plot a rough graph...maybe a day or two. Once the leak starts, I think we've got another day before it becomes critical for the inner door. If the inner door can hold the pressure, then we may be fine."

She looked at him, and could see even through the helmet that Joe's usual casual expression was absent. "But you don't think it will."

"No. If you want my honest opinion...?"

"Might as well."

"I figure the door will blow right in as soon as the pressure hits six or seven atmospheres. Then we die very fast."

She nodded again.

For a long time neither of them said anything. The buzzing hum of *Athena* ceased, then faintly restarted. She chuckled suddenly.

"I could use a laugh. What's so funny?"

She looked upward, grinning faintly. "I just realized, it must look like Swiss cheese, or a beehive, by now. All those holes spaced all over the floor..."

Joe chortled. "I'll bet it does. And you'd better watch out where you walk now."

She glanced down. No sign of movement below. She watched a few minutes, but saw nothing yet.

More minutes passed.

"Joe," she said finally.

"Yes?"

"We've done a hell of a lot, haven't we?"

He snorted. "Let's not start the predeath farewell yet."

"I can't help it; I'd like to be ready."

"Maybe I shouldn't have told you the odds."

She shook her head. "Joe, I wanted to know the truth."

"Well, maybe I should have told you the *other* odds."

She stared at him, puzzled. "*What* 'other odds'?"

He pointed up. "Up there? That's Madeline Fathom. Madeline Fathom *Buckley*, a woman so far out of my league that I didn't even realize just how far out she *was* for years. But for some reason she took a hell of a liking to me. She's crazy enough to *marry* me.

"She's also just crazy enough to figure out some way to rescue us, because that's exactly what she *does*. So I figure that our *real* odds are pretty damn good, because I'm down here, and she's up there, and that's *not* the way she wants it."

She laughed suddenly, and gripped his hand. "I guess you're right."

"Damn straight. She held up *Mars* when it was trying to collapse on us, what's a meter or two of ice?"

Without warning, a thundering thrumming noise vibrated *Zarathustra* like the string of an enormous bass, a sound like a jet in an earthquake. "*What the—*"

At the same time Joe let out a whoop that almost deafened her, even over that frightening noise. "*That's it!*"

"What? What's it?" She couldn't imagine what could be making a sound like that, but Joe obviously knew.

"*Athena!* They've built up pressure! They've let her break through and take on the whole damn Europan ocean as a feedstock!" With a little difficulty, Joe spun his seat around in a victory circle. "The odds just went way, way up, like one in two now. They don't have to move *Athena*, and the fact that we're still *hearing* that beautiful, beautiful noise means that the pressure of the ocean hasn't kicked *Athena* back up her bore. She's taking everything Europa has and vaporizing it out the back."

Lights flashed. "Joe?"

"I hear it, Maddie! Good news!"

"*Very* good news, Joe!" Helen could hear tentative, strained relief in the other woman's voice. "So far she's holding, and Jackie says if she stays put another few minutes she'll be confident that nothing's going to move *Athena* out of position. You can almost *see* the pressure rising."

"Which leaves you one problem."

"We're working on it. The solution may involve explosives."

"With you involved? I'd be disappointed if it didn't."

Helen glanced down as the two continued their conversation, and dropped carefully back down to the rear window. With this new sound, who knew what might happen?

And there it was. A shimmer in the depths, almost invisible. *Please, God, not that same thing. Let it have learned its lesson.*

She knew that *Zarathustra* would almost certainly not survive another confrontation.

The shimmer again. No, wait. *Two* shimmers now. Now one. *What am I seeing . . . ?* She tried to make sense of the vague, phantom shapes. *Could be one big creature that's sometimes lighting one part of its*

*body, sometimes two. Light seems to be a signaling
device here, at least for some species; that's why the
one creature still has eyes. Maybe it's also a lure. I
suppose if you can see and a lot of other species can't,
you might be able to parlay that into an advantage
even here. Lure wouldn't make sense in that case,
though.*

The lights faded into the distance . . . then returned
from the same direction. Like the other, it was a little
closer . . . *Hmm. But that wasn't the sharklike motion of
the first thing. That was something approaching, then
backing up. Something curious, I think, checking to
see if what it's seeing is a predator. It might still be
dangerous, but it's not moving the way a shark circles.*

Still . . . "Joe," she said, "I hate to interrupt, but I
think *Athena*'s noise has attracted another visitor. You
should probably strap in."

"Damn. Maddie, I have to go." Joe swung himself
into the pilot's seat, grasped the manipulator controls.
"Not seeing much on the camera. What've you got?
Not another of those things, I hope."

"I don't *think* so. It's not moving at all the same. I
haven't tried doing anything to get a range on it, but
if I assume the thing's generating about the same level
of brightness and that the water's about the same level
of transparent as it was last time, then it's roughly the
same size." The distant-but-a-little-closer light seemed
generally similar in shape, maybe a little misshapen,
a bulge partway down. But on this scale, fish, sharks,
dolphins, and submarines had similar shapes.

Suddenly the misshapen section moved, separated.
*Two separate animals! One staying near the other,
maybe touching the other! Mother and child?* The two

shapes hovered motionless now; they were somewhat similar, both fairly long, probably a similar body plan to the huge predator. The smaller one was only a few meters long. The larger one seemed broader, not just longer but more heavily built.

She wished that she dared brighten the lights to get a look, but she didn't want a repeat of the last encounter. Maybe these things wouldn't react that way... but they might. And if it *was* a parent and child, the parent would likely react—like many Earth animals' parents—with extreme violence to any perceived threat.

Once more the two rejoined, retreated—though this time to just the limit of visibility—and waited.

"Talk to me, Helen."

"I'm seeing a pattern of curiosity. Approach, wait, back off, wait. Whatever it is wants to find out what these strange noises and objects are, but wants to make sure it's not some kind of threat. Lots of animals have similar behavior on Earth, and it's a perfectly sensible strategy; new events and creatures have potential to benefit you, but they're also potentially dangerous, and you have to be very careful how you approach them."

Now the joined shape moved forward, even closer; they separated, and the smaller one darted off to the side and up—on the side farthest, she noted, from the whining rumble of *Athena. Now that's interesting. I wonder what it's up to?*

The larger creature hung motionless; she could just barely make out some projections fore and aft that might be tentacles or fins. *That would be similar to the other creature, and again the same body plan we've found in the biosphere of our favorite alien visitors.*

The smaller creature crossed back over the field of view, closer, but moving quickly, still blurred. There was a bright flash. "What the hell...?"

"What is it?"

"That flash looked like one of our rear lights."

"The things can mimic packaged LEDs? I'm impressed."

"Maybe... but it looked almost like a reflection."

"Nothing says animals can't have reflective parts. Isn't that why things like cats have that eyeshine thing going on?" Joe asked.

"Well... yes," she said, trying to figure out where the small creature had gone now (though "small" was relative; she was pretty sure that even the smaller one was bigger than General Hohenheim). "But I meant it looked like a flash from a *mirror*. The reflective material in cats' eyes doesn't really look like that."

"Oh. Well, I—"

Helen gave a gasp of startlement as the smaller creature suddenly swam into view from the side, and halted, almost framed in the center of the rear viewport, hanging only ten meters from the end of *Zarathustra*.

She stared, her mind almost blank, and heard herself say "Oh... my... *God.*"

"What? Helen—!" Joe didn't dare unstrap in case it was an emergency. Then he looked in the part of the monitors that covered the rear camera. "Jesus!"

Hovering in the center of the gently-glowing lights of *Zarathustra*, now drifting forward, now easing back, the creature stared at *Zarathustra* (or... *at* me?) through three large, golden eyes, each between a pair of complex tentacles. The whole creature was perhaps

306 Eric Flint & Ryk Spoor

four meters long, the streamlined body triangular in cross-section with flaring fins that rippled to move it in its cautious approach-and-retreat.

But that wasn't the source of Helen's disbelief; even the fact that the creature, with its multibranching arms and large eyes and tripartite beak, gently gaping and closing as the thing focused its triple stare from one point of the strange invader of its world to another, looked eerily like the reconstructions of *Bemmius Secordii* could not have shocked Helen into near-speechless incredulity.

No.

What kept her staring raptly back at their visitor, what had Joe sitting immobile and unresponsive to Madeline's increasingly insistent calls, was what those complex, jointed tentacle-arms were gripping.

Shining silver in the light, shaft curved in strange yet deliberate ways, yet utterly, instantly recognizable. Artificial. Metallic. Impossible.

A spear.

Chapter 41

"Bemmie? There's a living *Bemmie* down there?" Jackie said, incredulously. "I don't believe it!" She drove another securing spike down, making sure *Athena* was now thoroughly immobilized. She let the fountain of steam blow her backward, kept working her body to shake off any ice that tried to form. *Less is forming now, a lot less. Temperature is really starting to go up.*

Helen gave a laugh that still sounded like a woman half in shock. "Don't believe it. That's not *Bemmius Secordii*, or even an adapted version."

"Huh? What do you mean?" A.J. demanded. Jackie wiped off her faceplate and moved over to where they were starting to assemble a rig to try and break through the ice. "What else *could* it be?"

"There's several morphological differences I'm seeing—small ones probably from your point of view, but enough so I'm pretty sure this is a very different animal; for example, the forward manipulative tendrils *bifurcate*, they don't trifurcate twice and then bifurcate, and there's four stages, so they have sixteen fingers instead of eighteen. If there *were* actual Bemmies living in Europa—after being bioformed to fit the environment—they died out millions of years ago. I can't imagine such a lifeform staying stable for sixty-five million years. But I *can* easily imagine that other lifeforms, maybe domestic ones that then went feral, could eventually evolve to intelligence, and to us they'd look very similar indeed." There was a catch in her voice. "Enough that it does, I admit, get to me. I'm . . . meeting Bemmie, or as close as is possible."

"I do not understand, though," said Horst. "How can they have metal? That is an *ocean*. No refineries, no forging, nothing of that sort. And what sort of metal could they use in that salty sea, that would not dissolve too fast to use?"

"Well," said Joe, "I can answer the last question. According to the spectral returns I can get off our friend's spear—a spear he's now using to gently poke our hull, and if he starts getting near the wrong areas I'm going to have to find a way to discourage him—he's using something that's almost pure titanium."

"*Titanium?*" The disbelief was echoed by multiple voices. "Joe, are you sure you're getting the right breathing mix down there?" asked A.J., only partially in a joking tone. "Hallucinations are starting to sound like the more reasonable explanation for what you're seeing."

"I know it sounds crazy, but blame *your* sensors for what I'm seeing, not my air. Which other than being a lot more, er, fragant than Helen or I would like, is just fine, thanks.

"Damn. I wish there was some way to get a good high-bandwidth channel down there. I'd like—"

"Hey!" Joe said. There was the sound of *Zarathustra*'s wheels spinning in water. "Yeah, watch where you stick that thing, guy," he muttered. He spoke up again to the others. "Our native explorer was getting awfully close to the lock. He backed off when I revved, though."

Jackie was thinking, even as she helped A.J. move one of the supports for the icebreaking rig into place. "Titanium. Why does that seem familiar somehow?"

It was something about Ceres, she suddenly thought with certainty. Something she'd heard, something that the news had included...

And then she had it. "Helen, back on Ceres—the plants and other engineered sessile things. Didn't the report say some of them seemed to be concentrating metal?"

"Oh..." Helen went silent for a moment, and then continued, "Ohh, now, that's *very* clever, Bemmie. You *knew* you were preparing to colonize somewhere completely underwater, so how would you deal with that problem? Make a way to *grow* your tools, of course. Then even if a disaster happens to your infrastructure, you're not stuck back before the Stone Age."

A.J. scratched his head; this was a very silly-looking gesture when one was wearing a suit. "Er...I guess, yeah, that's actually very smart, but...*titanium?*"

"It's not at all unprecedented," Helen said, sounding more certain. "Some varieties of Earth plants— horsetails, and I think nettles—can have upwards of eighty parts per million of titanium. Design a plant or something like it that concentrates titanium into its tissues and give that concentration some useful advantage for the plant, and the general trait will probably propagate itself for a long, long time. And when this species reached intelligence, perhaps it found these very tough species and started farming them, choosing the most tractable and performing a sort of... of *bonsai* on them, creating spear trees or something like that."

"Spear trees. I like that," A.J. said with a grin. "So what's Bemmius Newguy doing?"

"*Bemmius Novus sapiens*, so to speak, has come back. He has eyes, so I wonder if he can see inside here. Sometimes I think he can see me."

"He might," Joe said. "I dunno if he's going to realize that you're a separate animal."

"Separate or not, I'm going to try to communicate with him," Helen said. "They use light patterns for *something*, so I'm going to see if I can get anything from him using light."

"Just be careful. Don't want to trigger a feeling of threat."

"I'll be careful, believe me. I'm going to use the spot illuminator on my helmet, not the main lights on *Zarathustra*. That shouldn't be panic inducing."

"Well, keep us informed," Jackie said. "We need to concentrate on getting you out of there."

"Yeah," Joe said. "And soon. That seal's really starting to go bad, and I expect a leak any minute now. Do we expect explosions?"

"Not yet, I'm afraid," Madeline responded, trying to sound cheerful. "First we have to get far enough down that what I have left will be able to break up everything and let us remove the chunks of ice."

"What, my super-spy wife is running out of things that go *boom*?"

"I'm afraid so, Joe. Everyone thought I'd brought a far larger supply of, to quote the military jargon, 'energetic materials' than we could *possibly* need and I was wasting valuable space and mass; now I wish I'd brought three times as much. As it is I'm probably going to have to improvise something."

"So what, you're going to bash on it with hammers?"

Jackie managed a laugh. "Basically, yes. Unfortunately, the specialized digging equipment that was supposed to be used for digging a base at Enceladus is way too big to fit through the bores we've made. So, we've rigged the heavy cutters and punch machines we got from *Odin* for machining to provide the force to drill or drive holes into the ice at intervals; then as we can break off chunks we can throw them away. Since *Athena* isn't moving anymore, we can get the power from her—she doesn't need any motive capability. When we get far enough down, Maddie blows the rest to pieces and we pull *Zarathustra* up. We've got a winch already set to do that on the line holding you."

"Heh. You sure your name isn't Montgomery Scott?"

"What?" She blinked. Then light dawned. "Oh, I didn't know that was his first name."

"Your geek powers are weak, young girl," A.J. said in an exaggerated bass voice.

"Bah!" she sneered with a grin that relaxed the tension in her gut. "*I* am the actual captain of a *spaceship!* Even if my spaceship *is* on the ground at the moment. That gives me more geek cred than all of you except the general *combined!*"

A.J. and Joe laughed together. "Aye, Captain, that it does!"

"Far be it from me to compete in your geek wars,"

Helen said, a smile in her voice as well, "but I'd point out that a super-spy who helped fight the first interplanetary ship-to-ship battle probably outranks you, too."

"Hey, are you *trying* to deflate my ego?" demanded A.J., instantly adding, "No, don't answer that, of course you are. But my ego is impervious to your puny attacks!"

Her side displays showed the general and Dr. Masters looking somewhat bemused at the juvenile byplay. "Don't worry, General. It relieves the tension."

"If it gets the job done, Dr. Secord," Hohenheim said gravely, "I really do not care if you decide to start wearing clown makeup on your suits."

"I want pictures," said Joe.

"If that happens," Maddie answered, "I will certainly get you some. Now let us concentrate on this so we can get you out of there."

Joe's voice was suddenly deadly serious. "Yeah. You'd better."

With a sinking feeling in her gut, Jackie was sure she knew what Joe was about to say, and his next words proved her right.

"Indicator just went red. Outer seal's sprung a leak," Joe Buckley said. "It's just a guess...but I'd say we have less than a day."

Chapter 42

One day.

The thought kept coming back, and Helen kept chasing it away, even while she flashed the light in a simple pattern. One flash. Pause. Two flashes. Pause. Three flashes. Pause. Four flashes. Pause. One long pulse of light. Pause. One flash...

The oceanic Bemmie—for she could not honestly prevent herself from thinking of it that way, although she was convinced it was really no more related to the original *Bemmius Secordii Sapiens* than human beings were related to *Troodon*—hung not more than three meters from the window, pulsing with faint light. It was clearly interested in what she was doing, but so far she didn't see *understanding*.

One day.

Once more she drove that thought backwards. *It doesn't matter! I will do everything I can in that day. If I'm not coming back, I will record everything I can. They'll finish salvaging Zarathustra even if we die—they've come this far, they're not going back without our bodies if they can help it.*

And that means that everything I record now will live on, even if I don't.

That meant a lot. It meant more than she could easily describe. Two pulses. Pause. Three pulses. Pause.

Suddenly the creature backed away, with an almost convulsive movement, seeming to *run* back to the larger creature...which, Helen now guessed, might be the equivalent of a horse, or—given the size—a riding elephant. "Oh, please, don't run away." *What caused that?* she wondered. The most obvious explanation was that a large predator had just showed up, but looking around, she saw nothing, and there were no sudden movements in the water suggesting something big nearby.

A few moments later the oceanic Bemmie—*Bemmius Pelagica Sapiens* Sutter, *maybe?*—slowly eased back towards *Zarathustra.* It seemed no longer bothered by *Athena's* rumbling but constant racket; this time it made no effort to stay on the far side of the rover.

"How's it going there, Helen?"

"Well, he ran off suddenly just a little bit ago, but he's coming back."

The creature stopped where it had been before, tentacles waving in a more agitated fashion. *I hope I haven't somehow made it—*

The whole animal flared a lovely blue-green for a moment. Then it was dark. Then it flared again, twice in succession. Dark. Three flares.

A chill of awe went down her spine, a shiver of triumph combined with disbelief, even as she shouted *"Yes!* Joe, he understands, he understands, Joe, *we are communicating!"*

Joe dropped down as quickly as possible, to see the beautiful aqua color spark out one long flare and then fade . . . followed by a single flash. Then two. "I'd cross myself if I were Catholic. I can't believe it." He bounced back up to the controls and she heard him telling the others.

She flashed back once. Then a long flash.

A pause, then it flashed twice, followed by a long flash. She gave it three.

It suddenly did a triple loop in the water, and then flashed four, then five, then six, strobing so fast she could barely count, then spun around, bobbing and weaving, and she was suddenly laughing, tears starting from her eyes, because despite the alien, almost monstrous face, despite the tentacles waving in a black abyss a hundred kilometers deep, tentacles surrounding a tripartite mouth that could have ripped her to shreds, she saw something else, a young being exploring a frontier who suddenly realizes it had found something completely unexpected, something so *wonderful* that it could not contain the excitement. "It's excited too, Joe, we're not dealing with something that can just count, it can *feel*. Just like us. I'm absolutely sure of it. It's doing the equivalent of jumping up and down in joy."

What now? I can't waste this time. She had given this some thought, but now that the moment had come, it took a moment to figure it out.

The helmet lights were, like most lights, arrays of LEDs. Normally they were on or off with varying levels of brightness . . . but you *could* make them project patterns. And she was sure that *Bemmius Pelagica* could see patterns; it was generating very complex ones on its skin at the moment.

Two flashes. A plus sign. Two flashes. An arrow. Four flashes.

She started the pattern repeating, and the Europan Bemmie stared, obviously trying to figure out what in the ocean this strange thing was up to now.

Joe was watching her. "You know, there aren't going to be any Earth math books where he comes from. Meaning no offense, but what the heck makes you think he's going to know what a plus sign means?"

She smiled. "I don't think he knows *now*. I'm wondering if he can figure it out."

After a few more repetitions, she changed the pattern. Now it was one flash, the plus sign, two flashes, the arrow, and then three flashes.

She did one more—adding two and three to make five—and cycled through all three patterns for a while.

"I think I'll call him Nemo."

"He doesn't look much like a clownfish."

"What? No, not that old movie. I mean because I actually have no name for him, which is what 'Nemo' meant in Verne's novel."

The newly-named Nemo was still watching; not entirely to her surprise, she saw flickers on its hide that looked like attempts to replicate the two symbols.

With abruptness that startled her again, it flashed brightly, a single long pulse. *I think its saying "stop, wait"—I was ending the other sequences with a long flash.* She paused the cycle, waited.

"Nemo" hovered, motionless, as though concentrating. Then he produced one flash. Slowly, a reasonably clear plus sign materialized on his back. Then another flash, followed by a slowly-developing arrow, and Helen found herself holding her breath, chest so tight with tension it *ached*.

One flash. Followed almost immediately by another flash.

"*Yes!*"

She sent a single flash followed by a long pulse; she hoped that would be a good symbol for "yes"; she'd already used it that way once.

Nemo spun like a top for a moment, then stopped, flashed three flashes, a plus, then seven flashes, quick as blinking—and then a long flash.

"Oh, oh, you are so very smart, you are smarter than I am, I think," she said, half-babbling. "You want to see me solve your problem." She sent back ten flashes, using the suit's circuits to make them as quick and clear as Nemo's own.

The tentacles flashed wide open and a wash of rainbow colors went over Nemo. Helen looked around the cabin, thinking. *I want to get past just these number games. We've established we can think, that we understand each other wants to talk. But I don't have* time.

Zarathustra wasn't built all that different from *Thoat* in many ways, and it was meant as a fairly long-term exploration vehicle. There was a small table, bunks, various devices for displays, conferencing, a lot of food and food wrappers, drinking containers—

That's it.

She grabbed up some of the wrappers, found one of the utility knives.

"What's up?" Joe asked apprehensively.

"Faster communication," she said briefly. "You're not an expert with paper folding or anything like that, are you?"

Joe shook his head, puzzled. "Um . . . no. Why?"

"Models. I think—I hope—he can see in here, and he's *got* to be able to recognize shapes. I think." Helen was cutting furiously, grabbing a drinking container and squashing it down flatter. *Thank God I used to fake up models and sketches all the time in my field work. Been a long time since I used those skills, but I'm not trying for accuracy here.* She paused and turned towards the port, to see Nemo floating even closer. *He's trying to figure out what I'm doing.* She turned back, focusing on the task at hand. *I don't think he'll leave any time soon.*

Sure enough, Nemo was still floating there several minutes later, although he'd drifted back and forth apparently trying for different viewing angles. By then, she had a crude model of Nemo; it was an elongated, flattened shape with a set of three tentacles in front (which were then ended in a bunch of narrow cut pieces—she hadn't even *attempted* to replicate the full branching design), and three slender ones at the back. She moved to the port and placed the little model in the center of the rear port, shining her light directly on it.

"Oh-ho, I see what you're up to," Joe said. "I might be able to do stuff like that—engineers make models too, you know. What do you want next?"

"*Zarathustra,* about to scale with that. Use one of those bottles as the body." She was rolling a ball out of some of the paper available. *Make a body...*

Seeing that the light was focused on something, the creature she'd named Nemo came closer. It was clearly much less cautious; the session of communication had made it feel that whatever this strange thing was, it wasn't trying to hurt him. Now the sea-dwelling native was within a meter of the viewport, holding its spear well away, and all three eyes focused on the tiny model. Already, Helen thought she could read something in its body language; it was puzzled. *Probably at least partly because it can see into Zarathustra, something you didn't encounter with most creatures. And most creatures don't generally draw attention to their insides, either,* she thought.

"Here," Joe said.

She was startled. Joe had put removable caps along the sides of the moderate-sized bottle, using quick-seal from one of the small repair kits, and they looked quite like wheels. A couple of straws, bent, were the manipulators, and some transparent plastic stuck on both ends showed where the ports were. "Better than I would have done. You're fast." She took the tiny doll-like paper figures and stuck them inside.

"You were staring at Nemo longer than you think. I also heard you muttering some anatomical notes to yourself."

She did vaguely remember that; her xenopaleontological brain was obviously continuing on autopilot. "Anyway, thanks!"

She put the second model next to the first, and turned the Nemo model to face *Zarathustra* at a short distance. The creature tilted itself sideways, seemed to be considering what it was seeing from all angles.

"How's the leak?"

"Not too bad yet. It hasn't really hit the growth phase."

She watched some of Nemo's "fingers" brush curiously at the port, near the models. "Joe...if the hatch does give way...Well, I was thinking. Our suits are mostly carbonan, and that's awfully strong. Isn't it

possible they'll survive, if we're not in the way when
the hatch itself goes?"

"Possible? Yeah, I think so. Especially if we stay
toward the top; it'll have to compress the air down,
and there might even be a bubble of reasonable size
left when it's done. But if we do, that only gives us
a few more hours."

"The suits are charged up pretty—"

"That's not the problem. Right now *Zarathustra's*
reactor's doing the work for us, but if we get immersed,
our *suits* have to keep us warm—and that's not a
major design consideration for a spacesuit, where
usually you're more worried about how to get *rid* of
excess heat."

"Oh." She did not relish the idea of dying of hypo-
thermia, and recognized that Joe's scenario was all
too likely. "How's progress up top?"

"They're making progress . . . but it's awfully slow.
It's *hard* to chop through ice when you need to make
a pretty damn big hole." Joe did not look optimistic.

Oh no. "It's still getting thicker, isn't it?"

"Not terribly fast . . . but every millimeter it's thicker
is that much more they have to take off the top."

A flash caught her attention. She saw Nemo, almost
rigid in the water, motionless, starting to sink slowly.
Before she could decide if that meant something bad
or not, it relaxed slightly and moved up, stretching out
one single tendril-like finger and touching the glass
exactly opposite the clumsy model that represented it.

Then its arms curled in, and out, covering its own
body. It reached out the single tendril, pointed, did
the same gesture.

Me. This is me!

She flashed once, then a long flash. *Yes.*

Nemo flashed colors, then zipped up, pointing to the larger model, then reaching out, brushing all of *Zarathustra* that it could reach. *You?*

Yes.

Fingers shaking, she picked up the model, opened the one end and took out one of the tiny figures, putting it between the *Zarathustra* model and the Nemo model.

Then she moved her whole body across, into full view of the alien creature. She pointed with her finger to the tiny doll-like shape, then used her arms and hands to cover all of herself.

Nemo seemed to *almost* understand. But he was clearly also puzzled, and she couldn't blame him.

"Here," Joe said, and she found herself holding another Bemmie-like model, much larger than the first. "That's what you need."

"Wh...oh, of *course.*"

She took the larger model and put it on the far side of Nemo. Then, making sure the creature was watching, she moved the Nemo model (having to reattach one arm at one point) over to the larger creature, putting Nemo on top of the bigger one. She then put the doll-figure into *Zarathustra.*

She repeated this several times, until suddenly Nemo spun around, flashing once, then a long flash, a pause, one flash, long flash. *Yes, yes!*

Nemo streaked up to the port, closer than it had been before. One arm pointed directly at Helen, and then pointed at itself. One of the others, simultaneously, was spreading, touching *Zarathustra*, then pointing off into the deep at the hovering larger Europan creature.

These things are the same. You and me. Zarathustra *and my riding beast.*

She laughed for the sheer joy. *Yes. Yes. Yes. Yes.*

Nemo seemed to feel the same thing, and Joe laughed as well, watching the creature go through a gem-sparkling dance. Then Nemo zipped around, moving away from the window, surveying the *Zara-thustra*. She could see it dodge away *quickly* when it approached the radiators too closely. *Didn't have to learn that predator's lesson; he felt the heat and avoided it.* It came to the front window, touched the manipulators very gently, brushed the front port, tugged cautiously at the rope that tethered them. Nemo seemed very interested in that, enough so that both Helen started to wonder if Joe needed to make him back off. *If he decided we're somehow stuck, he might try to* help *by cutting the line. I don't know if he could break that stuff, but we sure as hell don't want anyone trying.*

But just as Joe started slowly reaching for the manipulator controls, Nemo backed off, flickering with many colors in patterns similar to the ones she'd seen in his earlier "thinking" moments. He drifted cautiously, very slowly, towards *Athena*, and his extended tentacles began to riffle in the disturbed water.

The alien backed away very quickly, then came back to the rear port and hovered there, waiting, or thinking.

Helen was trying to think of what else she could communicate. *Damn. We never expected in our wild-est dreams that we'd end up in a . . . a "first contact" situation. I know people have devised all kinds of programs and plans for this, but none of that was loaded on* Zarathustra… *and we haven't got the band-width to transfer much of anything. What else can I say to him with what little we have?*

Nemo's arm reached out, encompassed itself, then pointed into the depths. Then it reached farther, touched *Zarathustra*…

…and pushed the craft up slightly.

She stared. The creature repeated the motions twice. *Nemo's figured it out. Maybe from* Athena's *presence. Maybe from the way we've clearly been fastened to something that goes up through the ice. But Nemo has it.*

The gestures were clear. *I come from down below. You come from up above?*

Yes, she sent.

She could only imagine what the Bemmie-like creature must be thinking. The spear showed some level of civilization, but there must be limits; here was a being on, at best, the level of one of Earth's most ancient civilizations, discovering an entirely new order of life, one that lived above the roof of the world. As great a shock as an ancient Inca or Roman encountering a fallen spaceman—perhaps even more, because while many religions taught that the heavens were a bowl over the world, the limits of that bowl were not obvious and tangible, cold and indestructible.

Whatever else it was thinking, it seemed curious now about the ice above. It drifted up, and pulsed, and flinched several times. "What *is* Nemo up to now?"

Joe rubbed his chin. "I really don't know." He watched the creature move along above them, occasionally twitching sharply. Joe stiffened. "Hold on a sec…"

He touched the controls, brought up the record

of the cameras on that side, played it back. Suddenly she understood. "The digging sounds. It's flinching whenever the ice is getting hit heavily."

"Yep. You told me these things would probably be sensitive to sound and vibration, and between *Athena* and our friends with the power tools, it must sound like a factory on overload around here."

Nemo of Europa swam quickly back to the viewport, made multiple gestures; pointed to them, pointed up, pointed to himself, and down, then opening its tentacles wide, finally moving the expanded arm up. It repeated that sequence twice, then flashed *yes. Yes.*

That enigmatic communication finished, Nemo moved swiftly off and hooked himself to his patient steed. An instant later, the larger creature lunged downward and disappeared into the gloom.

First contact was over.

But what have we started?

Chapter 43

"We can't put this off any longer," Madeline said, finally.

"But you said—"

"I *know* what I said!" She sighed, shook her head. "Sorry, A.J.; we're all on edge, and exhausted, and that's part of the reason I'll have to try it now. Brett checked the trend for me, and it's clear. There's no way we can keep up this pace much longer, not with the sleep limitations and physical stress this work's putting us under."

She gestured, and saw A.J. and the others finally really *look* around, not just let their eyes drift over the slow, steady change they'd been making, and she could hear little murmurs of startlement, even awe.

The bottom section of the ice was chopped down more than a meter lower, over an area wider and longer than *Zarathustra*—eighteen meters by four. Far above were scattered vast amounts of ice, dug out over the last twelve hours by the absolutely incredible effort of seven people who knew they were running out of time.

"You've all done *miracles* here. All of us have. That's something like a hundred tons of ice we've broken, chopped, dragged, thrown, somehow gotten out of the way. We've made Europa's weak gravity work for us, we've found a possible way to rescue our friends, and we've all pushed ourselves to our uttermost limits. We just can't keep it up for another six hours. Even the general is slowing down, and to be honest, sir, I thought you might be a machine for a while there."

General Hohenheim chuckled. "I am, alas, only too human, as our current predicament rather proves." *He's still carrying that guilt. I suppose he always will.* "But you are, as usual, correct. You are not in top shape yourself. The ice is getting slowly thicker beneath us, and while we have been keeping ahead of that, I presume we will not much longer?"

Even as they were talking, Jackie had triggered another series of hammering impacts from the jury-rigged jackhammer array. Horst, Mia, and A.J. stumbled down, sweeping up the fragments, throwing them as far as their weary arms could manage. Madeline could see that now even the smaller pieces were not clearing the high edge; the far side of the depression was starting to pile up with debris, and there wasn't all that much distance between that and the edge of the hole they were digging. "No, General. According to the plot, we're just about holding even now. Oh, we could probably drive ourselves a little harder and keep going for an hour or two more . . . but we may need those reserves when we *do* get *Zarathustra* up. She has her own problems."

"As you say. Very well. Cease operations!"

Madeline had to admire the general's tone of command; the others stopped instantly. "Please clear the area *immediately*," the general continued. "Agent Fathom will be setting her charges and we will have to detonate as soon as possible."

A.J. stood for a moment, alone in the center of the hole they had made, and she winced for a moment at how even his *pose* showed his exhaustion and worry, the clenching of his hand as though he would try to pound his way through the ice by main force. Then he turned and walked in slow, floating steps to the far side and ascended.

Last shot.

She weighed her options, then called the doctor over. "Petra, I need to be very sharp right now, and I don't have time."

Petra Masters frowned, then shrugged. "You know, of course, all the reasons not to do this. But I can't argue the situation is not dire. I'll give you a *very* small dose of the stimulant. It will take the edge off your exhaustion, clear your mind."

"That's all I ask. I don't need excess energy for this, I just don't want to be foggy while I'm working with explosives."

She barely felt the injection, which Masters administered through the designated area of the suit. "Thank you, Dr. Masters."

"Good luck, Maddie."

The others were silent; she wouldn't have been very surprised to find they were holding their breaths, except this would take too long.

"A.J., Brett, you've been taking the impact echo data, correct?"

"As much as we could," A.J. answered. "I think there's still a meter and a half to go."

"Pretty close. There's a small area where it's a little

thinner," Brett said, "but a couple others where it's a little thicker. There are a few weaker lines, though, places I think where the crack was originally and the ice formed around the old ice. I think your best chance is to take advantage of that."

"Can you send the data to my suit, so the VRD will do an augmented reality overlay?"

"Can do," A.J. said. A pause. "There, try overlay file code 'Icebreaker.'"

She smiled. "I will."

The ice suddenly glowed with color at the code activation. She could see complex lines of various shades—red, blue, green—making a ghostly X-ray vision of the structure of the ice. *God, it's thick. These charges . . . if I don't put them in the right place, I'll barely dent this ice.*

They were running out of the self-embedding spikes, too, but there would be more than enough; she had twelve of those, and only seven charges, designed to be placed in the holes the spikes made. She surveyed the whole area carefully, conferring with Brett's models, while the others waited, silent. "Joe, Helen, are you there?" she said.

"Still here. Pressure in the lock is three point one atmospheres. Still holding, though, no sign of the inner seal weakening yet."

"How about your . . . visitors?"

"No sign since he left a few hours ago." Helen's voice was wistful. Maddie couldn't imagine what it must be like to, in effect, have come face to face with the creature that changed your entire life, but it must be something incredible.

"I'm setting the charges. With luck, we'll break up

the ice over you and be able to haul *Zarathustra* up through the hole. At the least we should make big enough cracks that we can widen the hole and *then* get to the point we can haul you out."

"Hey, I'm all for that. Dibs on Hotel Europa's shower."

"Joe? The universe may not be able to kill you, but I can," Helen said darkly.

"Save the murder of my husband for later," Madeline said. "Stand by. I'll give a countdown to the detonation when I'm ready."

There.

Seven tiny points, now illuminating her vision, scattered at what would to someone else seem almost random across the hole the combined available crew of *Nebula Storm* and *Odin* had dug. But they were placed as well as both she and Brett could guess to produce maximum effect.

Quickly she moved to each point, drove in a spike, removed it, put in the miniature shaped charge, set the remote detonator, moved to the next. It seemed to take forever; she almost *sensed* the ice below her, slowly but surely adding another millimeter of thickness every few minutes. *Why* it was getting thicker she had no idea—Larry and Andrew hadn't figured out a good model yet, either—but the fact was it *was* getting thicker, and she had to hurry.

But only an idiot hurried with explosives. So she hurried only in her heart, but took all the time and care she needed with the charges.

Finally.

She bounded up the terraces to the top. "Everyone down behind the barriers." She surveyed the area, made sure everyone was, in fact, behind the barriers before going there herself. "Joe, Helen, we are about to detonate. Fifteen seconds."

She triggered the arming signal. Seven dots in her display went from amber to red. "Ten seconds. Nine. Eight..."

Please. Any power that's listening...please let this work. She suspected there was nothing listening, and a part of her chided herself for even *thinking* such nonsense which was probably left over from her horrid childhood...but at this moment, she didn't care. "Three. Two. One. Detonation."

There was sound now, carried very well by air vastly thicker than Earth's. A blurred stacatto of quick sequential blasts, jets of pulverized ice and white-gray smoke of the explosives themselves shot into the air. Fragments rained down around the edges of the depression, skittering across the ice towards their barricades, but nothing actually reached them except tiny pieces.

She was up and moving instants later, skidding to a halt at the edge, looking down.

Seven circular holes were clearly visible, and there were cracks showing across the surface. But the telemetry showed that only a few cracks really went all the way through...and they would freeze back up, very soon.

No.

"Come on, everyone! Let's finish breaking this up and get *Zarathustra* out!" she called, forcing as much optimism into her voice as she could manage. But inside, she was already feeling the cold, cold certainty.

We've failed.

Chapter 44

"It didn't work."

Joe could hear the certainty in Helen's voice. He nodded. "Yeah. They didn't send down the data, but I can see that there's only a few cracks that got through. The chances they can finish breaking all that up... aren't good."

Zarathustra swayed slightly. Joe had gotten used to this over the past days; he figured that it came from a current that ran along under the ice. The current wasn't terribly fast, but then with Europa's gravity and the buoyancy, *Zarathustra* wasn't very heavy, so they swung somewhat to and fro on the rope that it was suspended from.

I'd worry about that wearing through the rope, if we had to hang here for a few more weeks. But at least that's not a worry anymore.

"What's the pressure up to?"

He checked. *Not good.* "Almost four now." *And I think six is going to be the limit.* "I—crap!"

Something had just *zipped* past him, just outside of the front viewport.

Helen's face lit up. "He's back!"

Sure enough, the same tendrilled, tripartite shape was now drifting in front of the rear viewport. Helen lowered herself down and waved. Somewhat to Joe's surprise, "Nemo" waved back. Then it pointed down. Helen looked, then stiffened. "Joe—take a look through the rear cameras."

Rising up from the depths, slowly fading into visibility, were several more shapes. Each large shape shed a smaller one which continued to rise, until there were six or seven members of what Helen had tentatively called *Bemmius Pelagica Sapiens* (which, if he recalled his scientific nomenclature right, would mean the intelligent open-ocean Bemmie) drifting near the lower end of *Zarathustra*.

Joe stared. Looking carefully, he thought he could make out some differences. "I wonder if those notches along the side are natural or identifying marks, like tattoos or the scarring in some Earth societies."

Helen looked with obvious interest at the others, staring at what appeared to be symmetrical patterns of little nicks or notches in the edges of the fins at each of the creature's three body ridges. "I never noticed that before. I'd think it's artificial, but it's hard to tell."

One of the other creatures—somewhat larger—shoved Nemo out of the way and made a flailing backward gesture which, to judge by the manner in which all the others moved swiftly away, meant something like "back off" or "clear the area." Once the other creatures were away, the newcomer moved to the same location Nemo had spent most of its time, and suddenly flashed several times, generated a clear plus-sign on its back, and flashed several more times, ending with a long flash.

"Oh! He's testing what he's been told. Joe, how many flashes was that?"

He played it back for both of them. "Six and seven— so thirteen."

Carefully, Helen sent thirteen flashes in response.

The large newcomer backed off immediately and the . . . seven, Joe finally managed to determine . . . oceanic creatures entered into an obvious conference, combining eerie calls that the outside microphones could only sometimes record with extremely fast flickering displays. He could also make out that several of the creatures had some sort of harnesses on them, with flat things that he had to assume were bags of some sort attached to the harnesses.

Three of the . . . well, *people* . . . now approached. The center one . . . "That's Nemo there, right?"

"Yes, it is. He's the one with a three-notch pattern on his fins."

The three stopped in front of the viewport. For a moment they hovered, motionless, and then Helen gasped. *"Look!"*

On the back of one creature flickered the shape of one of his own kind, grasping tendrils and all. Nemo, in the middle, projected a simple arrow shape, the same one Helen had used for "equals." And on the other creature . . .

A crude figure, with a somewhat indistinct head, but two arms and legs attached to a body. *That's us.*

We equal you.

Helen laughed, an almost teary sound in her voice, and flashed back *Yes. Yes. Yes.* "Joe, they *do* understand pictures, not just models like I was afraid." She grabbed her portable computer, unrolled the screen to its maximum size and put it against the window. Joe saw her engage the drawing function and sketch quickly: *Human* ➔ *Bemmie.*

Yes, flashed Nemo. After a moment, the others also flashed *Yes.*

The triad flashed excitedly; the sudden appearance of the bright computer display obviously changed things in several ways. Then they flashed another set of images.

"What...hm." The first image was something like the oceanic Bemmie, but the hands were effectively missing, and it looked broader. "Oh," said Helen, "it's the things they're riding on, the ones they've left back down there." The next symbol was the arrow again, and then an obvious sketch of *Zarathustra.*

"Heh," Joe chuckled. "They want to know if this is our riding beast. Which is sorta is, but..."

"Yes. We sort of agreed to that before, with Nemo, but...I want to try to get across that it's *used* that way but we *made* it...how, though...?"

Joe thought a moment, and an idea came. "Hey, give me access." He sketched in the air for a few moments, then sent the image to her display.

On the screen a picture of *Zarathustra* glowed, with an arrow pointing to pictures of the riding creature, a Europan spear, and a recognizable sketch of the harness and bags he could see on one of the Europans.

That triggered a furious sequence of flashing and near-ultrasonic calls between the creatures, culminating in them swarming around *Zarathustra,* tapping and poking gently at various parts. A couple of them also circled around the location near *Athena,* and hovered near the ice above, which echoed with the pounding of the others trying to get through.

"Joe, can you generate a model of this whole area? A sketch-level one?"

Joe thought a moment. "I think so. All the data's here, and *Zarathustra*'s data-processing was meant to allow it to be used as a mobile base." He checked the parameters. "Yeah, it's easy if you're talking stuff to display as simple sketches."

She explained in detail, and Joe grinned. "That might work. Might work *real* well."

A few minutes later, the others had gathered again near the end window. Joe sent the first picture—a sketch of the two of them inside of *Zarathustra*, which hung suspended from the ice above, and the seven Europan natives hovering nearby, and farther away and down the bigger shapes of the riding creatures.

Yes, flashed Nemo after a moment. He clearly understood they were showing him what was around them.

"Great!" Joe said. "Next one coming up."

He zoomed the scene out. Everything in the first scene was still visible, but now they could see the thickness of the ice, and above the ice a bunch of other human figures.

The Europans considered this new idea, and hesitated. Then Nemo flickered uncertainly, and then generated an arrow, followed by *yes*.

"What?"

Helen smiled. "That's 'equals yes'... I think he's asking, *is this true?*"

She sent *Yes*.

Nemo echoed the *Yes*, after conferring with the others.

"I like the fact that he's apparently being allowed to keep the lead, even though that bigger guy seems almost certainly more like a boss," Joe said. "Okay, now for the payoff."

He animated the image, showing the people on the top trying to chip through the ice, and *Zarathustra* trying to get through from below.

Apparently the idea of *moving* pictures like that was novel. An explosion of flashing and haunting calls began, and went on for several minutes before Nemo and the others came back and looked again at the animation. Several more minutes went by with them watching. Then Nemo talked with its friends for a few more.

Then the three Europans moved so they were vertically arranged. The one on top showed some crude human figures. The one in the middle, Nemo, showed a line obviously meant to represent the ice. The bottom one showed a very simple *Zarathustra*, not much more than a lumpy oval, with two human figures inside.

Helen flashed a *yes*.

Then, very slowly, flashing like a video being stepped through frame by frame, the two figures from the bottom were shown moving up, then disappearing from the bottom creature and appearing on Nemo, and finally appearing with the others above the ice.

Yes! Yes!

Joe moved up, grabbed the manipulators, and started punching at the ice overhead. He couldn't do much, but he figured the symbolism might work.

The Europans watched, and then the one on the top turned to its companions and they talked. Then they swam down, away, heading for their riding animals, all of them, almost fading to invisibility.

And then they were visible again, riding up, *charging* up with a vengeance, and the tentacles at the front of the riding creatures were bunched up in a peculiar fashion, and they went *past Zarathustra*, streaking by at what seemed immense velocity, and slammed, one by one, into the ice above.

Joe gave a *whoop* of triumph, and activated the communicator. "Heads up, everyone—we've got a second work party on the job, and they just *might* make the difference!"

Chapter 45

"Holy *shit!*" Helen heard A.J. say. "I *felt* that! What the hell's going on?"

"It's the native Europans, the...the oceanic Bemmies, whatever we should call them!" she answered, feeling a grin spreading across her face. "Or, I should be accurate, it's their riding beasts charging into the ice."

In the background she heard a barely-audible murmur from what sounded like General Hohenheim. *If I heard right, I think that was German for "God be thanked."*

"That...just might do it, Helen, Joe." Madeline's voice was filled with genuine hope. "At the least it might keep the cracks we already made from permanently freezing." She raised her voice. "All right, everyone, this is it—we've got to give whatever we've got left!"

The light-radio link went silent, the others now driving themselves to match—maybe even exceed—their earlier pace for one last burst. The echoing *thud* of the multi-jackhammer alternated with duller, heavier impacts as the riding creatures struck the underside of the ice.

Joe watched, too; there was a bemused expression

on his face. "Not to look a gift worker-squid in the tentacles," he said, "but they haven't known us more than a few minutes. Why the hell are they working so hard to try to help us?"

"Why do human beings work so hard to save a beached whale—a whale that might die anyway?" she retorted. "Because you feel a kind of kinship, and if you *can* help, why not at least *try*?" She felt a strange surge of feeling that combined empathy with joy and the terrible tension of hope, felt tears sting her eyes.

"Well . . . I'd better do what I can. I don't know how long the manipulators will take it, but no point in trying to save them for later."

Joe locked himself in the control seat again and started methodically hammering at one spot in the ice above them, one impact after another, punching rhythmically and steadily.

And now I sit and wait. She tried to fight off the feeling of helplessness; it was stupid and counterproductive. So was that vague feeling that she was being useless, sitting there waiting for everyone else to get her out. *You made contact with them. You started the whole thing. You got lucky, of course—lucky that a local genius like "Nemo" was the one that found you—but you didn't do half bad, Dr. Sutter.*

But it was *still* terribly hard to just sit, and wait, as the ice stubbornly repelled every attempt to break it, silently and steadily trying to rebuild itself from the ocean around them.

She watched the next creature gather itself, launch upward, slam into the ice. *Perhaps that's one of their normal defensive—or offensive—tactics. Still, I simply can't imagine they can keep doing that very long.*

They were still living flesh—flesh, based on her own analyses, not much different from their own. Animals had limits like everything else, and she doubted that even Nemo would risk damaging his mount too much for these strange creatures he had found.

But they didn't stop, and she saw cracks now, slowly expanding. *They're* doing *it!*

She repeated the thought to Joe. "They're doing it, Joe! I see the cracks from the *underside* now. If they can meet our people in the middle—"

Joe grunted, jabbing again with the manipulator. "Maybe . . . they will. Damn. Next time," he punched with the other side, "I'll put an automated punching function into this thing. The designers simply neglected some of the most basic capabilities!"

She tried to keep her face serious. "Oh, yes, Joe. We'll have to submit a critical report to the designers when we get home."

He glanced back with a grin, but then looked back and to his side. "Damnation. Four point seven atmospheres."

"Any sign of the inner door weakening?"

"The humidity sensors twitched on one side. I think it's starting."

Her hope was suddenly dwindling. "We don't have much time left, do we?"

He shrugged. "An hour, maybe. Maybe as much as an hour and a half. I wouldn't worry about it; the way everyone's driving themselves, either we'll be out of here in that time, or they'll all collapse before it happens."

One hour. She sat silently, watching the frantic motion outside, hearing the unceasing pounding from above and below. But the ice was *hard*, it was thick, it was tough. It was the armor of a world. *And there's nothing that can soften it.*

She suddenly sat fully upright, so suddenly she bounced off the seat. *"Of course!!"*

"Of course? Of course *what?*"

She paid no attention, dropping down to the display screen. She linked to the drawing application again, sketched furiously, then put the display up to the window.

But no one was looking. Joe was still hammering away at the ice above. Nemo and the other Europans were stubbornly jabbing at the ice with their spears as they sent their mounts against the impregnable roof of the world. *No one's going to see this!*

She glanced up. *Oh, but I can* make *them look.*

She bounded up beside Joe, who glanced over but kept up his work. "Helen, what—*whoa!*"

The rear lights flared, a detonation of brilliance that illuminated the Europan ocean for a moment with light that it hadn't seen in all its aeons, a light that seemed to suspend each Europan and its mount in empty space, sharp-edged shadows racing away into the infinite darkness, all pointing back towards *Zarathustra.*

Everyone froze; even from above came a faint "What was *that?*" from Jackie.

Helen was not surprised to see Nemo recover first. The Europan swam quickly over and saw her back at the rear port, holding the display, pointing to it. The creature stared with all three eyes at what was there for a moment, then rushed up, flashing to the others. The other Europan people hesitated, then jetted over to *Zarathustra*, examining it carefully. Then, as two of them began to start their beasts battering the ice again, the other five—Nemo included—began pushing on *Zarathustra*.

"Whoa! What the—Helen, what did you tell them to do?"

She turned the display toward him.

He stared at the outline of *Zarathustra*, the radiators prominently blinking, and at the animation of the radiators being pushed up. *"Helen, you genius!"*

She laughed. "You think it could work?"

He grinned savagely. "I think I can give us a better chance." He activated the comm. "Mia! Mia, I need the access code to the direct reactor controls."

"What? Why do you need that?" Her voice was exhausted and concerned.

"Because that thump you just felt? That's the radiators of *Zarathustra* getting pushed against the ice, and I want—"

She let out an expression in Norwegian that *had* to be one of surprised joy, but Helen couldn't even guess at the words. *"Ya, Ya,* of course, you want to run the reactor as hot as possible! Wait!"

A few moments went by, and then Mia was back. "Here, Joe!" She rattled off a series of numbers and instructions. "That should do."

Helen took the display and marked the radiators as glowing even brighter, pushed it to the window. One of the other creatures—she thought it was the big one, the boss—saw, flashed *yes* back. The Europans moved their grip to a bit farther away.

A faint squealing noise became audible, vibrating through *Zarathustra* like fingers on a blackboard. It deepened, and she could now see small bubbles coming from the edge of the radiators visible in the cameras. "Joe, I think it's starting to *boil*!"

"Ha! The hotter the better! I think I can crank this until we're a little over two hundred C! *That* should get us through!"

"Better than that, Joe!" A.J.'s voice was excited, confident now, and just hearing that made Helen feel better. "With *that* much hot water around, there's *no* way it's going to keep building up more ice in that area. Matter of fact, now that I look at the old display, the ice was a little thinner right about the area that the upwelling plume from the radiators probably was most of the time."

Zarathustra jolted, dragged forward a couple of meters. "Now what are they up to?"

Helen looked. "I think . . . Joe, they're moving the radiators so that it's weakening the ice in a wider area."

"They're smart. These people are *very* smart. And even with their metal-trees or whatever, they're probably not very far past the tribal stage. I'm not sure human beings would be this smart in the same situations."

"Don't underestimate your own kind, Joe," Helen said, shaking her head.

"We still need to hurry this up," Joe said. "Pressure's almost five atmospheres, and now I *do* see a humidity rise in the inner seal."

"Damn." That was Madeline's voice. "We need some way to take advantage of the weakened ice. I can set the winch pulling—"

"Wouldn't hurt, as long as you can keep it from burning itself out pulling."

"I don't care if it catches *fire* as long as it runs until you're up, or . . . or time runs out."

"Yeah, but with my luck it would catch fire, explode, and blow up Europa just *before* you got me up. So be careful."

She heard A.J. grunt. "That's not bad, but that thing isn't going to put much stress on something this big. You need something that covers this whole *area* to push you up, and—"

"*Athena!*" Larry Conley shouted suddenly. "Mia, shut *Athena* down for a few seconds!"

"What? Larry, are you insane?"

"No, I'm completely sane!" The astrophysicist's voice was earnest. "Let the pressure drop, just a little! Even a *tenth* of an atmosphere will be something like *eighty tons* of force pushing up in the area we're digging!"

There were a few moments of tense silence, then Hohenheim's voice came through clearly. "Stand by to do as he says, Dr. Svensen. Mr. Tamahori, can you give us a timing estimate based on the model we now have refined of the behavior of this chamber? How long should we shut *Athena* down for in order to produce a short drop in pressure without risking a catastrophe?"

"Ha. General, everything you're *doing* down there risks catastrophe. But hold on . . ." A few more tense moments passed. "Mia, I make it five minutes, thirty-three seconds optimum."

"Understood. General?"

"Are we ready, Agent Fathom?"

"As ready as we can be, General."

"Then proceed, Dr. Svensen."

Athena's roar suddenly ceased. Helen felt as though she'd been struck deaf for a moment; she hadn't real-ized how *accustomed* she'd become to that rumbling background to everything. Despite the change, the Europans barely bobbled *Zarathustra*, keeping the furiously boiling radiators pressing against the ice, which was eroding at a visible rate.

"Okay, listen, Joe. Brett says that if this works at all, it'll happen right around the end of the period, probably about the time we have to restart. That's when the upward pressure will peak." This was Madeline's voice, the voice of the agent in control of a situation. "When that happens, if it works, there will be short surge upward that will let us pull you out. You *must* shut down the reactor, put it back to standby power, because you don't want to burn any of *us*, as soon as that movement starts. Set it up now, a deadman switch, so you just have to let go."

"On it."

Now it was back to waiting, but Helen felt the press of time less. She'd thought of something that helped, she'd taken action, and now the only question was if it would work in time.

"Pressure's five point two atmospheres. Humidity really starting to climb. If I start to see water for real in there, Helen, I want you to get up here *right away*, understand?"

She nodded. She had no desire to be in the way of a piledriver of water with the alloy and carbonan door as a leader. *In fact*, she thought, *why take chances?* She climbed up to the copilot seat and strapped in, making sure her helmet was secure.

Zarathustra quivered, jolted upward, even as they heard the bellowing rumble of *Athena* begin. "Are we . . ."

And suddenly it was the earthquake in reverse, as the huge rover *heaved* up, icy blocks rising, shifting,

cracking, Nemo and its fellow Europans streaking
away, the mounts halting their charge and retreating,
then everything dissolved in spray and ice chips and
foam. *Zarathustra* was moving, tilting up and then
tilted *down* as a tremendous, broad surge of icy water
shoved everything aside with implacable, irresistable
force—and then began to subside, a little, faster, and
the ice collapsed, a shattering, crushing force banging
on the sides of the rover, and she heard herself curse
and covered her head instinctively as *Zarathustra*
rolled—

and the rolling stopped.

Silence, marred only by the distant rumble of *Athena*
and creaking, crackling noises faintly coming through
the hull. She opened her eyes and looked.

Zarathustra was stuck, half-in, half-out of the ice.

But the rover's hatch lay just above the frozen
surface.

Chapter 46

Every ache in A.J.'s exhausted body vanished as he saw the familiar suit emerging from the hatch. He grasped Helen's hand, pulled her to him, and for long minutes the two of them stood there, holding each other, and to him there was nothing else in the whole universe except knowing she was finally with him again.

Finally he let go, just enough for her to pull away a bit and look up. He knew he had as many tears on his face as she did on hers. "Doc, you did damn good."

"And you."

Glancing over, he saw that Joe and Maddie were just releasing their own embrace, and became aware of clapping all around them.

"Mr. Baker," General Hohenheim said, with a broad grin that made him look ten years younger, "Dr. Sutter, Dr. Buckley, and Agent Fathom. It is good to see we are all reunited. It is time, I think, for us to stop pushing our luck and get back to the surface, would you agree?"

"Almost, General," Helen said. "But I've got to thank our new friends, if I can."

A.J. blinked. He'd almost forgotten about the fact

they'd discovered *aliens*. "Holy Jebus. I'm losing all my geek points. Hold on, Helen!"

He saw her hesitate on the threshold of *Zarathustra*. *Can't blame her; I don't know if you'd get me back into this thing if I'd just been stuck in it for that long.*

Zarathustra now sat with its rear wheels in the air, the formerly-boiling radiators held three meters above the floor. The forward port was now far below the surface. "It's starting to refreeze now."

"That's *good*," said Helen. "Don't you see? If we can keep *Zarathustra* running—if I can leave the computer plugged in, put the display in the front port, we can keep communications going!"

He *had* thought of it, but only as she was saying it. But he *could* go one farther. "And now we can download some of the real First Contact packages and load them into *Zarathustra*. Get some of the experts on Earth working on this and combine it with the contact you guys already made? We'll be *talking* with these guys in no time." He looked down. "Oh my God."

Hovering only a short distance away was something so like the models of *Bemmius Secordii Sapiens* that he had a chill pass over his whole body. It was like looking back in time, or through a portal to an alternate world. *Maybe it's* exactly *like that.*

Helen had retrieved her portable screen from the far end of *Zarathustra* and placed it on the forward port; *Zarathustra*'s front console screen lit, showing the display as the Europans would see it.

It showed *Zarathustra* half-through the ice, and a repeating animation of two figures getting out and being greeted by others. Along with this, Helen kept flashing the signal for *yes*.

The aliens watched for a few minutes, and then A.J. saw one—that he guessed *had* to be the one Helen called "Nemo"—flash *yes*.

All seven aliens slowly reached out and linked tentacles like grasping hands, until all seven were twined into a single line. They raised their third arms, pointing up, and in unison, flashed *yes*.

"General," A.J. said, "They get our thanks, and seem pretty glad that we succeeded. And Helen's right, this is *the* opportunity... not just of a lifetime, of all our lifetimes. I want to leave one of the big displays here, one that's big enough to cover the whole front window."

"I cannot think of a better use. But how can we make them understand that we still want to talk?"

"Helen's already shown us how smart they are. I've got an idea. Let me work on it a little."

"We're all just about at the end of our strength," Maddie reminded him. "And we have to get out of here soon."

"These guys deserve my last efforts today," A.J. said. "Larry had one hell of a last-ditch idea, but I don't think it would've worked without these people pitching in and doing *their* best."

"I can't argue there."

God, I'm tired. Not twenty anymore. Not even thirty anymore. But I'm not dropping off yet. It's not too hard, not with all the tools I have available...

It took him only fourteen minutes; he figured at the top of his game he could have done it in ten. But the animation playing now showed the people leaving *Zarathustra*, but leaving a big display which showed the people on it. Then it showed the Europans leaving, with the big rover staying alone on the screen.

Then, in the animation, *Zarathustra* started pounding on the ice in a pattern: one, two three . . . one, two, three . . . After several repetitions of the pattern, Europans swam up, and the display was shown flickering as though talking to them.

"Please understand," he murmured, as the animation played again and again. He heard Helen murmuring the same thing. "You guys have figured out everything else we threw at you, just this last one . . ."

It was a complicated idea to try to get across with pictures, especially when it was hard to know what those pictures *looked* like to their opposite numbers. But obviously they looked like *something* because the communications had gone well enough before. *They must use their own light a lot. I wonder . . . could Bemmie, the original group, have tried to make biological replacements for all the things an amphibious being might be giving up—like fire, reliable light, and so on?*

The biggest creature gave the single long flash that meant "stop" or "no" in the impromptu code; A.J. stopped the display.

The aliens conferred for a few moments, then one swam over and examined the manipulator, pushed at it gently; A.J. let them maneuver it. They pushed it toward *Zarathustra*'s hull until it rapped three times.

"Oh, *I* get it. Yeah, you're probably right. Hold on, guys . . . ."

"What is it?"

"Uniqueness of sound. The signal has to be something they can hear a long way away *and* be able to tell it's us, not something else." The modified animation showed *Zarathustra* banging on its own lower hull in the one-two-three rhythm. "Carbonan hitting ice might not be quite so obvious, but carbonan hitting metal alloy? You're not getting *that* sound anywhere else."

The aliens were signaling. *Yes. Yes.* And on the backs of three, the image of *Zarathustra* being left behind while the oceanic creatures swam away to something blurry that seemed to be where a *lot* of them lived—"a *city!*" Helen murmured—and waited; then *Zarathustra*'s arm struck its body three times, three times again, and Europan people swam out of the fuzzy "city" and came to hover in front of *Zarathustra*.

"They understand!" Helen said.

"They do. And we can go home."

A.J. rose from the controls, then waved along with Helen. The Europans waved back. *Maybe it's a gesture they alrady use, or maybe it's just an obvious greeting and farewell for anyone with manipulating members. I don't know.*

Reluctantly, Helen followed him out of *Zarathustra*.

They rejoined the others and turned and looked back at the rover. "You know," Joe said, "a part of me has never been happier to get *away* from a vehicle. And the other part of me is gonna miss *Zarathustra*."

"Same here," said Helen.

"Well," Madeline said, "If this area stays reasonably intact, people *will* come back here. Maybe even to swim with our alien friends. The pressure isn't beyond human diving technology."

"Not sure *I* would be up for that," A.J. said. "But I'll bet a lot of people would. And with your permission, Maddie, General, I'm going to lay both cable and relays all through the tunnel leading here so that there's a guaranteed connection. We *can't* drop this ball."

"Of course," Madeline and General Hohenheim said

together; the two chuckled. "As long as it is equipment we do not need to return home," Hohenheim continued, "you may use anything you like.

"We now know we are not alone in this universe," he said, "and we will make sure they, also, are no longer alone."

PART V

Restoration, n: 1) an act of restoring or the condition of being restored: as a) a bringing back to a former position or condition : reinstatement; b) restitution; c) a restoring to an unimpaired or improved condition; 2) something that is restored; especially: a representation or reconstruction of the original form (as of a fossil or a building).

Chapter 47

"All secure?"

Madeline checked all the telltales once more; all the ones that mattered for this maneuver showed green. "All secure, Horst."

They were the only people aboard *Munin* and *Nebula Storm*. All the others—Joe, General Hohenheim, Helen and A.J., Jackie, Petra, Larry, Brett, Mia, Dan, and Anthony—all of them were now aboard *Odin*, stowing away all supplies, preparing for their departure.

She looked at the main display of *Nebula Storm*, to see the oddly-tilted view of Europa Base—the living quarters, Hotel Europa, the circular track and armature of the centrifuge. The structures remained standing; there was no good reason to pack them and bring them along on this trip back, and perhaps future visitors would find them useful, if they survived.

Athena, too, was staying. Despite its glitches the melt-probe had performed heroically, but it had no purpose on the return trip. If anything remained for *Athena* to do, it would be here, on Europa. Mia and A.J. had carefully shut the probe down into storage mode, locked into its support structure above the last hole it had made, braced to withstand even another monster quake.

The view was tilted because—with muscle power, mechanical advantage, and judicious application of *Munin*'s jets—*Nebula Storm* had been turned around to be sitting at an angle on the ridge into which it had crashed. *Munin* now sat *underneath* the IRI vessel, locked to it by the best umbilical restraints they could devise.

The fact that *she* was here to pilot *Nebula Storm* and that Horst was piloting *Munin* had been settled in somewhat acrimonious debate. The general, it turned out, was more than capable of flying *Munin*, and had intended to do so for this final maneuver. However, he had been overridden. "General, our endgame for this entire adventure relies on your presence," Maddie had said. "I am expendable, you are not." She had silenced Joe with a gesture. "I know that isn't a popular way to state things, but it's easier if we address this directly. I am also the person who *landed Nebula Storm* after flying her tandem, and similarly Horst is the one with experience—much more experience, now—in flying *Munin*."

The general had, grudgingly, accepted this logic.

And now we come down to the end. "*Munin*, we are coming up to launch window. Is everything a go on your end?"

"All green," Horst reported.

This will be trickier, Maddie admitted to herself. With the nozzle now gone, she really couldn't use *Nebula Storm*'s main rocket anymore. *Munin* would provide almost all the thrust this time, until it was necessary to dock with *Odin*. "All living quarters folded back and locked. Tether release mechanisms armed."

"Acknowledged," Horst replied. "*Munin* engines now readied on standby. Launch window in ten seconds."

"*Nebula Storm* maneuvering thrusters fully charged, ready for use. Model reports all operations within parameters. We are a go for launch."

"Understood, *Nebula Storm*. We are go for launch. General Hohenheim, please confirm."

On the tight-beam communicator, the general's voice was steady and certain. "All telemetry shows green. Launch window has arrived. Launch when ready."

"Beginning countdown," Maddie said, and took a deep breath. The automatics would stil do most of the work, but this cobbled-together vessel, modeled or not, would almost certainly need the human touch to fly straight. "Ten seconds to launch. Full control of *Nebula Storm* attitude jets now assigned to *Munin*. Override controls on *Nebula Storm* show green."

"Five seconds," Horst picked up the countdown, "Prepared to launch ... two ... one ..."

The belly thrusters of *Munin* activated first, rearing the double ship up until it pointed upward at an angle of eighty-two degrees. Then the main drive cut in, a rumble, then a roar, and the implacably heavy hand of acceleration pressed down on her. *I am so weak now; even with all the exercise in the centrifuge we have all weakened. Bone structure, at least, hasn't shown much deterioration. If this works, we will have better options for keeping us fit on the way home.*

"We have liftoff from Europa," she reported, and could not keep the excitement and triumph from her voice. "*Nebula Storm* and *Munin* are up and accelerating." A higher-pitched jet sound. "*Nebula Storm* maneuver jets firing automatically for pitch and yaw. Minimal roll tendency."

Don't need to endure much of this. "Past the halfway mark, all green. Yellow now on course—"

"On it," Horst said, cutting her off. The side jets of both *Munin* and *Nebula Storm* fired. The plot went green again. "Course now optimal within projected limits. Main burn concluding in three, two, one, *zero!*"

Even as she said it, the main rocket went silent. "On course for rendezvous," she said, and heard the responding cheer. "Matching burn at Europa L1 point in less than one hour."

She let herself relax, read a few chapters of the latest novel she'd had transmitted from Earth, and rechecked all systems again; this took up the time until they were closing in on the matching burn.

"*Odin*, this is *Nebula Storm* and *Munin*," she said. "We are now on approach to match with you at the Europan L1 point. Confirm you have us on radar and visual?"

"Confirmed, *Nebula Storm*, *Munin*. Telescopes have you on visual and are tracking. Radar shows you on approach with minimal deviation from projected path. Proceed with matching burn."

"Roger, *Odin*," Horst said. "Rotating both vessels."

The joined vessels performed a lazy somersault and stopped, oriented now one hundred eighty degrees from their prior heading. "Rotation complete. Orientation now correct. Closing to rendezvous location. Beginning matching burn in three, two . . ."

The roar of *Munin*'s engine, transmitted through their mutual connections, was shorter this time, as some of the prior burn had of course been necessary to climb some distance out of Europa's gravity well. She checked the instruments and smiled. "Relative velocity of *Munin* and *Nebula Storm* now five point six meters per second."

She could see *Odin* now, the once-elegant ship now little more than a cylinder drifting in space, the old mass-driver units cut so short that they were barely nubs showing at one end. "*Munin*, *Nebula Storm* is initiating separation in ten seconds."

"Initiating separation, understood. *Munin* standing by."

And here we go. "Separation . . . now."

The tethers and umbilicals were severed in a precise sequence, ending with a tiny burn of one of *Nebula Storm*'s underjets that set both ships slowly drifting apart. Her smile broadened as she saw the results. "Separation complete and successful, *Munin*."

"*Munin* also shows full and successful separation. Proceeding to dock at hangar. Good luck, *Nebula Storm*."

"Thanks," she said.

She watched *Munin* move away towards *Odin*, and waited while the still-huge EU vessel loomed closer. No point in killing her speed until she was very close.

Once she'd done that, though, the tricky part began. "*Odin*, this is *Nebula Storm*. Prepare for docking and integration."

"Acknowledged. We are ready, Maddie. Come home."

"On my way."

She used the maneuvering jets to position herself directly "ahead" of *Odin*, opposite where *Nebula Storm*'s old rocket nozzle was now installed. She could vaguely see a blackish circle with her unaugmented vision, but by kicking in full assisted display she could see a tapered tunnel built directly into the center of *Odin*. Even as she watched, bright white LED panels blinked on, positioned all along the length of the tunnel on the four main axial directions. It was a landing strip in three-D. *That will help the automatics.*

"In position. Accelerating to docking."

She nudged *Nebula Storm* forward. At a hundred meters, the closing velocity was a meter per second. When she reached twenty meters, she decelerated, to ten centimeters per second.

The automatics triggered tiny lateral burns. *Nebula Storm* drifted sideways imperceptibly, a few millimeters a second, until the opposite-side laterals activated, making *Odin* utterly stationary before her, just looming up now in all directions.

Two meters and she triggered another burn, a centimeter per second, as the sharp nose of the ancient Bemmie hull entered that tunnel. *All up to the automatics now . . . and to the design and engineering skills of Brett, Mia, Joe, and Horst.*

A sudden, tremendously short burst from the jets, and then there was a jolting impact that echoed through the ship. At the same time she heard other sounds, tiny clicks, subsidiary clacking noises, and green lights blossomed across the panel where things had been dark a moment before. One glowed amber, then flashed to green.

"*Nebula Storm*," Hohenheim said, "docking is complete. All connections have been made. Welcome back, Agent Fathom."

She sagged back in her chair. "Thank you, General."

"Please wait a few moments. We will begin to spin the ship up to full rotation. Then you may exit."

"Acknowledged."

"In addition," Hohenheim continued, "we are now not two ships, but one ship, on a single and final mission. I do not think it is appropriate to call this vessel by the name of either of its parts."

"I would agree," Madeline said. "Did you have a name in mind?"

"I do," the general said, "and one I think is most appropriate and in keeping with current namings beside."

"Ha!" came A.J.'s voice. "Then I know what it is!"

"I have no doubt you do, Mr. Baker." The general's voice was amused. "And you are a man of dramatics; go ahead, then, tell us."

"You sure? Don't want to steal your thunder, so to speak."

Even Maddie laughed. "By all means, go ahead, Mr. Baker."

A.J.'s voice was suddenly serious, the same tone as when he had christened *Nebula Storm* those many months ago. "Okay, than. Born of the power of *Odin*, wielding the force of the *Nebula Storm*, this is *Mjölnir*, Thor's Hammer, short of handle, mighty in power. Thrown out into the solar system we both were, and now we return!"

The others clapped. "A good name indeed, General, A.J.," she said. "And I think appropriate in another way."

She unstrapped herself, feeling that *Mjölnir* was already rotating, and let the living quarters extend themselves outward. "We are also now a weapon."

Chapter 48

"We are on course, General." Jackie said. "Ready for Oberth maneuver in...ten minutes."

General Hohenheim chuckled.

"What is it, General?"

Hohenheim glanced towards Anthony LaPointe, who was sitting to Jackie's right. "Recollection, Dr. Secord. Those precise words were spoken to me once before... by Dr. LaPointe, as I recall...and the maneuver did not turn out to be quite as routine as we thought."

There were laughs around the engineering room which was now *Mjölnir*'s bridge. "Well," A.J. said, "this time there's just one ship making the turn, so we're not going to get into an argument with each other."

"Indeed. And we are no longer encumbered by Mr. Fitzgerald's presence." He looked at Madeline, who was strapped in nearby. "Speaking of the quite unlamented Mr. Fitzgerald, are we prepared for our approach in-system and an encounter with his presumed superiors?"

"I believe so, General. A.J., Mia, Horst, and Brett, with some added input from myself, have gone over every system of significance very carefully." She nodded to Horst.

"Your codes were invaluable, sir," Horst said. "There were a *lot* of backdoors into the code placed there by whoever set up the system in the first place, and it was very adaptable code; all Fitzgerald had to do was download something sent to him from back home and it would be accepted into the system with top priority. But A.J. and I, we are quite sure we have... neutered, I think would be the right word... all of this code."

"Right," said A.J. "It will *seem* to act, and we can send back dummy signals that will make it appear to whoever's doing it that *Thor* is responding—thank Brett for that, he'll be able to simulate the response just fine. We can even see what they expect and decide if we want to go along with it for a while."

He felt a grim warmth. *All is prepared.* "Very good. I will of course remain invisible until the... denouement, yes?"

"That is indeed the plan," Maddie said cheerfully. "Either they'll act or they won't; if they don't, your appearance will *still* be the nail in their coffins. If they *do* act, you'll have something new as well as something old to talk about."

Hohenheim nodded. "And when, exactly, do you think they will make their attempt?"

"Honestly? I don't think they really will. No matter *how* they do it, having *Mjölnir* crash at the end of the trip will look suspicious, and they can't be a hundred percent certain that we haven't sent sufficient evidence somewhere they can't reach. If they *do* attempt it... Whenever we're near the inner system and in the midst of some delicate maneuver. Their intent, remember, will have to be to cause a fatal, preferably utterly catastrophic, accident which wipes out any trace of the whole debacle. Earth orbital insertion would be my guess."

"Yes," Anthony concurred. "There it will be easy to make the orbit go wrong, send us into reentry. A landing through Earth's atmosphere, that will not be so survivable."

"And they could get a lot more people killed," Joe said darkly.

A.J. shrugged. "They *could*, but if they do it at all they'll be controlling that part of the show, or they would if we didn't cut them off at the pass. They're stupid in some ways, but they have no reason to kill anyone they don't have to. Calculate the *way* you want the orbit to go wrong and you can determine our crash-landing spot pretty easily."

"One minute, General," Jackie said. "Everyone strapped in?"

"All locked down," Larry said. Everyone was gathered in *Mjölnir*'s control room to watch.

Once more, Jupiter loomed up in all its incomprehensible vastness, no longer a rounded giant moon-shape but a cream and brown *wall* that seemed to rise from the infinite depths and recede above back into unbounded space. They were nearly as low down as *Nebula Storm* had been on her pass, as low as they dared fly the cobbled-together vessel, and this time they were calculating the maneuver to increase their speed in a particular vector, one that would take them *in*-system with tremendous velocity. The Nebula Drive would be kept to a minimum for some time, then redeployed to guide and slow them in their final approach in-system.

"Twenty seconds. Main nuclear drive reports all

ready." Mia gave her own smile. "And this time it will *work*, General."

"I certainly hope so."

Madeline took up the final count. "And...five. Four. Three. Two. One. Z—"

The deep-thunder roar of the nuclear rocket vibrated the control room with absolute power, erasing Madeline's voice, sending bone-deep vibration through Hohenheim's bones like the drone of a billion giant bees. *We are practically on top of the rocket here; I had forgotten what it sounded like.*

Mjölnir lunged forward, dumping mass at high speed, exchanging it for even more velocity, screaming around the largest of the planets at a speed so great that even mighty Jove could not stop it. The thunder went on and on, water ejected in hundred-ton lots behind the combined IRI-EU vessel and giving *Mjölnir* the greatest speed of any human-crewed vessel ever constructed.

And then the rocket cut off, and the stillness rather than the rocket was silently deafening.

"Anthony, report. How is our course?"

There was a pause, and then the French astronomer grinned. "It is perfect. We are precisely on course, to the limit of what I can measure." He turned his chair to face the others. "My friends, we are truly on our way *home!*"

When the brief but heartfelt cheers subsided, Hohenheim nodded. "And our E.T.A. at Earth?"

"As we calculated—one hundred eighty-two days, almost exactly six months. Which, I must assure you, is incredibly fast."

"Fast?" A.J. said, wrinkling his brow. "We went

from a zero standing start at Ceres and caught you in less than half of that."

"Ha! Yes, very fast. Ceres was much closer, in the asteroid belt, and you could accelerate all the way, as could we. In this case, we cannot accelerate any more, all we can do is coast, and then use your Nebula Drive to slow us *down* at the end, with *Mjölnir* using the last of its main drive to do the final matching burn."

"Still," Madeline said, "don't be too impatient. We have plenty of supplies to last, and with the delays in construction, we may *still* get home before the ship that was supposed to rescue us gets out of drydock!"

A.J. seemed satisfied with the reply, and Hohenheim nodded slowly. "Yes. I would like that very much. We have saved ourselves, and to get home this way...it is a fitting tribute, in a way, to those who could not finish the mission. We have joined together, and we return what we can...home."

Chapter 49

"God above—wherever 'above' is out here," A.J. moaned theatrically. "I ache *all* over." He glared, not terribly seriously, at Petra Masters. "You *enjoy* our suffering, don't you?"

Dr. Masters smiled thinly. "If so, Mr. Baker, I must also be a masochist. One point two gravities is a bit much, but we spent far too long in microgravity. Now most of us can stay in higher gravity for significant periods, and after only two and a half weeks I am already seeing a noticeable improvement in bone density." She pointed. "Are you going to get in on this tournament, or not?"

A.J. tagged in and the 3-D display shimmered to show the *Ryu-Chi Warriors* tournament matches.

Helen looked on in bemusement. "A.J. and Joe I knew about, and I suppose Mia and Brett aren't a great surprise, but I must confess I didn't expect *you* two to be . . . into these sorts of games."

Petra Masters raised an eyebrow as A.J. chuckled. "Do you mean that an English doctor can't enjoy breaking a few virtual bones? I assure you, there are a few patients that make it a quite cathartic release."

"And I realize it may seem beneath my dignity," Hohenheim said, "but such games were, I must confess, a staple of my youth. When I wasn't outdoors doing something more active, that is." He glanced over. "Ah. I see it is you first, Mia."

"At least I get a chance to cause *you* some virtual pain with some virtual gravity," A.J. said to Petra.

"Don't get too ahead of yourself, Mr. Baker. You have yet to reach the finals, which is where we shall meet."

A.J. tried not to snort too loudly. "I seem to recall *you* were the one insisting we set the difficulty level at 'novice,'" he pointed out. Looking up at Madeline, who seemed satisfied to observe on the sidelines, he went on, "Now, if it was our Supergirl, I'd concede."

Maddie shook her head. "Oh, no, I think you'd probably beat me. That's a pretty specialized kind of game, and I've only played them a couple of times."

Privately, A.J. suspected she only played "a couple of times" because that's all it took for her to master them. Instead, however, he said, "Have you gotten any info back from Nick since we left?"

"Just a little while ago, in fact. He said to let everyone know that the proper reception is arranged and we're to dock at *Meru*."

A.J. couldn't keep a rather sharklike grin from his face, and he saw it echoed on several of the others. "Proper reception arranged" meant that they were ready to move against Osterhoudt and his immediate allies, and that the press conference had been arranged according to specifications. "Eeeexcellent," he said, steepling his fingers.

The virtual ring echoed to shouts and grunts as Mia, playing the hulking powerhouse Vargas, tried to land a solid punch on her opponent; the computer, being somewhat clever even in novice mode, had put her up against Calamet, a combat dancer who used speed and stealth moves. Finally, though, Mia figured out that broad sweep attacks could brush Calamet's defenses aside and put him off-balance momentarily, which allowed Vargas to hammer his opponent. "Nice!" he said approvingly. Mia clearly hadn't played these games very often, but she'd approached the problem like an engineer, and taken her opponent apart.

"So, Doc Petra," he said, "what about the drugs? Did you get results on them? I know you were testing us with light doses."

"Good preliminary ones, A.J.; I believe that is partly why we are seeing good progress now. The side effects—though we obviously have a very limited group here—seem relatively minor, except for Dan who had an obvious sensitivity, possibly actual allergic reaction and who has thus not been taking them. It does appear his progress is significantly slower than the rest of you. Because of that, by the way," she looked to both Hohenheim and Madeline, "I wish to have Mr. Ritter permanently assigned to one of the acceleration cabins. This is the only way I can think of to hopefully get him to match us; since we all have to—pardon the pun—rotate in and out of the cabins, and he will not, this will give him a significantly longer time in high-gravity."

Hohenheim shrugged. "I see no reason why not, as long as the constant exposure will do him no harm—and as you are the medical officer, that is of course your judgment to make." A.J. saw Maddie give an assenting nod as well.

At that point Joe's fighter, the reptilian Orochi, was kicked violently out of the ring. "Ouch! Too bad, Joe. I guess you'll have to wait for the next round."

"Or maybe Maddie and I will just head out for a walk by ourselves," Joe said with an easy grin. Maddie took his hand as he floated over to her. "Well, after the first round is over, anyway," he corrected himself. "I want to see if *you* make it past the first."

"Well, well," A.J. said, ignoring his friend's feeble barb, "it's *your* first round, Doc Masters. Good luck."

Masters fumbled slightly with the control gestures, but Shun Hashimura, the bishonen martial artist she'd chosen, walked onto the ring with only minimal clumsiness. "Oh, blast," she said. "I'm up against Ryuken. He's *such* a bastard."

A.J. knew she wasn't just referring to his personality—though the game backstory certainly made the word fit. He was also one of the best fighters in the game and getting him in your first round was ... unlucky.

The two squared off against each other and the refereeing master raised an arm, then let it drop.

Shun Hashimura spun low, long black hair whipping out, twining around Ryuken's legs before he'd so much as taken half a step; the long-haired boy then did a handspring-kick to Ryuken's face, landed on his feet and whipped his head about, yanking the hapless virtual warrior around and hurling him so high into the air he disappeared in a twinkle of light. "Perfection in Beauty," the judge said, with a bow to the assembled watchers. "Victory, Shun Hashimura."

A.J. slowly transferred his gaze to Petra, whose smile was failing to hide her self-satisfaction. "'Tis true, Mr. Baker, that I insisted on the novice setting," she said,

and her voice was almost a *purr*, "but I don't recall
in the least that I said it was for *me*."

He burst out laughing. "Okay, fine, you had me
fooled. Good! See you in the finals—if Brett or the
general don't beat us there."

"Unlike the good doctor," Hohenheim said, "I am
quite rusty. But I will try to put up a good fight."

It was Hohenheim's turn next. A.J. leaned back.
"Good thing I didn't decide to actually go for a bet.
I would've bet you wouldn't get past the first match.
Ouch." He shook his head. "Anyway, I'm glad you've
got good data."

"Excellent data, and I've already written most of
two papers I'll be wanting to present. How about
you—Oh, *good* one, General!"

"Oh, he'll be feeling *that* in the morning," A.J.
agreed, watching Onikami trying to drag itself to its
feet before the general's Tankero closed the distance.
"Me? Well, I'm not the research and publish type, but
I've been working with Helen to help put together
some of her reports. Joe, too."

Now it was *her* turn to look at him with a raised
eyebrow. "For a man who isn't the publication type,
you have quite a large set of publications. Two hundred, last I looked."

He shrugged, a bit embarrassed. "Eh. Yeah, my
name is on that many, but in a lot of them I'm just
giving people better eyes, I didn't do a significant bit
of the *real* work."

"You're up, A.J.," Helen said, nudging him.

"Are you reminding me because you want to see
me humiliated?"

She laughed and gave him a quick kiss, which was

of course what he'd hoped for. "No, not really. I'm glad just to see how we can all just *relax* for the most part now."

"Same here," A.J. said. *Okay, Zellie Tenjou, let's show 'em what you've got.*

"Yep, I told you," Joe said as the tiny girl in her pink and powder-blue stepped into the ring, "he *always* picks the harmless-looking, cute ones." He looked pointedly at Zellie's short skirt. "The ones that kick *really* high."

A.J. felt his face go red. "Shut *up* and don't distract me, Joe!"

"You're right, sorry," Joe said contritely. A pause. "After all, you've got all the distraction you need right there."

Chapter 50

"*Mjölnir*, this is *Meru* control. All other traffic has been cleared from your area. Continue your approach and prepare for docking." The professional voice of the controller shifted to a more personal tone. "And *welcome home!*"

"Thank you very much, *Meru*," Madeline said. "But please, let's save the welcomes and celebration until after we dock. I don't think any of us are going to relax until we're actually *there.*"

"Understood, *Mjölnir.*"

She glanced over. The cameras were focused only on her and showed nothing of the rest of the engineering-area-turned-bridge of the *Mjölnir*. This was a good thing, since General Alberich Hohenheim was sitting not far to her right, and his continued survival was still something that needed to be kept a secret. They'd been in secret communication with Glendale and, through him, with the relevant authorities on

Earth. They were bound and determined to see that those responsible for the destruction of the *Odin* were brought to justice.

She looked at the display clock in her helmet. *Five minutes.* ·

Jackie took the central seat with a smile. "With your permission, General?"

"I am still a secret for these few minutes," Hohenheim replied. "The *Mjölnir* is yours, Captain."

"Everyone strap in," Jackie said. Madeline complied and brought up her own controls. "Anthony, Mia, prepare for final burn."

"I have verified our matching burn calculations," Anthony said. "Mia has the numbers. Beginning *Mjölnir* rotation for burn." A few moments passed. "Ship rotation complete," Anthony said. "Main burn countdown begin."

The last few seconds were ticking away. Looking at *Meru* and, beyond, the perfect blue-white globe of Earth, she was struck by a cascade of memories: *Nike* approaching the threatening mass of Phobos; the *John Carter* careening out of control; turning a corner to come face-to-face with a Tyrannosaurus Rex on Mars; desperate panic as she thought her husband had died mere seconds before she rescued him from a pit on Ceres; landing *Nebula Storm* on Europa; watching *Zarathustra* descend into the freezing depths; waiting in the dark as the power of her suit faded. She felt a sudden sense of wonder. How had they survived all that?

Mjölnir roared back to full life, one final thundering blast from the nuclear rocket that had, once, belonged to *Nike* and had traveled from Earth to Mars and all the way to Jupiter and now, at last, returned like its namesake to the place from which it had come. *Now, if ever...* she thought. The ideal time to disrupt their homecoming, to send them to destruction, it was this moment, as they approached Earth, to send them hurtling into the atmosphere and burn all the evidence to ash.

But nothing untoward happened. She smiled; honestly, she hadn't *expected* anything to happen; even for their opponents, the risk of such tampering was too great. But it was still an immense relief. She felt the gentle force of the deceleration, the vibration thrumming through her, a familiar yet still thrilling sensation, and a comforting one, one that assured her that everything really was going to be all right.

Then it cut off. Hisses, tiny shots of vapor as the attitude jets were used to kill the last remnants of motion, adjust the very final course.

Everything was still. Andrew turned from his console. "*Mjölnir* now stationary with respect to *Meru*. *Meru*'s crews are attaching cables to bring us in and complete docking."

Without warning, he let out a whoop that almost deafened everyone in the control room. "We have *done* it!"

The cheers were echoed around the room... and from the radio, as well. "We have indeed," Madeline agreed. Her eyes went to the Earth, slowly turning below, searching for a particular spot.

One last loose end...

Goswin Osterhoudt was fairly certain that there was no way his involvement in the disaster that had

overtaken the *Odin* could be discovered. Not enough
of his involvement for any legal charges to be brought
against him, at least. There would inevitably be rumors,
of course. But there were always rumors about powerful men like Osterhoudt. Only the scandal sheets
would ever print them, and who paid attention to such
reports? No one serious; certainly no one in position
of authority.

Some of Fitzgerald's underlings had survived, but
they didn't matter. None of them would have ever
known anything about their ultimate employer—and,
in any event, the three survivors had not been in
Jupiter orbit when the catastrophe occurred.

The wreck of the *Odin* was somewhat more prob-
lematic. It was, naturally, a piece of evidence of
deception all on its own... but again, there were ways
of making sure certain things were kept quiet. There
was far, far too much to lose for the IRI or Ares to
risk disrupting a potentially profitable relationship
with the EU over what was now over and done with.
There would, perhaps, be quiet backroom deals and
apologies—without names and behind nondisclosure
agreements—but nothing that would truly threaten him.

Still, Osterhoudt prided himself on being a practical
man, as well as a smart one. It was always possible
that, in the heat of the moment after the ill-fated
expedition's return, rash actions might be taken against
him by one or another of the more impetuous police
agencies. Which was why he was now at sea on his
private yacht, off the coast of Malta and well into
international waters.

Very few people knew he was here, at least at the
moment. His transmissions were still routed through

one of his private homes in Germany, one that was technically supposed to be a secret. In all likelihood, of course, nothing untoward would happen. In which case, he could simply finish a very pleasant and private vacation before returning to Europe.

He sat down in one of the comfortable, well-cushioned chairs and activated his own access network. Once full encryption was established and keys exchanged, he was able to view the current situation with perfect safety. The news channels, of course, were all focused on the approach of *Mjölnir*. He found himself leaning forward, chided himself for tension, then laughed a bit. *Of course I'm tense. No reason for me to hide it, here.* His stomach tightened slightly, and he debated having a drink, but decided against it. *Best to be as clear-headed as possible. Just in case.*

For the next half hour, the news channels devoted themselves to pointless chit-chat between news announcers and various experts brought in for the occasion. The truth was, space travel was boring unless something disastrous happened.

There was a slight hope in Osterhoudt's mind that such a catastrophe might transpire, given the jury-rigged nature of the spacecraft involved. The *Mjölnir* was now close enough for cameras to depict in detail its rather grotesque construction.

But it was only a faint hope. The surviving astronauts had been able to cobble together the craft and bring it all the way back from Jupiter orbit. How likely was it that they'd fail now, at the very end?

And it didn't matter, really. There would certainly be repercussions, of course, for what was far and away the worst disaster in the history of space flight. It was conceivable that Osterhoudt might lose his position as the Chief Operations Officer of the European Space Development Corporation. But the ESDC would provide him with a suitable retirement package, just to maintain the needed facade—and, when all was said and done, he was already a very wealthy man.

The news channel abruptly cleared away the chattering heads and showed the docking bay of the space elevator. "*Mjölnir* has successfully docked with *Meru*," announced the newscaster, a bit breathlessly. "We should be seeing the crew disembark at any moment."

And, indeed, within a few seconds the hatch swung aside and the survivors of the Jupiter expedition began coming through.

Madeline Fathom came first, followed by her husband Joe Buckley. Then, A.J. Baker, Helen Sutter, Larry Conley, and a dark-complected woman whom Osterhoudt presumed to be the Ares engineer. What was her name? Second? No, Secord. He couldn't recall her first name.

She was followed by the first of the survivors of the *Odin* disaster, the tall, blond engineer Horst Eberhardt; immediately behind him was a smaller man with brown hair. Osterhoudt recognized him as the French astrophysicist LaPointe. Then came—

When the next man's face came into view, Osterhoudt was paralyzed with shock.

Hohenheim? But it was not *possible*! He was supposed to be dead! The broadcasts from the *Mjölnir* had explicitly said so. Why—?

Some of Osterhoudt's confusion was shared by the newscaster, who was babbling away. Hohenheim approached the camera and looked directly into it.

"I am General Alberich Hohenheim, formerly commander of the European Union vessel *Odin*," he said, "now in joint command of the vessel *Mjölnir*."

His harsh tone softened a bit. "I must first apologize to my family and my friends, who have suffered much at my supposed loss. I can only say I hope you will understand once all is explained."

Osterhoudt finally grasped the truth, the only possible explanation: that he had been tricked. *A lie. A fabrication maintained for* months... *and all with only one possible goal.*

"What happened to *Odin* and *Nebula Storm*," Hohenheim continued, "was no accident. It was a disaster caused by the actions of one man, making use of illegal and covert weaponry placed upon *Odin* ..."

This was far worse than Osterhoudt had anticipated. But he took a deep breath and calmed himself. He was still outside of any territorial waters, after all. He had access to as fine a communications suite as existed almost anywhere on the planet, and had half a dozen excellent lawyers on his payroll. He simply had to remain calm and stay at sea for a while, while he conferred with his legal staff and other advisors.

Hearing a slight noise, he turned in his seat and saw that the yacht's captain had entered the cabin. The man had a peculiar expression on his face.

"Mr. Osterhoudt..."

"Yes?" he asked impatiently. There was no time to waste.

"We've been hailed, sir. By an Italian destroyer. They say they're planning to board."

Osterhoudt stared at him. "Board? But... They have no right to do so!"

The captain cleared his throat. "Perhaps so, Mr. Osterhoudt. But whether they have the right or not, what they *do* have are seventy-six-millimeter guns—the front two of which are pointed at us—not to mention surface-to-surface missiles and torpedoes. So I don't believe we have any choice in the matter."

There was no point arguing with the captain. Clearly enough, the man felt his obligations to his employer only went so far.

Osterhoudt heaved himself out of the chair and clambered up the ladder onto the deck. By the time he got there, he recognized the sound he was hearing. A helicopter was already on the way.

His yacht had a helipad, naturally. For a man of his stature in business affairs, that was a practical necessity as well as a matter of prestige. Within a couple of minutes, the helicopter had landed and two men were disembarking.

Both of them were wearing uniforms of some sort. Osterhoudt didn't recognize them, but he wasn't really familiar with the Italian armed forces.

It was only when the men were within a couple of meters that he belatedly realized the uniforms were those of a police force. Something called the EU Transnational Police, apparently, according to the insignia.

He hadn't known the EU even *had* a police force of its own. He'd never had much contact with police agencies. A man like Osterhoudt dealt with legal authorities frequently, of course, but the ones they dealt with were the ones who gave orders to policemen. Not policemen themselves.

Abrupt bastards, as you'd expect. "Mr. Osterhoudt, you're under arrest," said the larger of the two.

Osterhoudt put on his best derisive expression. It was quite good; had served him well over the years. Just short of an outright sneer, but clearly conveying the sense that those upon whom the expression was bestowed had severely transgressed both reason and polite custom.

"That's preposterous. Just for starters, we're in international waters. You have no authority here."

The policeman who'd spoken smiled thinly. "I'm afraid we do, Mr. Osterhoudt. There's a long list of charges, which includes conspiracy to commit murder. But the first charge is piracy." The smile widened slightly. "Pirates, as you perhaps know—this has been well-established legal practice for, oh, centuries now—can be apprehended on the high seas by . . . oh, just about anyone."

His associate spoke up, for the first time. "Certainly by anyone"—here he drew forth a sheaf of documents from his jacket—"carrying an arrest warrant issued by the European Union's official police force."

The policeman who'd spoken first unclipped a pair of handcuffs from his belt. "And—oh happy chance—carrying suitable manacles," he said.

His partner's smile now bordered on an outright grin. He waved the arrest warrant in the direction of the destroyer. "Not to mention half a dozen seventy-six-millimeter guns. They can fire up to eighty rounds a minute, you know. So I really recommend you put up no resistance."

"This is preposterous. *Piracy?* That charge will never hold up in court! I've never even *been* on any vessel other than my yacht or a few other similar ships!" Osterhoudt wasn't *resisting*, but these people had to

understand how ludicrous—how unacceptable!—this
entire situation was. *Piracy?*

The second officer shrugged. "Not for us to judge
what holds up in court, sir," he answered. "But as for
you being *on* the ship, you're being charged under
Article 101(c) of the United Nations Convention on
the Law of the Sea, as extended during the debates
on Mars to include space. And Article 101(c), sir,
specifically includes inciting or facilitating an act of
piracy—whether present or not."

The first officer opened the handcuffs. Osterhoudt
stared at the grotesque things and a dreadful leaden
weight seemed to fill his stomach as he realized that
all his words did not matter. The specific *charges*
didn't even matter. They were sufficient to the purpose, which was...

"Turn around, Mr. Osterhoudt. And extend your
hands behind your back." There was no concealing
the satisfied tone in the policeman's voice. "As I said,
you're under arrest."

Chapter 51

The airlock door opened, and standing in it was a slender—*too slender*, Nicholas thought—figure, helmet off, golden hair cascading in perfect order, as though she had just stepped out from a salon. Camera lights flickered, but the small crowd held its place as Madeline Fathom floated forward and to the side to let her husband join her. A.J. Baker popped through next, waving with childlike mania, Helen Sutter grinning tolerantly behind him. Larry Conley was next, his face narrower than it had ever been before, and then Jackie—followed by the first of the *Odin* crew, Horst Eberhardt, and his friend Anthony LaPointe.

And then emerged the towering presence of General Alberich Hohenheim.

A sudden, complete hush fell over the room as Hohenheim walked slowly to the nearby cameras—a hush that exploded into questions and confusion, and then quieted again as he began to speak: "I am General Alberich Hohenheim, formerly commander of the European Union vessel *Odin* . . ."

But as he spoke the rest emerged from the airlock—the white hair of Dr. Petra Masters, Brett Tamahori grinning brilliantly as he stepped into *Meru*, Dan Ritter, and finally Mia Svendsen.

Suddenly Nicholas found himself leaping forward, seeing surprise and then welcome on the familiar faces, even as Hohenheim continued his short, measured address. The next few moments were simply a blur—a very *happy* blur—of hugs and handshakes and greetings whose words were different but every one meant "welcome home."

Slowly he became aware that cameras were still flashing, and there was clapping in the audience, as well. He wiped his face, realizing with surprise that he was crying.

It made him feel somewhat better that most of the others—even the cocky A.J. and laid-back Larry Conley—did not seem entirely dry-eyed either. "I seem to have gotten a bit carried away."

Madeline had gotten a tissue from somewhere and was very expertly dabbing away her own tears without in any way marring her appearance. "It's good press . . . and honest press, too," she said with a smile.

He returned the smile, gazing around at his colleagues and friends. "I must confess . . . It was one thing to know you were safe; but after all this time, something quite different to *see* you all here, and alive."

He turned to the group from *Odin* as Hohenheim joined them, his short initial statement finished. "General, I did not know your crew, but I personally offer my sympathies for your losses."

General Hohenheim nodded. "I thank you." He looked over Glendale's shoulder, and Nicholas knew what he was seeing. "Ah. Already."

"You had requested this, sir," he pointed out. "I

believe that there was no one—in fact, still *is* no one—who would insist—"

"Except, perhaps, myself. And I *do* insist." General Hohenheim drifted forward, straightened himself on a handhold, and saluted the two men waiting; they returned the salute, but did not look happy.

Hohenheim smiled faintly. "Director Glendale, I was the commanding officer of *Odin.* What happened there was, ultimately, my responsibility, no matter what excuses others might make for me. My guilt and ultimate punishment—or, perhaps, reward for later actions—is not mine to decide, nor yours, nor that of the world which is seeing such drama. I want my name tried and cleared, or convicted, in as clear and legal a fashion as I wish to see Mr. Osterhoudt tried."

The rest of the *Odin* crew—Horst, Mia, Anthony, Petra, Brett, and Dan—started to protest, then quieted. Horst moved forward. "Then at least remember to call us, sir. When the court-martial begins."

"I assure you, Mr. Eberhardt," General Hohenheim said, "I will not *neglect* my defense. I hope I can count on you all for testimony, if needed?"

Horst and the others nodded vigorously. Madeline added, "And I believe I speak for all the former crew of *Nebula Storm* when I say that we will also happily testify on your behalf, if needed."

"Very good, then. Do not *worry* on my behalf, then. I am sure we shall meet again, all of us. And even if not..."

The smile that broke across the face was startling, a boyish grin as bright as the dawn. "... even if not, my very good friends, we have shared the most *amazing* adventure, have we not? An adventure which would keep a man proud and strong to the end of any days, I think."

He turned back and left with the two UN police, back straight, head as high as weightless movement would permit.

Nicholas watched him go, and even the crowd was quieter until the general had disappeared from sight.

"Well, Nicholas," Madeline said, "I see we have quite a reception. I suppose they expect interviews?"

"You *know* they do; you helped arrange this, after all."

"Indeed I did. But I think one of the spinning lounges would be a better setting."

Nicholas agreed, and led them from the non-spinning central hub of *Meru* to the outer, spinning living area.

"Nicholas," Helen said as they walked, "pardon my ignorance, but space construction is still a weak point with me. Meru is basically a huge tower sticking out from the Earth—why don't we feel weight up here? I know that it falls off with distance, but..."

Nicholas nodded. "It does, and faster than you think. Given the distances you've traveled, I suppose being a mere forty-two thousand kilometers up is very close. But it's still well over six times the distance from the center of the Earth that you are at the surface, so even if you *did* feel the gravity here, you would not feel much—it's less than one-fortieth of Earth's." He smiled wryly. "Space construction isn't *my* strong point originally, either, but I've had to learn a lot of the little factoids. In any case, even if gravity were noticeable up here, we are in actual fact not on a tower, but a bulge on a string that has a big weight another forty-two thousand kilometers above us, and are effectively in orbit—and thus freefall. So," they entered one of the larger meeting rooms of *Meru*, "we have to spin to sit down, just like everyone else out here."

Nicholas again took note of the fact that his friends looked more worn, thinner than he remembered, and also that when they sat down, most of them seemed to *drop* into their seats. *They've spent a long time in very low gravity, with non-ideal equipment and supplies. The doctors want them very soon, and I'm not going to argue.*

The press, and a few other guests, filed in and took their seats. Nicholas stood as soon as they were all settled. "Thank you all for coming, and for your great restraint so far. I want you to know that we very much appreciate the courtesy.

"Now, before we get started, I have a few announcements. First, I reserve the right to cut this conference off at any time; many of you can probably see that the crew of *Mjölnir* is not at all in top shape, and as soon as this conference is over they are *all* going to medical for testing and rehabilitation.

"Second," he said, now smiling at Helen, "I received official word only shortly before *Mjölnir* arrived: the United Nations is preparing to vote—any moment—on a resolution to declare Europa and its inhabitants a nation."

"Oh, thank God." Helen's preferences had never been in doubt, and he saw the sentiment echoed on all the other faces on his side of the table.

"Of course, I rather expected this. Perhaps a more interesting part of the declaration is that Camp Europa is to be a historical site; some of the equipment will doubtless be reused, but your landing and survival will be commemorated."

"What about the *Zarathustra* and the Bemmies?" Diane Sodher asked. Nicholas decided to just let the questions start. *Why not? Now that they're back, we have time.*

"I was about to get to that," he said. "Engineers from at least a dozen countries are currently working on designs to establish a safe and flexible working environment to permit long-term contact with our alien friends. As soon as an alternative exists, *Zarathustra* will be removed and likely become the centerpiece of the commemorative site."

"I thought there was considerable concern about contaminating other worlds with our own bacteria," asked another of the news people—*Hazumi Kishimura*, Nicholas remembered. "Won't this pose challenges for sending more people there?"

"That feline has completely escaped the flexible container," A.J. replied. "We didn't decontaminate before the crash, we were *living* there for months, we've undoubtedly dumped all kinds of our bacteria somewhere on that moon. We'll want to be careful not to contaminate them with something dangerous if we can, but heck, I suppose there's just as much chance they've got something *we* don't want to catch, either."

"Dr. Sutter, what was it like?" Diane asked. "To come face to face with the first alien species we've ever met?"

The room went silent, all watching Helen—who looked very uncomfortable for a moment.

Then she started to *think* about the question, and Nicholas could see the tension smooth away, replaced by a struggle to find the words. A few more moments went by.

Finally Helen shrugged and smiled. "What was it like?" she repeated. "I wish I could tell you. I don't know if there are words—and I'm not Nick, I'm not someone who makes speeches often. I do lectures." She shook her head, eyes now looking far away, back to an icy world with a black ocean beneath. "What was it *like*?" she said again. "It was ... it was *magic*. It was like opening a door, your front door, a door you open every single day and step out and go to your work, like opening *that* door and on the other side isn't your front yard and some steps like you've seen before, but a jungle where a pterodactyl soars high overhead and something taller than three houses stacked atop each other turns its head and looks down at you, curious, wondering. It was like taking a little jump, hopping over a curb you've stepped over a thousand times before, and finding you're *flying*, that somehow the wonderful, unbelievable, magical *impossible* has happened and you, *you* are the one person it's happened to in all the world, and even if other people learn how, you're the first, the one who stepped off the ordinary ground and *flew*." Her voice was unsteady, tears shimmered in her eyes. "It was *magic*."

In her words, for a moment, Nicholas *felt* the phantom chill of discovery, of the utterly unique moment in history, and the whole room was silent.

Finally, one voice spoke. "Just exactly like that," Joe Buckley said quietly. "Hey, for someone who doesn't do speeches, that was one damn fine improv, Helen."

The laughter rippled out, and on the heels of the

laughter came more questions. Nicholas let the interview go on for some time, making sure that each of the crew of *Mjölnir* got at least one answer. *History will record them all, and I'll make sure that none of them look back and say "Damn, I should have said something."*

Finally, he stood. "I think that's enough, people. Our friends need a lot of recuperation time."

"One more question, Nick," Hazumi said, and looked over to the others. "*Bifrost* was originally built to rescue you, but you managed to rescue yourselves. Now that she's built, will any of you go back? To finish your original mission?"

"Before they answer that," Nicholas said, "I should make my last announcement.

"As you say, *Bifrost* was originally designed as both a replacement for two lost vessels and as a rescue vessel. Now that *Mjölnir* has arrived home safely, it has been decided to take the time to expand and revise the design. There are pieces to be salvaged from *Mjölnir* which will likely serve again in *Bifrost*. The decision doesn't have to be made *now*." He looked back at his friends. "But if you do want to go . . . I'm sure any one of you would be more than welcome."

"I'm sure we would be," Maddie said, rising slowly. The others stood with her. "And I think . . . perhaps . . . some of us will. But . . ."

"But," A.J. continued, "we've spent *years* out there, and I, for one, am not ready to continue traveling the solar system in a controlled-environment cheesebox."

"Couldn't have said it better," Joe Buckley said, and slid an arm around Madeline's waist. "Our honeymoon— and yours and Helen's—wasn't exactly romantic, either."

He looked out the viewport, where the huge blue and white and brown of Earth was slowly passing in eternal circles. "The solar system's not going anywhere soon, and we've been away a long, long time.

"It's time to go home."

Chapter 52

"Do you remember that first fossil we found, back in Montana, more than fifteen years ago?" Helen asked.

The question was more rhetorical than anything else. Three of the people in the *Meru*'s medical observation deck had been involved in that discovery. Jackie had found the fossil, Joe had been with Helen when she first saw it, and A.J. had been drawn into the investigation only a few days later.

"Sure do," said Joe. His eyes were on the huge blue, white, and brown globe of Earth below, which—now that the the medical staff had given the all-clear—they would finally be returning to, after so very long. "You're thinking we've come full circle, aren't you?"

Helen shrugged. "In a way, yes. Emotionally, at least. Nemo and his folk aren't *really* Bemmies, if I wanted to be biologically precise about the matter. But..."

"What's the difference?" A.J. said. "They're descended one way or another from the people whose fossil we found, aren't they? And what's most important is the term itself. 'People.'" He paused, his tone full of wonder. "Bemmies are people now. Not fossils, not abstractions, not ancient history. People, living right here in our own solar system. In stellar terms, just a block or two away."

He grinned. "Hell, even the United Nations agrees. Unanimous resolution. How many times has *that* ever happened?"

A little chuckle swept through the deck. A short time ago, the vote had been announced: the United Nations General Assembly had voted to classify Europa and its inhabitants as a nation.

That would no doubt have come as a surprise to Nemo and his folk. Who knew if they even had the concept of a "nation"? But the issue was really one derived from human history, not alien history. True, the Bemmie descendants on Europa did not—yet, anyway—belong to the UN. But the Bemmies were a people, sure enough, and entitled to all the rights pertaining to any sovereign nation. There wouldn't be any fiddling with colonies or protectorates or such.

Of course, the unanimous vote over and done with, the wrangling had already started. Where, precisely, did Bemmie territory *begin*? At least one prominent school of thought insisted that it only began where the moon's ocean existed. And therefore it was perfectly legitimate for human nations and enterprises to create settlements on the surface of Europa, where, after all, no Bemmies lived nor *could* live without human assistance.

And were the Bemmies one nation—or many? No one knew. Yet, at least.

There was just as much wrangling on the flip side of that equation. However many polities the Bemmies were divided into, exactly which human polity or polities was to be the one *sending* them ambassadors, when that time came?

(*If* that time came, some people insisted. But their number, never large to begin with, was dwindling rapidly. Helen smiled to herself and glanced at A.J. and Joe. Their dream had finally become reality. Whatever else might come, the expedition to Jupiter had settled once and for all the question of whether space exploration was worth the cost.)

Was the United Nations itself to send ambassadors to the Bemmies? But the United Nations had never before sent ambassadors to anyone. Ambassadors were sent *to* the United Nations, not from it. To now do otherwise brought at least the suggestion that the UN was to become a state of its own. That thought was enough to produce a ruckus in practically every nation on Earth, none more so than the United States and China—who, each for its own reasons, were particularly touchy on the question of national sovereignty.

But if there was no supranational regulation of human-Bemmie relations, any number of unfortunate developments might occur. Even possibly outright disasters. All anyone had to do was look at human history to imagine an arms race between clashing Bemmie nations, each seeking advanced weaponry from different human nations.

Or from corporations out of control, she thought. And *there* is another ruckus.

The news of Osterhoudt's arrest was now on the front page of every major newspaper in the world and was usually the lead story in every major television newscast. The second or third story, at the very least.

The European Space Development Corporation's officials were scrambling frantically to distance themselves from the actions of the company's Chief Operations

Officer, and it looked like they might be successful—at least in keeping themselves from being arrested on criminal charges. It did now seem as if Osterhoudt had not directly involved any of the ESDC's other officers in the scheme which led to the catastrophe that killed most of the *Odin*'s crew.

But even if they managed to avoid prison, there was no longer much doubt that the careers of those corporate officials were over. Indeed, it was now deemed likely that the ESDC itself would be destroyed. At best, it would be subjected in the future to regulation and oversight so strict that it might as well just become an official agency of the European Union.

Oh, indeed. Ruckus after ruckus after ruckus. The controversies were in some cases so sharp that many commentators were prone to using the term "crisis" in every other sentence.

But it didn't really *feel* like a crisis to most people. And the reason was because for most people the news that another intelligent species had finally been discovered was a source of hope rather than anxiety.

Not all, of course. Any number of religious figures and denominations were unhappy at the news, and in some cases downright livid. But most of the world's religious currents and all of the major ones were taking the news reasonably well, if not exactly in stride.

And on a positive note, the profession of theologian was undergoing a sudden rise in popularity and was likely to be booming for at least a generation. Enrollment in religious schools was climbing sharply.

It helped that the Bemmies on Europa obviously posed no threat to human beings. True, there might be some species out there in the galaxy—perhaps related to the Bemmies, perhaps altogether new—which could and would threaten humanity. But that was a problem for another day, and probably not a day that would come anytime soon. One other thing that the Bemmie expeditions of the past few years seemed to have definitely established was that interstellar travel was possible, but extremely slow. There wasn't much likelihood that a fleet of invading aliens would be appearing in the Earth's skies. Not today, not tomorrow—and judging from the record, not for millions of years if ever.

Very few human beings, even ones prone to hysteria, can really work themselves into a panic over a threat that might loom eons after their death.

And in the meantime, there were those images and videos of Nemo and his kin that the expedition had brought back. Enrollment in courses that might lead someone to qualify for space exploration were now booming even more than enrollment in theological schools. And there was a veritable slew of babies being named "Nemo."

"Yes, full circle," Helen said finally, realizing the others had also paused, lost in their own thoughts. "But the close is also a beginning. I always wondered when our discoveries concerning the Bemmies would eventually end. Now, I know. Never. We'll be at this the rest of our lives. So will our own descendants—and if Bemmies are any gauge, those descendants of ours will still be around tens of millions of years from now."

Silence fell over the people on the deck again. It seemed enough—more than enough—just to watch the planet below in its stately rotation.

They'd known that species came and species went.

But the great fear that had always lurked somewhere in the back of every intelligent person's mind had now vanished.

Yes, species came and species went—but life continued. So, it now seemed certain, did intelligence. Not the intelligence of your own species, beyond a certain time, most likely. But what did it matter? A descendant species would keep the spark alive, and that species would surely have others to share the universe with.

Whatever else, the universe was not and never would be a dumb, mindless thing. For the people on the observation deck of the *Meru*, that was an assurance of immortality than no previous generation had ever enjoyed. Not personal immortality, to be sure, but it was still immortality.

"Millions of years..." Madeleine murmured.

Joe smiled fondly at her. "If you're in charge, at *least* that."

The observation deck airlock opened and a tall Indian officer stepped through. "Your down capsule is docked and cleared for departure, ladies, gentlemen. Your luggage has been loaded. Whenever you are ready, we can depart."

A.J. bounced to his feet, grabbing his carryon that lay near his chair. Helen smiled at the movement. *A few weeks in medical have done wonders for us all; now it just feels* heavy, *not oppressive.*

"Wait," Horst said. He reached into his carryon, and drew out a dark green bottle.

Helen and the others stared in disbelief. "There is *no way*, absolutely *no way*, that you've had that with you all along," Joe said bluntly.

"Naturally not," Madeline said. "So *that* was what Nicholas had to talk to you about."

There was a *pop!* as the champagne cork ejected itself to bounce around the room. "Yes," Horst said. "Since we could not partake in any such celebration until the medical staff cleared us, I asked Nicholas for one bottle...for our departure." He looked around. "One toast?"

There were no wineglasses, but plenty of little water cups; it didn't take long for everyone to get a small cup of the bubbly liquid. Horst looked at her. "Helen?"

"Me?"

"Of course," A.J. said, and Jackie continued, "You kinda started it, didn't you? Shouldn't you...close the circle?"

For a moment, she didn't know what to say.

But then she did. *Close the circle.*

She raised her cup. "To the end..."

The others began to echo her, but she shook her head, smiling.

"To the end...of the beginning."

MORE . . .
ERIC FLINT

MORE . . .
ERIC FLINT

MORE ...
ERIC FLINT

THE BELISARIUS SERIES with David Drake

THE MANY WORLDS
OF DAVID DRAKE

THE RCN SERIES
With the Lightnings
Lt. Leary, Commanding
The Far Side of the Stars
The Way to Glory
Some Golden Harbor
When the Tide Rises
In the Stormy Red Sky
What Distant Deeps
The Road of Danger
The Sea Without a Shore

HAMMER'S SLAMMERS
The Tank Lords
Caught in the Crossfire
The Sharp End
The Complete Hammer's Slammers v.1
The Complete Hammer's Slammers v.2
The Complete Hammer's Slammers v.3

THE BELISARIUS SERIES
WITH ERIC FLINT
Destiny's Shield
The Dance of Time
Belisarius I: Thunder at Dawn
Belisarius II: Storm at Noontide
Belisarius III: The Flames at Sunset

CHARLES E. GANNON
Alternate History and Space Opera on a Grand Scale

"Chuck Gannon is one of those marvelous finds—someone as comfortable with characters as he is with technology . . . . Imaginative, fun . . . his stories do not disappoint."   —David Weber

CAINE RIORDAN

Fire with Fire • 9781476736327 • $7.99
Nebula Finalist! An agent for a spy organization uncovers an alien alliance that will soon involve humanity in politics and war on a galactic scale.

Trial by Fire • 9781476736648 • $15.00
Raising Caine • 9781476780931 • $17.00
When reluctant interstellar diplomat Caine Riordan returns from humanity's first encounter with alien races, sudden war clouds burst.

RING OF FIRE SERIES (with Eric Flint)

1635: The Papal Stakes • 9781451639209 • $7.99
Up to their necks in papal assassins, power politics, murder, and mayhem, the uptimers need help and they need it quickly.

1636: Commander Cantrell in the West Indies
9781476780603 • $8.99
Oil. The Americas have it. The United States of Europe needs it. Enter Lieutenant-Commander Eddie Cantrell.

STARFIRE SERIES (with Steve White)

Extremis • 9781451638141 • $7.99
A resurrected star navy hero attempts to keep a fragile interstellar alliance together while battling an implacable alien adversary.

"[T]he intersecting plot threads, action and well-conceived science kept those pages turning."—SF Crowsnest

---